"I wish I understood why the Marquess of Furness would want to marry me when he must know so many more suitable ladies. Surely many of them would bring a dowry as well as noble antecedents. It cannot be for love, when he has not spoken a word hinting at any feelings for me, and how could he, when he hardly knows me?"

"I own I am surprised to find you expressing romantic nonsense at your age and with your education. Furness knows what will suit him."

"Yet he must know of others with the same qualifications. Why choose me?"

"He met you, formed the opinion you would be a well-behaved marchioness, unlikely to be extravagant or wish to figure in society or set up your will against his. He is ready to marry again as soon as may be. His reasons matter little. You should be rejoicing at this opportunity. As your father, I would be derelict in my duty if I failed to arrange such a very advantageous marriage for you."

"I see." Gillespie's evasiveness confirmed her formless suspicions. Some very significant benefit must attach to her marriage, not only to allow for the acquisition of even a small estate but to allow her father to dispense with her services as a copyist. He was not clever about money, but they had never exceeded their budget (except in the matter of Benedict's school fees) until his illness.

His face cleared. "Excellent! You are prepared to receive Furness's addresses, then. I knew your sense of duty would overcome any foolish female hesitation."

She dared not correct his assumption.

Praise for Kathleen Buckley

Kathleen Buckley's five previous historical romances published by The Wild Rose Press:

AN UNSUITABLE DUCHESS

MOST SECRET

CAPTAIN EASTERDAY'S BARGAIN (3rd Place, Historical Fiction, OKRWA IDA 2019)

A MASKED EARL

A DUKE'S DAUGHTER

Her second novel, *MOST SECRET*, was a finalist in the 2018 Oklahoma Romance Writers of America (OKRWA) International Digital Awards, Historical category, and in the 2019 Next Generation Indie Book Awards, Romance category.

Her third novel, *CAPTAIN EASTERDAY'S BARGAIN*, placed third in the Historical Fiction category of the 2019 Oklahoma Romance Writers of America (OKRWA) International Digital Awards.

Portia and the Merchant of London

by

Kathleen Buckley

This is a work of fiction. Names, characters, places, and incidents are either the product of the author's imagination or are used fictitiously, and any resemblance to actual persons living or dead, business establishments, events, or locales, is entirely coincidental.

Portia and the Merchant of London

Contact Information: info@thewildrosepress.com

Cover Art by *Jennifer Greeff*

The Wild Rose Press, Inc.
PO Box 708
Adams Basin, NY 14410-0708
Visit us at www.thewildrosepress.com

Publishing History
First Tea Rose Edition, 2021
Trade Paperback ISBN 978-1-5092-3486-8
Digital ISBN 978-1-5092-3487-5

Published in the United States of America

Dedication

For M.L., D.S., and D.H.

Chapter 1

Early August, 1741

Portia Gillespie's mother said, for perhaps the fifth time, "I don't know how we are to pay Benedict's school fees."

Portia sighed. Neither did she.

A week earlier, when Thomas Gillespie had not emerged from his study fifteen minutes before supper, Portia had tapped on the door to remind him. It was not like him to lose himself in his work so late in the day, as he always had an appetite by that time. When she received no response, she knocked a second time. Silence. He might be so involved in a translation that he had not heard. Would he be more annoyed at an unexpected intrusion or at not being summoned promptly for the meal? She opened the door.

Half a dozen books and a sheaf of papers lay scattered on the floor. That, more than the sight of her papa fallen forward across his desk, alarmed her. Had he merely nodded off in the warm afternoon? He would be upset to find his reference volumes fallen, the pages perhaps crumpled, and his papers all out of order. Hesitantly she went forward and shook his shoulder and murmured, "Papa?" For one heart-stopping moment when there was no response, Portia thought him dead. Then she steeled herself to touch his hand and found it warm. She chafed it. Was that not what one did when someone swooned? Or spirits of hartshorn: that was the thing. Mama had a vial of it. She had used it to revive Benedict once when he fell off the stair rail while sliding down. She did not like to leave Papa as he was, but she must fetch help.

By the time she, Benedict, and their footman had carried him to his bed, her father had opened his eyes.

"You fainted," Eliza Gillespie said to her husband. "How do you feel now? Shall I send for a doctor?"

He frowned on the left side of his face and gabbled. Frowned in perplexity, and attempted to speak again, with no better result. The doctor, on his arrival, called it apoplexy and proceeded to bleed him. Cook was set to making a panada, her answer for all sorts of illness, which, as she said, "goes down easy if there's no currants used, and never troubles the stomach nor bowels." Benedict had to be sent out to buy a lemon for the dish, the footman having already been dispatched to the apothecary for a tonic recommended by the doctor. Mama set the maid to work organizing Papa's bedchamber: fetching a small side table from the attic to hold sickroom necessities and moving Mama's clothing and the contents of her dressing table to the unused bedroom.

Consequently, it was not until the next morning that Abby, the maid, came to Portia with several sheets of paper clutched in her hands.

"Begging your pardon, Mistress Portia, but these here was on the floor in the master's study with his books, and I'm mortal afraid of putting them in the wrong place."

Her father being particular about the organization

of his desk, in spite of the number of books and documents stacked on either side of it, Abby's concern was not unreasonable. Portia took the sheets. One belonged with the article he had been working on, and one was a letter he had begun to one of his scholarly friends. The third was a letter from Radford's School, with the amount due for Michaelmas term: so much for housing and food, so much for tuition, laundry, miscellaneous expenses. The fourth sheet contained numbers scribbled almost at random, degenerating to a scrawl, the ink smeared where it had not yet been dry. Her father must have been writing when he collapsed and knocked it and half a dozen books and other sheets onto the floor. After they moved him, Portia had had no time or thought to spare for tidying the study.

The numbers were too large to be sums of money, at least in their household! Nor was there any indication of pounds or guineas. Well, she would put it aside for now and return the first two to their appropriate piles. The letter from the school was more urgent.

Portia opened the door of the sickroom. Her mother looked up from her chair near the bed. Portia whispered, "May I speak with you?" and beckoned. Setting aside the smock she was sewing, her mother rose and glided out to the passage. Her face was damp with perspiration. The weather had been hot and the windows of the sickroom were closed to prevent any stray breeze from causing a chill.

"Mama." She showed her mother the letter.

"Oh, dear. We must wait until your father is well to deal with it."

"Dr. Royce has given no indication of how long he may be incapacitated." Or even whether he would live or die.

"No one can be certain of the outcome of an illness," Eliza pointed out. "We must do all we can to promote your dear papa's recovery. Except cupping. I will not agree to cupping." Mama had seen her younger brother cupped, a treatment involving heated cups applied to the skin. The experience had given her an aversion to the therapy.

Portia was no advocate of it, either, having heard her mother's description of poor Uncle William's suffering during the procedure. "The doctor will be returning tomorrow. Surely after that he will have some idea of how long it might be until Papa can at least give us instructions on how to pay Benedict's fees. We have some time yet before the beginning of the term. But if the second bleeding does no good, I think we must deal with it ourselves, for I do not think repeated bleeding can benefit Papa."

"But Portia, dear, the doctor says it must in time reduce the congestion of blood to the head."

"To do it once to reduce the congestion is perfectly reasonable, I suppose. How can it be advisable to do it again and again?"

"But if it does not succeed the first time, Dr. Royce says—"

"Mama, you saw how much he took. Would you not be concerned if someone lost that quantity of blood from an injury?"

"Well…I would, 'tis true. But physicians bleed patients then, too."

"It may be justified if the patient is a headstrong young man who will not keep to his bed unless he is made weak enough to be unable to leave it, but even then it seems an odd way of proceeding." If any benefit could be derived from bloodletting, they must certainly permit the doctor his way.

In the end, she and Mama compromised: they would permit Gillespie to be bled once more. If there was no improvement, the course of treatment would be discontinued.

By the next day, he was slightly more alert, though his right side remained useless. He appeared not to understand anything they said and could only make garbled sounds himself.

"He is improving, my dears, which proves the bloodletting works." Eliza beamed at Portia and Benedict. Mama's reddened eyes and the shadows beneath them testified to the hours she had spent sitting at his bedside, though Portia had risen in the middle of the night and taken her place in the sickroom. Mama had no doubt been too worried, and perhaps too exhausted, to sleep. That night Portia sent her mother to bed early and sat up with her father the greater part of the night. Her heart ached for him: his brilliant mind, his care for his family, his company while she assisted him with his writing.

But in the morning he was listless and showed no interest in eating. Dr. Royce tutted and recommended cupping to improve the appetite.

Mama refused to permit it. "My little brother suffered terribly, and in the end it did no good at all, and he died."

"We must continue bleeding, then, madam, to decrease the congestion of blood."

"You have taken a pint each day," Portia pointed out. "How much more can my father lose? And how can he improve by being bled when he is weaker today than he was yesterday?"

"Six days is not too long to continue the treatment. Everyone knows bleeding is beneficial for a number of ailments, and it has been endorsed by leading physicians since ancient times. Some recommend releasing more than a pint. I do not expect a young lady to understand medical matters."

Eliza Gillespie was staring down at her fingers, moving them one after another. Before Portia could marshal her argument against prolonged blood loss, she said, "But if you took a pint a day for six days, that would be near a gallon."

"Only three-quarters of a gallon, Mistress Gillespie."

"Which is near enough a gallon, to my way of thinking, sir," Portia said. "Mama, I think you are not willing to pursue this treatment?"

Her mother pounced on the suggestion. "No, indeed. We must try how we can increase my husband's appetite and support his recovery by other means."

Royce huffed in irritation and departed, promising to send his bill.

It was not a good week. Papa grew restless. His left hand plucked at the coverlet, and intermittently he uttered disjointed syllables. Portia preferred to think of them as "syllables" rather than noises. Her mother sat with him, mending, and speaking to him in her low, pretty voice. Perhaps it was wrong to wonder whether her inconsequent chat consisting of gossip, commentary on the weather, and what Cook was making for his next meal was more of an annoyance than encouragement to rest and get better. Thomas Gillespie did not ordinarily tolerate prattle, but if he could not comprehend her words, her voice at least should be soothing. Or possibly his agitation resulted from his improvement.

And he was improving. His expression alone made it clear he did not care for the panada, even though it contained lemon, sherry, and a good deal of sugar in addition to the boiled bread crumbs, even without his sharp but unintelligible comment. Eliza, who had brought it up to him, was reduced to tears. The stress was wearing away her accustomed placidity. Portia took the offending dish away and instructed their cook to make a caudle instead. The alcoholic content should have a mellowing effect on Papa. Then she returned to the bedchamber.

Eliza had managed to stanch her tears. Portia drew her into the passage, shutting the door.

"We cannot leave your dear father alone!"

" 'Tis only for a few moments. I think we must have at least one more person to sit with Papa. You are worn to a bone, and while I am not—yet—we two cannot continue this way."

Her mother's eyes filled again. "To bring in a stranger seems so unfeeling, as if we did not care about him. Yet with one of us in attendance on your father and the other sleeping, Benedict is left to his own devices. I'm sure I do not know if he is studying."

Or slipping out to do whatever it was he did when he absented himself from home for hours.

Mama sighed. "I suppose we could hire someone to sit with him part of the day, perhaps a man? We cannot send William on errands when he must be here in case your papa needs…that is…"

"Requires a man's assistance in a valet's capacity."

This morning, Thomas Gillespie had made it perfectly clear he would not tolerate a female's assistance with his more personal care. "I wonder if Papa would like Benedict's company for a few hours each day? Abby and William might each also spend short periods with him. They would at least not be strangers to him."

"How could I ask it of Benedict?"

"Why should he not involve himself? He could study or read quietly, as he does anyway to prepare for the term."

Her mother contemplated the matter. "That's very true. He often does his lessons in the study under his father's eye, after all. It may be reassuring to your papa to see Benedict is not neglecting his work."

Chapter 2

Even with Benedict and the servants sharing the nursing duty with Mama and Portia, Mama was half distracted. Mistress Crump, their cook, did not appreciate having the invalid dishes she prepared sent back uneaten, with instructions to prepare a posset or caudle or custard instead. Neither Portia nor her mother was well rested as they divided the night watch. Thomas Gillespie showed signs of increasing irritability and restlessness.

However, Benedict had agreed readily to sit with his father, and Papa did seem to enjoy his presence, in spite of Benedict's intermittent commentary on whatever book he was reading. Oddly, this did not annoy Gillespie, who sometimes grunted in response to a comment, or nodded or shook his head in reply to a question.

Portia was sitting with her mother while Benedict read in the invalid's chamber. They had seldom had the chance since the Unfortunate Event as Mama called it, with the household routine all disordered.

"It is time I lie down for a while so I am ready to sit up with him after William prepares him for the night." Eliza closed her sewing basket and stood up.

Portia chose her words carefully. "Mama, if Papa is not better in another week, I think we must do something about paying for Benedict's Michaelmas term."

"I had quite forgotten. That is, not forgotten exactly. I've been preparing a list of what he will need, apart from clothing, which is already ordered. I suppose we cannot wait much longer to make payment. Which reminds me, Abby says Smith, the butcher, will expect the month's account to be settled. We always pay it on the first of the month, which is more than a week ago now. There are some other tradesmen's bills outstanding as well." Evidently seeing her daughter's mystification, she continued. "None of us thought about it that day, after you found your papa, nor indeed until yesterday, when Abby went to get some bones for soup. Smith understands the household is all upside down; he merely reminded her."

"Then let us pay it and the others today."

"I don't think we can, Portia."

She knew almost nothing of banking except that Gillespie visited his banker on quarter day when his investment income was paid and came home with money. He then gave Portia and her mother their pin money for the quarter, with a smaller sum to Benedict. "Did he not give you the month's household allowance before his attack?"

She had seen her father entrust the month's money to her mama, with his usual admonition not to overspend their budget, even though there was usually a shilling or two left from the previous month. Much as she loved him, she could not help but think that after so many years of marriage it was unnecessary to remind her mother to be frugal.

"I am afraid your papa would say I have spent too much this month," her mother burst out. "We must get by until quarter day, and then all will be well."

"Do you mean we cannot afford to pay our bills?"

"It is not as bad as that." Her voice quavered. "We can pay them. It's what we are to live on until next quarter day that worries me."

"Almost six weeks? How much of the housekeeping money is left, after those bills?"

"Four shillings, tuppence, and a farthing. Please don't look like that, dear. You know we paid Dr. Royce and the apothecary out of it, for they do not like to carry an account. The aqua vitae regia Royce recommended was rather expensive, then there were the special foods for your father—lemons for caudle, port, sherry, Rhenish wine, rice, more eggs than we usually need. If we are very careful and use my pin money to make up the deficiency, we can scrape by. I think we almost can, if we need not buy any more medicines or wines."

"Where does your housekeeping money come from? Does he withdraw it from the bank each month?"

"I suppose so, as he gives it to me by the month."

Which was to say, her mother had no idea.

"You say we can almost get by. I have eleven shillings and a few pence, if it will help, Mama." She saved a portion of her own pin money, as she seldom bought any but necessities. An old maid had no need of fripperies.

Her mother bit her lower lip. "I do not like to ask it of you…but we will need food, kindling, candles, and who knows what else, for the remainder of the month. We must eat very simply and cheaply, and reserve your pin money in case we need something more for your father. However, I do not know how we are to pay for Benedict's new clothing, which is already delivered.

Not that it would come out of the housekeeping, but I do not know where it would come from. Your dear father would have provided it."

"Mama, never mind the clothing. I'm sure the shop will take it back. He could wear last year's with a few alterations. He's only grown taller, not fatter. But where is Benedict's tuition to come from? Can we delay paying Radford's School until the term begins? And how will we get the money if my father is not able to see his banker to receive it?"

"I don't know."

Papa gave her mother the money at breakfast on the first day of each month. She was sure at times the bank had not been open the previous day. He might, of course, have withdrawn it a day or two in advance. Knowing Gillespie well, she doubted it. If he was hard at work writing or tutoring, he sometimes did not leave the house for several days at a time.

"The chances are he withdrew the whole quarter's budget at one time and then doled it out by the month. If so, it would surely be in the study."

"Portia! You cannot mean to pry into your father's desk!"

"We cannot know when Papa will be able to resume control of financial matters. We need money for next month. We also need money to pay for the new school term." Which brought them back to where they had begun, and Mama went off to lie down with a lavender compress on her forehead. If Papa had not recovered sufficiently by a week before the term began, they would have to discover how to have the quarterly income paid out.

****

Although she had not admitted it, searching her father's desk felt awkward and simply wrong. She did find the money box, however. Having observed her father's habits while assisting him, she had not anticipated great difficulty. The two bottom drawers were locked and therefore the likeliest place to look. Now, where to find the key? There was a small box of wafer seals in horrid colors in an unlocked side drawer. Her father used the more sedately colored wafers in the center drawer. She tipped the disks of purple, bilious green, pink, and yellow out on the desk. Two brass keys fell on top of the pile.

The money box was in the second drawer, and the smaller of the keys opened it. The contents bore out her opinion of Thomas Gillespie's methodical habits. The box held three drawstring bags, two bearing little pasteboard tags inscribed in the precise, crabbed hand her father used when he was not writing at speed to capture his ideas as they came to mind. The one marked "household" contained enough for September, which would bring them to quarter day. The second bag was tagged "SDT" and contained almost five shillings. The third bag was embroidered with his initials. Perhaps it had been a gift from her mother early in their marriage, as the style resembled the monograms on the handkerchiefs she made for their family. It held two shillings, nine pence. They might be able to scrape through until the end of September without running much into debt, if they curtailed all purchases not absolutely necessary.

But where was Benedict's tuition?

****

"I don't know how we are to pay Benedict's school

fees."

"I think we must see Papa's banker," Portia replied.

"Do we know who he is?"

"Not by name. I do know he banks at Pimling's. I am sure they will be able to tell us."

"To approach Mr. Gillespie's bank seems so intrusive." Eliza Gillespie twisted her handkerchief, a nervous habit which was very hard on the delicate linen. "I could sell my pearl necklet."

"I believe you should keep your necklace, in case some dire problem arises," Portia replied.

"What could be more dire"—Eliza's voice had risen on the first five words but was abruptly moderated as she remembered someone might hear—"than failing to educate Benedict?"

They kept their voices low when discussing their current difficulties. The bedchamber doors and windows had been left open, Benedict having pointed out that this made the house cooler. Medical thought might hold it best to keep an invalid warm and out of drafts. When the patient was fretfully trying to push his bedclothes off and he—and everyone else who entered the sickroom—was perspiring freely, it was time to use common sense. "For if he were in a fever, we would be advised to bring it down," Portia had pointed out. "We must simply not speak where he can hear of things that might worry him while the weather is hot."

Dr. Royce had been insistent that the invalid not be upset. "You might not think him able to understand, but I have treated sufferers from similar attacks, and it appears that they often comprehend though they may not be able to respond. 'Tis best not to risk his being worried and suffering another apoplectic fit." This was the only advice Royce had given them with which they both agreed.

The moment Portia feared had arrived. It was now necessary to give up the pretense that he would certainly recover in time to deal with their problems. "If Papa is not recovered by Christmas, and we cannot determine where he found the money to send Benedict to school, we should withdraw him from Radford's. You might sell your necklet to pay for an apprenticeship for him." She had hoped not to have to mention this possibility.

"I cannot bear it, Portia. Benedict must at least finish school, even if we cannot contrive to send him to university, though it would break your papa's heart to think of it. Pray excuse me, dear, I must speak with Cook about something." She hastened from the study, pressing her much-abused handkerchief to her mouth as she departed, stifling a sob.

Eliza Gillespie had grown up the sheltered only daughter of a man in very comfortable circumstances. She had not been trained to manage a household, and as best Portia could determine, nothing had been expected of her beyond genteel behavior and the accomplishments of a well-bred lady. Unfortunately for all concerned, her father was in trade. When he died, her much older half brother encountered setbacks in the business, wiping out the money that would have supplied her with a good dowry and therefore with a good marriage. In one way, this had worked in her favor, as she was thus able to fall in love with and marry Thomas Gillespie.

She was not of a practical bent, but as Portia's

father made all the important decisions, this posed no difficulty. Portia gave her full credit for being an excellent wife and mother, while wishing Mama possessed a more resolute spirit. However, she was spending hours each day with Gillespie, reading to him either from such books as Portia thought he might enjoy or else from any correspondence that contained no upsetting news, or simply talking to him about the events of their day. Portia read to her father also, usually from some scholarly paper sent to him by a friend or from his books in Latin, French, or German. Mama had been taught French in her youth although Portia suspected she had never been able to carry on any but the simplest conversation. Eliza Gillespie had given her daughter her early lessons in that language, but it was from her father she had acquired fluency and learned Latin and German, both more by circumstance than by Papa's intention. As he was a prodigious writer of essays, articles, and books on various aspects of scholarship, as well as carrying on a voluminous correspondence, he found it helpful to have someone with a good hand make clean copies. His own penmanship suffered from the speed at which he wrote in his desire to move on to the next project.

As her mother was clearly not ready to contemplate a visit to Pimling's, Portia must try to puzzle out how much money they had. It would be sensible to prepare before going to the bank in any case. She sat at the desk in the study to review the household accounts she had found in the other locked drawer, with her father's business correspondence and banking records. It would have been easier to spread out the ledger without the barricade of untidy piles of books her father had been using, scraps of paper, letters, and notes for future articles sticking out of them. She did not feel she could move them. Papa had once summarily dismissed a maid for shifting them in order to dust and polish the desktop. Not that he could cast his daughter off for the same sin, but she hoped he would eventually be able to return to his usual activities. When he did, he would expect to find everything as he had left it. Her mother had timidly suggested he would not like Portia to be going through his papers, but her own representation that they must find the funds to pay Benedict's tuition carried the day.

The account book with the housekeeping expenses was current to the date Papa had collapsed, with entries clearly set forth. Gillespie's quarterly income was shown, as were fees for tutoring, translations, scholarly articles, and books which contributed varying amounts. Their expenses were subtracted. Each month, a few shillings and pence were left over and then vanished like fairy gold, going back for a year or more. Papa could not be spending it all on books, and there was nothing else he bought. She would be aware of any addition to his library. When he did buy one, it came from the used book stalls, and those purchases were noted.

The missing money did not add up to much. Still, it was troubling, an additional mystery. Nothing in the ledger or any of the other documents showed Benedict's tuition payments had ever been made, though her brother had certainly attended Radford, his father's old school, for the last two years.

They could withdraw the amount of Benedict's fees from the bank, if the bank would release them on her mother's instruction. Portia feared such a course. The amount on deposit must be left intact against extraordinary expenses. If Papa were able to resume his tutoring and writing within a few months, all would be well. If he could not, their situation would be difficult indeed. They dared not use the funds in Pimling's.

Perhaps their income had declined from previous years. But going through the earlier ledgers yielded the same result. Her father must have some other bank account or other source of money, but where? Portia realized, as her mother perhaps did not, that the remaining money must be hoarded. Their only realistic hope of sending Benedict to school was to find out where the previous years' tuition had come from.

****

Portia dragged her unwilling mother to see Papa's banker. Their expenses continued to increase despite having discontinued the doctor's and apothecary's attendance. Before his stroke, Gillespie had told Mama she might order necessary clothing for Benedict, who kept growing. She had done so, and now the clothing had been delivered, and they really could not afford to pay for it.

Her mother murmured, "I hardly like to bother you about the matter, Mr. Wallace, when Mr. Gillespie may recover soon and all will be well."

"The doctor was not hopeful my father will recover quickly, sir. Even if he does, the doctor could not say whether he will be able to resume tutoring and writing. With the decrease in his income, I fear we shall be in difficulties before he does. Indeed, we are already faced with unexpected bills as a result of his illness." Portia would as soon have dealt with the bank by herself. But

Wallace would be more willing to speak with her mother than a spinster daughter.

"It is best to deal promptly with financial concerns," the banker replied.

As her mother seemed unlikely to contribute anything further, Portia went on. "The most pressing problem is Benedict's school expenses. While we could withdraw money for them from what my father has on deposit with your bank, if he does not recover soon, we may need that money for future expenses not covered by his quarterly income."

"I am sure the grocer would give us credit, Portia, dear. And we may have enough coal to cook if we are careful, as it's summer and we do not need fires in the drawing room or bedchambers."

"Mama, you are forgetting we are already behind, with all the extra expenses we have had to pay, with the doctor, apothecary, and food suitable for invalid dishes. But tuition is the great problem."

"Unfortunately, I have no answer for you, Mistress Gillespie, Mistress Portia. The income from his investments comes in, and most of it goes out for your living expenses. His fees for his writings and tutoring are paid to Mr. Gillespie in person, I assume. Have you searched his desk? Or mayhap he keeps a money box elsewhere in his study?"

"I found a box with the rest of the quarter's housekeeping budget, and two other purses, though they did not contain much. I suppose I must next search for anyplace he may have concealed money. That is a very good thought of yours, Mr. Wallace." Portia contemplated going through every one of the books on the shelves. Might there be banknotes between the pages? It would not take many of them to pay for another two years of schooling for Benedict, as the smallest denomination of currency issued was for twenty pounds. If there were a few of the larger notes—two or three hundred pound notes, or a five hundred pound note—they could stop worrying, at least for the moment. Though this was the merest wishful thinking: an entire family might live on two hundred pounds per annum, if not very comfortably. The best she could hope for would be a few guineas.

Wallace was frowning thoughtfully. "I recall your father meant to come in to discuss the situation before Master Benedict's first term. Let me see now, when would that have been?"

"Benedict entered Michaelmas term two years ago."

"Then sometime in late spring or summer two years ago your father mentioned it. Ah, of course! We had met by chance the day the highwayman Dick Turpin was hanged. What a crowd there was! That would make it, hmmm, mid-April, I suppose. I haven't thought of it since."

"Did he not come in?"

"If he did, he must have spoken with someone else. Egad, of course he must! My mother fell gravely ill around that time, and I went to be with her and the rest of the family. Between leaving and returning, I was gone over a month."

"Is there any way of determining who saw him?"

"Not unless he borrowed or deposited money or arranged for the sale of investments. He did none of those things, as we can see from his account. I will inquire, but it is doubtful anyone will recall an appointment with a client years ago, when it led to no bank business."

****

Much of the next week was spent on a ladder, searching the books on the upper shelves in the study. Might one volume be false, merely a hollowed-out box? Many of them were large enough to conceal a number of guineas. She took them out, gave them a brisk wipe with a rag, flipped through each, and replaced them after determining no cache of money lurked in or behind them on the shelf. She did not overlook the possibility of a concealed panel, though that was a feature more likely found in a silly novel than in real life.

Her legs ached from bracing herself on the ladder as she needed both her hands for the chore of dusting and searching. Now every book on the upper shelves had been examined. Benedict insisted on looking behind every painting in case one should conceal a cavity. He looked under carpets, under the desk, behind its drawers, under the chairs, and anywhere else anything might be hidden in the study. He found two buttons and a farthing.

The next day and a half were spent sitting on the floor, searching the lowest three rows of shelves. At least they were not dusty, although crouching or kneeling exercised a different set of previously unused muscles. Benedict helped somewhat, though he kept wandering off to tap the paneling in other rooms, pry at the mantel pieces, and twist the bulbous tops of the newel posts.

She had put off examining the shelves at standing and desk height, where the most commonly used books were kept. Papa often directed one of his students to fetch this or that volume or to look something up. He would scarcely hide banknotes or anything else of value there.

But at the end of the least used section was a small, cheaply bound commonplace book, out of place, wedged between a Hebrew text and the end wall. Her father kept his books in strict order by subject and author. Instead of merely leafing through its pages, she opened it.

The first page was headed *Benedict's tuition 1739*. Under it was an amount similar to that in the school's recent letter regarding the payment due. Beneath that, a slightly larger sum was noted, with SDT written beside it, followed by deductions at regular intervals. Most were dated at the beginning of the month: a few shillings here, a crown or a pound there. Once it was five pounds in the middle of the month, with the crabbed note, "From sale of rights to *A First Hebrew Grammar* to L. Prescott, Paternoster Row." At the bottom of the page, a balance remained. The next page, 1740, followed the same pattern though with the addition of the balance from the previous page. More deductions. The third page began with the balance from the previous page and the current year's tuition cost. The entries looked nothing like the household accounting. Portia frowned over it for long minutes.

The second bag in the money box had been labelled "SDT."

Chapter 3

A little less than two weeks since Thomas Gillespie had been stricken down, the letter came. Portia had been dealing with all the correspondence addressed to Mr. Gillespie. Most had been from his scholarly friends and acquaintances or former students informing him of their academic progress at university. A few concerned potential students for tutoring. She had written brief replies, explaining that he was ill and would respond when he had recovered. She never failed to say a little prayer that the said recovery would be rapid as she penned these messages.

This letter was different.

Mr. Gillespie,

As I have not seen you this month and have received no communication from you, I shall give myself the pleasure of calling upon you in the next several days.

The signature, if it could be called that, was an elegant, swirling flourish which might be a monogram, though Portia could not make out the initials.

Old Jury, Cheapside, at the Sign of the Scales

Who might Papa have been visiting so regularly that cessation of his visits would cause concern? She thought she knew all of his closest friends; some had come to the house occasionally, or he had mentioned visiting them, if they were infirm. Many of them were his age or older, and all of them were scholars or at least took an interest in scholarly pursuits. She had seen letters from most of his correspondents; one of her tasks was to file them. As the letters usually contained analysis of some point, Thomas Gillespie sometimes consulted the correspondent's previous letter or letters. She had never seen one like this, and the penmanship was distinctive, too, being a good, round commercial hand, very easy to read, except for the flourish which signed it. To question Papa about the strange letter, alas, was impossible, both because of the language problem and because he must not be disturbed. Biting her lip, she decided there was nothing for it but to ask her mother.

"I'm sure I don't know of any of his friends or acquaintances who would live in Cheapside. Oxford, Cambridge, Edinburgh, Dublin, Rome…someplace in one of the German states, I can never recall the name. The German language is so un-English. A good many small towns here at home, of course. And two or three publishers here in town."

Portia wished ardently the writer had given a fixed day for his visit. No matter. She would reply immediately, informing him that her papa was unable to receive visitors at the moment by reason of ill health. But before she could sit down to write, she was called away to deal with a kitchen catastrophe.

The cat, finding a plump chicken unattended on the work table, had nibbled the skin off the breast and begun to set its delicate fangs into the meat when Mrs. Crump returned from the pantry. Now she stood lamenting, a performance worthy of Covent Garden, while the cat crouched unrepentant under a chair.

“As nice a hen as I’ve ever seen, and just the thing to tempt the master’s appetite, loving poultry as he does. Now it’s spoiled and that beast not even ashamed of itself.”

Mrs. Crump was a good cook but given to dramatic utterances.

“Oh, nonsense. It is to be made into soup, not roasted or served whole. Rinse it off, and be sure you chop the meat small so my father does not choke on it. I am sure it will be very good. Do not take on, Mrs. Crump. We all understand how it happened that you and Betty were both out of the kitchen at the same time.”

No sooner had she calmed Cook than Benedict arrived by the servants’ entrance, full of some amazing thing he had heard about a clock that kept time on a ship at sea. When she tried to escape his explanation of why such a thing would be important, her brother whispered, “Portia, I need to talk to you.”

A boy of fourteen years seldom wishes to speak privately with his elder sister.

“The study, Benedict. Mama is in the drawing room.”

He shut the door. “Portia, you haven’t said anything about my going back to Radford, but I overheard you and Mama talking about it. About how there’s no money.”

She had instituted a number of economies and stressed to her brother that he must be careful of his clothing and be sparing in his use of candles, explaining that their income was somewhat reduced, with Papa unable to tutor or write his articles. Adolescents are heedless; who could imagine that Benedict would notice how worried she and Mama were?

"We have been hoping Papa would be able to tell us how to manage. But we must make shift to work something out soon, and I promise you we will." They might have to take money from the bank and hope that by Christmas Thomas Gillespie would have recovered enough to explain where the next term's tuition would come from. She did not like to rely on his recovery.

"No, but wait, Portia. I'd as soon not go back to school. I could go to sea in a pinch, or get work with an instrument or clockmaker. That would be far more interesting and useful, too, than studying Greek and fusty old stuff. And as for Hebrew! Who needs to know it but a churchman?"

"Benedict, gentlemen attend grammar school, even if they don't go on to university. You know how your papa feels about a good education. And you like studying."

"I don't mind school or study. It's the subjects I don't like. Arithmetick is useful, and natural philosophy, too."

"I think Papa believes you will follow in his footsteps. To be a scholar is not inappropriate for a gentleman, but to build clockworks and the like is only a skilled trade."

"It's mechanics and mathematics that change the world, not the writings of the old Romans and Greeks. Except for Euclid. He invented geometry, you know, which is used in surveying land, fortifications, and in aiming cannon. Then there are steam pumps. Who knows what they could be used for, besides pumping water out of mines?"

"Not I, certainly. Did you speak with Papa about

this?"

"I did, after my first year, when I discovered that Radford's did not teach anything of interest other than some mathematics. I spoke with the headmaster. He wrote Papa and claimed I'd argued with him. I didn't, Portia! I merely pointed out that except for Euclid, the Greeks were pretty useless if one wished to build more and better machines. Papa talked to me when I came home at the end of term."

He did not have to explain further. Portia could well imagine how the talk had gone.

"It isn't as if I could have refused to go back to school. Well, you know how he is."

Yes, indeed.

"He would be terribly disappointed. However, we cannot consult his opinion, though we can guess what it would be. Perhaps we could write the school, explaining he is ill, and ask if you could return for the following term."

"Oh, excellent! Meanwhile, I can get work to help you and Mama."

"We are not that desperate yet, if we need not come up with your tuition. Now I should explain matters to Mama."

Portia sought out Eliza, who greeted her by remarking how fortunate it was that Papa was now able to eat a more normal diet. 'Twas indeed, as the cost of preparing flummery caudle had worried Portia, the Rhenish wine, oranges, and lemons being so dear. Though they had best rely on fish and cheaper cuts of meat than chicken.

"This serves to convince me that good invalid care serves as well as bleeding or cupping."

"Probably better, Mama. Now, I have just had a most illuminating conversation with Benedict, which may solve our most urgent problem."

Chapter 4

With one thing and another, Portia never did sit down to write to the correspondent she thought of as "Old Jury." This omission was brought forcibly to her mind when Abby sought her mother out in the little room where Portia was engaged in mending and her mother was making underdrawers for Benedict. No need to purchase those!

"Ma'am, there's a gentleman asking for the master."

"Who is he, Abby?"

"Says his name is Solomon Toll'ee-something, and he has business with Mr. Gillespie."

"Oh, dear. I suppose I must see him?" She glanced doubtfully at Portia.

"I'll come with you, Mama. Is he in the drawing room?"

"Not knowing him, I didn't like to have him in the house without you agreed, ma'am. I left him on the step."

"But he's a gentleman?"

"Well, he dresses and talks like it…"

When the visitor was shown into the drawing room, Portia understood their maid's hesitation. The man's coat, waistcoat, and breeches were of a good tobacco-brown cloth. His bow was graceful but not elaborate. However, there was something slightly foreign about him.

"Mr.—?" her mother inquired, delicately.

"Solomon de Toledo, madam, to see Mr. Gillespie on a matter of business." His voice was well bred and utterly English. A Spanish or Italian ancestor, perhaps, which was really not much odder than the many English people who had French forebears.

"I fear my husband is unable to see visitors, sir."

His dark brows rose slightly. "May I ask what the impediment is?"

"He has suffered an apoplexy and is not himself. He is unable to conduct any business at the moment."

"I am very sorry to hear it, Mistress Gillespie. I would not have come had I not expected to hear from him early this month and wondered if a message had gone astray."

He sounded as though he accepted her mother's statement. Why would he doubt it? But while his question had been perfectly polite, Portia had caught a trace of underlying skepticism.

After a slight pause, he asked, "Is he able to receive a visit from a concerned acquaintance?"

"Oh, dear, I don't think it would be wise. He is unable to, er, enunciate clearly, which makes him very irritable, and he must not be excited in any way, lest he have another fit."

"Are you by any chance a publisher, sir?"

On entering, the gentleman had included Portia in his bow. Now he turned his gaze upon her. His eyes were dark, penetrating, and suggested keen intelligence. "No, Mistress Portia."

"You know my name?"

"Your father mentioned he had a daughter of that

name." He sounded amused. "And, er, Master Benedict, of course."

Mr. de Toledo must be acquainted with her father then, not merely a business connection, though if he had not come about one of Papa's books or articles, what possible commercial interest could they share?

"If you could explain the nature of your business to my mother, mayhap she"—Eliza Gillespie cast her a panic-stricken look—"could assist you. My father cannot speak or write, and we are not quite sure how much he understands. Though he has improved, and we trust he will continue to do so, if he is not troubled."

"Portia…" her mother protested. They had not previously revealed how disabled he was.

"I see." At a guess, Solomon de Toledo was debating with himself. "In that case, I had best explain that I lent money to Mr. Gillespie for Master Benedict's school fees."

"Oh, dear."

Oh, dear, indeed. At least it explained where the money had come from. The deductions in the commonplace book must indicate payments her father had made.

"I suppose," Mama ventured, "you lent him the money against the book he was writing? *Etymology of the Hebrew Language*?"

"Ah…no. I think it might be best if I returned in a month or two."

Mama drew breath to answer.

Portia spoke first. "Mr. de Toledo, I believe we should discuss this now."

"Portia, if it's business, it should wait, surely."

"I suspect it may be something we ought to know

now."

"Then to be blunt, I am a moneylender. Two years ago—"

"A moneylender? Oh, no," Eliza Gillespie protested faintly.

"Mama, I have been dealing with the finances since Father fell ill. It will be best if you leave this to me." Since finding the commonplace book, Portia had been deeply concerned. She had not allowed herself to think of her father borrowing to educate her brother, particularly when he obviously lacked the resources to repay the loan.

"You cannot entertain a male visitor without a chaperon, and I feel quite ill myself."

"Ask Mrs. Crump to give you a glass of that soothing cordial for low spirits, and have Abby attend me here."

"Abby gossips."

"Then I will dispense with her chaperonage. Find something to keep her occupied out of the way. We will leave the drawing room door open. As I am almost an ape leader, why would anyone see any impropriety? No one will even know. I will have to answer the outer door if anyone comes," she added to de Toledo. "I doubt anyone will, however."

"You are not an ape leader, Portia." However, Eliza Gillespie's desire to quit the presence of that terrifying being, a usurer, was greater than her concern over a hypothetical threat to her daughter's reputation, thank goodness. Mama glided from the room, leaving the door open.

"Please be seated, sir." Portia perched on a straight chair. "I have been wondering where the funds came from to pay my brother's tuition. I found notations of amounts and what appear to be payments for his first two years. There was no entry for what I suppose would be the amount of this year's loan."

"No, he had not yet come to me to arrange it. Mr. Gillespie might have received enough from some other source to cover Benedict's next installment of tuition. I was surprised not to receive his scheduled payment, however."

"Old Jury, Cheapside! You are the one who wrote to him a few days ago."

"I did. If he has been ill, no wonder he has neither paid nor applied for another loan."

Portia bit her lip and stared at her clasped hands. "It is not clear to me how much the payments were to be. The amounts varied."

This time, de Toledo seemed disconcerted. "Mmmm, given the variations in your father's income, there was no set amount. We agreed he would pay whatever was left from his month's budget. Of course, when he received a payment for his writing, he paid more. "

"My God, the interest will be ruinous." Visions of debtor's prison rose before her eyes.

"Mistress Portia, let me help you to the sofa before you faint."

"I'm not going to faint."

All the same, she found herself leaning on his arm while he escorted her the few steps to the divan and before she knew how it happened, she was reclining on it. It was not something a decent female should be doing in the presence of a man, unless he were a family member. She struggled to sit up.

"I'll fetch your maid."

"You probably won't find her easily, and I don't need her. I really am not going to swoon. It was the shock, realizing what a sum my father owes you, and the interest as well." The sum itself was not enormous. What did they have that they could sell? Thomas Gillespie owned some valuable books, but she (or her mother, rather) could not sell them while her father lived. However had her father come to make such a mistake as to borrow money from a usurer rather than his bank? Having done so for Benedict's first year of school, perhaps expecting payment for his book to cover it and the interest, why would he borrow again, when it failed to do so? She would have to write Radford's School and let them know her brother would not be returning.

"Mistress Portia, you need not distress yourself about interest." He seated himself in a straight chair nearby.

"Mr. de Toledo, I dare not ignore it. Our debt will continue to increase, even if my father never borrows anything more. You must have realized by now that at the rate my father has been able to repay you, it would be years before he paid off even the principal. With the interest…" Her eyes stung with threatened tears. She blinked them away and swallowed hard. "He may never be able to resume tutoring or writing his books and essays, which I dare say he counted upon to pay back your loan."

Papa's books had never brought in a great deal of money, despite being quite popular in their limited audience. How could Thomas Gillespie have expected to earn enough to pay even the minimum payments a moneylender would expect? “I can’t think why you would have lent the money to my father if you were fully apprised of his income.” Here her voice faltered. The man was a moneylender. He would take their last penny, and when they could pay no more, Papa’s books would be sold, her mother’s few pieces of jewelry, and ultimately the lease on the house would pass to him. Perhaps she could get work as a governess or instructress in a girls’ academy as she was sufficiently well educated. Her wages would not support the rest of the family, however. Benedict might have to go to sea.

“Mr. Gillespie explained his circumstances to me. I don’t think he understood—”

Footsteps thudded in the passage. De Toledo rose and faced the door as Benedict called out, “Portia! If you really think—” He came to an abrupt halt in the doorway. “I beg your pardon, Portia. I didn’t realize you had a guest. Sir,” he added, with a jerky bow.

“That is why you should not speak before you enter a room. I suspect you have something you are bursting to tell me, but perhaps your news will wait?”

Benedict blushed remarkably. It was the fault of the fair hair and skin inherited from their mother. He had her chiseled features as well. It was quite unfair, when Portia’s face and coloring came from Papa. She liked her hazel eyes, but her hair was an undistinguished brown, and her face inclined to the square.

“Yes, certainly. If you will excuse me, please?”

When he remembered his manners, one might think him almost an adult. Then at times he might have been ten. Fourteen-nearly-fifteen was an awkward age.

“You must be Benedict.”

She could not see Solomon de Toledo's face, but her brother's answering grin reassured her.

"I am, sir." Benedict's gaze was speculative. She did not miss his inquisitive glance at her.

"Mr. de Toledo, this is my brother, Benedict. Benedict, Mr. de Toledo and I were discussing some business matters."

"Your servant, sir." Benedict bowed again and spoiled the effect by adding provocatively, "I expect you'd like me to cut and run."

"Where do you pick up such expressions, Benedict?" He would not have dared to use it in their father's presence.

"It's a sea term meaning to cut your anchor cable and sail away quickly. I've been studying the vocabulary so that if—"

"That's quite enough. Why don't you go down to the kitchen and ask Mrs. Crump to give you a slice of that breakfast cake."

"Shall I ask her to send up a tea tray?" He blushed again, no doubt remembering how scant their supply of tea leaves was.

"It's not necessary." She stared at him in a manner which she hoped made it quite clear his presence could be dispensed with.

"Good day, sir. Sister, I'll tell you about Wilkes the apothecary later," he added teasingly. When he went out, he closed the door behind him out of force of habit.

De Toledo turned back to her and resumed his seat. "That is why I offered Mr. Gillespie a loan with no interest. Your brother needs an education. I imagine he is aware of your family's current difficulties and has offered to go to sea."

"He is torn between the Royal Navy, where he thinks he might rise to be a captain, and the East India Company ships. He thinks India would be interesting, and he assures me there are fortunes to be made there."

"From what I have heard, life on a naval ship is no very pleasant thing, even when we are not at war. He has also failed to take into account that to rise high in our navy he must have the right connections. He is correct about India, but no ship is safe. He might as easily die as make a fortune or gain high rank. The East Indiamen do tend to sink."

"He's almost fifteen."

"I remember being that age." He smiled wryly. "He needs another year or two at Radford's and then mayhap to be sent to university. Your father told me he's intelligent and studious. He wanted Benedict to have a university education as he himself did but admitted that it was too soon to plan on it."

"I never understood how he thought we could afford it. A grammar school was one thing, university quite another." Though even the grammar school tuition had proven to be out of the question.

"He hoped to earn more from his writing. I was not sanguine about his prospects, but Mr. Gillespie wanted Benedict to study for a gentleman's profession. I suspected your brother was an active lad, from certain things your father mentioned, and suggested he might prefer business to Greek grammar. Mr. Gillespie was not ready to give up his ambitions for the boy so we agreed to postpone talking about university. Under the circumstances, I will mention that a university degree is not necessary to rise in the East India Company or perhaps a merchant house."

"It sounds as though you and my father discussed the matter a great deal." She could understand how her papa might have spoken at length with Mr. de Toledo about matters which had little to do with securing a loan. The man was somehow very easy to talk to. It was probably an asset in his business.

"We did."

"And yet you lent him money at no interest, which I find hard to believe. Indeed, I cannot think how he found you."

He blew out a breath. "He almost did not. He learned of me through the merest coincidence."

"Are there moneylenders who lend at no interest? For it seems to me it would not be a very repaying business."

"It would not. And I do ordinarily charge reasonable, though not extortionate, interest."

"Please explain to me how it came about, sir." If she understood, she might have some idea of how to deal with the problem.

"Your father went to his bank before Benedict's first term, when he realized he could not afford the tuition. His banker being absent for some reason or other, he spoke with my cousin, who was employed there. David could not authorize even so small a loan in Mr. Gillespie's circumstances, but told him he had a cousin—me—who sometimes loaned small amounts and recommended your father apply to me. I should add that David is no longer with the bank. He has too active a sense of humor and is much happier working in a relative's import business."

"Was it not rather cruel of him to send my father to a moneylender?" Though he had received a loan, and at no interest, too, if Mr. de Toledo could be believed.

"David's joke was on me rather than your father. In my family, I have a reputation for being soft-hearted. Apparently, my cousin described me as a small, private banker. Your father explained his problem, and while we were discussing the importance of education, I decided to lend him the money."

"Just like that? Surely you realized he would have trouble paying you back?"

"Well, yes. He warned me it might take him some considerable time. I told him I was not pressing for repayment according to any set schedule."

"Mr. de Toledo, did it not occur to you that if my father dies before the debt is paid, you may never be paid?"

"Mistress Portia, I've lent money for almost ten years, ever since I left grammar school. More recently I have, er, gone into other businesses, and those are doing well. Your father reminds me of my paternal great-grandfather, with whom I lived for several years when I was a child. I wanted to help Mr. Gillespie and I could afford to do so, even if he was never able to pay me back. He would not have accepted charity but agreeing to very flexible payments allowed him to send his son to his own old school and permitted me to, er, do a good deed in a naughty world."

"That's from *The Merchant of Venice*!"

"It is a quotation I've always liked. Do you—"

Chapter 5

The door opened, and Benedict stuck his head into the room.

"Sorry! I didn't mean to interrupt again, I just assumed…After I went to the kitchen, I went up to see Mama to tell her about Mr. Wilkes offering to hire me to make deliveries. She's upset about something. I don't think it was about Wilkes because she hardly seemed to be paying attention. But she moaned and said I should talk to you."

"About what? Working for him as a temporary position? If you go back to school—" But how could he?

Benedict, who had edged into the room, stared down at his shoes, and brushed crumbs off the front of his waistcoat. There was a spot of jam, too. Portia sighed. It might come out. Mama had a receipt book with helpful household hints, including how to remove stains.

"With Father so ill, I think it best to remain at home at least for the next term in case you and Mother need me."

Benedict had fastened upon the "if." Before she could think how to respond, de Toledo spoke.

"If your father knew you meant to miss a term at school, he would surely be distressed. You know how important he thinks a good education."

"I know, sir, but…" Benedict's eyes sought Portia's. *Help!*

"Benedict understands that we are in some difficulties because of Papa's illness and wishes to assist us. I don't think doing errands for Mr. Wilkes is the best choice, however." And how were they to conceal Benedict's presence at home from Papa, who might understand good deal?

"Master Benedict, your sister and I have been discussing the matter. It's in your best interests and your family's, too, that you continue your education at Radford's School."

"Do you not have some reading to do, Benedict?" She did not want to continue in her brother's hearing a discussion which might encourage him to hope he could give up formal education.

"I could review my books from last term."

"That would be a very good idea."

"Before I forget, Portia, Mama mentioned something about entertaining a gentleman. I didn't quite follow what she meant, but she said to tell you. Female stuff, I suppose."

Then he was out the door, leaving Portia blushing. Maybe Benedict had not understood the message but she did: she had spent far too long alone with de Toledo, part of it with the door closed. Her own face burned with humiliation.

Was there a polite way to tell him he must leave? It was not a situation that had occurred with any visitor in her memory. Ladies and gentlemen knew when to call, how long one might stay, and that a gentleman should not be alone with a lady who was not a relative, particularly not with the door closed. It would be different if one of the pair were elderly. She, of course, was at her last prayers, but the moneylender was in the prime of life for a man, no more than four or five years older than she. And they still had matters to discuss. She hurried into speech to cover her discomfiture.

"Sir, while I agree on the importance of education, under the circumstances my family should consider alternatives." It was a pity that she could not think what those might be. Making deliveries for Wilkes? No. Going to sea? Definitely not!

"As a friend of your father's and his, mmmm, financial advisor, I really think Benedict must complete his schooling."

"While I agree with you, sir, I must discuss this with my mother. She does have a half brother who may be able to help." Portia's lack of confidence in this solution must have come through in her voice.

"You should talk to your mother and any other advisor you can think of. Then let us revisit the matter to be sure your brother receives the education he will need no matter what career he pursues. Er…you have my direction from my letter to your father? I do know it's improper for a young lady to write a man, but surely if 'tis a matter of business, it is permissible. You would write an attorney or a grocer, would you not?"

"Oh, certainly. That is quite a different thing. I will write when we have worked out what to do, whatever it may be. Thank you, Mr. de Toledo. You have been most obliging."

He bowed, turned toward the door, and paused. "There is something I can do for your father, which may be acceptable. My own father is a physician. To oblige me, I am sure he would see Mr. Gillespie. He studied both at Leiden and Edinburgh and is accounted an excellent doctor. He has to be; his father and grandfather were also physicians. Unless you have a doctor who is treating Mr. Gillespie?"

"We had one in several times after my father fell ill. He bled Papa and when it seemed to do no good, he recommended cupping. Mama would not agree to that. Then he wanted to continue to bleed my father. I did not feel we should allow him to be bled further, and so we dismissed the doctor." And they could not afford further fees. "In spite of my father not being bled again or cupped at all, he does seem to be improving."

"I promise you, my own father is no great advocate of either practice. May he call upon you? There would be no fee."

She would have refused if it meant further debt. Still, it would be reassuring to have a second doctor's opinion, particularly for Mama, who was all but worn to a thread with worry.

"If you think he would be willing to see my father without a fee, I can't refuse. We have been nursing him as we would for any ailment, and he does seem better, but—" She shrugged.

"I will ask him to come as soon as possible. Now, I fear we have been closeted together far too long. I'm sure that was what Benedict's message from Mrs. Gillespie meant. Madam, good day to you."

"And to you, sir."

****

Portia Gillespie was so unlike what he had imagined that Solomon feared his surprise had been obvious. When he met with Gillespie in the coffee house the first few times, he had inquired about his family's health and Benedict's progress at school. He always did speak a little with his clients in part to ascertain how they were going on, and because it was good business. Men were less likely to cheat or default on a debt to an acquaintance rather than one they regarded merely as a bloodsucker. His meetings with Gillespie had lengthened as he discovered how much the man reminded him of his great-grandfather and Gillespie realized Solomon had received a gentleman's education, even if not at university.

They had become friendly as Gillespie had talked of his work and interests. His daughter acted as his amanuensis. " 'Tis a saving of money, for otherwise I would have to hire some needy fellow to assist me. It gives her something to do and makes her feel useful," Gillespie had said. "A pity she did not take after her mother. 'Twould have been easier to find her a husband." The brisk young lady met at the Gillespies' home was not the faded, aging spinster he expected. Was Thomas Gillespie blind to his daughter's charm? Or was her unmarried state the result of his inability to provide a dowry? Or because Gillespie kept her too busy to meet suitable men?

What a pleasant young lady. Not too young, either: she must be four or five and twenty. Gillespie had told him she helped with his essays and books when the rheumatism in his hands bothered him. Gillespie alternately worried about her future and yet admitted he could not do without her assistance.

She was devoted to her family, too. The skin under her eyes was blue-smudged, either from lack of sleep because she sat up with her father at night or because worry kept her awake. They should have some decent woman to act as nurse for at least part of the day; not all were gin-soaked slatterns. Given their financial woes, he could not suggest it nor offer to advance money to cover the cost. His ordinarily agile brain could not produce a reason for why a sickroom attendant should count as part of Benedict's school expenses. She would not consider indebting the family still more to spare her mother and herself the additional labor of caring for Gillespie, however much of a toll it took upon them.

Families. His own parents worried about him, which was ridiculous at his age but perhaps understandable. Mother had actually told him that if he insisted on making a business of arranging marriages, he should make one for himself. But he intended to postpone taking any action until his various business interests and investments were thriving. In fact, it was difficult to know what lady would want to marry him, given certain of his decisions. Banking was a respectable business; moneylending was not. A gentleman might invest in a merchantman's cargo or in property. Buying and selling odd lots of merchandise was trade, and therefore crass.

Acting as a matchmaker for a fee was vulgar, although certain ladies of the beau monde would sponsor girls with no relatives able to bring them out in London and did well from it without doing anything so ungenteel as charging a fee. The young lady would naturally require gowns for her introduction to society and all the accessories that they would require. The bills from the dressmaker and milliner might be inflated, with the sponsoring lady receiving the difference between the actual bill and the bill provided to the chit's guardian. The cost of needed lessons in dance, deportment, and the like suffered the same fate. Such tricks worked best with country gentlemen whose pockets were deep and whose acquaintance with London was slight.

His brothers and cousin could not understand why he had not gone into banking ("real banking," David called it), or the Levant trade, or trained in medicine, like their eldest brother. His mother sighed over him.

After he last dined with the family, when the tea tray was brought to the drawing room and his mother finished brewing the tea, she had drawn him aside. She said tentatively, "Your brothers and Blanche are all married. I wish you might find a bride. I know you could not like a girl who is hardly out of the nursery or who is foolish, but the Vergers' daughter, Susan, is not too young and is sensible. I cannot think why she has not been snapped up already except that her standards are high. I do not mean she is hoping for a title, merely a man of intelligence and good character."

"Mother, I want my children to be brought up as Jews."

"Well, of course."

"Mistress Verger is not a Jew."

"No, but she has reared Susan very carefully. I don't speak merely of her accomplishments but also of her deportment, interest in charitable work, and even her education. Susan would be an admirable wife for any gentleman."

When he was younger, Solomon had sometimes suspected he and his parents did not communicate successfully. Apparently, the problem still existed. "Mistress Susan is not a Jew."

"Of course she is. I know for a fact the children

were raised in our faith."

Solomon filled in the unspoken "more or less." "The child of a non-Jewish mother is not a Jew. Mistress Verger did not convert, so her children can't be considered Hebrew."

"Oh, pooh, Solomon. She would have had to go to Holland to convert, and she could not very well have gone on her own, even if she or Jeremiah had had the money to send her."

"Mr. Verger's father changed his surname from Verga to try to pass as English." This had no bearing on the current Mistress Verger's failure to convert, being merely another thing his great-grandfather Alvaro would have disliked. It was perhaps hypocritical to bring it up, as his mother's family, the Mendeses, had altered the spelling of their name to Mendys.

"What of it? I am perfectly sure many of the families descended from the Normans no longer spell their names as their ancestors did. It's not as if he were deceiving anyone."

"Then why change? He might as well have kept his Portuguese name. Everyone knows his religion."

"Precisely, dear. And Susan and the boys are considered Jews."

"Not by our law."

His mother frowned, something he rarely saw, as she worried about wrinkles. "That is your great-grandfather speaking."

"He was very devout."

"Yes, and I do not object to that aspect of his character. He was brilliant and often kind. He was also ridiculously prejudiced. He might have been living in medieval Spain, and he wasn't even born in Spain! His disapproval cast a gloom over your grandfather's second marriage, in spite of there being no chance of children."

"He was never rude to Grandmother Sybil."

"No, that I will admit. She may never have realized he considered it a mésalliance. I hope not, because she was a delightful stepmama-in-law, if there is such a relationship. I do wish you were not quite so much like him."

If you had not sent me away when I was little…

She said judiciously, "I don't say he was not a very fine man. I know he did not approve of what he called *conversos*, but he never spoke a word about it when your brother Vidal converted. After all, his own grandparents accepted Christianity rather than leave Spain. I suppose the idea of converting for safety did not seem utterly strange to him. He must have ignored the fact that there is no Inquisition in England. It does not appear to me that English Christians are very devout, except the Dissenters, and they are kept down, thank goodness."

"Great-Grandfather would have said, 'They may someday acquire the power to impose their beliefs on all.' " Admittedly, it seemed unlikely; the English might have grown moderate as a result of their religious wars.

"I should not have agreed to let you live with your great-grandfather. Your papa wanted you to know your grandfather better, and it never occurred to us your great-grandfather's influence would be so strong. If I or your father had imagined such a thing, we would have managed somehow to hire a woman to mind you."

It was no one's fault. His mother had been in poor

health for several years after Blanche's birth and had all she could manage caring for the baby. The nursery maid was too busy to have time for any child but Samuel, who was beginning to walk, or rather, run; he went directly from crawling to dashing. The older boys, twelve and fourteen, spent their days with their tutor. At six, Solomon was old enough not to need a nurse and too young for a tutor. He had been sent to live with his grandfather and great-grandfather.

"Grandfather was busy with his patients. Grandmother Sybil was busy with their home. Great-Grandfather had time to spend with me."

"Sometimes when you speak, Solomon, I can hear him as clearly as if he were in the room. It rather worries me."

"I suppose I picked up his way of speaking." Solomon's own speech sometimes took on Great-Grandfather's subtly foreign intonation and turns of phrase when dealing with his clients. Why did he do it? Ordinarily he sounded like any other educated Englishman.

"You took on his attitudes, too, and I fear they will not bring you happiness." Her face was troubled. "Mothers always wish their children to marry, but I am not sure you should take that step until you are settled in your own life. Or settled in your mind."

"Am I not? I have modestly successful business interests, I know what I want in a wife"—*so why am I am reluctant to look for a bride?*—"which should mean I am settled. I'm past the age of being an irresponsible young man about town."

"Now that is one thing you never were. You've always been responsible. While I could not wish you to be guilty of the usual excesses of young men, I also wish you were not so very serious. However, by 'settled,' I meant you must decide what you really want."

He intended to say he knew precisely what he wanted: to honor Great-Grandfather Alvaro's traditions and their shared religion and to marry and enjoy the warmth and love of family life. Before he could utter the words, he knew he was mistaken, or at least that it was not the whole truth. But before he could puzzle out what was lacking, his mother was speaking again, and he put the question aside for later.

"If you are to marry," she said slowly, "you must consider two things, at least. The first is, how would a really observant Jewish wife regard your habits? You do not always keep the Sabbath, and I'm sure you do not observe all the dietary rules. Your great-grandfather would be dismayed if he were not dead. I was extremely glad not to have to live in the same house—your father and I could not have done so, fortunately, given the size of Alvaro's house—and indeed, your papa and I and our fathers all agreed that we must have our own home. It was put in the marriage settlements."

The thought of his parents occupying the same residence with Great-Grandfather was not one Solomon could imagine without a shudder. They had Christian neighbors and friends and mixed with them without worrying too much about strict adherence to religious laws that, as his father said, seemed to have little relevance in the modern world.

"I attend the synagogue. I don't eat pork"—*if I can avoid it*—"and you are not appalled by my lapses"—could they be called lapses when he simply did not feel the rules were the central tenet of his religion?—"by which I conclude some young ladies of our faith would not object to my ways."

His mother conceded the point. "That is the second point to consider. Are you able to support a wife in the manner those girls and their families would expect?"

A very good question. The real problem might be that marriage to a moneylender and occasional matchmaker would not confer an acceptable social status on his bride. "I do have some investments."

"If you gave up moneylending in favor of some other occupation, it would be easier to find a wife. You could get a position with the Levanter Trading Company, Solomon. The less common languages you learned from Alvaro are an advantage you could put to good use."

Great-Grandfather spoke half a dozen languages, including Turkish, Italian, and Dutch. As a child, he had spoken the Ladino dialect of Spanish. Solomon had forgotten much of what he had learned from him, having had little practice since Alvaro's death.

By Alvaro de Toledo's standard, Solomon was a very bad Jew. He would also not have regarded moneylending and matchmaking as suitable occupations, not like being a physician or a rabbi. He might have considered banking or importing acceptable.

"He told wonderful stories." *Na! Kontará un maasè de los de abásho. Listen! I will tell a story of the dead.* They were often grim: tales of persecution, of accusations by a neighbor of unchristian practices which brought down the wrath of the Inquisition. Sometimes they were tales from where their family had lived after leaving Spain: Turkey, Italy, Holland.

"Your father told me some of those stories. They were frightful. I fear Alvaro's early years gave him a rather melancholy view of life. There is no reason you cannot be successful, have a pleasing bride, and live a good life. This is not medieval Spain."

"I haven't been looking for a wife, Mother. If I remember where this conversation began, I only said I wanted my children raised as Jews."

"You were raised as a Jew, dear, if not such a very strict one as your grandfather or great-grandfather. You ought to give some thought to marriage. I hope you don't mean to be an old bachelor!"

"Well, no. But you are correct that I should have a little more to offer a prospective bride."

"Which you could do with no difficulty, if you took a position with a trading company or bank."

"But I would like to be successful on my own merits, not by using family connections." That was the influence of John Barlicorn—now Earl of Barlyon—met during the period he had lived with his grandfather and run free when he wasn't doing his lessons or listening to Great-Grandfather's stories.

"No one doubts your intelligence, Solomon. Nepotism is perfectly respectable, and far more common than succeeding with no one's help. In some families, the eldest son inherits the family business, or the title and property, and 'tis understood the second will go into whatever profession family tradition dictates, and their families help them advance. Your father preferred to let each of you decide what would best suit you. Mayhap it would have been better if he had told you what your career was to be."

"I do not think I would have enjoyed being either a physician or a rabbi, Mother."

"No, and he would never have insisted on it or even suggested it. But although he has never said so, I am sure he would rather you engaged in some other occupation."

"I'm not doing badly with some investments."

"Oh, excellent. That's respectable." She tilted her head to one side, like a bird intent on a juicy bug. "That friend of yours, the one you brought to dinner occasionally years ago…what was his name? It was an odd one that always made me think of the countryside and farm laborers. He was a poor lad, but didn't he buy and sell used goods? I had the impression he did rather well at it, though he was quite young. He was so good for you. He countered your great-grandfather Alvaro's influence. Why did you stop bringing him home?"

"After I moved to my own rooms, we met there or in a coffee house usually." From John Barlicorn, Solomon had learned to get along with Christians and to fight. They had traded positions then, and Sol had taught Barlicorn what he knew about the importance of contracts and negotiation, how to put one's money where no pickpocket could get it, and even better, where it might breed. The recollection lightened his mood momentarily.

What an inconvenient memory his mother had! He had not brought Barlicorn to dinner in a dozen years. His friend had discontinued his visits when he first began to become known in London's underworld. Solomon should tell her Barlicorn was dead, which was the rumor he had spread. But she had been quite fond of his friend and thinking him dead would grieve her.

There was no chance of his family encountering the new Earl of Barlyon. He could say John had taken ship for the colonies, but then she would wonder how he fared, and he could not claim not to know his destination. If he made up something, she might ask any visitor from the Americas whether he had heard of John Barlicorn. His mother peered at him inquiringly.

"Ahhhh…" He could not lie to her, and she was true blue and would keep a secret. "You remember he was living on his own"—and how his mother had worried for him, although hundreds or thousands of orphans scrambled to make a living in the streets—"having run away from home. He went back to see how his mother went on and discovered his stepfather was dead and he had inherited the land. So he stayed to manage it and take care of his mama."

"I am very glad to hear it. Why did you not tell me when you learned of it?"

"I thought I had. Or you might have asked."

She sighed. "I often wondered. I was afraid to know what had happened to him."

Chapter 6

To Portia's surprise, Dr. Benjamin de Toledo called upon her family the following day, throwing Eliza Gillespie into confusion. Portia had not mentioned Solomon de Toledo's offer to her, assuming that it would come to nothing. Mr. de Toledo's father would be too busy or unwilling to involve himself when he was contacted through an intermediary, unwilling to sacrifice a fee. She had also feared his visit would upset her father.

Benjamin de Toledo was shorter than his son and substantial without being at all fat. His relaxed manner set them both at ease. Of course, her mother was most confident when a man was present to make any decisions, at least if the man in question dressed and talked like a gentleman. Unless he was a moneylender; no matter how seemingly well bred, a usurer fell into the same category as highwaymen, violent lunatics, and rabid dogs. The doctor's lack of pomposity reassured Portia, and the laugh lines at the corners of his eyes called to mind his son.

He spoke directly to Thomas Gillespie when he examined him, a gentle flow of comments about current events which required no response from a listener. Portia and her mother hovered in the background. Her father did react to two or three remarks. What his head jerk or grunt meant was anyone's guess.

"Do you have any favorite dish you would like for dinner, Mr. Gillespie?"

Her papa grunted. One half of his face scowled.

Her mother hurried into speech to cover the embarrassment of her husband's inability to reply. "Dr. Royce recommended nothing but gruel and broth to prevent the risk of choking. Though we did add oatmeal caudle for variety."

"Very sensible for the first stage of recovery, madam. However, you might add custard, blancmange, rice pudding, and any soft food which does not require much chewing. Syllabub is another possibility. If there are any foods that Mr. Gillespie particularly likes which fall into that category, I think he would appreciate them."

Her father raised his left hand and brought it down sharply on the bed.

Seeing Dr. de Toledo puzzled, Portia explained, "My father is in the habit of slapping his desk smartly to reinforce some point he is making. It's startling the first time. I believe he agrees with you."

"Ah." He turned back to his patient. "Sir, you seem to be making good progress. I apprehend you are bored, however. I think your family reads to you for an hour or two each day?"

"We do, Dr. de Toledo," Eliza assured him.

"Perhaps if you could read to Mr. Gillespie several times during the day, even if not for an hour at a time, so as not to strain your voices?"

This time Gillespie's hand rose hesitantly and dropped on the coverlet.

"We can, sir. My brother can read aloud also."

"I see you are tired, and I will take my leave of

you. Your servant, Mr. Gillespie."

Mama scurried off to speak to Cook after thanking the doctor, leaving Portia to offer refreshment and express their thanks more profusely. He agreed to a small glass of claret and made several more suggestions, all of them sensible and more to the point, inexpensive. This seemed to indicate his son had spoken to him of the family's circumstances.

"Dr. de Toledo, I and my mother, too, are more grateful than I can say for your visit. Please tell me how much we owe you. I fear it will be some time before we can pay you…" If indeed they ever could scrape up the money.

"Mistress Portia, my son asked me to call upon your father. He has the greatest respect for Mr. Gillespie's scholarship. There is no fee, no more than if I were called to the bedside of a family member."

"He did say you would do it without charge, but I did not feel he should impose upon you. Yet I admit we were anxious to have a physician's opinion as to my father's condition. Thank you again. It is a relief to know he is better and to have an idea of how to go on. Please thank Mr. Solomon de Toledo for me."

"I will. Solomon so seldom asks me for a favor or assistance that it was a pleasure to grant it. Please send for me if Mr. Gillespie's condition seems to worsen. Upon the same terms as this visit." He paused. "Since we are speaking of my son, may I urge you to accept his help? I suspect that worry for your brother's education is contributing to the strain I see in your mother and yourself. He needs an education in order to gain any suitable employment."

She bit her lip. "I know, Dr. de Toledo. But how

can we incur more debt that we may never be able to pay?" In two more years, when Benedict finished at Radford's, they might all be in debtor's prison.

"If I understand the matter, you might scrape by on your father's investment income if you practice the most rigorous economy. Isn't it true that the only real debt you cannot pay is what you owe Solomon for Master Benedict's schooling?"

"Well, yes."

"He has lent the money at no interest, with no set time for repayment. No doubt if your father is able to resume his writing, he will make payments as he has been doing. His *Elementary Guide to Hebrew Grammar* is masterful, by the way. Solomon admires Mr. Gillespie and shares with him the belief that your brother should receive a good education. There is this, too: anxiety for Benedict may affect Mr. Gillespie's recovery. If your brother does not leave for his school, his presence at home cannot be concealed. My son has other sources of income and does not wish you to worry about repaying him until you are able."

She had nothing to offer to counter the doctor's argument. In fact, she could think of a host of objections to any other course of action.

"We have been considering an apprenticeship." An apprenticeship for Benedict, paid for by Mama's necklace, brought problems of its own. It must be a gentlemanly trade, and those were likely to require a large fee. She had heard a Levant merchant's apprenticeship premium could be as much as a thousand pounds.

"Mistress Portia, an indenture for apprenticeship must be signed by a justice of the peace. I am not an expert on law, but I suspect that as your father is alive and may recover, your mother lacks authority to arrange an apprenticeship. When Mr. Gillespie is able to resume his normal life, he would almost certainly object, would he not?"

A craft with a consideration they could afford would be one Papa would never accept. Periwig maker? Hosier? She shuddered, imagining his reaction to such an occupation.

"I believe the indenture would then be null and void," he continued. "The fee would probably not be returned; it isn't, when the apprentice runs away or is turned off for his faults or dies."

If Benedict were to help support their family eventually, he must complete his schooling.

"I know you are correct, sir. Even if he served his apprenticeship, it's unlikely he would earn much for years, or perhaps ever."

"I suggest you send to my son to make the necessary arrangements. Or shall I ask him to call upon you?"

She should speak with her mother about it. Oh, fiddlesticks! Much as she loved her mother, she could not pretend that she would be able to make any decision more difficult than deciding the week's menu.

"If you would, please." Benedict's future was in Portia's hands.

****

Her mother was upstairs when Abby came to the library to tell Portia "that foreign gentleman" was in the parlor. Their house was not sufficiently elegant for the chamber to be called a drawing room. Although she had been expecting his visit, her heart gave a skip. For one ridiculous moment, she thought of going up to tidy her hair and kerchief. She might have done it, but for the risk of alerting her mother. Benedict, thank goodness, was out of the house.

"I hope my father's report of Mr. Gillespie's condition has reassured you, madam. And your family, too, of course."

"Dr. de Toledo was all that was kind and made several helpful suggestions, one of which my mother is employing at the moment. Reading to my father," she added. "Please be seated. Unless it would be better to talk in the library? In case it is necessary to make notes or draw up an agreement?"

"I brought a notarized copy of your father's contract. As you can see, it bears no interest and contains no penalties or set schedule for repayment. I know you have been worried about Mr. Gillespie's debt and about additional debt."

He passed a sheet of paper to her.

The terms were brief and clearly stated. She perused it, saying, "Thank you, sir, for I cannot help but be concerned about the debt."

Portia did not know whether to be disappointed or relieved. On the one hand, if they had had to agree to and write out terms, he would have had to remain longer, and they would have had to use the library. Meeting a man alone was bad enough. Meeting him in a room farther removed from intrusion would be fatal to a lady's reputation. Her cheeks felt warmer than could be accounted for by the heat of the day. Perhaps it was because today she was more aware of him. She could find no fault with his deep red suit and waistcoat, and while he wore no lace at his throat or wrists, the effect was very attractive. He looked like a gentleman. She had never liked a man so well on short acquaintance. Or longer acquaintance, for that matter.

She returned her attention to the document somewhat unwillingly. If she could believe the notarized copy, her father's loan was indeed interest-free with payments due at the borrower's convenience. When she looked up, he asked, "Will you permit me to advance funds for another two years at Radford's, Mistress Portia?"

"I fear I must, Mr. de Toledo. Your terms are more than fair. They're embarrassingly generous. But if my father has not recovered by the time Benedict leaves school, we must find some employment for him which is not too…" What could she say, after all?

"Not too demeaning. I would add it should also pay adequately."

"If only it were possible, perhaps he could contribute a little toward what you are owed. And now Dr. de Toledo has assured us no medicines are required, I can see how much we can allot to paying you." Shallow it might be, but she did wish it were not necessary to worry so much about expenses. The parson might advise one to trust in Providence, but any rational person knew that Providence took no particular interest in one's comfort. One's mind should be fixed on higher things. But it was very difficult to concentrate on Heaven when one wondered how to pay the butcher and lacked the coal to keep warm.

" 'Tis only two more years, and then if Master Benedict wishes to take a post with the East India Company or in some other respectable business, we will have no trouble finding him a place. It is a pity trade is held in contempt by many. As things are, a man who does not inherit a good income or a productive property has few ways to earn money if he wishes to remain a gentleman. Some of those ways require the sponsorship of a family member or friend in order to rise. Like the Navy."

"I agree, and yet…" She had meant to say that business coarsened a man. However, de Toledo was gentlemanly, if not a gentleman, being far less acceptable than a banker. Some professions were not unsuitable for a man of good family: the law, the church, the army. She could not think of any commercial enterprise which would be acceptable. A man might be able to use his connections to secure some undemanding post in the government which would pay enough to live or at least be a supplement to his income. Inspector of the Royal Table Linen, perhaps. Then he would hire someone at a fraction of his pay to do the actual work. Alas, her family possessed no relative or friend able to help Benedict to such a post.

"Or there is always a good marriage," de Toledo added.

"But why would any young lady with a dowry marry my brother, assuming he were old enough to marry?"

"Such things happen. 'Tis more likely if the young man is titled but poor and the lady's family wishes to make a good family connection. However, we cannot consider marriage a possibility until he is older."

"I wish marriage were not the only profession open to a lady." She had not meant to let the words escape her, often as she had thought them recently. She had been uneasily aware for several years that she had faded into spinsterhood, without being able to do anything about it or provide for her own future.

She had considered the more successful local tradesmen, but she could not quite imagine herself marrying Smith, the butcher, or James Grace, the haberdasher. Her father's acquaintances were genteel older men, but financially most were in hardly better circumstances than he was.

"A lady may be a companion or a governess."

"She may manage to support herself thereby, but she can be of little assistance to her family, and will likely be very poor when she is too old to work."

"That is true, I admit. Well, we are agreed Benedict will return to school?"

"I can see no other course."

"Do you wish to consult your mother?"

"I should have done so. However, I know she would agree and being asked would only make her uncomfortable."

De Toledo's smile conveyed a world of understanding. He had kind eyes. "It is better to deal with someone able to act decisively."

Was that a compliment? Perhaps it was a mere statement of fact.

"Thank you, sir. I need not take much more of your time. However, I would like to know how my father made his payments."

"We met at a coffee house, which would not be suitable for you. But there is no need to worry about paying immediately, as you need not worry about the interest."

"How can I make payments to you?"

"If I were worried about the money, I would never have lent to your father. Let us deal with repayment when your household is on a more stable footing. At that time, perhaps I could call upon you at intervals. Let us now consider how to facilitate Benedict's return to school."

The prospect of visits from a moneylender should have been horrifying. Instead, it was rather cheering. The thought of the necessary arrangements with Radford's School brought her down to earth with a thump.

"Mr. de Toledo, regarding Benedict's fee for the term, how am I to pay it? I go to the grocer and other shops to pay, but although I know my father has sometimes written instructions to his bank to remit money to someone, I am not sure his banker would accept my mother's signature as authority."

"I shall send it to Radford's as I have sent the previous fees. I met Mr. Gillespie at the coffee house to give him the money for the coach fare and incidental expenses. I will deliver it to you."

"Thank you, sir. That relieves my mind of a great worry. I hardly liked the idea of sending payment by the post."

"Not when the post boys are robbed with tedious regularity, Mistress Portia. I have a more secure method of sending payments. Does Benedict travel to his school by himself?"

"He has been going by stage with a friend, accompanied by the friend's family connection who is a tutor at Radford's."

"Will that arrangement hold for this year?"

"Yes. We have not told them Benedict might not

be able to return to school. First we kept hoping to find that my father had an account in another bank or a substantial sum of money hidden in the house.

"It may seem odd we were so ignorant of our financial situation. Papa managed the accounts and expenses himself, which I can understand, as my mother does not excel at figures." There was an understatement, if ever Portia had uttered one. "Once I reviewed the banking and household records, I could not understand how we had ever had enough to cover the school fees, if there was no other account or hidden money."

"This is not the first time I have known a man's family to be unaware of their finances. Does Mr. Gillespie take Benedict to the coaching inn to meet his fellow travelers?"

Here was another problem. "He did."

Solomon took a small notebook and pencil and jotted a few words. "I will see to it he gets there." Returning it to his coat's capacious pocket, he withdrew two folded sheets of paper and passed them to her. "This is the contract I have prepared in duplicate. Please review it and tell me if you disagree with any point. It is essentially identical to the one your father signed."

The agreement was short and lacking in legal jargon, stating merely that Solomon de Toledo would lend to Portia Eleanor Gillespie such sums as might be necessary to pay for Benedict Charles Gillespie's school expenses at Radford's School, including books, board and lodging, and other living expenses, coach fare, and incidental costs associated with his education not otherwise specified, at no interest, the principal amount to be repaid at the borrower's convenience.

"This is more than fair," she admitted. She went to the escritoire to sign both copies.

Solomon signed and sprinkled the sheets with pounce. "May I hope you will inform me when your papa is able to receive visitors?"

"I will. Thank you for your help. You've been very kind. I'll see you to the door."

When he was gone, she breathed a sigh of relief that the question of Benedict's school term had been settled, though the debt still bothered her. What a decent, thoughtful man he was. She had not found those characteristics among her male acquaintances, not with any regularity, at least, and not with a man who was young and not unattractive. If she had…

Mama would need to be revived with hartshorn if she knew how long she and de Toledo had been alone behind a closed door. At that door's opening, she started guiltily, only to see that it was Benedict.

"Mr. de Toledo seems like a good fellow," he remarked chattily, and dropped onto a chair. "Even if he does think I should continue at school."

"Whatever brings Mr. de Toledo to your mind?" she inquired. She feared she could guess.

"Don't you remember you told me not to rush into a room without being sure there were no guests? Or something like that. I stopped outside this door to listen and make sure I would not be intruding."

"And stayed to listen?"

He grinned. "You were discussing me, Portia. Of course I stayed."

"I hope you don't make a habit of eavesdropping."

"If I hear my name mentioned, how can I resist?"

"Try. It's not the action of a gentleman."

"Think how you would feel if people were plotting about your future behind your back."

Which was not uncommon when one was female, as she very well knew. She was not going to try to tell him he was too young to have a say in the matter. "Your opinion should be taken into consideration, but you do need an education, and how would Papa feel if we allowed a temporary setback to deprive you of it?"

Benedict winced. "It's not so much how he'd feel as how he'd make us feel. When I told him I didn't see the use in learning Hebrew, he looked at me in that disappointed way, as if I'd taken to gambling or picking pockets."

"He has very high standards for a gentleman's education."

"Portia, they're what men learned a hundred years ago. Besides, you can't make money with them."

She could not deny it. Her father's scholarly preoccupations to the exclusion of everything else was why they were in their present straits. "Amassing a fortune should not be our primary aim in life."

"I don't want a fortune. I do want to be able to buy a book sometimes and not worry about paying bills, as you have had to do since Father fell ill. Our goal in life should be to increase our knowledge."

Portia smiled at this pompous statement. "And that is our father's opinion also."

"Yes, but Portia, I'm talking about real knowledge. Useful stuff, like steam power. Still, I don't think I'd mind going to India. It would be interesting, and it's a practical career. Mr. de Toledo has been very obliging, hasn't he? I wonder if he could help me to a position with the East India Company."

"We could hardly impose on him more than we already are. One of Papa's colleagues may be able to help you find a place."

"Portia." Benedict's tone was edged with exasperation. "I like some of them, but they're old, their ideas are old, and they're all poor as church mice, too. Their idea of suitable work would be as a tutor or a curate. It would be no improvement on"—he flung one arm out dramatically, and barely missed sweeping Eliza Gillespie's Delft vase from a side table—"this."

Suffering a pang at discovering Benedict also chafed at their circumstances, Portia said, "But what makes you think Mr. de Toledo might be able to assist you? He's a moneylender, but if he lent money to Papa…" Did Benedict know where his school fees came from? What had he overheard or worked out? Then, too, she could not complete the sentence "he must not be very successful." He had claimed to do well enough, which was no proof, because men were rather boastful. Though Solomon de Toledo had offered to assist Benedict to a position once he completed his schooling, and he might know someone among the bankers or importers of his faith.

"Given what we know now, it would make you wonder how he came to loan Papa money," he allowed. "But Portia, while speaking like a gentleman is no guarantee of being plump in the pocket, his suit was good and I think nearly new."

"Was it? I would have thought it Sunday wear for a modestly successful small tradesman or an attorney's clerk, perhaps."

Her brother snorted. "The cut and tailoring is

everything. You can tell the difference in ladies' clothing, can't you?"

"Of course. But I wouldn't have thought you could."

"I wouldn't know a good female gown from a cheap one. Most of the boys at Radford's are like me. But there are a few Honorables, like my friend Ferdy, who's a viscount's son, and even Baron Westersea. His father died before Westersea was out of leading strings, so his mama did not want him to go to school far away. The boys who come from good families or have wealthy merchant papas have finer linen and better coats and breeches. More of them, too."

"Good families? Benedict, ours is a good family."

"You know what I mean. People who don't have to think about how many candles they can use or how much coal they can burn in the winter." He went on. "I used to believe Papa had a mind above discomforts like cold. Part of his Stoic philosophy, you know. It's really just because we have too little money, isn't it?"

If she were honest with herself, she would admit that she also had assumed they lived as they did from Stoic principles rather than poverty. "It is true that we depend upon a rather small income. To accept straitened finances gracefully is certainly part of Papa's philosophy. To bemoan our situation, when we have enough food and a roof over our heads, would not be helpful. "

"I've been thinking, Portia. Mr. de Toledo is a pleasant gentleman. He seemed to like you. I wouldn't mind having him for a brother-in-law, and then we needn't worry about being obligated to him because he'd be one of the family. He's certainly preferable to any of the other fellows who have come skulking around you."

"That is a ridiculous idea." Though de Toledo was pleasant, and she had been more impressed with him than with the two or three potential suitors she had discouraged. "Please don't mention this subject to Mama."

"No chance of that! I remember how she went on and on about Mr. Mannering when she thought he was going to offer for you."

Chapter 7

"It's strange," Eliza remarked. "When I read to him, my dear husband seldom does more than growl at me."

"Probably it is because you read him his letters and bits of your own correspondence. There is not much scope for a response. The growl may signify his opinion of the writer's opinion or indeed the writer, rather than being aimed at you."

"My dear, I hope you are correct. Does he grumble when you read to him?"

"Sometimes. Occasionally he snorts. I only once made the mistake of starting to read a letter I had not myself read first. I came upon a passage Professor Gilchrist had larded with Greek words. Although I know the letters, I have never had occasion to pronounce entire words. My father was not amused by my efforts." He had in fact been furious. Portia had begged his pardon and implored him not to agitate himself lest he bring on another apoplexy. He had been in a black mood for the rest of the morning. Thomas Gillespie did not suffer fools gladly.

****

Solomon delivered the money for incidentals himself. Ordinarily he used a reliable messenger for such errands, but he wanted to assure himself that all was well with the Gillespies. As it fell out, when he inquired for Mistress Gillespie and Mistress Portia, only the latter was available. When she entered the room, she smiled and her pretty hazel eyes sparkled. Was it because her father was improved or was she pleased to see him?

"My mother sits with my father at this time in the mornings and reads to him. Benedict attends him in the afternoons, I take the evening, and Mother sleeps on a trundle bed in their room at night," Portia explained.

Mindful of the family's economic straits, he declined her offer of refreshment. "I wanted find out how Mr. Gillespie goes on as well as deliver the money." He passed her the purse.

She glanced curiously at the little bag in her hand. "This seems like a great deal—unless it's all pence," she remarked with an uncertain chuckle.

He mentioned the amount. He had hoped she would not raise the point.

"For incidentals? Oh, you've included the coach fare, I suppose."

"No. I will take care of that separately. It's merely for incidentals. Clothing, you know. Boys of that age always need clothing. A little pocket money. A visit to the barber? Quills and paper and ink. It all adds up."

After a moment, she murmured, "Thank you. Thank you for everything, Mr. de Toledo. My mother is more at ease, now that she need not worry about Benedict. And I, too, of course. I had wondered about clothing him; Benedict will persist in growing. Won't you stay for a cool drink? It's very warm today."

He would like to spend a few minutes more chatting with her. "I won't keep you any longer. You must have a great deal to do to get your brother ready to leave for school, with Mr. Gillespie ill."

"Oh, yes." Her shoulders slumped slightly. She must feel she was carrying the weight of the world.

"Master Benedict departs for school from the George in West Smithfield, I think?"

The traces of worry returned. "Yes."

"Then I will deliver him this year, and either turn him over to his friends or wait with him until they arrive."

"Oh." She chewed her lower lip in embarrassment or perplexity. "It would be such an imposition on you, sir." However, she had not refused.

"How else is he to get there? You certainly cannot escort him and return alone, and you would not want him to go by himself. He's near fifteen, of course, but still…"

"He's near fifteen," she agreed. "And I cannot think of anyone I could ask. No one reliable, anyway."

"It's settled then. They leave the Friday before the term begins?"

"Yes."

"Then it's only a question of your making sure he's ready to go that morning."

"Thank you again. I don't know how we could have managed without your help, Mr. de Toledo." She turned abruptly to pick up a basket of mending and remove it from the settee. Then she seemed not to know what to do with it. Had she done so to blink away tears?

"Thank you for your time, ma'am. You have my direction, in case…?"

"Yes."

"Your servant, Mistress Portia." He bowed and left before either of them could find a reason he should remain.

But he found himself wondering what else he could do to make life easier for Portia Gillespie. No, for the Gillespie family, of course. Perhaps he would think of something later.

****

He was still mulling the question of how best to aid the Gillespies when his clerk (actually more of a precaution against robbers and aggressive clients than a help in the office) announced a visitor. What he actually said was, "Cove as wants gelt to see you."

The fellow was not a previous client, though he was representative of many of Solomon's usual clients. That is to say, he was well dressed, spoke like a gentleman, needed money, and was evasive. He showed Solomon his card but did not give it to him.

"Sorry, I have only this one with me, I find."

He did not want to leave any proof of his visiting a moneylender, Solomon concluded.

"A friend—an acquaintance, really—recommended you," Philip Pomeroy said.

"His name?"

Pomeroy smiled deprecatingly. "I think he'd prefer I not mention it."

As if revealing his name would be a breach of confidentiality, when Solomon already knew about a former client's financial problems. Either the fellow was the merest chance acquaintance, no names exchanged, or he was one of Solomon's rare failures.

Pomeroy's story was simple, if not quite the same as that of most borrowers. He had an opportunity to join in a lucrative investment, but he must do it quickly, if he were not to lose out to some other investor. At the moment, he was low on cash.

"It's all going to dower my oldest girl, who's betrothed to Tiverton's second son."

Ah. He had seen the announcement in the newssheets. No wonder Pomeroy was short of cash: it would take a substantial dowry for a mere gentleman to marry a daughter to a viscount's heir presumptive, even though there was an older brother who could produce an heir. The advantages of an alliance with a titled family made it an excellent investment.

"Your bank will not lend you the money?"

"It's conservative. The dowry will take most of my money on deposit, accumulated over years to establish my daughter and sons. My estate does not bring in a great deal of income. I do have money in the Funds, but I'm reluctant to sell out when I need a relatively small amount to buy into the new investment."

"How much do you need?"

"A thousand pounds. I do have money coming in very soon. Unfortunately, it won't be soon enough."

Solomon had made larger loans, though not often. It would nearly empty his own bank account. On the other hand, he too had money coming in soon.

"Er, perhaps I should ask your rate of interest before we go further."

The man was not an oblivious fool. "Five per cent."

"That's no more than my bank's rate!"

"If your bank would make the loan. I keep my interest at the legal rate"—or sometimes lower—"but my clients cannot get a bank loan for one reason or another. Most moneylenders charge more. Someone who had anything of value would take it to a pawnbroker, or sell it outright."

"I've a cargo of sable pelts coming from the Baltic. I can't sell them until they arrive."

"Do you have proof?"

"My bill of lading." Pomeroy held out a folded sheet.

It appeared to be authentic and listed a fair-sized shipment of pelts. Solomon might not know a great deal about the shipping trade, but he did know the going price for furs. The cargo would more than cover the amount borrowed.

"When is the *North Sea Venturer* due?"

"The last I heard, she was eight or nine days out, according to an officer on a newly arrived merchantman."

"And when do you need the money?"

"Tomorrow at the latest." A rueful smile. "I lost too much time waiting for a decision from my banker, then trying to convince several friends they should lend me the money or part of it. It's a better risk than the tables, after all."

Though not as much fun as taking a chance on dice or cards, and perhaps they knew more of Pomeroy than he did.

Having never taken a cargo as security, he should ask Hawkins's opinion as a ship owner and importer. "I will give you my decision this afternoon. At four of the clock?"

"Can you not do it sooner? My opportunity to invest in my friends' enterprise is almost lost."

"Unfortunately, I have arrangements to make and other appointments." All true and had the advantage of not revealing that what he needed was advice. "We might meet here at two, if you do not mind risking my being a few minutes late."

Pomeroy agreed. When they shook hands, the man's palm was damp. Still, most of Solomon's clients had reason to be nervous.

By two o'clock, Solomon was also feeling some anxiety. Hawkins had not been in his office. He had gone to visit a ship moored near the Isle of Dogs. According to his clerk, he was not expected to come back to his new Leadenhall Street office that day.

"Mr. Hawkins might stop in at the old Wapping office on his way home. Then again, he might not, if he and his lady have some engagement tonight." Lady Emily Hawkins was foisting him on the beau monde in spite of the gossip about Hawkins having been a pirate and the fact of his having more recently been exonerated of a murder charge.

"Is Mr. Timothy in?" He had met Hawkins's friend and right-hand man once. He was razor sharp and very likely aware of the legal ramifications of accepting a bill of lading as security for a loan.

But Timothy was with Hawkins and out of reach. Simon Hayes, Solomon's man of business who would likely also be able to advise him, was out of town, combining his honeymoon with inspection of possible investments. Marriage. An increasingly desirable state, judging from the way it had caused Hawkins to cut back on his workday, move his office to a more salubrious area, and expand his social life. Hayes appeared happy with his new state, too: his bride enjoyed touring manufactories.

"Have you a decision for me?"

He had been going back and forth since this

morning. He could have consulted David, had he not been too proud to ask for help. If all went well, he would make money on his loan to Pomeroy. If something went wrong, he would lose a thousand pounds. Such a loss would not break him, though it would be an annoying setback. If he could lend money against cargoes, it would expand his business. It would be more respectable, somehow, more like investing in a cargo than moneylending. It all came down to the same thing, of course, but for gentlemen, appearances counted.

Chapter 8

It might have been expected Eliza would be worried about the additional loan. Instead, she was relieved.

At the news de Toledo had advanced enough money to pay for Benedict's new clothes with some left over, her mother remarked, "How thoughtful! Then everything is settled, and we can be comfortable. I confess I cannot like having dealings with such a person, but he has behaved very decently. I suppose he looks up to a man of such accomplishments as your papa's."

Portia doubted Solomon de Toledo's education had lacked much, judging from his conversation. It was a relief to find her mother reassured even if she herself was not quite comfortable about their growing debt. Though Benedict's matters were well in hand, their family situation remained precarious.

Somehow they must make up for the loss of Papa's tutoring and writing income. She could obtain a position as a governess or instructress in a female academy. However, either post would require she live on her employer's premises, out of the question when she was needed at home. Nor would it be well paid work. If only she had learned to play a musical instrument, she might be able to give lessons. She had never had the opportunity to acquire musical skill.

Perhaps it was no loss, to judge by her singing voice. Her talents did not lie in that direction.

One would ordinarily turn to a family member for advice, but who? Her mother's older brother lived in London, but the two had never been close. From certain things her mother had let fall, Uncle Edwin viewed any contact from his sister as being a veiled attempt to ask for money. She herself had met her uncle only three or four times. Were there not connections of some sort on her father's side? He had come from Warwickshire, near Radford's School, as he had once said the coach journey was short. Papa talked of his experiences at the school, although his reminiscences were uninformative. He spoke of something called Coventry godcakes, which were a kind of mincemeat tarts, and of being soundly caned for the usual sorts of youthful offenses.

Thomas Gillespie had a number of friends in and around London, though he kept in touch mostly by correspondence. Still, she had met many of them at one time or another, and half a dozen ranked as family friends, who came to visit or to dine occasionally. She could ask advice of them, the sole drawback being that while they were scholarly, they were not particularly practical or knowledgeable outside their field. Then she remembered Seth Brigginshaw.

"Mama, how does Father know Mr. Brigginshaw? It cannot be in a professional connection, can it?"

"Why, no. I'm sure your papa has never had a case before the Court of Chancery, which is where Brigginshaw practices, you know. Or in any other court, either. I think they must have met in university. No, I'm wrong. Once or twice Brigginshaw made a reference to events when they were boys. Mayhap he also attended Radford's. They are friends of longstanding, certainly."

Seth Brigginshaw proved to have more to offer than sympathy. "I am sorry to hear of his ailment. As stout as I am and with the law as a demanding mistress, I should be more likely to fall into an apoplexy than Tom. Yet I don't think I'd care to be chained to a desk all day as I suspect he is. No, I'm in and out to go to court or to call upon my clients, and I seldom go anywhere by chair or hackney. We both grew up in the country, Mistress Portia, and I'd be there yet if I could make a living in a smaller town, for I like to breathe clean air when I stretch my legs. Mayhap Tom would have done better to follow his father's business, but he wanted to be a gentleman."

"But my father is a gentleman." Portia's grip on her glass of sherry tightened. Her papa never forgot he came of the gentry, even if he seldom spoke of his family and his youth.

"Ay, like his father, but the family had no money though they had land. There was coal on their property, however, and old Gillespie went into business with a fellow that had the money to mine it. They made a comfortable living, the demand for coal in Coventry and Birmingham being what it is. Otherwise, I don't think the Gillespies could have afforded to send Tom to Cambridge. Tom didn't want to be connected with such a common business, or any business, and I think had no head for it, neither. He'd no brothers, so a cousin went to work for his father, which was a good thing for the cousin, if not so good for Tom."

"I see." But Papa's "investment" income was surprisingly small if he had inherited the coalfield.

Brigginshaw said, "I don't know this from your papa, who prefers to forget his money comes from common coal. It's what I worked out from hints here and there. By the time old Gillespie died, not so old, neither, only a few years older than Tom and I are now, he'd saved enough of his coal money to dower the girls in spite of using part to buy out the original investor. You've aunts, you know, married to decent country gentlemen.

"The cousin inherited the coalfield, because it wasn't entailed. What use was it to a man who was only interested in dead languages? He couldn't have managed it, and his cousin wouldn't have managed it for him.

"His father knew it, too. He settled as much money as he could on Tom, the same as went to each of the girls. It's invested, which is the source of his income. I'm sorry to say they were not on very good terms by then, his father being angry with him for wanting to profit from a business he scorned to take part in, and Tom wanting him to sell out to remove any hint of a connection with vulgar commerce. If I'd been old Gillespie, I'd have had a portion of the profits from the coal go into the Funds for Tom so he could pretend it came from gentlemanly investments.

"But family squabbles can be bitter; I see it all the time in my profession. The cousin had improved production and profits, and the old man had come to look on him as a son. Your father felt he should have inherited or at least got half. He wouldn't have minded that connection to the mines then. Asked me to write, demanding a fair share. The answer came back in six words: 'I'll see you in Hell first.' "

"It does seem rather unfair."

"What, that he not get a larger portion? He might have had a case at law had he not agreed to the settlement, with no provision for increasing it. It's as well he did not try to fight it. He'd probably have lost, though it might still be making its way through the courts. It is hard on you and your mother and brother."

Of course her papa would have agreed to a small settlement without taking into account possible increases in the profits. It was all of a piece with his borrowing money he had little hope of actually repaying: failure to consider consequences and outcomes. She had not told Brigginshaw about the loan and did not intend to.

"With my father being unable to tutor or write, and with some additional expenses because of his illness, I must find some way to supplement our income, Mr. Brigginshaw. It must be something I can do at home, and I will admit I have no accomplishments I could teach, unless someone wishes his daughter to learn Latin or French or German or the Greek or Hebrew alphabets."

"Quite unlikely, I fear. You've been in the habit of assisting Tom as his amanuensis, haven't you? Write a good, clear hand, and quick, I'll be bound?"

"I have been and am."

"You were wise to come to me. My partner and I always need documents copied, and our clerks can't keep up, they've too much else to do. We pay legal copyists by the page. May I rely on you not to make your margins unreasonable wide?"

Relief at having secured employment, and at what seemed a good rate of pay per page (possibly because she had promised to be niggardly with the margins) distracted her from Attorney Brigginshaw's revelations about her father's earlier life. It was surprising she had never heard anything of it. She might ask Mama, though her parents had not met and wed until Thomas Gillespie came to London. She did not think her mother had ever met any of the Gillespie family or connections.

As it fell out, she had only taken off her hat and gloves and inquired of William how her father did, when Solomon de Toledo arrived.

"I don't wish to intrude, but I found a book Mr. Gillespie might enjoy."

"It's kind of you, sir. He is not able to read yet, but my mother and I often read to him as Dr. de Toledo suggested." She invited him into the drawing room and offered refreshments, which he rejected.

"William, please tell my mother Mr. de Toledo has called."

The footman shifted uneasily. "The mistress is laid upon her bed with a megrim, Mistress Portia. And Cook sent Abby to the fishmonger and grocer."

Even their rather unsatisfactory footman knew she should be chaperoned. Portia ignored the hint.

"I will take my leave of you, Mistress Portia." Solomon, as she could not help thinking of him, had understood the message, too.

"Don't go, Mr. de Toledo. William will leave the door open." Still not quite proper, but she would not turn him away so abruptly.

At her invitation, he settled himself. She thought he felt the awkwardness of the situation. She did not. He had been more than kind, was a friend of her father's, and had brought a gift. Each of those things demanded he be treated as an honored guest. She was exceeding grateful for any help in her family's current plight.

He held out the volume, handsomely bound in calfskin. " 'Tis a satire in Latin by a Norwegian author, *Nicolai Klimii Iter Subterraneum*, though it was published in Germany. It reminds me of *Gulliver's Travels*, being a fantastical tale of travels inside the Earth and observations on the religions, relationships of the sexes, morality, and natural philosophy of the beings living there. I thought he might enjoy it if he is sufficiently recovered."

"In some senses, he is. He comprehends a good deal of what is read to him. But his speech is—" She faltered. "Not as much improved as his understanding. He can speak a word or two, but it is still somewhat slurred."

Mr. de Toledo was certainly kind, but his very kindness put Portia in mind of the Trojan horse by which the Greeks entered Troy. Somehow he had infiltrated their family's life. The analogy was unfair. Her papa had very obviously spent considerable time talking with Solomon when he made his payments, making an acquaintance of him. That bond, however thin, had contributed to Solomon's willingness to give them assistance when he discovered Thomas Gillespie was incapacitated.

From the hall came a cough: William reminding her of the proprieties.

"Thank you for bringing the book, Mr. de Toledo. I look forward to discussing it with you. And so will my father, I am sure."

"I will be most interested in your views, Mistress Portia. Your comments might be as amusing as the book." He rose and bowed.

Their almost clandestine meeting was at an end. Portia wished it were not.

Chapter 9

Sol,

Meet me at Job's Coffee House this afternoon about two.

A.H.

Hawkins's reply to Solomon's query was terse, even for Hawkins. With a sinking feeling, Solomon reviewed his ledger, answered a letter from an uncle in Amsterdam, and made a list of things to do the next day, before setting out for Job's. He had not visited John Barlicorn's old haunt since the previous October, before Barlicorn vanished from London. There were coffee houses nearer his office, and others nearer Hawkins's new office, all of them livelier and better appointed than Job's. Even without Barlicorn's presence, it would likely still be a place where the patrons minded their own business and a meeting between a rich ship owner and a moneylender would go unremarked, if not unnoticed.

Hawkins had a table to himself, his expression enough to scare away anyone looking for conversation. As Solomon approached, he was already beckoning a waiter. The boy set down the cup as Solomon pulled out a chair.

"Hawkins? I trust Lady Emily is well?"

The grim lines around his mouth vanished as if by magic. "Blooming. You did a good day's work when you matched us."

"I'm glad to hear it. Long life and all that sort—"

"You wanted to know how long it would take before the *North Sea Venturer's* cargo was cleared at the Custom House." The lines were back.

"I don't know anyone else who gets the *Lloyd's List*, except Easterday, and I don't know him well enough to approach him. And it would be as bad to go to Lloyd's Coffee House."

Hawkins's "Ha!" did not qualify as a laugh. "No, anyone you approached would be suspected of being on the brink of insolvency."

"Well, yes. I thought best to ask your opinion by post. Although it's good to see you again. You're the only one I know who might be able to guess at how long ships bringing in freight from foreign parts might have to wait." His cousin David Mendys or one or two other family connections would know, but Solomon's family thought him self-sufficient and he chose to keep it that way.

"Sol, the *North Sea Venturer* was reported going down in a storm by the captain of a schooner who saw her struggling. Nothing he could do for her, against the wind and waves. What's your interest in the *Venturer*?"

Solomon stared down at his coffee bowl. It now seemed as unappealing as Thames water. "I made a loan secured by the client's interest in a cargo of furs. It seemed safe enough. I would have asked you, but you were out for the day, and he needed the money almost at once to invest in something else."

"He hasn't let you know the ship is lost?"

"No."

"Huh. Letting you know would be the honorable

thing, but on the other hand, many men would try to raise the funds to repay you before mentioning it."

"Which would you have done?"

"If you'd asked me ten months ago, I'd have said, the latter. Now, I'd break the news as soon as I heard and assure you I was working on finding the money to repay you."

Solomon took out a little commonplace book and thumbed back two or three pages. "You don't happen to recall the exact date you heard of it?"

Hawkins frowned, counting on his fingers, and muttering, "This hasn't been a very interesting week, as far as shipping is concerned. Last Monday the Easterdays came to supper. That might have been exciting. They're expecting an addition to their family. I was praying Mistress Easterday didn't discharge her cargo at the dessert course, for she gives new meaning to the term 'great with child.' " His grin broke. "Easterday mentioned the loss of the *North Sea Venturer* as an example of how even the most skilled sailor may lose in a contest with the sea. He knew the captain."

Solomon waited patiently as Hawkins scried in his coffee bowl, frowning slightly. Finally he said, "It was the previous Monday I heard. I remember because while we were talking of it, I was brought word of a fire in the hold of one of my ships."

"I hope no one was injured? Was the ship much damaged?" Had it burnt to the waterline, he would surely have heard of it.

"No, nothing to signify, either men or ship. The blaze was put out before I arrived. Several crates were damaged, that's all. It did take the rest of the day to determine how it happened. The bottle-head who thought he'd have a rest and a pipe there won't sail for me again."

"He came to me in the midmorning, a week ago this past Monday. The day you were out of the office."

"Was—" Hawkins did not continue as the boy approached their table to refill their bowls.

Solomon nodded at the lad and murmured, "Thank you." The server bustled away.

"—it insured?"

"I don't know."

"When you say he secured the loan, what do you mean?"

The cautious way Hawkins phrased his question suggested there was a good deal more to know about bills of lading than Solomon had previously realized.

"He left the bill of lading with me."

"There are two possibilities. Either he did not know that possession of the bill of lading is commonly taken as proof of a right to the cargo, in which case, I suppose he is not involved in shipping and might not have heard the news, or else he intended to chouse you."

Marriage had improved Hawkins. He used not to be tactful.

"As he came to me the same day you heard of the ship sinking and was urgent to get the loan, I would be a fool not to conclude he meant to cheat me."

"I asked about insurance, because if the furs were insured, you might be compensated for their loss, unless your borrower has already made a claim."

"Could he do so without the bill of lading, Hawkins?"

"It's not a question I've ever dealt with. I'll make

inquiries at Lloyd's, both to find out if there was a policy taken out, and if there was, whether it's been paid. Even if he did make a claim, it may not have been paid yet, as the underwriters tend to be cautious if they have any suspicions about the insured. Worth looking into, anyway. If the claim has been paid, they'll want to know about his fraud. I hope you aren't bit too badly."

"It's been a costly mistake but worth learning. I'll survive it."

"Who was the fellow, anyway? Mayhap I know something of his reputation."

"One Philip Pomeroy, of Oakleigh Grange, near Devizes, Wiltshire. He was only in London on business."

"Never heard of him. It does strike me as curst suspicious he came to you the very day we heard the news."

"Just so. However, his daughter is to marry one of Lord Tiverton's sons, so he can hardly be a rogue. I will write to him in case he was ignorant of the loss."

****

"…An' I come to you 'cause Peebles what lives in the next street said as you was fair to him when he needed the doctor for his wife's broke leg an' I don't know what else to do. The parish don't pay out enough to feed the horse and keep us alive, and without the horse to pull the wagon, my son won't have his trade when he's well." The woman ran down finally and gazed at him beseechingly.

Any sickness or shortage of work put the poor in danger of starvation or eviction. This washerwoman might be no more than forty years, younger than his mother. She looked a muscular seventy.

"So all you need is a bit of money to keep you and your son while he is too ill to work. Money for your rent, for food for all of you and the horse, and for whatever the apothecary recommends." He asked how much her son brought in per week when he was working, and how much she earned for washing. "Then you, your son, and his little girl live on about fifty pounds a year, Mistress Milson."

"Never thought of it that way, but I s'pose we do. Sometimes a bit less, sometimes a bit more. We don't do bad, then, Mr. Solomon."

"I will lend you one pound a week for two weeks. That should give you enough to get what your son needs from the apothecary and make up for his lost income. Come back in ten days, and tell me how he does. If you need another loan, we can arrange it then. The interest will be one percent per year." He had never seen Mistress Milson before, but he had heard of her: a thrifty woman, not addicted to gin, who washed and sometimes cleaned for others as much as she could, given that she also cared for her granddaughter. Even the child worked, stuffing dried lavender, herbs, and flower petals into little linen bags.

"Bless you, Your Worship!" Her eyes were filling. "I'll pay regular as soon as Harry's on his feet again."

"I'm no judge. 'Solomon' will do." He opened his ledger, entered her name, the date, the amount, and the rate of interest before counting out two pounds. He suspected he would charge no interest if she did make payments faithfully. If she could not, perhaps he could arrange for her to clean or cook for some of his friends who could afford occasional help. For those who lived day to day, any illness or accident spelled disaster.

Sometimes he found his occupation quite melancholy, in spite of thinking of himself as a small, informal bank and believing he was generally able to assist people no one else would help. He needed to do something to improve his mood. Visit a coffee house to idle away an hour or two with friends, attend a play?

It was unnecessary to visit the Gillespie home again. Nevertheless, he found himself strolling down an undistinguished street between Red Lyon Square and Bloomsbury Square, approaching a certain narrow house. It could do no harm to inquire after Mr. Gillespie's health again and see if they had all they needed. He asked for Mistress Gillespie and was informed she was out. Mistress Portia was at home, which was gratifying. The maid led him to Gillespie's study where Portia sat at the smaller desk. She had been writing, though she carefully pushed the sheet away as he entered and smiled at him.

She was prettier than he had remembered. Her eyes called to mind shadowy groves in a park: green, gold, and brown together. He would like to take her to Vauxhall Gardens some summer evening. Impossible, of course. Even if it were possible, her family or friends would be present, and he would never have a chance of strolling in the Dark Walks with her.

"Mr. de Toledo. I was not expecting you. Won't you sit? I apologize; Abby should have shown you to the drawing room. The parlor," she added, as most of those who lived in that street would call it.

"Thank you." He moved a straight chair from its position in front of Gillespie's desk to face the student desk. She was nervous, and her long fingers bore traces of ink. From the stack of sheets at her left, he guessed she was copying rather than writing a letter. "Is it something of your father's?"

She blushed, a sight he had not expected ever to see, as composed as she was.

"No. I am doing some copying for an attorney."

No need to ask why. Of course she was worried about money; any sensible person would be, in spite of his having assured her she need not worry about the debt for Benedict's schooling.

****

Rain brought a respite from the heat and drought, and the air cooled somewhat as summer slid toward autumn. Father was a good deal better than he had been, certainly. He was able to sit up in a chair part of the day. His speech was still garbled, and it was unclear how much of his family's speech he comprehended. Mother sewed and talked to him when she wasn't reading to him. She said he seemed to listen. Portia read him the letters from his friends and students, some of which he appeared to understand. When Benedict visited him, usually with some book in hand to read aloud, their father gazed at him. He might be attempting to smile. They all hoped it was a sign he would eventually recover.

Almost every day brought some encouraging sign as Thomas Gillespie began to emerge from his fog. Eliza fluttered into the study one afternoon and announced, "Your papa spoke today. It quite startled me. Is it not the best news?"

"It is. How did he happen to speak? What did he say?"

"I had been reading Cousin Cecilia's latest letter to him, and he scowled on both sides of his face, I vow he did."

Portia found Cecilia's letters irritating herself. "What has Augustus done now?" Mama's cousin's son featured largely in her letters. Thomas Gillespie's opinion on one occasion was that the boy should have been sent to school early, or else caned frequently at home. But Augustus having lost his father in his third year, neither of these courses had been implemented.

"Cecilia did not go into detail, so I am not quite sure, but she is dreadfully afraid the magistrate will order him to enlist. And your papa very clearly said, 'Good!' "

The following day, her mother interrupted Portia's scrutiny of the household ledger. There must be some way to reduce costs still further. Eliza dropped into the chair before the desk with less than her wonted grace.

"I was reading an old issue of *The Gentleman's Magazine* to your papa, and he spoke again."

"Then he is greatly improved. At least, I suppose so?" If what he said had made sense; her mama did not seem much encouraged.

"I cannot wish he should remain bewildered, but this was perhaps not the best time for him to be attending."

"But you were reading to him."

"Yes, and I know he follows when Benedict or I read to him, for sometimes he snorts or growls, just as he would do if he were of sound mind. No one could expect him to become incensed over the article I was reading. Such dull stuff! But it was something he might ordinarily find interesting, though I expect he had read it before.

"Then Abby came to the door to tell me she had

found a shirt of Benedict's and his second-best breeches, both covered in mud, folded up under his mattress when she turned it. We were a little late with that project this year, because of your papa's illness. I told her to wash the shirt and brush the breeches as best she could and then we would see what parts had spots that might be removed. She said he would not need them for school, and that's when your father positively bellowed, 'School!' He was very agitated."

Portia wiped her pen and set it aside. "What did you tell Papa?"

"I repeated several times that Benedict was leaving for school in a few days. Even then, he seemed uneasy. I am not sure he understood me, however, for he seemed quite put about." She drooped. "Then he muttered, 'Hell.' Poor man, it must be terrible for your papa, not being able to make himself clearly understood."

"Did you not explain about Mr. de Toledo having called and arranged everything?"

"Do you think I should have told him, Portia? I feared it might alarm him."

"If he was concerned about my brother going to school, he might well wonder how it was to be managed, since he cannot be aware that we know about his borrowing the money."

"I suppose I must tell him," she said.

"I will inform him, Mama." She did wonder whether he would be relieved or irritated they had discovered the truth and handled the arrangements.

She was not sure how he felt about it, even after she told him. A series of expressions flickered across his face: surprise, chagrin, annoyance? They succeeded each other either too quickly or were too mixed to be easy to interpret. Finally he mumbled, “School, good,” and managed a half smile.

She smiled in reply. “You needn’t worry about anything, Papa. Mr. de Toledo has been extremely helpful, and we will manage until you are well.” Then, as her father sagged in his chair, she asked if he wished to lie down to rest, a suggestion he agreed to with a jerky nod.

“Would you like Benedict to sit with you after supper?”

“Ay,” he managed as she helped him to the bed.

That had gone well. Her father was improving every day.

Chapter 10

The weather continued warm but without further rain. Benedict should have an easy journey to school. By the date of his departure, Papa had expressed a slightly garbled but comprehensible admonition to Benedict to apply himself to his studies. He added, the words coming with more difficulty as his energy flagged, that they would look forward to a joyous Christmas when Benedict came home. Portia did not attach any particular importance to this statement in spite of it being somewhat out of character for their father. He must expect to be completely recovered by then.

Benedict's departure exhausted Gillespie, and it was therefore not until the following day that Portia considered how he would miss her brother's presence. They had begun to take tea in his chamber after supper, to preserve the pretense of ordinary family life, as he was still not steady enough on his feet to venture downstairs. He had been in good spirits all day, for once not impatient at his continuing disabilities. He even seemed to be hugging some secret satisfaction to himself. He must have been worried about Benedict and was relieved that he was back at school.

When her mother paused to sip her tea after relating that Augustus was now a cornet in a troop of horse, Cousin Cecilia having been able to purchase his commission, Portia broached a subject likely to be more welcome to her father.

"Mr. de Toledo asked to be informed when you were ready to receive visitors. Should you like him to call? I gather you are social acquaintances besides having a business connection."

Gillespie started to speak, then stopped. His gaze focused somewhere beyond her.

When his attention returned to her, he said only, "No." Perhaps he felt the response was too curt. "Not yet."

She supposed he would prefer not to see his friends until he regained his old fluency of speech.

****

Dear Father, Mother, and Portia,

As you will have concluded from receipt of this, I have arrived at Radford's. I will not describe the journey, having done so last year and the year before, too, except to say that we had a very merry time, thanks to the baskets of food you and Danver's mother sent, and Mr. de Toledo presented me with a package of confections, including coriander seed biscuits, burnt almonds, sugar puffs, and several other things which I do not know how to name. He admonished us not to eat them all at once, for fear of being made ill, and Mr. Elliott, the tutor, who is Danver's uncle, you know, assured him he would make certain we did not surfeit ourselves. But Mr. Elliott is not so old that he did not eat his share. However, you will be pleased to hear that we shared our repast with an old lady and her granddaughter who were mightily pleased by it. They must hardly have had enough for the coach fare, as they had brought no more than a bread roll and an apple apiece. Before you think to ask, I have also written to Mr. de Toledo to thank him for his generous gift, and appended Danver's thanks also. There is enough of the confectionery left over to keep us supplied for several days, if we are prudent.

Now, as to my studies this year, which will be of more interest to my father...

****

Thomas Gillespie's optimism was borne out. By mid-October, he was able to speak clearly, with only a slight slurring when he was tired. He was able to walk around his chamber and indeed the whole first floor with the aid of a cane. Mama had the trundle bed removed from their chamber and resumed her place in the marital bed, and Gillespie declared himself ready to attempt the stairs to the ground floor. The prospect worried Portia and her mother, but the attempt must be made. Thomas Gillespie wished to resume his normal routine, and neither Portia nor her mother could contemplate putting up with his irritability over his absence from his study and his usual occupations. His maiden descent of the stairs was made with the assistance of William, overseen by Eliza and Portia.

Once seated, he surveyed his desk. Mother was almost visibly quaking with anxiety lest he should find anything out of place. Portia was not worried, having taken the greatest care to arrange everything as it had been the day of his collapse. Gillespie's eyes fixed on the Radford letter and the sheet of numbers.

Portia said, "Abby found those sheets on the floor. They must have fallen when we moved you to your chamber."

"Hmmmph." He dismissed William brusquely with

an awkward wave of his hand. "Don't hover. Close the door behind you," he added to Eliza and Portia. She glanced back from the doorway and saw him twitch a folded sheet out of a book by his elbow. Despite the slight drooping of the right side of his face, his look of triumph was unmistakable.

"He is impatient to resume his usual routine," Eliza murmured. "I suppose he has been thinking of the book he was writing and chafing at the delay."

"I wonder if he will be able to write easily enough to begin again." Portia had been writing letters for him since he had been able to organize his thoughts and speak fluently enough to dictate them, though he had been able to read them himself days before and had immediately demanded that William bring him his unopened correspondence. His signature was still shaky.

Within half an hour, Gillespie was calling for her from the door of the study.

As she settled at the smaller desk, her father dropped a folded letter into a drawer and then locked it. She had never heard of Bertram Keswick, to whom he wished to write, nor did the body of the letter clarify the matter. The message consisted of only two lines: *I received your letter upon the very day I fell seriously ill and have been unable to reply until the present. I will write to you at greater length in the near future.*

"Send it by William. The Sign of the Quill and Tome, Chancery Lane." His smile was slightly crooked.

When she sealed the letter and left the study, her papa was still smiling.

****

"Your dear Papa's mood is marvelous improved

since he began to recover his health."

Portia agreed. "I imagine he hated being dependent upon others to read to him, among other things." He had begun dictating to Portia his replies to the letters received during his recovery. He would resume dictating his work in progress on *Etymology of the Hebrew Language* once he had caught up on his correspondence.

One chilly day, summoned to his study to take down another letter, he began by directing her to address a letter, already folded and sealed. He had written in his own hand, most likely as practice. It was directed to Bertram Keswick, to whom he had written the day he had come downstairs for the first time since his apoplexy. She remembered that later in the week when Gillespie told her to send William for a hackney.

****

"Have you heard the latest wonder?" David Mendys signaled the serving boy to bring more coffee.

"I've heard several astonishing things recently. The customers at a certain chocolate house wagered on whether one of their number who had fallen into a fit would live or die and prevented a doctor from attending him, lest it affect the outcome. Then there was the piglet dressed in infant's clothing—"

"Phoo. I mean Sturgis, the blast furnace man."

"Very rich, I hear. Not likely to come to me." Solomon drained his coffee bowl as the boy approached with a pot.

"Particularly not as he died several months ago." His cousin said nothing more as the server filled their cups.

"Was that surprising? He can't have been a young

man."

"Between fifty and sixty years of age, I believe. No, the thing that's set London buzzing is his will. He had no children—none that lived, anyway—and left most of his wealth to a cousin. A scholar or some such thing. By all accounts, in the will Sturgis paid back a good many snubs he and his people received at the cousin's hands and said he hoped the inheritance might allow him to achieve the level of society he aspired to. He meant it as a sneer, according to the report I heard."

"I've noticed there's something about a will that brings out the worst in those on both ends of it. But if the death was months ago, why is this the latest in gossip now?"

"The fellow missed the reading of the will. They weren't close. The circumstances were unusual, and it's only in the last week the heir contacted the attorney. A young clerk with an active tongue heard the details and found it too tempting not to pass on to his friends."

"Embarrassing for the family."

"Mmmm." David turned his bowl in his hands. "Mayhap you will be congratulating me presently. I hope to be betrothed."

"Daughter of someone in the Levanter Trading Company?"

"Uh, no. She's the daughter of a baronet. He's not well inlaid. He does have excellent family connections which will be useful."

David had always said it was as easy to court a rich girl as a poor one. "I hope your match is not solely a business decision." His mind wandered to Portia Gillespie.

"Well…no. She's very pretty and has a sense of

humor. Her father doesn't mind my being in trade and a Jew. Neither does her mother. Can you believe it? They have four other daughters and four sons, and not a penny to bless themselves with, as they say. But Petronella says she likes me because I'm sensible but not dull."

"Felicitations. When is the happy event to take place?"

"It's not actually certain yet. Her family wants to meet mine. To make sure there are no near connections who peddle old clothes in the street, no doubt. If we pass muster, the wedding will take place in about a month, at Uncle Gerard's house. Special license, of course."

"Neither of you intend to convert, then."

"Well, no. I don't need to, because it's not as if I plan to stand for Parliament or hold an office. The Crispins would be glad to marry one of their children to a Red Indian or a Moslem, if only there was a good settlement involved. Though I will say, I don't think they would force any of them into an unwelcome marriage," he added fairly. "The whole of both families will be invited. Uncle Gerard's dining room will seat all of us. He's undertaken to serve nothing that will offend our more observant family members."

"In return for which, they will overlook the fact that those foods have undoubtedly been present in the kitchen?"

David laughed. "We've all made some accommodations."

Solomon conceded the point. "I wouldn't be able to eat at an inn or ordinary if I insisted on observing the dietary laws. In Spain, our family conformed to

Christian practice, so…" He shrugged. It hadn't done much good there. "When I lived with Grandfather and Great-Grandfather Alvaro, I was very devout, not that I had much choice."

"And like him, you refused to adopt English habits here. Except you aren't very observant."

"I was a trial to my parents, the first few years after I returned to them. When I was a little older, I came to understand the necessity for cutting our coats according to our cloth. Great-Grandfather had died by then, so at least I wasn't disappointing him."

"But neither did you make any attempt to blend in. Being a moneylender to kings is respectable, but what you do isn't. Better than being a peddler, of course. It's none of my business, except you're my cousin, but your family must wish you were in some other occupation."

"They do," Solomon admitted. "At least, my mother does. Father hasn't said anything, but he wouldn't. I suspect my brothers are embarrassed, but they don't upbraid me for it."

For once David's good-humored face lost its levity. "Why would you do that to your family? Lending money and making matches isn't the dearest wish of your heart, is it?"

David, considered the least clever of his family, and frivolous as well, had occasionally shown himself uncomfortably perceptive. Solomon took several moments to answer, and began with the second question.

"No. It isn't." He tried to formulate his response to the first query. "And…I don't know?" Humiliatingly, it came out like a question.

The boy came around with more coffee and asked

if they wanted anything to eat. They both shook their heads. Solomon cradled the coffee bowl in his hands, enjoying its warmth. He was a rational man: it should not be this difficult to understand himself.

David remarked, “If a fellow loves what he does, sometimes he doesn’t care if it’s not very profitable. Or if it is lucrative, he may stick with it even if he hates the work, at least until he can afford to do something else. But you don’t love it, and you don’t make much.” He inhaled the steam from his own cup. “It’s an insight I got from a night-soil man. Now that’s not work anyone would want, but he told me he earned very good money making his rounds for four hours a night, and working as a porter during the day. He was saving to buy a little shop. He thought by the time he’d saved enough, his oldest boy would be able to take over his route. A smelly, nasty job of work, but worth it for the money.”

A restorative sip of coffee gave Sol an interval to consider. It was not enough. He needed to think about his cousin’s question, and not in a coffee house, amid bustle and talk.

Solomon wrenched the conversation in another direction. “It’s as well Great-Grandfather Alvaro is not still alive. He would not have attended your wedding.” David would understand he was avoiding the issue and most likely understand why.

“I suppose it’s like sowing one’s wild oats only without the usual actresses and opera dancers,” he observed, reverting to the previous topic.

“Not entirely without them, David! I’m no Puritan.” He should see about forming a connection with a suitable female to banish Portia from his imagination.

“Usually one gets tired of wild oats by your age. Couldn’t you have run away to sea or taken the King’s shilling by way of flouting both your great-grandfather’s and your parents’ expectations?”

“I don’t really enjoy taking a wherry on the river, and the idea of being sent to foreign parts to shoot at other inoffensive fellows is distinctly unappealing.” His cousin was correct: he could not have rejected his parents’ way of life and Great-Grandfather’s beliefs more thoroughly if he had enlisted or gone to sea.

This time David let it go.

“If my suit is acceptable, will you be my groomsman, Sol?”

“Of course.”

David asked, “Did you see *The Merchant of Venice* a few months ago? The one with Macklin, the Irish actor?”

“I did.”

“What did you think of it? I’ve heard he studied for the part by going out to the markets and talking with Jews. It seems a novel concept.”

He ignored his cousin’s ironical tone. “Macklin does have a very natural manner on stage. It was a relief not to see Shylock portrayed as a clown or buffoon. It is too bad he made Shylock more villainous, for while his demand for a pound of flesh was utterly unreasonable, at times I can understand his motive. To be made use of and yet treated with contempt does not suit my notions of gentlemanly conduct. Further, Antonio knew the terms of the loan. Now, an unsophisticated borrower may not understand how to calculate the interest he will owe, but Antonio was engaged in trade himself and should have known better than to agree to such conditions. I deal with arrogant men like Antonio and fools like Bassanio every day. I would not have lent Antonio tuppence."

"I will wager you'd have lent Bassanio the money."

"You would lose, David. I meet men every week who expect me to lend them a few hundred pounds to give them a chance to win the hand of some wealthy widow or heiress. And that is all it is: a chance. If they fail to succeed in their courtship, they have no way to pay me. As a gamble, I prefer cards or dice. If they have something to recommend them, like a title, I might agree to find them a bride with money."

Chapter 11

When Papa came home, Mama greeted him uneasily. One glance at his slight frown was enough to explain her restrained tone. If he were not angry, he was at least displeased. What a change from his demeanor when he left.

"Will you lie down for a while before dinner, Thomas? I am sure you must be tired after going out for the first time. Perhaps you would like a glass of that soothing cordial? I will have William assist you upstairs."

"Don't fuss, Eliza. I will not go upstairs when I should only have to come down again in an hour or two. Have William bring a bottle of Madeira to my study. Then I do not wish to be disturbed until dinner."

Mama smiled uncertainly, murmured an assent, and left the hall with a faint rustling of her petticoats and gown, a sound heard only when she was agitated. At other times, Mama somehow contrived to glide soundlessly. She would not question her husband about his change of mood.

He stood by the little console table, one hand resting upon it, the other upon his cane. He must be worn to the bone by his excursion though it had not caused his speech to slur.

"Let me help you with your greatcoat, Papa." He would surely need assistance, if he needed his stick and the table for support.

"Thank you, Portia. I confess I am somewhat weary. I would not let your mother know: she would keep me an invalid."

She folded the heavy woolen coat over her arm. "May I see you to your study?"

He accepted her other arm, saying, "You're a good daughter."

He was seated behind his desk, already uncapping the ink bottle, when William brought in a tray holding the wine and a glass. Portia loitered long enough to see him pour out a glass and be waved brusquely away. William left on her heels, closing the door carefully behind him.

"I never knew the master to have a bottle in there before, Mistress Portia. Mortal careful of his books and papers, he is."

"He must have needed a restorative after going out. And there isn't much on the desk at the moment." Papa's usual barricade of books had been set aside on the small desk; he had not yet continued working on his *Etymology*. Before his illness, he had written or researched every day, including the Sabbath, to her mama's distress. Still, he was not fully recovered yet. Before the apoplexy he had been vigorous, but being confined to bed or his chamber had weakened him. He might be waiting to regain his health before continuing with his work. She did wonder where he had gone today. What had happened to annoy him? Though mayhap he had only been irked to find himself not as ready to resume his normal activities as he had supposed.

"William, did my father mention where he was

going, when he sent you to fetch the hackney this morning?"

"That he did not, mistress."

****

Portia had only just returned with several documents to copy for Attorney Brigginshaw when her mother found her putting away her gloves and mantle.

"That odd Mr. de Toledo is here to see your father. He says Gillespie wrote, asking him to come. How could he have written unless you wrote it for him?"

"He asked me to address a letter to Mr. de Toledo, Mama. He can write, if not very neatly, especially if he uses a pencil. It's difficult for him to avoid blots with ink. I assumed he wrote to thank him for his assistance with Benedict's tuition." And for the book he had sent as well, she trusted. Best not to mention to Mama she could not imagine how Papa was to make further payments on the monies de Toledo had lent. He had done nothing to resume his tutoring, though he was now sufficiently recovered to do so.

She could make payments from her earnings as a copyist, but would Solomon accept her money? She might let him think it came from Papa, but when her father did resume his payments, Papa would find out. He would not be pleased at her meddling or to discover she was working for pay.

"I don't think he should be disturbed, do you? If he fell into another apoplexy, I don't think I could bear it."

"I will ask if he invited Mr. de Toledo to call. If he did, we cannot refuse to admit him, without Papa worrying because he has not come, or becoming irate that we refused to admit him."

Eliza sighed. "You are correct, of course."

"Of course I sent for de Toledo." Gillespie spoke as he did to a student who had failed to understand some quite simple point, with the same slightly smug expression.

Her mother was in the parlor, making polite conversation. No doubt she was congratulating herself on being able to comment upon the parts of Niels Klim's adventures underground which Portia had translated for her. Otherwise it would be laborious work to find a topic one could talk about with a moneylender. The weather would have been exhausted as a topic long since and Eliza would not ask about his family because that would be too familiar. Portia entered to hear her inquire, "Do you attend the theater, Mr. de Toledo? I have heard some new actor, David Garrick, has been much praised for his performance in Richard III."

"I do, madam. I did not see that play myself, but friends did and are full of his excellence. One said he was so natural that one might have thought oneself observing the real Richard." Seeing Portia at the door, de Toledo rose and bowed.

"My father is expecting you. If you will follow me?"

Portia would have liked to linger in the study. She had missed seeing Solomon regularly since Benedict had been sent off to Radford's. The arrangements had required a number of meetings and also the exchange of several letters, though she should not have been writing to a gentleman. But how else to settle all the details when her mother was really not able to cope with them? And they had been business letters, not personal letters…more or less. She should have written, then had her mother sign. But then the reply would have been sent to her mother, and while she herself would have ended up dealing with it, it would not have been the same, and Mr. de Toledo would not have added his pithy observations on life and events. His visit to bring that amusing book had been an oasis in a desert. If he were to become a regular caller, he might be induced to spend some time in the drawing room as well as the study.

To her surprise, her father did not keep Solomon—Mr. de Toledo—long. Only fifteen or twenty minutes elapsed before she heard his step in the passage. She popped out of the drawing room before William could open the outer door.

"Won't you stay for a cup of tea?" Fortunately, they had tea, and of a good sort, which Papa had brought home the day he returned from his unstated errand in the hackney though he could not have gone out only to buy it. Now that she thought about it, he had had money enough for the hackney fare and a few pence over in case he needed refreshment. The amount was not sufficient to buy tea, which was a new and troubling thought.

Their visitor's pensive mien puzzled her. His expression mirrored his state of mind, except when he troubled to conceal it as he had at their first meeting. She had not seen that impassivity since she had told him of Gillespie's illness. After their frequent consultations over Benedict's tuition and travel, discussions which had sometimes wandered far afield from those topics, she had become convinced he really was not worried about prompt repayment of his loans to her father. He could not be uneasy about her father, who had been in good health and spirits a mere hour ago.

"Yes, do, Mr. de Toledo." Her mother had come to stand behind her. "I don't know if I ever thanked you for the trouble you took in making sure Benedict returned to school. I know it was a relief to Mr. Gillespie."

At her mother's intervention, de Toledo smiled and permitted himself to be persuaded. Eliza directed the conversation into topics suitable for entertaining a gentleman in the drawing room. De Toledo made suitable, often amusing responses. Portia sat like a lump, unable to think of any trivial remark to volunteer and scarcely able to comment when Mama directed a question to her: "Don't you agree, Portia?"

At last, as Mama took a sip of her bohea, Portia demanded, "May I ask why you appeared to be in a brown study when you left my father, sir? Did he say something to worry you?"

"Portia!" Eliza set her tea bowl down on its saucer with a *clink*!

"Ma'am, Mistress Portia." A pause. "I was only surprised. Mr. Gillespie paid off the sum he had borrowed from me."

"For this term's tuition?" If he had, it would have taken more from their quarterly income than they could spare without leaving them penniless.

"No, Mistress Portia. He paid the whole amount."

"Thank God," Mama breathed. "What good news."

Portia and Solomon traded glances. Considered dispassionately, the sum was not a fortune. She found herself unable to regard it unmoved, as one quarter's tuition and associated costs equaled four-tenths of Thomas Gillespie's quarterly investment income. Was it possible he had received enough from his publisher to pay Solomon in full? Impossible. She could not recall how much her father's payments totaled over the last two years, but they were insignificant compared to two years' tuition plus Michaelmas term this year. Could he have withdrawn the money from his account at Pimling's? If so, they would have very little to fall back upon. She felt quite ill.

Her mother failed to notice; de Toledo did not. "Mistress Portia, I don't think you need be apprehensive."

"What is there to be apprehensive about?" Eliza Gillespie inquired. "I vow I am quite relieved to know we do not now owe you money, Mr. de Toledo. Not that you haven't been most obliging, but small amounts owed to the butcher, tailor, and coal merchant are one thing, and, ah…"

"A larger sum owed to a moneylender is quite a different matter. I do understand. Thank you for your hospitality, ma'am. I must be on my way now."

Portia stood up. "I will walk to the door with you and have our footman fetch a hackney for you."

"That would be kind."

"Good day, Mr. de Toledo." Her mother seemed to find nothing peculiar in Portia offering to escort their guest to the door before a hackney had been summoned.

The drawing room door was closed to keep the heat in, and with William dispatched to the hackney stand, they could be private.

"Sir, do you know how my father made shift to pay you such a sum as you were owed?"

"I don't know as a fact. He did not tell me. But does your father have a cousin named Sturgis? I have a reason for asking."

"I have no idea. I've never met any of my father's relations, if they are still alive. I don't think he cared for them; I believe they were very common people and engaged in trade. Though they must have been somewhat successful, for I remember Papa mentioning a cousin of his who was also educated at Radford." Mr. Brigginshaw had spoken of a cousin who had inherited Papa's family's coal mine. Regrettable, but it had happened years ago; she had not given it any further thought. The present was quite enough to cope with.

"Was the cousin's first name Nathan?"

"I don't think I ever heard a name mentioned." Could it be the cousin who inherited the coal field? From Brigginshaw, she knew she had relatives her father had never mentioned. Papa might have half a score of cousins. "On the only occasion he referred to a cousin, he was speaking of the importance of education for a gentleman and how it was wasted on those who would then go into trade like his aunt's son, the ironmonger's brat." Should she mention her conversation with Brigginshaw? No: it reflected badly on her papa, though he was correct that a gentleman did not take part in trade. Still, under the circumstances, it would have been as well if Thomas Gillespie had been able to compromise his principles enough to secure a comfortable income. She did not care to reveal their sordid little family squabble to Solomon de Toledo, whose people sounded delightful.

"I see. Well, I don't think you have any need to fear Mr. Gillespie has beggared himself by paying me."

"How can I not, when as you know I have become all too familiar with our family's finances?"

"Try." In spite of the chill passage, his smile warmed her. "And if you find yourself in difficulties, I'll lend to you—to your father, that is—on the same terms as before. But I don't think he'll need my services." His light tone was tinged with regret.

Hooves and wheels clattered to a halt outside, and footfalls announced William's return.

"Hack's here, sir."

She saw de Toledo slip a coin to the footman, who grinned and bobbed his head in thanks.

"Goodbye, Mistress Portia."

"Goodbye, Mr. de Toledo." She watched him spring up into the coach. The boys her father had tutored displayed much of the same energy but not Solomon de Toledo's control and grace.

"With your father restored to health and no debt to worry about, all our troubles are now over," her mother said when Portia returned to her chair near the fire. Portia wished she could agree, but her heart was mystifyingly heavy. She ascribed it to apprehension about the source of Gillespie's payment to Solomon, despite the latter's reassurance.

Chapter 12

Gillespie began to work on *Etymology of the Hebrew Language* again, though for fewer hours each day than he had been accustomed to devote to it. He had done nothing about resuming his tutoring activities, probably because his speech still tended to slur when he was tired. Without the additional income from preparing boys for university, or remedying defects in the education of boys to be sent to grammar school, their income would scarcely be adequate for the necessities. Payments for his writing were sporadic at best and seldom large. It was not a subject she dared discuss with him.

She was spending less time working with him than she had after he first began to recover. It was no longer necessary to read his correspondence to him or write his replies from dictation. His handwriting was less precise than it had been, so she would have expected to be asked to copy his letters in a fair hand. He did have her copy some of them. All were his usual scholarly correspondence. But sometimes one went out, written in his own hand. She could not well question him, and though on one occasion she was sorely tempted to sort through the half dozen William was taking to the penny post, with the excuse that she wanted to confirm an address, she dared not do it. The footman might mention it to her papa. Later she could not remember if it were about this time she had noticed a letter on paper far too expensive for any of his usual correspondents. It lay on the desk when she went to his study to ask about some trifling matter. He had been reading it but immediately refolded it as she approached, which only drew her attention to it.

****

Not generally a pessimist, Solomon did not look forward to the family dinner at Uncle Gerard's home. It was not only that he expected some social awkwardness: the arrival of a letter from Hawkins had set the seal of gloom upon the day. He even considered—briefly—sending a letter of his own to the Mendyses claiming he had fallen ill and begging their pardon for missing the festivity. The only ailments he could think of were smallpox and leprosy, which would worry his mother.

There was no hope for it; he must clothe himself in his best suit and try to support David. Ordinarily, he would be happy to make the sacrifice. At this moment, it would be difficult to pretend he was not a failure. Pretend? Was he a failure? He supported himself as well or better than many of the lower professional class. He lived comfortably by his own efforts, had money put away in case of setbacks, and invested in the government Funds and in various commercial concerns. His Mendys cousins were far more successful in business. His father and his brother Vidal earned adequate incomes and loved the practice of medicine. Samuel was doing well in Jacob Levy's business of importing precious and semi-precious stones, and Daniel had been taken into the Mendys trading company, Uncle Mendys being lamentably short of sons. They seemed to enjoy their work.

He was not sure he even enjoyed lending money, however satisfying it was to help people out of their difficulties.

All of which only reminded him of the letter:

I inquired among my friends at Lloyd's about your Philip Pomeroy. For a time, he frequented the coffee house, acting the part of a successful businessman among men who deal in thousands of pounds, like a lap dog swaggering among lurchers. As you noticed, the bill of lading in your possession was endorsed to him. The original consignee of the pelts declined to say why he transferred it. My guess is it was extorted to conceal some misdeed or in payment for a gambling debt, probably his son's. The cargo was not insured.

Something smelled about the transaction. Recalling his address, I asked an acquaintance of Emily's about the fellow. He—the acquaintance—lives near Devizes and is also county gentry. I did not tell him the reason for my curiosity, only saying I'd heard his daughter was to marry one of Tiverton's sons, which I supposed meant the Pomeroys were either rich or socially prominent or else the young lady was very beautiful. The following is a much boiled-down account of what I learned. "Wrong upon every head." He laughed. "They have little money, live retired, and the girl is a plain old maid." He went on to say Tiverton's heir presumptive met her in Bath where she had gone with her father in the hope the waters would ease his rheumaticks, which are very troublesome. It is his one expedition every year. The younger Tiverton was with his older brother who was recovering from some lung ailment, and the two being thrown together, he fell in love. They share a passion for garden design. The nub of it is, Philip Pomeroy of Oakleigh Grange, near Devizes, being almost seventy and able to get around only with the help of two canes or crutches, cannot be your Pomeroy.

Upon further investigation, I learned that your Pomeroy has numerous minor creditors, though always managing somehow to pay before the bailiffs are brought in. I suspect him of being a sharper among other things. A day or so after defrauding you, he left town. 'Tis rumored he sailed for the New England colonies or mayhap Virginia. Or Atlantis or Abyssinia or where you will.

A.H.

Which explained the curt letter from Oakleigh Grange disclaiming any knowledge of Solomon de Toledo, sable pelts, or a loan, and asserting Mr. Pomeroy had not visited London in ten years. In a postscript, the writer added that the matter would be referred to his attorney if any further such communications were received. The signature did not resemble the one on Solomon's contract with the man he knew as Philip Pomeroy. Easy enough to get someone else to write a letter or disguise one's own hand. However, the information Hawkins had passed on proved Solomon had been taken in by an impostor.

No point in thinking of his mistake now. The moss green velvet suit, worn with the oyster-white silk waistcoat embroidered with gillyflowers and ferns should impress the family of the girl David hoped to marry. Solomon, his father and mother, his brothers and sister and their respective spouses, as well as another cousin or two, and their maternal grandmother, were to be present to meet the Crispins. Only the prospective bride, her father, brother, and an aunt who was Petronella's companion/chaperon, lived in London, their other connections residing in County Durham. They would be outnumbered by the Mendys family and its de Toledo relatives. If any of the Crispins present were not in favor of the marriage, they might find it uncomfortable.

How did anyone have the courage to face the challenges of such a union? Deciding in which faith the children would be reared, what careers they would follow, very likely other things which had not occurred to him. The first decision would settle many of the others, of course. If they were brought up as Jews, the sons would not attend university, not in England, and would not hold positions in government. If the mother were Jewish and married a titled gentleman, could the oldest son inherit the title if he were not Christian? Probably not, unless he converted. Of course, the father would likely insist on their being raised as Christians. Presumably these questions had been dealt with, or would be, perhaps in the marriage settlements. Still, as long as David was happy, it didn't matter.

"So..." His cousin drew him aside on his arrival. "Petronella's people have met most of us before, except you and Grandmother, and they'll be impressed with her. Earl's daughter, after all."

Granted, he had been an earl with nothing left but his title, an entailed estate, two sons, and two daughters. The marriage settlements from the girls, one to a wealthy Scottish tobacco importer who wanted a connection to the Mediterranean trade, the other to Simon Mendys, had wiped out the earl's debts. Less than a month after the second profitable wedding, the heir apparent and his brother arranged for a physician to declare the earl of unsound mind and agree that he should be confined in a suite of rooms at the manor, which had the beneficial result that he could not gamble away any more money or possessions. While Solomon did not approve, he sympathized with their motivation.

"What I started to ask," David went on, "is would you mind not mentioning you lend money? I wouldn't want you to lie, but could you, er, circle around the truth?"

"Easily." His cousin quite understandably did not want anything to cause Sir Peter Crispin to break off the negotiations. He doubted any of the Crispins would ask about his profession, and he would not mention it.

He was mistaken. After the introductions, the first member of Petronella Crispin's family to speak with him at any length was her aunt, a stiff-backed, chilly-eyed spinster lady of a certain age.

"Your father is a physician, I understand. Do you also practice medicine? I understand it is quite a tradition in your branch of the family."

"No. I fear I do not have the aptitude for it. One of my brothers does, however."

"Not a profitable profession, I imagine, Mr. de Toledo."

"I suppose it might be, for a few fashionable practitioners, but as a rule, it is not." His father might not be in demand in court circles but did well enough. Dr. Benjamin de Toledo, like some other medical men, had begun to question whether the ancients actually knew everything about medicine and the human body. Given the many advances in other branches of learning, why should medicine not progress, too? Benjamin de

Toledo was particularly sought after for the treatment of fevers, especially for recurring agues, as he had no religious prejudice against the use of Jesuit's bark and was careful not to call it by that name when speaking to his patients, many of whom abhorred anything associated with papists, even if it would abate the fever and chills.

"Are you engaged in importing, then, like Mr. David Mendys and his father?" Augusta Crispin's raised eyebrows demanded an answer.

"I am not an importer myself, but I do invest in cargoes, and also in properties. At the moment, I have an interest in a shipment of sable pelts." Which was true, even if the furs were now at the bottom of the Baltic Sea. He knew better than to mention the odd lots of merchandise he still bought and sold. Jobbing would not impress her.

She pursed her lips. "Not a very secure livelihood, I imagine." Her gimlet eyes evaluated his suit and the lace at his cuffs and neck cloth.

Spends all his income on his clothing, she might be thinking.

"It's a hard way to start. I take my gains and invest part in the Funds and the rest in more properties and cargoes."

"Hmmm."

He was wondering what that meant, until he noticed her eyes were fixed on something past his shoulder. Risking a quick glance, he saw young Mr. Talbot Crispin and Alafair Mendys in earnest conversation. Alafair's cheeks were glowing with pleasure at Talbot's admiring gaze.

Hmmm, indeed.

Chapter 13

17th November

Dear Portia,

I write to you only. I hope you will not share it with Mother or Father, for it would worry the former and anger the latter. First of all, I am not in trouble. I have been thinking about my studies a great deal, and I really do not see the point of studying Greek and Hebrew. I do not want to spend my life as a tutor, which is the only career for which my current studies would qualify me. Mr. Elliott mentioned in passing the cost of sending his older brother to university, and some of us have been talking about the future.

I came to understand our circumstances when we were searching in Father's library this summer. I have deduced that Mr. de Toledo (who is, in my opinion, a trusty-Trojan) advanced the money for this term. We cannot expect him to support me at university, especially when from what I hear, university would not be truly useful unless I became a parson or perhaps a lawyer or went into politics or some government service. But in order to advance in those professions, I would need some connection or sponsor to get me a post. It would be foolish to waste money sending me to Cambridge only because our father studied there.

I wish Radford's taught more Arithmetick, and more natural philosophy. I have been reading Sir Isaac

Newton's Mathematical Principles of Natural Philosophy*, which my friend Norton brought with him. You should hear what he says about the ancients! Fortunately,* Principles *was translated some ten or twelve years ago. I would not like to have to read it in Latin. Newton's ideas are far more interesting than old wars, which have no relevance in the modern world, and fusty old notions of nature, like the belief that a mother bear licks her cub into shape. Anyone who thinks about it at all must realize that is foolishness. Kittens and puppies do not look like full grown dogs and cats, nor do infants look like adults, and none of them require to be licked into shape. I have spoken with boys here at Radford's who live in the country, and they say the same is true of horses, sheep, and cows. Why would a bear cub be born formless when other animals are not? I do not suppose those old Greeks had ever seen a newborn bear cub and simply made this story up. If they were wrong about that, they are likely wrong about other things as well.*

I know you cannot change Father's mind, but please hint to him that I'm not suited to be a scholar. I want to study something that's actually useful.

I hope you and Mother are well. Will you please send me another shirt? I fear one of mine suffered a mishap at the Guy Fawkes bonfire, and the woman who does the mending for us says it is quite ruined.

Yr brother,
Benedict

****

The thought of hinting to Papa that Benedict did not wish to follow in his father's footsteps made Portia feel sick. Since his recovery he had alternated between unusual cheer and irritability; both worried her. Gillespie had not been a light-hearted man before his apoplexy and had always been easily annoyed, less by casual mischances than by disappointment with another: a student, fellow scholar, or family member. Generally, however, he had at least affected an air of calm. She did not like to do anything to stir his ire. Still, the attempt must be made.

He often worked alone in his study now, writing notes or memoranda which he put away when she entered. Those carefully guarded sheets must relate to his book. Perhaps he was having trouble organizing his ideas for it, after his apoplexy and convalescence. He went out oftener than he had before his illness, always without explanation. Freedom from many of her secretarial duties did permit her to continue copying legal documents for Mr. Brigginshaw. She set those earnings aside for unexpected expenses…though she did wish she might have a new mantua. She had requested that the attorney not tell her father as she was sure he would order her to stop. She could not rely on Gillespie's nonchalance about their expenses.

She finally ventured to raise the subject of Benedict's future as he finished dictating a letter to a former student who was now secretary to a member of the House of Lords and therefore worth continued correspondence. "Papa, do you think Benedict suited to scholarly pursuits? When you were ill, Mr. de Toledo and I discussed what was to be done about his future if you did not make a full recovery, as we could hardly expect de Toledo to lend money for a university education when we already owed him for the Radford's fees." *And with almost no hope of ever repaying the debt.* "It seemed to both of us he is more interested in practical things than in the abstract."

"De Toledo respects scholarship. After all, he comes from a long line of learned men on his father's side, though he has chosen to involve himself in financial matters." His mouth thinned at the phrase. "Financial matters" was a tactful way of describing Mr. de Toledo's business. "We had many interesting discussions," Papa added in a warmer tone.

When he did not go on and did not appear distressed, Portia took heart. "I understand Benedict would not need to attend university to rise in the East India Company or in some merchant house. Mr. de Toledo was willing to help him secure him a position."

"He has been helpful. However, there is no need to trouble him further. My son is a gentleman and will receive a gentleman's education."

Portia bit her lip. She did not want to risk upsetting her father. On the other hand, she refused to pretend no problem existed. "How is it to be paid for?"

"You need not worry about such details, Portia. It is unsuitable for a female in good society to be concerned about money."

"And yet Mother and I had to worry about it and deal with it, too, during your illness." She was appalled when the thought emerged from her lips.

"I am not obliged to explain my decisions to you. I am well aware of what is required to educate a boy for a gentleman's life."

This conversation confirmed Portia in her decision to continue copying for Seth Brigginshaw. Papa, unobservant about household activities (except as they affected him), would not notice she often took a basket when she went out for her daily walk which now was invariably to Brigginshaw's office to pick up his work and return the completed copies.

In spite of her concern about expenses and the bills related to her father's illness, the household money for the month did not run out. This should have been reassuring, but while the warm autumn meant less expense for coal, that saving alone could not account for it. However, her father's request for imperial hyson tea, far more expensive than their usual black bohea, prompted even her mother to protest.

"Nonsense, Eliza. We can afford it. I have not tasted it since I left home and find myself longing for it. The flavor of green tea is much superior, and one need not add milk."

Her father returned from one of his mysterious errands a few days later and sent for her to see him in his study. His manner was strangely flustered. Perhaps unsettled more nearly described it, for he issued his instructions briskly.

"As your mother is out, please tell her to expect a delivery the day after tomorrow. The chairs and carpet are for the drawing room. I am not quite pleased with the appearance of the house. On Thursday, we will receive a visit from a nobleman who wishes to discuss his sons' education. Have the maid be particularly thorough in dusting and sweeping. Your mother should be suitably gowned and ready to provide appropriate refreshments. You must also look your best."

She curtsied and left the study without another word beyond, "Certainly, Papa," for what could she say? Rude and unfilial of her, mayhap, but if he expected even the richest member of the aristocracy to pay a tutor enough to cover the cost of new furnishings, her father was fit for Bedlam. He had always been somewhat arbitrary, and as proud of being the son of a Warwickshire squire and the nephew of a bishop as of his own academic attainments. His reputation was a perfectly legitimate reason for pride among scholars. In London society, a father who was merely county gentry, even a squire, conferred no great distinction, except over tradesmen and those even lower in the scale.

Understandably, Mama was in a ferment of anxiety over the threatened visit.

"I'll have Cook make Shrewsbury biscuits. Or would wiggs be better? I suppose it depends on whether we serve him tea or wine. Gentlemen do like wiggs with wine."

"I imagine Papa will offer him wine, and that will be sufficient. 'Tis not a social occasion, after all. He's only coming to discuss his sons' education. We will hardly see him, unless by chance. Or if we peek out the window when his carriage arrives," Portia added. Her mother would certainly never do such a thing. She herself might, if she were interested, which she was not, having met two or three of the fathers of the young men her Papa tutored. They were all unremarkable, middle-aged, and given to ponderous witticisms. This one would differ only in having a title.

As it turned out, she was wrong on almost all points. The Marquess of Furness had not spent long in the study before she was sent for.

"Lord Furness, this is my daughter, Portia. My dear, the Marquess of Furness heard that you sometimes assist me and requested to meet you."

Furness was not middle-aged, except perhaps by the reckoning of a schoolroom chit. She doubted he was more than ten years her senior, if as much. He was also neither thin nor stout, possessed aquiline features, and was not pockmarked. His hair, neatly tied back, was very fair. By his suit, he was both rich and fashionable, and the lace at his neck and wrists was of the finest quality. He bowed to a precisely calculated depth. However, had he determined the exact inclination suitable for introduction to a female of the middling sort? His face was rather austere, though his smile rendered it quite attractive, if chill. His subsequent dispassionate study of her face and form caused her to modify her first, favorable impression.

She curtsied to exactly the correct depth, murmuring, “Lord Furness.” She felt rather like a horse being viewed by a prospective buyer. Surely Papa had not suggested she would assist in the tutoring? Why would he? Furness could not be concerned his sons would form an attachment to her, as they must be too young unless he had begotten them when still at Eton or Harrow. Even if he had, meeting her would have put to rest any notion that a boy would fall into an infatuation with her.

He inquired idly about her interests and activities and seemed surprised to learn that she knew the Greek and Hebrew alphabets as well as the French, German, and Latin languages.

“Do you enjoy scholarly pursuits?”

She found most of her father’s work rather dry. “I enjoy using my mind, and I like to be busy.” Visiting friends and doing needlework would not fill the day. “And of course I am happy to be of assistance to my father."

"Unusual! I find most young ladies to be more concerned with fashion, shopping, and amusements than with intellectual matters." He could not quite conceal his distaste for her mantua. It was two years old, of cloth the color of amber, but quite unadorned. She had chosen it because the color suited her and it showed few signs of wear. After several minutes of chitchat, her father ushered her out of the room.

The men remained shut up in the study for some time.

When he had finally seen the marquess out, Gillespie paused at the door to the parlor. "That went very well. Now, I have some reading to do, if you will excuse me." She would have asked why she had been introduced to the marquess but was given no chance to do so.

She wished she could mention her concern to someone, preferably Solomon de Toledo. She could write, except that the business relationship which would have made it acceptable no longer existed. Too, it was clear that her father preferred not to continue the acquaintance. How embarrassing, when Solomon—Mr. de Toledo—had apparently regarded Gillespie as a friend. Portia could not think of him as anything else. There was not another soul to whom she could speak of her anxiety; her girlhood friends were all married and busy with their families. Unless perhaps Benedict? He was still a boy, but he was remarkably sensible in some ways. The Radford's School term was all but over, and Papa had instructed Cook to prepare a celebratory dinner.

"I suppose it is because Benedict is coming home,"

Eliza murmured doubtfully.

"And perhaps because Papa is now fully recovered?" He had never previously made much of Benedict's return from school; boys went away to school, came home between terms unless distance prohibited it, then went away again. Thomas Gillespie was a fond parent but not doting.

Her mother added, "He did say we had a great deal to celebrate." Hearing of the treats Cook had been ordered to supply, Portia feared for their household budget.

Her father's restored health was indeed cause for celebration, but he was strangely changed since his apoplexy. It might be no more than the consciousness of mortality. If so, it had taken an odd turn. As an admirer of the Stoic philosophers, she would have expected that his near encounter with death would have inclined him to muse upon the Stoic virtues of prudence, morality, temperance, and courage. Instead he spent money on furniture, rich foods, and wine, all things which he would previously have considered unimportant. His greatest happiness had been study and the writing of learned articles and essays. While he still wrote, he also went out, seldom mentioning where he was going or what he was about. She had spoken to her mother about these perplexing alterations to his habits.

"I do fret over our recent purchases, Portia, but your papa has always been careful about our expenses. He knows best what we can afford, I'm sure."

Portia would have liked to ask Dr. de Toledo whether changes in behavior were to be expected after an apoplexy, but the arguments against writing Solomon de Toledo applied to his father as well.

The day following Benedict's arrival, Father sat at the head of the table, gazing at his family either benevolently or perhaps smugly. Portia had become increasingly uncomfortable over the last week or two. He had taken to closing himself in his study. He might be reading. If he were writing, he did not need her assistance. His self-satisfied air had begun about that time.

He raised his glass. "We all have a great deal for which to be thankful. Benedict has completed another term and, I am told, done well. I have recovered my health. I have recently received an inheritance. Last of all, the Marquess of Furness has invited us to spend Christmas at one of his estates. Let us drink to our future."

Her mother and brother's blank expressions suggested they were as dumbfounded as she. They all raised their glasses, however. After drinking, Benedict recovered enough to exclaim, "First-rate!"

His father's brows contracted. "While I appreciate your enthusiasm, Benedict, I wish you will purge such peculiar cant words from your speech and leave them to vagabonds and criminals."

"It isn't cant, sir. 'Tis a naval term for the largest ships of the line, with the biggest crews and the most guns, which are therefore the best. It seemed to apply," he ended apologetically.

"Let us leave naval jargon to the navy, for while its officers may be gentlemen, it is an occupation which coarsens them."

Eliza Gillespie uttered, "Lud! Who would think…?" and similar disjointed comments signifying amazement and gratification.

An inheritance explained Gillespie's lack of concern regarding their finances. Relief at discovering they were neither bound for the almshouse nor debtor's prison did not distract her from the puzzling end of his speech.

"Papa, why has the marquess invited us to stay?"

"He wishes me to evaluate his sons' academic progress, and he did not wish to bring them to town. I do not usually instruct boys as young as his, of course, but I did not feel I could refuse his flattering request. I can study the lads at leisure in surroundings in which they are comfortable and recommend some former student of mine who will best be able to guide their minds. At the same time, it will be pleasant to spend two or three weeks in the country at a nobleman's house."

While this explanation tripped glibly off her father's tongue, Portia could not imagine the Marquess of Furness welcoming a family like theirs into his home. Even her father, a recognized scholar, would hardly rank above a tutor—nominally a gentleman but still only a sort of upper servant in the marquess's eyes.

Her mother twittered something about needing to see about a new gown or two, both for Portia and herself.

"Nonsense, his lordship won't expect you to be fashionable. There won't be time. His coach will come for us early Wednesday morning. We will arrive that evening, if the weather does not turn. If necessary, we will stop at an inn."

Eliza squeaked, "Wednesday! Portia, tomorrow we will visit the haberdasher for ribbon to freshen our gowns. Perhaps new stockings, too. William must bring the trunks down from the attic."

She could not have had occasion for them since her marriage, and Portia had never been outside London. The idea was daunting. Yet to see the countryside and stay in a manor held a certain attraction. What a pity their host would be titled, making it impossible to relax and enjoy the experience!

Chapter 14

The week had been mildly vexing. He had spoken with two young men whose entire next quarter's allowance was already spent. Now that the new quarter was approaching and they would be spending Christmas with their families, the problem they had postponed thinking of loomed large. Fragments of the conversations recurred at intervals to annoy him:

"I'm an earl's heir. I've an obligation to live like one." By which he meant supporting a mistress, playing deep at the tables, buying and housing several horses, and sporting a prince's ransom in sleeve links, jeweled buckles, rings, and the like. The fellow was only two years short of his own age, old enough to know better, one would think.

Another could not grasp the simple fact that Solomon would not lend money if there were no possibility of its being repaid. "I need only a run of luck and I'll pay it all back, and interest, too," the young idiot offered. Gamblers always believed a run of luck would solve their problems. In Solomon's experience, they gambled it away again before rising from the table. This fault virtually insured that gambling hells never failed.

The third, old enough to know better, had sunk all his money into an investment scheme touted by a fellow he had met at an assembly. "Scheme" was definitely the correct word.

"He said the enterprise cannot fail, and as soon as he returns, it will be high tide with me. He must be out of town, seeking more investments to expand our business or perhaps staying with his family connections to celebrate Christmas. I need only enough to carry me through the next month or two."

The applicant did not know where to find him. He knew nothing of the promoter: they had no friends or acquaintances in common, though the plausible scoundrel claimed to have attended the same university—not at the same time, of course.

"He was busy organizing the undertaking," the prospective borrower explained. "Somehow I never got his direction."

Or his real name, or any references.

"Do you believe everything you are told?"

"No, of course not."

"Yet you trusted him based on a claim you had both been at Cambridge."

"He is obviously a gentleman. Gentlemen do not lie."

Solomon sighed. "Have you a wife, or children, or any dependents?"

The man stared as if he were being asked to put up one or more of them as security. "No."

Fortunate. "Do you have any income at all? Or any salable property?"

The client was beginning to show affront at what he felt were unnecessarily prying questions. "There's a pittance that comes in from an investment my godmother left me. About a hundred and fifty per annum, I think. Not enough to live on. Oh, and a cottage, too, in Suffolk. Just a mean little place. I'm told there's two rooms on the ground floor and four bedchambers above. It's not worth selling or renting out. There's an old couple who act as caretakers, who have a pension from my godmother."

Thank God.

"I can't lend you money based on a hope that your elusive acquaintance's investment will prosper and he will return."

The man stood abruptly. "This has been a waste of my time, then."

"Not at all. You have two choices. You may be able to find work, perhaps as a gentleman's secretary"—because the fellow had no skills beyond being a gentleman, which at least meant he could read and write—"or sell anything you own here in town that you do not wish to take with you, pay your bills, and move to the cottage. In the country you'll be able to get by on your income. You won't be hungry or cold and you will probably be able to keep a horse."

"A gentleman can't live in a hovel like a rustic on a few pounds a year." He bit his lip. "I've heard you arrange advantageous marriages as well as lending money."

"A marriage is a bargain like any other. Each side gives something and gets something. When the bride or her family are willing to make a good settlement to get a husband, they expect to benefit from the match. Do you have aristocratic connections? A very old, respectable name and family history?"

"No."

"Then you have nothing to offer. Believe me, the cottage appears to be your only choice, unless you can attract a wealthy widow on your own merits. I'm sorry, but honesty is essential in my business." On that note, the interview ended.

The corner of a letter peeked out from the book in which he listed appointments and things to be done. He really must do something about Lady Isabelle Baldock. She had written again. Not directly, of course, for she would never let her servants see a missive addressed to Solomon at the Sign of the Scales, Old Jury. It had arrived enclosed in a letter of only two or three lines from her downtrodden man of business: "Lady Isabelle is most anxious about the status of your inquiries. She trusts you will have a report for her by the end of December." The plea was unmistakable.

She had refused his first two candidates without so much as seeing them. The baron was not high enough in the order of precedence and too recent a creation in any case. The viscount he had dangled before her was too old.

"I have already had an elderly husband. I want one with some life between his legs. And, of course, a title which is not an insult to my descent." Lady Isabelle's father had been an earl, but she had been less concerned about living up to her ancestry when her perennially purse-pinched papa had set about finding her a husband. As a girl she had no more than passable looks and a dowry of two thousand pounds. She had been perfectly willing to settle for a middle-aged cit with a great deal of gelt. The late Mr. Baldock had been generous, giving her enough pin money to keep a family in comfort, in addition to buying her whatever she fancied.

It should not have been difficult to find her a

husband in spite of her exacting requirements, even a duke, as she had inherited everything Mr. Baldock owned. Apparently even needy noblemen had some standards. Her indulgent spouse had at her request tied up much of her inheritance in well-constructed trust funds, and the stocks were entirely her own. Many men could have accepted not having control over the greater part of her fortune. The problem was her well-earned reputation as a handsome termagant with no reluctance to speak her own mind and to throw things when in a pet.

He sighed, wrote an answering line to the man of business, assuring him that fulfilling Lady Isabelle's desire for a new husband was his highest priority, although given the season, the gentlemen he was considering for her approval were in the country. He would communicate as soon as he could after Twelfth Night.

The only bit of cheer was a boy of eighteen years who was a baron's third son. He sat slumped and white-faced and confessed his bills and expenses amounted to more than a year of his allowance. He admitted that when he first realized he had a problem, he had done nothing because he did not know what to do. He was terrified of telling his father.

Solomon drew out information about the family bit by bit. At last he said, "Your father may be angry. He will certainly be disappointed. I very much doubt he will cast you off, for from what you have told me, he is a reasonable man and a kind father."

"That makes it worse."

Solomon understood the feeling. "Of course you don't want to disappoint him, but it's the fate of parents to be disappointed by their children occasionally," as he himself knew very well. "My suggestion to you is go home—I suppose you can afford coach fare? Or can pawn something for it?—and talk to him. Explain to him as you have to me, and ask him to help you get a position so you can earn a living and perhaps repay him eventually. The East India Company is a good choice, or perhaps the Africa Company, or there's the church or law, though there's not much profit in those. It depends upon your abilities and interests. Talk to him."

The boy straightened his shoulders and drew a deep breath. "Thank you, Mr. de Toledo. I think I knew there was no other way, but you have confirmed it and—and made it easier somehow. I was fearing a painted devil." He paused. "That's in Shakespeare. It means—"

" 'Tis the eye of childhood fears a painted devil. *MacBeth*, Act II, Scene II, I think."

The cub was young enough to blush. "I wasn't sure if, er…"

"If Jew moneylenders attend the theater? Or read plays? I enjoy Shakespeare, though not, I admit, *The Merchant of Venice*."

"Thank you again, sir. You've been a trusty-Trojan, and I've taken your time. I should pay you something for your assistance, though I fear I won't be able to do so immediately."

Solomon smiled to take away the sting of his irritable remark. "I lend money for interest. Advice is free. Have a pleasant holiday with your family." That appointment lifted his spirits temporarily.

It had been two weeks or more since he had seen Portia Gillespie, which should not matter…except that it did. While his business with Thomas Gillespie was complete and at his last visit Gillespie had made it plain (without stating it explicitly) that he had no interest in continuing their acquaintance, Solomon still took an interest in the family. In Portia, anyway, and Benedict, too. As it happened, he had come across the first two volumes of *L'architecture hydraulique* by Bernard Forest de Bélidor at a secondhand book stall. He should deliver them; Benedict would now be home from school. Solomon might still hear his amusing or trenchant comments about the last month of the term. Surely the boy would be able to read French; every well-educated English gentleman did. If by some chance he did not, inspired by his interest in the engineer's art, he could teach himself to do so. Even if he were out of the house, Portia would be at home.

But when he presented himself at the Gillespies' door, he was startled to find the knocker removed. Its absence was meant to inform callers the family had gone out of town and was so unexpected that he stood staring at the less weathered paint where it should have been. He finally rapped on the door instead. Several attempts were required before the maid opened it.

She recognized him from previous visits. "The family's away from home, sir," the maid informed him. She offered him an apologetic smile, mayhap because he had tipped her on those visits.

"I am sorry to have troubled you to come to the door when I saw the knocker was off, but I understood the Gillespies have no family connections they might be visiting. Given Mr. Gillespie's recent ill health, I was concerned."

"Nor I don't wonder, for Cook as has worked for

them since Mistress Portia was only a bit of a girl, says they've never done the like. 'Tis the talk of the street, them going off in a coach with a crest on the door."

His grip on the parcel under his arm tightened. "What a great thing for them. Lord St. George, I suppose, as I believe he is a great scholar and must know Mr. Gillespie."

"Oh, no, sir. It was the Marquess of Furness asked them to spend Christmas at his estate. Whoever would have expected it? Something to do with teaching his boys, Mistress Gillespie said."

"Furness? His estate must be a very long journey at this time of year, for it is situated in Lancashire, is it not?"

"Might be he has one there, but it's to Essex they've gone. We'd none of us heard of the place, we servants, I mean, and I can't call it to mind now. William, our footman, did mention it to a friend at the livery stable, who said the nearest coaching inn to it is Chelmsford, which is no more than fifty miles, if as much. Or so he says," she added doubtfully.

"Ah, well, I'll call again when they return."

She took the sixpence he offered with stammered thanks. Gillespie's servants probably were not used to tips from his visitors, or not such large ones. They would be on board wages, too, with the family away.

He turned from the door, frowning. Furness! What ill luck had led to Gillespie encountering him? His opinion of the man had been formed at their brief accidental meeting at Vauxhall Gardens, and nothing he had learned since had altered it. Solomon had scored a hit in that engagement, but the memory was unpleasant. Furness would not appreciate Solomon having mentioned his financial difficulties before the others present at that meeting. He had even wondered, waking in the early morning hours, if the marquess might hire a bravo to slip a knife between his ribs. The others, belonging to Furness's class, would be safe from murder; they had pledged not to speak of what they knew. The marquess would trust their word as he might not rely on Solomon's promise.

Why would Furness, who bore himself as haughtily as a duke, invite the Gillespies to his country home? True, it was only the small Essex manor inherited from his father, a mere viscount of no great fortune or attainment. The thought gave him a moment's amusement, as no nobleman could be called "mere." Still, it was a signal honor for an impoverished scholar of only genteel origins to be included in a marquess's house party. That it should be held in Essex rather than Lancashire made sense, given that winter travel in the latter might be slow and even dangerous. But why invite the Gillespies?

He was still turning the problem over in his mind as he neared Old Jury. He could send the books to Benedict at Blackwater Hay, with a note inside the cover addressed to Portia. It would not do to write Mr. Gillespie, though he would ordinarily be the obvious person to warn. They had discussed scholarly topics for the most part and current events during their coffee house meetings. Even in connection with those subjects, Gillespie's partiality for the titled was evident. He would not be open to aspersions cast upon a marquess.

Portia was a sensible female, and it was for her he was most concerned. On the other hand, to write to a young lady to whom one was not betrothed would be scandalous (in spite of their having exchanged correspondence to arrange Benedict's school term). If anyone other than Benedict or Portia discovered the letter, the fat would be in the fire. Portia's reputation would suffer if it became generally known. If her father were the only one to learn of it, he would be furious with Solomon at least and perhaps with her as well. If Furness found out…it did not bear thinking of. The marquess might feel he had already suffered humiliation at Solomon's hands, unless he had forgotten about Solomon as being too far beneath him to remember. Being forgotten would be preferable.

He was approaching the door of his office when the thudding of heavy feet penetrated his distraction. He spun around and dropped to a crouch, ready to meet an attack in earnest as John Barlicorn had taught him years ago.

His bull-like attacker stopped short. "You're mighty nervous today, Sol," Ambrose Hawkins commented.

"Hawkins." He took a breath. "You seem to be in a hurry to see me. Is your bank refusing you a loan?"

A snort in reply. "Not likely. I was on my way to share some news."

"Come in. I've a decent claret or a good dry Madeira."

Solomon nodded to the brawny former boxer who presided over the front office. Rafe was slow in his wits, but his fists were still quick, and his appearance was enough to discourage robbers or clients who held a grudge. He was not able to write down the names of those who inquired for Solomon, which was a minor drawback. Those who already knew Solomon sent him a note requesting an appointment at a particular time. Rafe provided small sheets of paper for unexpected callers to leave their names and directions.

As soon as they were closed in Solomon's office, even before Solomon could offer him a seat, Hawkins burst out, "I'm going to have a child."

Solomon paused in the act of setting out glasses. "Really?"

"I mean, Emily is. We are. I'm going to be a father, and you're on my way to Cinnamon Street to tell Timothy, because I have to tell someone. Two someones is better than one. And I suppose I'll have to write my brother and sister and mother," he continued more temperately. "Though it's not the same as doing it in person."

"Congratulations! Claret or Madeira?"

"Uh, Madeira."

Their tumblers filled, Solomon proposed a toast to young Master Hawkins or young Mistress Hawkins. "As the case may be."

They passed on to a few items of interest to those in the City and on the Pool of London. When those topics palled, Solomon said slowly, "Hawkins, I discovered something today that I find troubling. I need your opinion. A family I know has gone to spend Christmas at the Marquess of Furness's place in Essex."

"I expect even the Devil gives house parties. I wouldn't care to attend one, however. Who's the family? Hard to believe Furness has friends, but odder things have happened." Hawkins held his glass up to admire the wine's tawny color against the fire in the hearth.

"The man is a scholar, a former client of mine."

"Huh. I don't see Furness as the scholarly sort. He's not the kind to bother with the common herd, either, or anyone who could not benefit him."

"No, that's what I thought, though I only met him that one time."

"Lord, what an affair that was! He was angry enough to chew nails, wasn't he?"

"Indeed." The memory made Solomon's blood run cold.

"Is it possible your scholar is some sort of relation to him?"

"No."

Hawkins's face went blank. "Does your scholar happen to be related to one of your prosperous banking families?"

"He's a Christian. And not connected to any Christian bankers, either. But it was a good thought, if you were thinking the marquess might be trying to scrape acquaintance with some wealthy family."

"I was thinking of ransom."

Solomon opened his mouth to protest, then closed it again. He could not dismiss the possibility, except—"His victim would have to be rich or be related to someone with wealth. And my old client…"

"Isn't? That scuttles that notion."

"I'm wrong." Several bits of information came together, like iron filings to a magnet. "He paid off what he owed me. Not much by your standards, Hawkins." *Or even mine*. "I heard something that may mean he has come into some money. You've heard of Sturgis, the man who made a fortune with his new-fangled furnace? He's said to have left his wealth to a cousin who is an academic."

"Then your fellow is now wealthy and worth squeezing?"

"I don't know. The family doesn't seem to be spending any great amount of money, as far as I can judge. My informant did say Sturgis paid back some snubs he received at the cousin's hands. That doesn't make sense if he left the bulk of his fortune to his cousin. Could the cousin have refused it? The scholar I know wouldn't enjoy being connected to a man he called an ironmonger's brat, no matter how rich."

"It sounds as if this man is a friend as well as a former borrower."

"I used to think of him as a friend. Then he fell ill and I met the rest of his family. We became acquainted while arranging for his son's next school term. After he recovered, he paid me in full, and that was that."

"He's cut your acquaintance, but you're still concerned about the family," Hawkins summed up. "Why?"

"The daughter is a pleasant young lady, and I've somehow become her brother's adopted uncle." Pleasant was too mild a word for Portia or not sufficiently complete. Pretty, intelligent, sensible, and resourceful would describe her and still not give the entire picture.

"Oh, that explains all. Yet I still do not quite understand what worries you about the visit, unless we've come full circle to ransom or extortion."

"I don't know what it is I fear, Hawkins. I am not easy in my mind, which may be only because Furness is involved."

"Not unreasonable. Yet what can you do?"

“I don’t know.”

Hawkins departed.

Who would know why Furness had asked the Gillespies to his home? While he dealt with several of his humbler clients who had either come in to make their regular payments or to request a loan of a pound or two, his mind churned the question. While reviewing the status of other accounts, his brain produced an answer. Portia Gillespie had taken on copying work for an attorney, some family friend. She had mentioned him by name. Solomon sat waiting for the ink to dry on his most recent entry, pursuing a wisp of memory. It began with a B, he thought. Ay, a B, and an odd one, not common like Brown or Baker. Briggs? No, Brigginshaw, in Chancery Lane. As of the last time he had seen her, Portia was still copying for him without her papa’s knowledge. However dire their situation, Thomas Gillespie would not have approved his daughter working. Or working for someone other than himself. The chances were she had continued as a copyist, the discovery of their straitened finances having made a deep impression on her. That being the case, she would have told Attorney Brigginshaw she was going away for a time over Christmas. As he was a friend of the Gillespies, she might even have told him why.

Chapter 15

Presenting himself at Brigginshaw's office, he requested a consultation on an urgent matter. The clerk asked the nature of his legal problem. Solomon told him that the issue was so sensitive that even to describe it to any but the attorney would be a breach of confidentiality.

"I see, sir. Let me speak with Mr. Brigginshaw." He scuttled away, the picture of a man who did not understand but was willing to leave any decision to his master.

On the way to Chancery Lane, Solomon had debated the best way of approaching Brigginshaw: Should he introduce himself as a friend of the Gillespies and ask straight out? Or work around to it? When the clerk returned and asked him to step into Mr. Brigginshaw's office, he still had not decided.

"Mr. de Toledo? Have I that correctly? Please, be seated."

"Thank you for seeing me on short notice. Yes, my name is Solomon de Toledo. I will say that while I am a moneylender"—because his occupation was not a secret—"this has nothing to do with collecting a debt. I am gravely concerned about the welfare of certain friends."

"Is their difficulty of a legal nature?"

One could interpret that phrase in two different

ways: Does their difficulty require an attorney? Or are they in trouble with the law?

"Not precisely. The nub of my worry is that the family, including a young lady, have been invited to a house party given by a man not of their usual circle, who is known to me as a scoundrel."

The attorney had been listening with detached professional interest. Now his eyes lit with curiosity. "May I inquire how you know of his character? Are you an associate of his?"

"Good God, no!" What a horrid thought. "I met him once. Six months ago, he twice attempted to blacken the name of another gentleman. I was present at the first attempt, at which he also tried to coerce an heiress into marriage. For convenience and discretion, I will refer to him as the Gray Nobleman. A friend I have known since childhood and would trust with my life told me the man's sister eloped with her favored suitor when it was learned the Gray Nobleman meant to have that suitor crippled."

"Surely you spoke with the head of the family about the wisdom, or unwisdom, I should say, of accepting the invitation?"

"I only learned of it after they had left town."

"Can you not write to your friends expressing your sentiments?"

"There are reasons which would make that inadvisable, Attorney Brigginshaw."

Brigginshaw raised his eyebrows.

"I am a Hebrew moneylender. Their host is a nobleman. The head of the family…has a great admiration for the aristocracy. The other members of the family might be inclined to believe me but are powerless. It is also possible a letter sent to one of them might be diverted."

"This sounds like the sort of novel one would not permit one's daughter to read," Brigginshaw remarked dryly.

"I know it does, sir, in part because I am suppressing the names of the parties."

"I do not see how I can aid you, Mr. de Toledo. It does not appear to be a question of law, or at least not of my specialty."

"No, I agree. I came to you because you know the Gillespies. Mistress Portia mentioned to me that she was copying documents for you."

"How well acquainted with the family are you?" The bald question suggested he had once again secured Brigginshaw's interest.

"I lent Thomas Gillespie money for Benedict's first two years at Radford's School, and for this year. During our many meetings, as he was making payment on the loans each month, we became friends." *Or so I thought.* "I met Mistress Gillespie, Master Benedict, and Mistress Portia after he suffered his apoplexy and visited them a number of times to make arrangements for Benedict's Michaelmas term. I delivered him to the coaching inn to meet his friend and a tutor for the journey."

The attorney laughed aloud. "Ay, and provided a hamper of confections, as I heard from Portia. She did not mention your name, only referring to you as a friend." He laced his fingers together and pondered. "This does put a different complexion on the problem. Indeed, it does. What is it you think I can do? Write to Gillespie to warn him of his host's character? What is your Gray Nobleman's name? I mean no offense, but I should like to inquire as to his character before taking any action, and Portia informed me only they were going to visit someone who might engage Gillespie's services for his sons. Unfortunately, I was out, calling upon a client, and her note was very brief and discreet."

"The Marquess of Furness."

The attorney straightened in his chair. "Dear me. Ay, that is disquieting. May I offer you a glass of claret, sir?"

"Thank you, Mr. Brigginshaw." Apparently the attorney had accepted him and they had more to discuss. "I take it you know something of Furness?"

"It is no secret there is currently a case before the Court of Chancery regarding payment of a dowry."

"Which Furness failed to pay?"

Brigginshaw smiled primly and remarked, "You seem unsurprised."

"I am privy to some information which I am not at liberty to share." Solomon returned the smile. "What I hoped you could tell me is why the Gillespies went to Blackwater Hay."

"Portia's note said a titled gentleman had invited them to his manor to meet his sons who needed to be tutored. Apparently there was some question as to whether they were ready for a tutor."

"I cannot imagine Furness inviting even a scholar of Gillespie's reputation to stay, and with his family at that."

"Now that I know it was Furness, I confess it seems wondrous strange to me. However, you are quite right about Gillespie's liking for titles. If the marquess invited him to help celebrate some Satanic ritual, my old friend might do it."

Solomon almost choked on a sip of his wine. "Surely not!"

"I beg your pardon, I exaggerate. Gillespie is a very brilliant scholar and a decent fellow, though he is wrong-headed about some things. He would, however, go to great lengths to ingratiate himself with a member of the nobility. Not being a member of the beau monde, it's unlikely he is aware of Furness's reputation. I am not of that charmed circle myself, but it employs attorneys and solicitors who are thereby aware of certain things." He absentmindedly poured more claret for Solomon and himself, sunken in thought. "This is a very troubling development." Brigginshaw puffed out a breath. "I believe you are right to worry, Mr. de Toledo. But damme if I know what either of us can do."

****

Portia found much of interest to look at, having never been out of London. It did not take long to conclude that Essex was home to a great many sheep, and that it contained a surprising number of brooks and streams. Fortunately, the weather had continued dry, as much of the land was flat and low-lying. Rain might turn the county into a quagmire in spite of the presence of ditches presumably meant to drain off excess water.

The estate lay a few miles beyond Maldon. Portia knew nothing of agricultural land, but the tenant cottages she had seen appeared ill-kept. The property was a manor, the house less grand than she had expected, and the grounds were not impressive. In winter the trees were bare-branched. In the spring and summer, the park might be pleasant and the parterre pretty if it were planted with flowers. She did not voice these observations to her father, who had been puffed up with either pride or satisfaction or both since announcing they were to visit the marquess. It was left to her mama to broach the topic.

"This is not what I would have expected of the home of a marquess," Eliza remarked. Her mother, though a cit's daughter, had seen the country homes of aristocrats.

Before she could say more, Papa cut her off. "This is not the marquess's principal seat, Eliza. Blackwater Hay is merely the manor inherited from his father, the viscount. As I am sure I mentioned, the marquessate came to him from his uncle. Furness's chief holding is too far north to make a Christmas visit convenient."

"Oh, of course."

Her mother did not appear convinced, a sentiment Portia shared. Granted, it was not an unattractive house, though of several different styles. The left front appeared medieval, while the right half, though of similar stone, did not quite match and contained symmetrically placed sash windows instead of tall narrow ones.

They were welcomed with as much formality as if it were a royal palace. The servants swarmed around them, all obsequious attention. They were ushered through heavy double doors at the left of the entrance hall into a reception room and promised refreshment and escort to their chambers at once!—as soon as the Marquess of Furness had greeted them.

Gigantic dark beams supported the ceiling high above them, and the tall, narrow windows certainly looked medieval. The stone walls had been sheathed in linenfold paneling, however, and a fire provided welcome heat.

Portia's mother sank onto a chair with a coat of arms embroidered upon its tall back. Her father surveyed the room with a faint, self-satisfied smile. "This is undoubtedly the oldest part of the house. I would guess that paneled wall"—he nodded toward the far end of the room—"was added to divide the original great hall in half."

"It can't be easy to warm a room with such high ceilings."

"Nonsense, Benedict. One cannot count minor details against a place of such age and dignity. A house like this is judged by quite another standard than a commonplace modern dwelling, packed cheek by jowl with others of the same sort. This is the best of England, my boy."

It was fortunate their papa was studying a series of paintings depicting famous battles, as Benedict's face had taken on an expression Portia interpreted as utter incredulity. She compressed her lips to avoid smiling, and thus encouraging him. While she could understand the attraction of a medieval manor, she did hope the bedrooms would be cozy.

The double doors into the reception room opened again, admitting a blast of chill air, and a footman intoned, "The Most Honorable, the Marquess of Furness, Viscount Ardrey."

Eliza Gillespie popped up from the chair like a Jack-in-the-box toy and curtsied deeply. Portia also curtsied. Thomas Gillespie bowed. Benedict was a trifle slow in doing so, having stared for a moment at that rare spectacle, a nobleman.

Furness made an imposing figure, clad in a very

formal suit of rich blue, though he was not wearing a wig. The marquess at home proved to be less intimidating than he had seemed at their first meeting. He smiled as he greeted them and inquired about their journey, bowing over Eliza's hand, then over Portia's, and holding it a little longer than necessary. The moment was broken by the hurried arrival of a timid, elderly lady followed by a footman with a tea tray and another with a tray bearing a punchbowl with hot punch.

She was introduced as the marquess's aunt, Frances Sedgewick, who was to act as his hostess. Frances and Eliza Gillespie recognizing each other as kindred spirits, settled to a comfortable chat. Portia sat wondering what she could contribute to her mother and Frances's conversation or what she and the marquess could converse upon, should he address her. However, Papa and the marquess retreated to one corner and put their heads together. They seemed to have a good deal to say to each other. Benedict was too fascinated by the room and furnishings to converse with her. She concentrated on sipping her tea and admiring the ornate silver tea service and was glad when the marquess suggested they would wish to retire to prepare for supper.

Frances murmured apologies for the shabbiness of the house as she accompanied Portia and her mother to their chambers.

"He's seldom here," she almost whispered. "There's the house in town, of course, and then there's Furness by Coniston Water, the seat of the marquessate."

Portia saw no need for apology for their

accommodations, in spite of the bed hangings and coverlet being faded and darned. The rooms smelled of beeswax and lavender and were better kept than their own home. The dark old furniture was somewhat rustic but suited the house better than the lighter modern styles would.

Once they had tidied themselves and changed their travel-crumpled clothing, it was time to go down to supper. As the party was small, talk was general, or should have been, if Eliza and Frances had contributed to the conversation. Too much in awe of the marquess to put themselves forward, neither did more than respond to direct questions. Again, though her father and Furness did most of the talking, the marquess addressed her occasionally. Benedict, who was not usually retiring in voicing his views except with his father, kept silent and concentrated on his food.

The marquess and Gillespie discussed the relative merits of living in London with its social and cultural attractions and living in the country with its clean air and lack of distractions. Portia speculated over the absence of other guests at what she had supposed was to be a house party. Then it occurred to her that as her father had been brought to Blackwater Hay to advise the marquess on his sons' education, Furness would not wish to subject his friends to the presence of even such a scholarly tutor as Thomas Gillespie. One could not feel offended by it; it was the way of the world. Nor would she have enjoyed being subjected to slights by aristocratic guests. But however were they to occupy themselves in such a small company?

During a lull in the men's conversation, she offered the only conversational gambit she could think of.

"Will we meet your sons tomorrow, Lord Furness?"

The significant pause before he replied alerted her that she had raised a delicate subject. Yet it was on the boys' account Gillespie had been invited to stay, with his family to cloak the visit in informality.

"Unfortunately, I have learned that the roads in the north are too difficult to allow my sons to make the journey. The youngest has already contracted a chill, too. But having arrived, you will remain to celebrate Christmas, of course."

How awkward. When her father said nothing, she murmured, "I'm sure we do not wish to keep you from town, where I dare say you would prefer to spend Christmas as your boys cannot be here. We could perfectly well return home—"

"Lord Furness will wish his horses to rest before undertaking another journey," her father said, cutting across the marquess's "I cannot hear of it. You are my guests, and I will not allow such an inconvenience to you." Instead of sounding hospitable, the words came out like an order.

"Oh, please do not think of going." Lady Frances spoke almost for the first time since they had sat down.

"How kind," Portia's mother faltered. Eliza, uncomfortable in an aristocratic household, however shabby, would clearly have preferred to depart.

Possibly aware that his manner had lacked something, Furness went on, "I think Mistress Portia and her brother have little experience of the countryside. They will enjoy riding out and seeing the sights. Maldon may be of interest. 'Tis only some six miles distant."

"I fear we will have to confine ourselves to

admiring your estate on foot," Portia said apologetically. "Neither of us has learned to ride."

A crack appeared in their host's cool assurance; for a moment, he was taken aback. "Hmm. Lady Frances, I am sure you can find a habit which will either fit Mistress Portia or can be altered to fit. And boots, of course." He fixed his pale eyes on Benedict. "As for young, ah…"

"Benedict, my lord."

"Benedict, of course. The attics must hold some of my and my brother's old riding gear he could wear."

"I will see to it in the morning, Furness. If that would be soon enough?" She glanced toward the narrow windows, where woolen hangings kept the dark and chill at bay.

"The morning will do, Aunt Frances."

"I would be glad to help you, ma'am, if I may?" Benedict offered.

Portia suppressed a smile. Blackwater Hay could offer her brother nothing more interesting than excavating in the attic, unless there were machinery of some sort to examine.

"Thank you, Master Benedict. Then I would have you at hand to check for size."

"If I could also be of assistance, ma'am?" It would certainly be easier for Lady Frances to be sure of a good fit if Portia were present, rather than having to have two or three habits and pairs of boots carried downstairs.

"Dear me, how very obliging of you, but…"

"My aunt knows I have a prior claim on your time," the marquess finished. "You will find the library of interest. I mean to show it to your father in the morning."

She would like to see it. Too, in the attics her gown would become dusty and might even be torn by some protruding nail. Portia did not have so many changes of clothing that she could be careless with one, particularly as she had brought only her better clothing.

"I look forward to seeing it," she said.

****

The library was not promising. One could not expect a scholar's library in the home of a country gentleman, even a marquess, but the collections of sermons and treatises on agriculture and husbandry, interspersed by a few philosophical works, plays, and novels seemed unlikely to appeal to her papa. Portia noted several books of some age which might repay investigation, and a book with receipts and instructions on household matters, written by a prior lady of the manor.

Thomas Gillespie gave the books little more than a passing glance, and remarked, "There is ample space for a good collection." Many of the shelves held ornaments or mementos from the travels of previous viscounts rather than books. He praised the windows, which would provide good light during much of the day.

The marquess addressed most of his comments to Portia, standing by her shoulder as she leafed through the more interesting volumes. He stood a little too close, and the nature of his remarks made her uncomfortable, being more appropriate to a flirtation than a tour of the house.

"Blackwater Hay is an unusual name." It was the only remark Portia could think of, and at least had the virtue of being something about which she was curious.

" 'Hay' is an ancient term, meaning a hedge or ground enclosed by a hedge or fence. I do not know how it came to be used here, though it must prove the age of the estate. The 'Blackwater' comes from the name of the nearby river, though you cannot see it from the house. Tomorrow we will begin your riding lessons. Once you are comfortable in the saddle, I will show you the estate."

Chapter 16

Solomon eventually ran his prey to earth in a street of middling houses, where he was pushing a small cart covered with a piece of canvas. He wore three hats stacked on his head.

"Abe."

His former client stopped abruptly and turned.

"Solomon! I don't suppose you'd care to sell your greatcoat? Or your hat?"

"No, I think not. I'm glad to find you in London. I feared you might be in the country."

"Not in the winter," Abe Schneider declared. "Peddling in the country is all very well in the spring, summer, and early autumn when the weather is pleasant. You get a feeling for when it's likely to rain and take shelter in an alehouse or in a cottager's kitchen perhaps. Mayhap I sell a paper of pins, or a packet of spices, or a ribbon or two. If not, I entertain my hosts by juggling and card tricks and news and gossip from town. In the winter, it's always raining, the roads are ankle-deep in mud, my pack gets wet, my clothing is soaked, and I suffer cruelly from chilblains. So I spend winter here, helping my uncle. He sells in Rag Fair, while I collect. If you can entertain the cook and maids, it's surprising how many cast-offs you can get even in a neighborhood like this. No matter how worn they are, someone will buy them in Rag Fair. The woman of the house often has something decent to sell to me, too. Ladies' maids are harder," he added reflectively. "They have better things to sell, but they take them to a shop as a rule. Still, one can often get stockings and smocks. But you did not come to talk about my business."

"No. I need to ask a favor, which may be inconvenient for you. You won't lose by it, if you can do it."

"I've finished my round or near enough. Can you walk back with me to my uncle's? We can talk about it on the way or go to a public house after I've delivered my day's catch."

The street outside the alehouse was growing dim when Solomon drained his tankard. "Will you do it? Can you, I should say. Your uncle may not be able to spare you."

"He'll let me go, as it's for a short time. He calls me an Englishman and despairs of me, but I'm his only living kin. He can hire the sons of the widow across the street. The oldest is lacking in wits but can push the cart, and the younger boy has wits enough for two. It's what Uncle does when I'm in the country. I'll give him part of what you pay me. It will all work out."

"You understand the danger?"

Abe shrugged. "Life's dangerous. I don't see this being a serious risk. Your fellow will never see me, and the female servants will like me. You lent me the money to care for my uncle when he had the lung fever. Of course I'll do it for you. When do we start?"

"Do you know Essex?"

"My usual circuit is in Kent."

"It was too much to hope for. I'll get a map. It wouldn't do to lose ourselves."

“A map is a good idea, but as it happens, I know the man who works that area. Old Isaac will tell me about the places he visits. I’ll only need to know his route immediately around the place you want to visit.”

“Is he in London?”

Abe laughed. “Solomon, tomorrow is Shabbat. He’ll be home this evening or in the morning at the latest. Probably this evening. He’s getting old. He doesn’t work as hard as he used to. I’ll talk to him tonight, if I can, or in the morning.”

“The sooner, the better.” The thought of Portia at the Marquess of Furness’s estate, ignorant of his true character, made him exceedingly uneasy.

“We couldn’t leave before tomorrow now in any case. Can you arrange for a horse for me? I usually go by carrier’s wagon. Riding would be quicker. And I will need to purchase some things for my pack.”

“Would you start tomorrow? I assumed you would not be willing to go until Sunday.” He made a mental list: advance Abe money for his peddler’s stock, find him a horse, purchase some articles of clothing for himself, write to David Mendys. He could not expect an answer before leaving. David would have to reply to him at the Maldon coaching inn, using Solomon’s nom de guerre. He would pass as a Huguenot.

Abe tsked. “You’re worried for your friends’ safety. Perhaps none of them is in danger of death or a crippling injury, which would be a permissible reason for violating the Shabbat laws. But what you have told me about this marquess suggests you cannot ignore the possibility. Best to err on the side of caution. It will not be the first time I have missed Shabbat: once I was caught in a flood and could not get home or to any

Jewish community. I could not even simply stay where I was. I don't believe the strictest rabbi would have insisted I should stay and drown. As you will need my help to make sure your friends are safe, I must assist you."

Solomon said admiringly, "You argue like a Jesuit."

Abe thanked him, laughing.

****

On arriving in Chelmsford, he inquired for someone who might sell him a horse, saddle, and bridle. He would need a way of traveling in the area around Maldon without having to hire a mount from a livery stable.

The man had three horses to sell. In the pasture, he pointed out to Solomon a handsome chestnut and a black with white feet and a white blaze on its face as being suitable mounts for a gentleman. At a little distance from the others stood a gray horse. He had always admired dapple grays, though perhaps he only thought so because he and his brothers had had a dapple gray rocking horse.

"That gray," he began.

The farmer laughed. "The gray's a joke hereabouts. Now, the chestnut has good paces and no vices"—he glanced critically at Solomon—"to trouble a rider who is not often in the saddle. The black gelding's breeding is good, but he's not a reliable jumper, and country gentlemen want a jumper."

"I can understand why the dapple might not appeal to many—" The mare was not as refined in appearance as his old rocking horse. She looked awkward, too.

"Ay, poor old Dumpling." The man laughed again.

"What's wrong with Dumpling, apart from the obvious? Is she old?"

"She's five years. She's not a comfortable ride—"

Solomon veered toward the gray, asking over his shoulder, "In what way?"

"Above a walk, she'll rattle the bones out o' your body."

"Bad paces."

As he drew near, she turned her head to gaze at him. As with some plain women, her eyes were her best feature: large, dark, and warm.

"Does she bite, shy, toss her rider, or kick out?"

"Nay, none o' those." The farmer frowned with the effort of explaining. "She's a friendly girl. I trust her to carry my granddaughter and my nephew. Now, I'll give you a good price on the black, some folk not caring for four white feet."

By then, Solomon was stroking the dark, velvety nose. Dumpling whiffled. He bent to feel her legs. Barlyon and his head groom had spent a good deal of time checking horses' legs. The mare stood placidly and nuzzled his shoulder, no doubt leaving horse spit on his coat. He could not detect any of the problems his old friend and the groom had described to him. Was a brief lesson or two in horse care adequate to choose a mount? Was this to be the same kind of experience as his ill-fated acceptance of that cargo of sables? He fired off several questions at the farmer.

"Good hooves and wind. Dumpling's not a gentleman's horse. Not much of a riding horse at all, except to carry children around the field or to the village. She's not fast or showy. I will say she's sensible and tough. Her rider will tire before she does.

I've trained her to pull a wagon, so she's useful at harvest. A hard worker." Detecting his customer's interest in the gray, he added, "She'd pull a chaise."

To the fellow's hesitantly requested price, Solomon asked if he could recommend someone who could sell him a saddle and bridle. In the end, over mugs of ale, he was the owner of a plain horse with its necessary equipment.

He trotted uncomfortably into Maldon at midafternoon, very glad to see the Blue Boar coaching inn at the end of the London road. Dumpling, cheerful and willing, really did possess uneven paces. She was not quite the right horse for his imposture, but she was a good choice for a London man who seldom rode.

Thank God for his old friend, John Barlicorn, now the Earl of Barlyon! While he had not attended Barlyon's wedding down in Kent—both having agreed his presence would be indiscreet—he had been invited to stay for two weeks in July. Life in the English countryside was as alien to him as medieval Spain would have been. No, even more strange, for he had grown up hearing his great-grandfather's tales of Spain. Not that he had been ancient enough to remember those days himself, but he had heard the old stories handed down from his elders.

Kent had been a revelation. Granted, he had visited the "country" homes of several of his more affluent connections, but as their owners maintained interests in the City of London, those rural retreats had been within a short distance of town. The Mendys family had a delightful place in Chelsea. However, Barlyon's estate lay far enough from London to be in the midst of hop fields and orchards and plantations of trees which were a crop, too, though a slow-growing one. John Barlyon had become intimately involved in agricultural matters though not so busy he did not take the time to teach Sol to ride.

“ ’Tis a useful skill, as I found when I returned from the dead. Once learned, ’tis never forgotten. I will admit that after so many years, I was out of practice. If you suffer from aching muscles, Aurelia has a salve which will help.”

Solomon had given some thought to changing his appearance for his visit to Maldon. John Barlicorn had once pointed out that if a man wore some eye-catching garment, those who saw him would see and remember the clothing rather than the face, but if he dressed in inconspicuous clothing, he might pass entirely unnoticed. He had purchased secondhand an unfashionable suit of good quality in a subdued plum, the sort of garments a country squire would wear. He could not do much about his hair; a wig would be ridiculous for traveling. With luck, no one would remember him as anything more than an unpretentious gentleman, no touch of London about him, taller than some and rather sallow. He would be Francis St. Julian, an estate steward of Huguenot ancestry, investigating the possibility of land for sale for his employer.

As he refreshed himself with a pint of ale, he mentioned his employer wished to buy a small property as a wedding gift for his younger son, “and not too near the family seat,” by way of explaining why he was looking in an unfamiliar part of the country.

Abe should already be in place a few miles beyond Maldon. They had agreed it was safer this way: Blackwater Hay was close enough to Maldon that word might get back to Furness that a peddler substituting for Old Isaac had been seen with someone resembling Solomon, which might make trouble for Isaac, "as I am not one of Furness's favorite people," Solomon remarked. Unlikely, perhaps, but he would not take risks with his friend's life.

He could easily ride from Maldon to the village Abe had made his headquarters, and to Blackwater Hay, if only he could arrange to meet Portia. Riding was not all he had learned from Barlyon. The coaching inn was busy, meaning few if any would take notice of him unless he distinguished himself for odd conduct. With that in mind, he found a fellow nearby who was happy to stable the dapple-gray mare for him and to have Dumpling ready for Solomon as soon as there was enough light to see.

The next day, he rode out to meet Abe. He was lodging with an old woman on the outskirts of Mundon, two or three miles southeast of Maldon, and about the same distance south of Blackwater Hay. Solomon found it without difficulty, using the map Abe had drawn based on the very detailed directions given him by Old Isaac. The landmarks, distances, and comments about the temperaments and hospitality of the more prominent householders boded well for his ability to find Mundon, Blackwater Hay, and anything else in the vicinity.

Abe greeted him with a grin and told the little old woman who had opened the door they would take a walk to the stream and water the horse. "My friend will want to stretch his legs, and I'll bring in a bucket of water. Two, if you wish."

As they trudged down to the stream, Solomon leading Dumpling, Abe with a bucket in hand, Abe said, "Old Isaac makes a point of stopping at Grannie Irons's on this part of his circuit. Two nights, as a rule, first as he sets out for Bradwell and Tillingham, then again on his way back. She's a poor old body, and the pence he pays for his bed and board is welcome. She's kind to animals, children, lackwits, mad folk, and most others. I don't know what basket she sorts Isaac and me into. He told me we can trust her." He cocked his head to one side, considering. "She's right proud her great-grandam was hanged for a witch."

"We can trust her because she's descended from a witch and proud of it?"

"No, because she doesn't like Furness. Her granddaughter works there and tells her things. She says she thanks God every day she's plain and no temptation to the marquess. Though he's not often here. Some say it makes him a bad landlord. Others say 'twould be worse to have him around, as he's said to take offense easy. The more I hear of him, the more I think you are correct to worry about your young lady."

"She is not my young lady."

Abe's lips twitched. "Your friend, then." While Dumpling drank, Abe continued, "I ambled past Blackwater Hay on my way here. There's a place a little before you come to the entrance you might use as a place to meet your lady."

"She's not my lady."

"Ay, ay, your friend, then. I'll mark it on the map for you. I'm sure you have a pencil with you, as well."

He did, of course, with his little commonplace book, in one of his coat's pockets. Abe added three little circles arranged in a triangle near the carriageway leading into the manor. "I think the house is about a quarter mile from the road. I couldn't go in, of course."

"Is there a gate and wall?"

Abe shook his head. "Grannie Irons says the family never worried much about keeping the riffraff out. They never had the money, either. The current viscount—the marquess—is the kind to want a gate, but he ignores the place. I didn't go in because if I'd called there, I'd have no excuse to go there with your message."

A quarter mile would not be too far for Portia to walk, if she were willing to meet. She might not agree or she might not be able to slip out of the house. Solomon could not contemplate the possibility Abe might not manage to pass his message to her. "If you can't see her—"

"I'll get it to her, be sure of it, if I have to bribe the maid. She's Mistress Irons's granddaughter."

"Will she talk about you to Furness or the other servants?"

"The servants don't talk to Furness without he speaks to them. Not a happy household. It's a good thing for us, as we'll have a spy in Blackwater Hay if we need one. The girl's not happy there, but she can't go home. Her mother's dead, and her stepfather…" Abe spread his hands. W*hat would you?* "Her grandma would take her in, but Mary, that's the girl, knows the brute would make trouble for the old woman. She'll leave Furness's as soon as someone else needs a maid."

After this reassurance, Solomon returned to Maldon by way of the road that ran by Blackwater Hay. Passing the marquess's den at midday posed a slight but acceptable risk; being unable to find the proposed meeting place would throw all his careful plans into disarray. He did not know how he was to endure the wait until Abe could deliver his message.

Chapter 17

The habit was old, she thought, as she had never seen one so ornate. Rose-pink with gilt buttons and the buttonholes embroidered with gold thread, it was the finest garment she had ever touched. It was a trifle large in the waist but wearable without alterations. The thin linen shirt with lace at wrist and neck had needed only to be washed and ironed.

The marquess turned Benedict over to a groom for instruction. "I will claim the pleasure of teaching Mistress Portia myself."

Her brother was jogging around the paddock, the groom beside him, before Portia was sitting comfortably in her saddle. Perhaps it was easier if one rode astride; the position required by the sidesaddle felt awkward. Her right leg was hooked around the horn in an appallingly unladylike and unnatural way which she expected would soon make her muscles ache. The peculiar way of sitting was not the only problem. Being almost alone in the stable yard with Furness, his hands adjusting hers on the reins, his eyes judging her posture, was too intimate. She should have a chaperon. Then she remembered her private meetings with Solomon de Toledo and blushed. She had not felt the need of an escort to protect her reputation with him. The difference was, his manner had been pleasant and friendly, if not impersonal, while Furness's gaze lingering on her face and body flustered her.

Furness said approvingly, “Very good. You don’t fear the horse. I expected you to be timid. Do you feel well balanced in the saddle?”

“I am not sure, my lord. I do not feel in imminent danger of falling off, but then, the horse is standing still.”

His sudden laughter made his face more attractive. “A point, ma’am. But we will start by walking our horses.” Portia admired the way he mounted as smoothly as if it were one movement.

“I will ride close beside you and catch you if you should begin to fall.”

“Thank you, sir. That makes me feel quite secure.” She hoped fervently she could stay on her bay mare. Benedict and the groom had left the paddock to ride gently in Blackwater Hay’s park, leaving her alone with the marquess.

“Let us circle the paddock a few times, then, until you become accustomed.”

Her horse, a placid creature, ambled round the field. The marquess rode beside her, keeping up a flow of idle talk: how many acres the park contained, how much larger was his home in Lancashire, the elegance of his London house. He interposed an admonition from time to time, gently correcting her posture or her handling of the reins. He was not as haughty as she had supposed at their first meeting, proving one should not judge too hastily. She might even learn to enjoy riding, though she doubted she would have any use for the skill after they left the manor.

****

Mary, the maid she had been assigned, said,

"There's such a crank Jew peddler in the kitchen, ma'am."

"Really? A crank?" Whatever that meant.

"Merry or jolly, I should say. Crank is the word, hereabouts."

For some reason Solomon came to mind, though by no stretch of imagination could he be wandering the roads of Essex with a pack of small wares.

"He juggles and tells such waggish stories we couldn't help but laugh out loud. He has thread, embroidery silks, pins and needles, all sorts of things. He has finer things, too, like silver buckles and gauds for the hair, and"—she lowered her voice in awe—"French lace. I never saw the like before. He asked if there was any ladies in the house that might like to buy some little thing. I wish he was our reg'lar peddler, but he says he is only obliging Old Isaac who's abed with an ague."

Portia would not ordinarily ask the name of a peddler, but curiosity niggled at her. "Is he Old Isaac's kin? Young Isaac, perhaps?"

Mary laughed heartily. "No, mistress, this one's called Solomon."

What a strange, uncomfortable coincidence. "I think I must go down to the kitchen and look over his wares." She could not imagine Solomon, her Solomon, juggling and entertaining the servants. It was not an uncommon name. She knew of a mercer in her own neighborhood whose name was Solomon. She was therefore not discomposed to discover that the peddler was not de Toledo. He was shorter and broader, with curly brown hair. She could hardly expect her Solomon to appear, merely because she wished she could talk with him.

He swept her a bow, exclaiming, "A young lady come to see my stock in trade! She is the sun!" The cook chuckled appreciatively. The kitchen maid, Rachel, giggled. Mary grinned and muttered, "Now as you're here, I'll be about my work," and whisked out.

Taken aback by his mountebank-like behavior, Portia stared at him. "I beg your pardon?"

"No, I beg my lady's pardon. Pray do not be angry with me. Remember, while no one loves a messenger who brings bad news, I am a bearer of good tidings. And the quality of mercy is not strained."

Could one of the servants have mentioned her name? Would a hawker know Shakespeare's plays? He was surprisingly well spoken. "I took no offense…Mr. Solomon, I think your name is?"

"Merely Solomon, ma'am, though I'm one of a pair."

"A pair of Solomons?"

"Aye, and I hope with wit to spare between us."

"I hope so, too." Had Solomon de Toledo sent her a messenger? Why not write? No, of course he would not write a lady…at least, not if anyone else would see the letter. To correspond with her about Benedict's schooling, when her father could not deal with the matter and her mother had given over the household's problems to Portia, might be acceptable. To write her here would be a mistake.

"May I show you some of the things I carry for ladies?" Without awaiting an answer, he opened his pack and brought out a cloth cylinder which he unrolled to reveal many pockets. "I have silver buckles for the shoes and for the hair, buttons, a prettily bound commonplace book for a lady to write down receipts or whatever else she wishes. Here is a fine Valenciennes lappet, and here is a length of exquisite Alençon lace." It was wound on a narrow, folded rectangle of surprisingly good paper wider than the lace. He met her eyes, then glanced down at his hand, moving his thumb to reveal a penciled flourish or monogram: SdT. He raised his eyes to hers once more.

"How long is the Alençon?" Portia managed to ask.

"Two ells. I know nothing of ladies' fashion, but I am sure you would find it interesting and useful."

So was Portia. The peddler Solomon's thumb again concealed the monogram. She asked the price.

"Two pounds, two shillings. Dear, but see the quality."

"I won't ask how it came here."

"The same way a deal of the brandy drunk by lords comes, I fear," he admitted cheerfully.

The cook was stirring something in a pot hanging from the crane, or trammel, as it was called in Essex. Rachel had gone to the laundry. The huckster lowered his voice. "If you haven't that much, give me what you do have. You need this lace."

She brought out the little drawstring purse she had dropped into her pocket before leaving her chamber. She said softly, "Only three shillings, sixpence, I fear. I do have a little more upstairs," but she should keep a few coins for vails at the end of her visit. Her papa had given her two pounds. She would not need more, he had assured her, with the nearest village having nothing to buy except a few things such as country folk found necessary.

"Three shillings, then," he whispered.

Ridiculously cheap for the lace, but the lace was not the point, she understood. She dropped the shillings into his hand.

His voice returned to its normal volume. “Nothing else for you? You’ve made an excellent bargain, my lady. May you wear it in good health. On your wedding day, mayhap.” He jingled the shillings so they clinked merrily, then somehow they made their way into her hand with the roll of lace. “Health and good fortune to all. I’ll be on my way.”

Portia stuffed purse, lace, and coins into her pocket and slipped out of the kitchen. Passing into the front of the house, she heard the murmur of voices in the study: the marquess must still be meeting with his bailiff. She continued up to her bedchamber to slide the rolled lace off the paper.

Mistress Portia,

I take the liberty of writing to you because I am gravely concerned for your safety and happiness. Do you know the reason for your family’s presence at Blackwater Hay? If you are considering marriage to the Marquess of Furness, I beg you will reconsider. If you are able to meet me alone, I will await you between dawn and nine o’clock each morning near the three oak trees about one-quarter of a mile west of the entrance to the estate.

The hand was unmistakably Solomon’s. She sat frowning over the little sheet of paper for some time. A clandestine meeting with a man would be shocking conduct. It would be worse than her meetings with Solomon in the drawing room at home, because there at least someone had been within call. Or would have been if their servants were not out on errands or upstairs cleaning or in the kitchen.

Whatever did Solomon's reference to marriage mean? Why would the marquess want to marry her? She had no dowry to attract a marquess. Unless Solomon was pondering marriage—*with me?* Where had that thought come from? No, ridiculous. He must simply be concerned for her, as a friend would be. He had been all kindness to her family, and she liked him for it. Though why would he ask about Furness courting her?

Furness's manners were polished. He had shown an interest in her spinsterish, unremarkable self, which should have been flattering. Her opinion of Furness, slightly modified by his manner to her since their arrival, had not completely altered. True, he had spent a good deal of time with her father and herself but had largely ignored her mother and brother. A schoolboy would be of little interest to him. Her mother, having come of the mercantile class would ordinarily be beneath his notice. As a guest in his house, however, the wife of a man he had chosen to cultivate, she was deserving of courtesy. One could hardly count his arrogance against him, as likely most noblemen were haughty. Why would they not be? The laws were made by them and for them. Wealth, too, gave advantages unavailable to those in straitened circumstances, which her family were, in spite of her papa's status as a gentleman. In a warm-hearted man, pride of rank would be tolerable. Or would it? The Greek word *hubris* occurred to her: a man's overweening confidence in himself that offends the gods and leads to his downfall.

It was hard to evaluate the servants' attitude to their master. They were more subdued, though no more polished, than the Gillespie servants, such as they were. Yes, and some of them had either not been employed at the manor long or had been hired temporarily. If he seldom visited the estate, he would keep the minimum number of servants to maintain the house. The shabby upholstery, draperies, and carpets testified to neglect, which might be understandable in a minor holding where he did not regularly reside. On the other hand, much of the furniture was not only old, but scuffed or scratched, some not even recently polished. Their own home was certainly worn, but at least the furnishings were cared for, despite their few domestics.

She would meet Solomon. She only wished it could be sooner than tomorrow morning.

****

Portia woke at about six o'clock, then had to wait, huddled under the bedclothes, for the first faint light of morning. Her fire had gone out, making it impossible to light a candle easily. Even with a candle to dress by, she would not have been able to find her way to the appointed meeting place in the dark. Before going to bed, she had arranged the petticoat and casaquin she meant to wear on a chair in the order she would put them on. Her jumps, smock, and stockings she had put under the covers beside her to warm by the heat of her body, as she did at home in cold weather. Dressing in clammy linen in a cold room was not an appealing prospect. The maid would not come to see to the fire until eight. The ladies' maid assigned to her would not arrive with a cup of chocolate for half an hour after that. Since arriving at Blackwater Hay, she had found it irksome to wait for them, when she was accustomed to rise at six. Now it was an advantage, as was the sparsely attended household. She had taken note of the various outer doors and found one into the overgrown garden behind the house. While she waited for a sign of gray around the window curtains, Portia scrambled into her undergarments in the warmth of her bed.

She tiptoed down the staircase, cloak over her arm. No servant would be using the front stairs. The marquess did not rise early or the servants would already be in evidence. He would not be dressing in an unheated chamber without assistance and a cup of chocolate, which would mean a maid to light the fire, a cook and a kitchen maid to prepare the chocolate, a maid to carry it up to his lordship, and his manservant to lay out his clothing and shave him. She had been acquainted with Furness only a few days, but his insistence on formality in all things told her everything she needed to know about his likely habits.

Portia made her way along the passage leading to the North Salon, as their host called it. Even the marquess hesitated to speak of a ballroom in what was really only a fair-sized manor house. It was sparsely furnished with a few chairs and tables around the walls, a harpsichord, and a number of large paintings of battles and classical scenes like Leda and the swan, in which the nature of the swan's interest was all too apparent. One might hold a dance there, if there were no more than twenty or thirty couples, or stroll in it for exercise when the weather was too wet or cold to go out, or let children romp there. Gentlemen could practice fencing in it. More to the point, a set of double doors opened onto a terrace and the garden.

Thank goodness it had not rained overnight, which would have made her excursion quite unpleasant. The flower garden was a rectangle, walled on two sides by the house, and on another by the wall surrounding the kitchen garden. Although she had strolled in it the previous afternoon to orient herself, it looked different in the dim predawn light. She knew there were several rose bushes and some ornamental shrubs placed more or less at random. None of them could possibly hide someone watching her, and yet her heart beat faster.

The garden's unenclosed side led to the lawn. She breathed a sigh of relief to be in the open with no tall shadows to threaten her. Picking her way along the path, she turned at the end of the wing. As long as she did not pass too near the east side of the house, she could reach the carriageway where the trees lining it would provide some cover.

No one was stirring in the entire wing, for no light showed at any window she could see. She hurried past. The servants had their quarters over the kitchen block. Well beyond the front of the house, she turned to stride toward the three oaks at the edge of the property. The road ran a few feet beyond them. She risked a glance up and down the track but saw no one before retreating to the triangle formed by the trees. The pale predawn light had not penetrated the dimness beneath them, offering concealment if anyone should pass. Where was Solomon?

A sort of breathy equine snort nearby, followed by rustling, startled her. She shrank behind the largest tree until she heard a low-voiced "Mistress Portia?"

His outline was barely visible in the shadow of a tangle of blackberry brambles a few feet away.

She recognized his voice. "Mr. de Toledo! Thank goodness."

He approached as she spoke. “I feared you might have difficulty escaping the house.” The words and his grim tone caused her to shiver. Truth to tell, she had wondered if she would be able to slip out, but that he should express the same doubt, and use the word “escape” was disturbing.

“Why did you come?”

“May I answer by asking you a question? How is it your family are the marquess’s guests? Are you related to him?”

“That is two questions,” she could not resist pointing out. “No, he is the merest acquaintance. He asked my father to come and informally assess his sons’ academic progress and to bring our family to make it seem nothing more than a Christmas visit.” Should she voice her own misgivings? Before she could decide, de Toledo spoke.

“But the boys are not here.”

“No, the weather made it unwise for them to travel so far. How did you—oh, your peddler friend, of course.”

“He asked whether there were any children in the house, as he had toys and gewgaws to keep them amused on rainy days.” A pause. “Has Furness been courting you?”

“Me?” It came out like a squeak. “Your letter mentioned marriage, but why would he want to marry me? He had only met me for a few minutes before we arrived here.”

“For your…” He stopped.

For my what? She must have been gaping.

“Has no one told you that Mr. Gillespie recently inherited a fortune?”

"A fortune?" Oh, for pity's sake, in her surprise she sounded like a simpleton. "My father has inherited some money from a cousin, but it wasn't any great sum. A few hundred pounds, I imagine."

His face took on the inward look she had seen on her father's when he was considering some thorny problem of translation. "Possibly I was misinformed. Nathan Sturgis, who I believe is your papa's cousin, was rich as Croesus. Have you seen positive proof of the amount of the inheritance?"

"No…have you?"

"No. But there must be some reason Mr. Gillespie and his entire family were invited to Blackwater Hay."

"I have wondered about the invitation. The marquess does not seem the kind to consort with commoners who are not even landed gentry. I will ask my father…" She bit her lip. To ask about the size of his inheritance would annoy him. He was strictly honest, as she knew from his admission on several occasions in his writings that another scholar had been correct and he had been wrong. Yet he had not mentioned the amount he had inherited, which was odd. Though he had been secretive about the state of their finances. The absence of the marquess's sons was understandable in view of the difficulties of travel, but Papa's lack of irritation at the wasted trip troubled her. This might merely be good manners and reluctance to offend a potential patron. Still, he had not revealed any annoyance even to her. Nor had he seemed surprised.

This time Solomon hesitated. "It might be better not to raise the subject, Portia."

"It would be awkward to explain my curiosity. Impossible, I should say."

He had called her by her first name. She could not feel offended. She often thought of him by his Christian name…well, no. His first name. If he thought of her as "Portia," it would be easy to make the mistake. Had she not done the same with his name at least once?

"It would certainly be better not to give him cause to wonder why you would ask, for all our sakes."

"I had better return to the house now."

They parted with the briefest civilities. A more conventional leave-taking would have been ridiculous, considering what they had been discussing. As she marched back toward the house, the whole thing began to seem like something from a daydream. In her distraction, she almost forgot to enter cautiously. She saw only one servant, however, a maid busy laying a fire in the drawing room, who gave no sign she had heard Portia pass.

She met Mary, her assigned maid, followed by another, hurrying toward her bedchamber. Mary stopped and murmured, "Oh, mistress, here you be, thank the Lord! Becky here was right gastered when she went to lay the fire and found you gone."

Becky dropped a curtsy and whispered, "And I bain't done with it yet, begging your pardon, m'lady." The maid's face turned red as any radish. Having flaxen hair and fair skin must be a trial for a shy country girl in service. She would always be blushing at something. Then Portia caught her own maid's warning glance at Becky. It might only be for putting herself forward, when the chambermaid was supposed to be unseen and unheard when she went about her work. Or was it because of the way she had addressed Portia?

She said casually, "I'm no lady. Not a titled lady, I

mean. You may finish laying the fire now. I woke early and went out for a walk. Mary, could you bring me a cup of chocolate?"

****

She found both her father and the Marquess of Furness still at table, lingering over coffee. It was unfortunate Furness was present, for she could not contemplate him now without grave misgivings. She would have preferred to have at least another hour or two to settle her mind. She could speak with her father and delicately approach the subject of why they were really at Blackwater Hay, if only she could get him alone. The ostensible reason for their stay at the manor, the opportunity for her papa to become acquainted with the marquess's sons, had not materialized. Thomas Gillespie had accepted their absence, excused by bad weather in the north and the youngest child's tendency to catarrhs, with neither surprise nor impatience. One could hardly show annoyance to one's host, particularly a nobleman. Still, his manner since they arrived had seemed strange.

The marquess and her father were laughing over some rustic foolishness of the nearest villagers when they had ridden out the previous day. Her papa had not ridden for many years, certainly not in her memory, yet having been the son of a gentleman, he had been taught to ride; evidently it was a skill one did not forget. The marquess had shown Thomas Gillespie the greatest condescension, as if he were an honored guest rather than a poor scholar brought to discuss tutoring the children.

And her father was bearing himself less like the scholar he undoubtedly was and more like the country gentleman. His transformation gave her yet another thing to think about. They had risen on her entrance, and the marquess had come forward to bow over her hand and escort her to the empty chair at his left, the right being occupied by Gillespie. The footman inquired deferentially what she would like for breakfast, providing a respite from the need to talk to the marquess and her father.

Chapter 18

Furness took her out for another riding lesson after breakfast; she almost liked him then. For a man who was often impatient with the servants, he was a surprisingly good instructor.

"Your brother is a born horseman," Furness remarked as Benedict rode off with the groom. "He only required a horse. Soon he will be able to ride alone."

"Perhaps it is not surprising, as Benedict is very good at cricket, too, I understand. I suppose all physical skills are related." She would have liked to see the marquess with Benedict. She might have learned more of his character by watching his interactions with a schoolboy.

"Riding comes naturally to a gentleman. You are learning quickly, too."

As she murmured a shy "Thank you, my lord," she wished she could believe the compliment. Legions of her muscles ached from the unaccustomed position and activity. "I fear it will be some time before I can do without an attendant."

"You will always be escorted by a groom or a gentleman."

"Oh, of course. Though it seems unnecessary if one is riding in the park of an estate like yours."

"Within the park, you would be unlikely to meet

with anyone who would do you harm. My bailiff treats gypsies, vagabonds, and poachers with the severity they deserve, insuring they do not trouble me or mine. However, if your horse shied and you fell, you would not be able to mount without assistance. It might be a long walk back to the house."

The first part of his calm statement chilled her. What would the marquess consider deserved severity? Would it extend to a peddler or to someone visiting his land uninvited? She hoped Solomon the peddler was safe and that her Solomon would take care. Then Furness was pointing out the view of the Blackwater River, which was really an estuary here, wide enough to contain islands.

Her chance to talk to her father came after her lesson. Furness's bailiff was waiting at the house to beg his lordship's indulgence over some urgent matter. Benedict had not yet returned from his ride, Eliza would be sitting with Frances Sedgewick exchanging household hints over embroidery, and deprived of the library and the marquess's company, Papa was at a loose end.

"Shall we admire the portraits in the long gallery?"

"We may as well. I have not seen them yet."

Portia had been shown them two days after arrival by the marquess, fortunately with her mother present. She would not have been easy alone in Furness's company in the gallery, which was some distance from the rooms where someone might be within calling distance.

The pictures were not noteworthy. She had seen few portraits, but the pictures she had seen, and the sketches and watercolors made by acquaintances, suggested that these were undistinguished examples. The wooden poses, muddy colors, and sometimes odd proportions could scarcely be true representations of the Sedgewick family, judging by the current marquess.

"A fine old family, even if neither the marquessate nor the viscountcy is a truly old creation."

"It was kind of the marquess not to send us packing when it was clear his sons could not be here. I suppose he received a message after we left town. How disconcerting to find you had come for no purpose."

"Hmmm? Ay, so I understand." He was studying with grave approval the likeness of a thin-lipped man with the long, curled hair of the previous century. Portia admired the gold and silver embroidery on his coat and waistcoat.

"I would have expected him to send us back to London when the reason for our presence was gone. Noblemen do not usually entertain the untitled, do they? Unless they are family connections or close friends?" Not that she knew much about the aristocracy, beyond what she had heard and brief contacts with the boys her father tutored. She could not recall any whose papa was above the rank of baron.

"Furness is precisely what a nobleman should be and would naturally treat a gentleman with courtesy."

Her papa was apparently blind to the failings of some of titled gentlemen. She had noted the same unwarranted respect in many of the older generation. "Still, I feel rather out of place, like a governess permitted to dine with the lords and ladies."

He raised his eyebrows. "You are the daughter of a gentleman and worthy to consort with the highest ranks."

True in theory, perhaps, but in practice their family's social circle was limited to scholars, professional men like Attorney Brigginshaw, and their wives. Her father met the titled as the laundrywoman or the chimney sweep met her mother.

"Still, he has behaved with great condescension, considering our reason for coming here."

He had moved on to a painting of three young children and a spaniel, who seemed no more than incidental figures in the portrait of the house. "You like him, then, Portia." It did not sound like a question.

She chose to take it as one. "I cannot say I actually like the Marquess of Furness. I don't dislike him. He has been a courteous host"—*mostly*—"but his manner is generally too reserved to make him easy to know."

Gillespie pursed his lips. "I fail to see how you could object to him. Furness has the air of a nobleman. A man of his rank must be expected to hold himself somewhat aloof from the common herd. He is not old or ill-favored. I know that last is important to females."

"He has been obliging in teaching me to ride. But his servants appear to dread his displeasure, and the tenant farms have an air of neglect." Was the decrepit state of the cottages and outbuildings the tenants' to remedy or the landowner's? Ultimately it fell to Furness's account. A landowner should make the necessary repairs if they were his responsibility or insist the tenants do so.

"Oh, bumpkins. No doubt they take good care of the crops and animals. That's what matters."

They had reached the end of the gallery. Gillespie turned toward the opposite wall with its windows. "Look there. That's Blackwater Hay land as far as you can see, inherited from his father, the viscount. There's another manor, as well, a few miles away. A good deal smaller, but still, a gentleman's estate, not merely a farm."

To Portia's mind, the view was not inspiring: gray and damp and empty.

"Furness is proud of his family and titles, and should be. He knows what is owing to his rank. You must respect it and show him all due deference. And some warmth," he added.

"Papa, you cannot mean I should flirt with him."

"Certainly not. That would be forward. Merely…hmmm…bestow upon him the degree of friendliness you would display to one of my scholars or a scholar's father. You have an easy way with them, without being familiar. Sir Thomas Roylott remarked upon your pretty manners."

This was proving unexpectedly difficult. She must change her approach. "Do you intend to continue tutoring, now that you have received an inheritance, Papa?"

"No. I think not."

It would make sense if the inheritance were sizable. A thousand pounds was impressive to anyone in their situation. If invested, what would it yield per annum? His records showed he made twenty or thirty pounds a year by tutoring, depending on the number of scholars. Unless his bequest brought in that much per year, he could not afford to stop teaching. He had already spent some of the funds. Thomas Gillespie's windfall seemed unlikely to improve matters.

Unless he had inherited a much larger sum; Solomon claimed Sturgis had been extremely wealthy.

Would her father conceal the real amount he had received? He might; he had always shown a certain contempt for ostentation, holding that austerity better befitted a serious man. She could imagine his admitting only to a small sum to keep her mother, Benedict, and herself from expecting luxuries and fripperies.

"Furness wishes to inspect his other nearby property tomorrow," he said unexpectedly. "He has invited me to come with him. 'Tis the sort of activity of interest to any country gentleman, if not to ladies. We will stay the night, as it is too far to ride there and back when the days are short. There is no knowing how long it will take to accomplish his business, either. We will return the following day."

"Mama and I will be staying here, then?"

"It would take too long to go by coach. The marquess and I will ride, which will be faster and permit us to go across country in places. The house is not occupied and has only enough servants to maintain it. You would not find it comfortable, and you would be bored, besides."

Blackwater Hay had only enough servants to maintain it, yet it was thought possible to stay here. "Is Benedict to go? Lord Furness says he is a born horseman. I suppose he would enjoy the journey and not care if the sheets are damp and the furniture dusty."

"He will remain here. An enthusiastic boy would be a distraction. You and your mother will no doubt find things to occupy yourselves. Sewing or reading or whatever you like. Benedict will be happy enough to ride here, I am sure."

The interview left her uncomfortable. She had not been able to confirm Solomon's suspicion and yet she could not dismiss it, and now she must wonder at the real reason for their invitation.

They met at the breakfast table to see Gillespie and the marquess off, as they were to leave as soon as it was light. Regrettably she had been unable to meet Solomon with the household up so early. Eliza Gillespie, smothering yawns, drank chocolate and nibbled a piece of breakfast cake. Benedict was full of questions about Pipperidge Rise, to which Furness replied briefly, "I leave that to my bailiff."

Her father had little to say. Trying to think of some remark to contribute, Portia finally said, "I shall miss my riding lessons while you are gone, my lord. Unless I might share Benedict's?"

Furness laughed. "He's like to leave you far behind. If he goes careering off, the groom will stay with you. Master Benedict really needs no groom in attendance, as quickly as he's mastered his lessons."

Benedict grinned and ducked his head, mumbling thanks for the compliment. Portia offered hers more sedately. She did enjoy riding, though her muscles still suffered.

The men departed, and Benedict, hastily swallowing his last quince preserve-laden bit of toast, bounced up, saying, "If you want to come riding, you'd best hurry into your habit. I'll send a message to the stable to have the horses ready."

"I need not ask how you like the country," Portia commented as they rode out of the stable yard.

"It's not so much the country as the riding. I never gave it a thought in town. Though there's a good deal of interest in how things are done that I never considered, in spite of knowing Tull's inventions were changing methods, though not quickly in this part of the country. They should be using the seed drill. The ploughs are practically antiques. I can't imagine how they manage to till as much as they do. As for the kitchen, which may be of interest to you, Portia, the turnspit dogs should be replaced by a clockwork spit jack."

"Not that we have either dogs or spit jack at home. I will miss riding when we go back to London."

Benedict, ordinarily gabby, was silent for several minutes before he turned in his saddle to address the groom. "Jem, I will not abandon my sister, and as you see, she is doing very well. We will not gallop. You need not follow too close."

The man nodded respectfully and fell back as they rode ahead.

"As to that," her brother went on in a low voice, "you may not have to give up riding. I've heard something I wanted to mention to you, but Mother or Father or the marquess are always around, or else some curst servant."

"Benedict!"

"Ay, such language. I have wanted to talk to you privately. You don't like the marquess, do you?"

"Don't you like him?" she asked, dodging the question. "I would have thought his making you free of his stable would have endeared him to you."

"I think he only did it to keep me out of the way. No, I don't like him. You should hear how the grooms and servants talk about him when they don't think anyone's listening. He's bad-tempered and close-fisted, and he knows nothing about agriculture. I apprehend that's why this place is so poorly kept up."

"I had no notion you had taken him in dislike." To

discover her little brother was as capable of duplicity as she came as a shock.

"Well, how could I? It would be rude to let our host see it. Father would not be pleased. He and Furness are thick as inkle weavers."

Offending their father might be the more important consideration for Benedict. When she did not immediately speak, he went on.

"I haven't been listening at doors. It's only that no one pays any attention to a fellow like me who's communing with a horse or eating an apple and watching the farrier shoe a nag."

How true. In her experience, no one noticed children or boys her brother's age if they were quiet, except their mother or their nurse. Not always their mother, sometimes, as she would have other things to do and think of.

"What I want to know is, why are we still here, Portia? Furness is hardly civil to his bailiff, yet he treats Papa as if he were a friend."

"Perhaps he respects our father's reputation as a scholar."

Benedict snorted. "Judging by his library, Furness is as interested in scholarship as a turnip. Is he courting you, do you think?"

Lud! "What?"

"You know. Meaning to ask you to marry him."

The idea was ridiculous. She almost said as much. Then she recalled Solomon's question and her papa's comment in the picture gallery about showing the marquess some warmth.

"I don't think it." To her own ears, her voice lacked conviction.

"I hope you're correct."

Then Benedict pointed out a heap of stone blocks which he thought might be the ruins of an abbey or a convent, "or some such thing," a topic which lasted them until they reached the stable.

Chapter 19

She had no qualms about going out the following morning to visit the three oaks, though there was a sharp wind and lowering clouds. With her father and the marquess away, her only worry was that Solomon would not come, thinking the weather would keep her indoors. Again she heard his voice before she saw him, his plain, dark coat blending into the deeper darkness among the trees.

"Mistress Portia."

She hurried forward. "Mr. de Toledo." Then she did not know what to say.

"I have heard that Furness and Mr. Gillespie are away." The uninflected statement made it possible for her to speak.

"Yes, so it seemed safe to come." *Safe?* What had made her use that word? "When we met last, you asked if Furness were courting me. My brother asked me the same yesterday. I now begin to wonder if he is."

"Can't you tell?"

The sudden amusement in his voice provoked a gasp of laughter. "I can't! He's been teaching me to ride and has been all that is courteous and attentive, but that is no more than gentlemanly conduct to a guest. That is what I assume, at any rate."

"If your family were his friends or connections, or if Mr. Gillespie were titled, I would agree. However, inviting your father and his family to spend Christmas here is unusual. If I were Furness, I would have had your father visit at some more convenient time of the year, like summer or late spring, and probably only for a week. Did it really not occur to the marquess that travel from the north might be difficult and mayhap impossible in December?"

Portia pulled her cloak more closely around her, shivering in the wind and from a certain internal chill. "It did seem strange. Yet why would he court me?"

"I would rather not answer until I receive confirmation of my theory."

"About my father's hypothetical fortune?"

"Yes. Both Furness's first wife and the lady he attempted to court a few months ago were exceptionally well dowered. If your father inherited Sturgis's fortune, he could afford to give you a fine dowry. The Marquess of Furness lives very lavishly."

"Not at Blackwater Hay!" How lowering it would be, to be valued only for a dowry.

"No, but there is no one to impress in this area. He never has guests here. Until now." He paused. "Any sensible man would seek your hand for your own natural attractions. Furness would require more than character, intelligence, and beauty, however."

She wrapped herself in Solomon's words as if they were a favorite, warm mantle. She should thank him for his opinion, but it had been phrased as an observation rather than a compliment. "You do not like Lord Furness. Or you know something to his discredit?" A moneylender would hardly be acquainted with a marquess, but it was not impossible he might come to hear something about him.

"Both. I would not judge him for seeking a bride with a dowry. It's not uncommon for marriages to be made for gain rather than affection. 'Tis the way of the world. But Furness is a harsh, vindictive man, which would make him an uneasy husband."

While she was wondering what Solomon knew of Furness and was not divulging, he added, "I would not want my sister to have anything to do with him or any man like him. I hope I would take whatever steps were necessary to prevent it."

"Oh." His matter-of-fact statement might have convinced her even without Benedict's remarks. "Thank you for warning me at such inconvenience to yourself."

"The inconvenience was not great." He shrugged. "Knowledge is power. I could not in good conscience leave you to face the marquess unprepared."

****

She would have liked to spend some time thinking about their conversation. Furness's housekeeper suggested she and her mother tour more of the house than they had yet seen. Frances declined to accompany them, saying, "Oh, I have seen it often and would like to finish this piece of embroidery, as I am nearly done with it."

The house revealed both the antiquity of its oldest section and the good taste of whoever had built the later parts. What a pity that signs of neglect were visible in places: marred paneling, plaster ceilings where repairs had been made with less skill than the original ornamental sections, threadbare drapery and carpets. These were apparent in the chambers Mrs. Hollis showed them. They would only look at the most interesting, she assured them, as it would be tiring to see the entire house and could take several hours. Portia suspected they were shown only the best rooms. Who knew what the ones they passed by, their doors closed, were like?

After the housekeeper released them, it proved impossible to escape Mama's private comments and her polite enthusiasm when Frances Sedgewick joined them. Then Furness and Gillespie arrived and discussed their visit to Pipperidge Rise. Or her father did; Furness devoted himself to questioning her about her day's activities and what she thought of the house. She was glad to be able to praise the dimensions and elegance of the architecture and the atmosphere of age and tradition in the older part.

****

As the marquess and Gillespie had been expected back in the late afternoon, the usual midday dinner was replaced by a light meal, and a more elaborate repast was served in the evening. It dragged on, through three courses of eight dishes each. The food was good, better than the Gillespies' cook produced at her best, but Portia had little appetite.

The service was in the French style with all the dishes set out around the table. When the first course dishes were placed upon the table, a very peculiar expression passed over Eliza Gillespie's face. Portia would have missed it had she not been looking at her. However, her mother helped herself to fricasseed chicken and several of the dishes seldom or never seen at their own dining table and appeared to like the artichoke pie in particular. Benedict tried some of every dish. Portia contented herself with small portions of the pease soup, roast duckling, asparagus, marinated fish, and pickles. Her father and Furness ate heartily. Frances ate sparingly though with enjoyment.

The fruit and ratafia creams, lemon jelly, coriander seed biscuits, sugar puffs, sponge cakes, custard cups, and marchpane in the third course were such as any middling family might eat. Not frequently, perhaps, or all at one dinner, but on occasion.

Finally the marquess's aunt rose to signal the ladies' withdrawal. Benedict began to rise as well.

"Gillespie, if you have no objection, the boy may stay. He is old enough to have a taste of port, surely."

Benedict's face lit. Being permitted to remain while the gentlemen drank their port must be not unlike the first time a girl wore her hair up. As she followed her mother out of the dining room, her brother was sitting very straight, trying to look taller and older.

She wished she might be able to retreat to the privacy of her chamber. Good manners forbade it, in the absence of some unassailable reason. A megrim or a female complaint, perhaps. Many ladies used the headache as an excuse to escape duties or events they wished to avoid. However, she wished to speak with her father about the marquess. After the men joined them, she could ask her father about some point of translation, allowing them to retreat to the library.

Her mother's voice pattered on with occasional interpolations from their hostess. Portia took her knotting project out of her pocket. The great advantage of knotting was that it was an easier skill than embroidery and she could do it without concentrating on it while still appearing to be occupied.

To her surprise, when the door opened, only

Benedict entered.

"Portia, Father asks that you come to the library."

"Are the gentlemen not joining us?" Eliza Gillespie inquired.

"I don't know, Mother. I was only told to request Portia attend upon Father."

Portia rose and gave her petticoats a twitch to shake out the wrinkles, tucked away her knotting, and took her leave. Benedict excused himself also.

"I wonder why Mr. Gillespie wishes to see Portia. So strange…" Her mother's next words were cut off as the footman closed the door behind them.

"Are you summoned to the library, too?"

"Uh, no." When they were out of the footman's hearing, her brother added, "It's about the marquess."

"What about him?"

"I think I'd best let Father tell you." He left her at the door to the library.

Taut with apprehension, she entered.

"Ah, there you are. Sit down, Portia. There is something we must discuss."

She waited attentively.

"I have good news."

"Is there to be another printing of *Greek Grammar Made Plain and Easy*? That would be excellent news. We could make the changes to it you have been thinking of." It was his most popular work.

"No, nothing so petty. The Marquess of Furness has asked for your hand in marriage." He beamed at her, a rare sign of approval.

The phrase "turned to stone" occurred to her. It precisely described how she felt. "He must have been joking." She forced a laugh, which emerged more like the coy titter she deplored in other females. Benedict's and Solomon's suggestion had come true.

The smile vanished. "The marquess is a serious man. He is certainly not given to vulgar frivolity."

"How can he possibly wish to marry me, Papa? Even if the nobility married for love, which I believe is not ordinarily the case, we hardly know each other. Nor would I be capable of fulfilling the duties of a great lady. I am ignorant of the beau monde; I have no idea of how to manage a household like this…"

"None of that matters in the least. You will learn. He knows his own mind and is set upon having you for his marchioness."

"I have seen no indication he was interested in me."

"You could hardly expect him to behave like a clodhopper courting a dairy maid."

"I would expect some sign of interest, however, if his offer were motivated by emotion. There is no practical reason for him to wish to wed me."

"Nonsense. You are a gentlewoman, attractive and well-educated. You are old enough to be sensible and to be a stepmama to his sons. I am sure he will show his regard when he makes his offer to you."

"Papa, I am not easy in my mind about this matter." She did not trust coincidences that arrived in flocks: a marquess seeking a noted scholar's advice on the education of his young sons, the boys' foreseeable inability to be present, his unexpected insistence they should remain, his sudden desire to wed her. No effort would have been necessary to persuade her father. Thomas Gillespie would revel in the opportunity to stay with a marquess. The inconsistencies also troubled her.

A warm-hearted man (Solomon de Toledo, for instance) might make a friend of anyone and perhaps even fall in love against his own best interests. The Marquess of Furness doing the same was as likely as her father befriending a costermonger.

Gillespie compressed his lips. Before he could respond, she hurried on. "While I may not be unsuitable in terms of my birth and education"—except that a knowledge of several languages was inadequate training for a marquess's wife—"it is only in tales that such unequal matches occur. If the marquess wants a bride, he has his choice of aristocratic females who would bring him family connections and a dowry." Her own education might have come at second hand, from reading her father's books to better understand his manuscripts, but she had learned to think rationally.

"Whatever his reasons, Portia, his mind is made up. Come, you cannot suppose that a man of his age is as impetuous as a boy. You are past the age of expecting a great romance, after all, and you know the legendary romances turned out badly."

She did: Romeo and Juliet, Lancelot and Guinevere, Tristan and Isolde.

"I don't expect a romance, Papa. But I am not quite comfortable with our host."

"That will come in time, as you learn the ways of the aristocracy. He has shown you very flattering attentions, has he not? He converses with you and is teaching you to ride. How better to show his regard?"

These were all very good points. Had they been speaking of some other young lady in a similar situation, Portia might well have agreed. "The marquess takes little interest in his tenants and land, from what I have seen when riding with him, and he is often curt with his servants. Can you not hint him away so I am spared having to refuse his offer, and he is spared the humiliation?" She could not explain her unease further without telling him Solomon had grave misgivings about Furness's character, and thus revealing she had met with Solomon. Confessing her clandestine meetings with a man was unthinkable. Still, she could weather his disapproval, much as she dreaded it, but she was not willing to expose Mr. de Toledo to his wrath. Or to Lord Furness's ire. Why should she think it might be dangerous? *We are living the eighteenth century, not the Middle Ages.* Nevertheless, the fear remained.

Her father sat up straight. "Impossible. I have given my consent. I will not now tell him my daughter is foolish and ungrateful for the condescension he has shown her."

"I wish you had consulted me before accepting this odd offer." Her response came slow; her mind had gone blank. She would have to face the marquess herself and turn him down.

" 'Tis done now," he said dismissively.

"It will be awkward to decline his offer when you have led him to believe his suit was acceptable."

Her father frowned. "You cannot refuse him."

"Are you saying I must wed the marquess? I cannot believe you would insist."

"Of course I accepted such a flattering and suitable proposal. Why would I not?"

"Perhaps because I had not agreed to it? If marriage among the aristocracy is a practical matter, how is his lordship benefitting from marrying me? On the basis of a few days' acquaintance with my aged self, he cannot have discovered such sterling facets of my character that he feels impelled to marry me." Anger had boiled up from nowhere or she would never have spoken thus.

He pursed his lips. "Daughter, there were sound reasons for my decision."

"Then please tell me what they are. I am of age. You cannot bestow me on him without my consent."

"You will be a marchioness. Our alliance with a noble house will be an advantage to Benedict. He will be able to make a good marriage and move in the highest circles of society."

She was distracted from her own fate for the moment. "What would constitute 'a good marriage'?"

He sat back and smiled. "The daughter of a viscount at least. I do not think we need look lower. A good dowry as well, for the connection to a marquess is a great inducement."

"I would not think being the brother-in-law even of a marquess would be much of an inducement when we are merely gentlefolk and not rich."

"A relationship, even by marriage, would be worthwhile for anyone. However, we need not worry about a bride for Benedict until he completes his education. Now, as to your wedding: Furness will procure a special license so the wedding can take place here. He does not wish it to be the subject of gossip and speculation as it would be if held in town."

"I have not agreed to marry the marquess."

He appeared to be sunk in thought. At last he replied, "Well, you must give him a chance to persuade you. Hearing him out would only be polite."

After a moment's hesitation, she agreed though

with a momentary qualm. She could hardly deny she owed Furness that much, her father having encouraged him to believe she would be willing to accept his hand.

"That's settled, then. Lord Furness awaits you in the little salon."

"He intends to address me tonight?"

"Ay, why not? He has been a widower for some time and wishes to conclude this matter as soon as may be. Goodnight, Portia."

Hot and tremulous, she made her way slowly to the salon. Previously she had found it one of the most comfortable of the public rooms at Blackwater Hay, as it was small enough to be warm, and shabby in the pleasant way of a room where people actually lived. Probably Frances used it as a sitting room when there was no company. The ornate drawing room might have been more to Lord Furness's taste for the occasion, but he would hardly like to turn his aunt and guests out of it.

A footman at the end of the passage opened the door for her. She had never seen one there before. He must have been assigned to that place for the evening for no other reason than to open the door and to receive the marquess's orders, if any. Not to act as a chaperon: the man closed the door behind her.

"Mistress Portia." He rose from a chair before the fireplace and came toward her.

She dropped a curtsy. A young lady might well think him the very pattern of a marquess: handsome, finely dressed, well spoken, with a commanding presence. "My father said you wished to see me, Lord Furness." Her voice emerged thin and uncertain.

"Please, come sit." He guided her to a settee with

one hand at her back. She was uncomfortably aware of it through her gown, stays, and smock. He seated himself beside her, angled toward her.

"Did Gillespie explain why I asked for this interview, my dear?"

"He mentioned you wished to ask me a question." Portia focused on her hands in her lap and willed them to unclench. While the fire had warmed the room, it could not be the heat from the fireplace that made her feel hot.

"Then you are aware of my regard for you."

"I—not really, my lord. I had no idea—" Lord, she sounded like a flibbertigibbet.

"My fault, I fear. It is unsuitable for a nobleman to display his most tender emotions, which puts him at a disadvantage with ladies who are not aware of the constraints we are taught."

Which was to say, a mere gentlewoman like herself. "I do not know what to say, Lord Furness."

"You need only say 'yes.' "

Her father expected her to accept in order to oblige her family. Her marriage to Furness would have advantages. In spite of her argument against it, even she knew a noble connection conferred benefits: preferential treatment at school or in employment and from tradesmen. It might not provide wealth, but the fathers of young men studying for university would be more likely to send their boys to Thomas Gillespie for tutoring because of his relationship with Furness. Though her father had spoken of not taking more students. Of course, he had the inheritance from his cousin Sturgis.

She would be a marchioness. Pretty gowns, jewels,

deference from almost everyone: what young lady could resist? But Benedict's opinion counted for something in spite of his being a boy, and Solomon de Toledo's obvious concern about Furness weighed even more heavily. Most would likely dismiss a Hebrew moneylender's judgment of a peer of the realm; she could not. She knew Solomon. She did not know Furness in any meaningful way.

She must answer somehow, before the silence stretched too long.

"My lord, this has come as a complete surprise to me." She bit her lip. What could she say to postpone answering? "I feel utterly unworthy of the honor of your regard. I must have time to consider whether I can do justice to the duties of a marchioness. May I have until tomorrow to reply?"

"Of course, my dear."

She unclasped her hands to rise, and the marquess, taking possession of one of them, pressed a kiss upon it.

"May I escort you to the drawing room?"

"I believe I will go to my chamber now, my lord, to contemplate…" What? What was she to do?

"Your future." Furness completed the thought.

"My future, yes. If you will excuse me, sir?"

He opened the door for her. "I will await your reply eagerly, Portia."

She swept out as sedately as possible, not to seem to be fleeing.

In her bedchamber, she sat for some time trying to still her thudding heart. The sensation of being overheated had faded, leaving her shivery. She had no more than twenty-four hours before Furness would demand her answer. Surely any lady would be thrilled to receive a proposal of marriage from a marquess. Her father considered it her duty to accept, and admittedly it would benefit her family. Why was she hesitating?

Chapter 20

A tap at the door made the breath catch in her throat. She did not want to talk to her father, or her mother, either, if she had come to talk about the proposal.

"Who is it?"

"Portia, it's me."

She jumped up and hurried to let Benedict in.

"Are you all right?"

"Yes, of course."

"You don't look it."

She sank down on the armchair, and after a glance at the stool before the dressing table, Benedict perched on the bedside steps.

"I'm not, Benedict. I spoke at random."

"Like the way you claim to be perfectly well when you've used a week's supply of handkerchiefs in a day or feel like vomiting," he remarked. "Did Furness ask you to marry him?"

"Yes." Presumably one's younger sibling learned things in the mysterious way servants always did.

"No wonder you look like a chicken that hears a fox. What did you answer?"

"I turned into a blushing, stammering miss and asked for time."

Her little brother guffawed. "And he was deceived?"

"I really didn't know how to answer. Papa told me it was my duty to accept. That was when we spoke in the library after supper."

"Like the way he decided I should be a scholar."

"Very like," she agreed grimly. "You knew when you told me Papa wanted to speak to me, didn't you?"

"I didn't exactly know. I'd heard some things."

She raised her eyebrows.

"I didn't put them all together until it was too late to warn you. The passage on the way to the library didn't seem like the right time."

"What did you hear?"

"Two or three days ago, Jem and the dairy maid were talking about 'our new young ladyship' when I went out to the stable yard. They stopped as soon as they saw me. I didn't think anything of it except that Furness must intend to marry. Who would think it would be you? A marquess, after all. Sorry."

"It surprised me, too."

"This afternoon I drank my little portion of port and stayed until Papa said I might as well be excused as I'd had enough to drink, and Furness agreed. I was glad to go. Port's stronger than I expected and believe me, the conversation is less interesting than you'd think. After I left the dining room, I thought I'd go out to the stable to give Treacle—that's the gelding I've been riding, you know—an apple. When I came in, the servants must have been at their own meal, for there was no footman or anyone about. The door to the library was ajar, and I heard Furness say to Father, 'Is there any question of her agreement?' Father said, 'Why would she refuse? She is at her last prayers, and she is a dutiful daughter. She will accept.' Who else could they have been talking about?"

"Are you certain you heard correctly?" *A dutiful daughter* should be a compliment. In such a context it was nearly as insulting as *at her last prayers*. Yet both were the truth.

"I'm not wrong about the words. You know I have a good memory, Portia. The proof is that he asked you to marry him."

Benedict's thoughts were often written on his face, unless he was upset. Now it was a *tabula rasa* as her papa would have said, devoid of expression. Her own face might be equally blank. She was an old maid, but it hurt to have her father acknowledge the fact. A tiny spark of resentment kindled.

"Did you hear anything more?"

"The marquess began to speak of a settlement, but I heard a door opening down the corridor—you'd think someone would grease the hinges in a nobleman's house, wouldn't you?—so I had to shab off."

"I take it you mean you left, Benedict."

"Fled, more like. Portia, do you know how much Father was left by that cousin?"

"No, he never said. I can't decide whether it's only a small amount or whether it's sizable and he doesn't want us to lose our thrifty habits."

Benedict snorted. "That's putting it tactfully. I believe it can't be large because if it were a great fortune, he'd have been merry as a grig. Wouldn't a fellow crow a bit if he were suddenly as rich as Croesus?"

She had to agree.

"The thing that I don't understand is why Furness would court you. 'Tis passing strange."

"He claimed to have formed a tendre for me. Though I've seen no sign of it. Noblemen do not show their softer emotions, according to the marquess. Yet I should have noticed something." Even if 'twere only a warmth in his eyes when he looked at her.

The question of why Furness would seek her hand in marriage and the exchange between their father and the marquess were troubling enough, without Solomon de Toledo's visit. She stared straight ahead, aware her brother was studying her.

"I think you'd be aware. Girls are, I'm told. My friends say their sisters think they're being courted if a man only smiles at them. Not that there is any reason he mightn't fall in love with you. You're an excellent sister and not homely. In fact," he continued, with an air of doing strict justice, "I suppose you're quite handsome. And you're not as old as Lord Furness."

"*Merci du compliment.*" She could not quite suppress an ironic inflection.

Benedict ignored it, or likelier yet, did not notice it. "It's true. But the marquess is as jealous of his consequence as Father is. I'd expect him to insist on a bride from a noble family, and one with a dowry."

"Papa isn't—" Her *pro forma* protest died on her lips. "I suppose he is, at that." He did not have an easy manner with servants or tradesmen, as if allowing them the same courtesy he would show to a fellow scholar would reduce him to their level.

"It's worrisome." Benedict fell silent, frowning slightly. Her brother disliked mysteries. He would pick away at any question of why or how until he understood.

He circled back to the very point that bothered her.

"While I'm sure any man might fall in love with you, 'tis odd Furness would and you not know it. I wouldn't expect him to care about love, anyway. Will you marry him?"

"I don't know."

"If you don't know, I guess you shouldn't, because if you wanted to marry him, you'd know."

"I haven't had time to think about it. Sometimes marriage is simply the sensible thing to do."

"I know that, Portia. It's about marrying money, or mayhap acquiring another estate, or useful family connections."

His matter-of-fact statement echoed her father. To introduce a lighter note, she replied, "Pish! Is this what you and your friends plan to do when you're old enough to wed?"

"Ho! Who wants to marry? At least until they've seen the world and had some adventures. No, some of the other boys speak of their sisters and brothers marrying or trying to. It sounds horrid. Witherby's mother wants to catch a title for his sister, Johnstone's brother is betrothed to a Glasgow tobacco lord's girl with red hair and freckles, and a few days before the end of term, Ames heard his older brother died of some inflammation in his entrails. He's the heir now, and his parents are already planning to find him a bride as soon as may be after he finishes at Radford's. He hasn't any younger brothers, and his father is a baron, so there's the title to consider. Of course I know all girls want to marry, because what else can they do? But would you want to marry Furness?"

"I would have a home of my own and perhaps children. I would be a marchioness. A relationship to a marquess would work to your advantage, as well."

"Witherby sounded happier about visiting the tooth-drawer than you do. But he'd been in pain for several days. Do you like him at all?"

"He has been very obliging."

"He's taught us to ride, to be sure, and let us stay in his house, which would not be much of a pleasure but for the riding. I hope you don't marry him. There must be someone in town you'd like better."

Solomon de Toledo came to mind. He would be a completely inappropriate suitor if he were a suitor, which he was not. He had never displayed any interest of That Sort in her, only kindness. He did seem to enjoy her company. But if he were her beau? Portia did not care to think what her father would say to such a match. The wrong occupation, the wrong religion, and very likely her papa could think of other objections. She sighed.

"There is no one." Solomon de Toledo was not in town.

"What are you going to do, Portia? If you dislike the idea, you should not marry him, even if Father sighs over the ingratitude of his children and makes you feel like the veriest worm."

"I don't know. It would help our family to be allied with Furness. He could use his influence on your behalf, which would advance your career. Particularly if you and he can convince Papa not to insist on your being a scholar."

"He's given up that notion and says I will be a country gentleman. I don't see how, for Furness isn't likely to support us, and you can't really be county gentry without land. Do you suppose his apoplexy affected his mind? Because he's different, isn't he? Mayhap it's only that I was away at school or because I'm older that he seems to have changed somehow."

"Having a brush with death and receiving an inheritance might have changed him," she conceded. "He is different. More than I realized if he no longer expects you to follow in his footsteps."

"He doesn't. Now he apparently wishes you to be a marchioness."

"I fear you are correct." She and her brother were close, and in spite of Benedict's youth and desire for "adventures," he could be amazingly shrewd. She needed advice. He would have to do.

"Benedict, you must not breathe a word of this to anyone, but I have heard that the marquess is not a good man."

He snorted. "I told you how he treats his servants and tenants. You must have seen that for yourself."

"He is worse than that, according to Mr. de Toledo."

"What does he say about Furness?"

"I will not go into detail as I think S—Mr. de Toledo told me in confidence, but he considers him dangerous."

"And you could not reveal your misgivings to Father because he does love a title, or if you did, he insisted you come in spite of them?" Benedict remarked cynically.

"I could hardly have remained at home with only the servants, with you and our parents gone." True, but misleading. "I did not learn of Furness's history until we were already here. Mr. de Toledo was sufficiently concerned to, er, contact me."

Her brother's eyes lit with enthusiasm. "Oh, was he Solomon the peddler I heard the servants talking about? It didn't sound like him, somehow."

"The peddler brought me his message. I've met Mr. de Toledo twice on my walks before breakfast. I must see him tomorrow."

"Good. He will know what to do."

"You have great faith in him," she said, amused in spite of herself.

"He's very practical in his suggestions. That's helpful."

"However do you know? I hope your opinion isn't based only on those treats."

"We correspond. I wrote to thank him for taking me to the coaching inn and for the sweetmeats and buns, and he wrote back, and then I did. Well, you know how it is: you can't not reply, at least if it's an interesting letter. I asked him about something, and no, I'm not going to tell you what. It wasn't the sort of thing I could ask Father. Sol's answer made good sense to me."

She would not have thought Benedict an enthusiastic correspondent. How little one sometimes knew of one's nearest and dearest.

Benedict knit his brows. "If I'd been able to ask our father, his answer would have been based upon the way things should be. Sol's dealt with the way things actually are. Much more helpful, you see." He took Portia's silence for lack of understanding. "If I had inquired whether it was permissible to eat jam tarts between meals, Father would have said one should not want to eat them. Sol would tell me I might do so in moderation, if they did not spoil my appetite for my dinner."

He had captured the essence of both. "I see. He does give sensible advice. I noticed it myself when Papa was ill."

"It's too bad he is not your beau."

"Papa would be…" She should not criticize her father whom they were obligated to respect.

"He would be furious and forbid you to have any contact with him. A bit cool, I'd say, considering how good Sol was to us."

The shortening of Solomon de Toledo's name finally caught her attention. "You call him by a nickname? Benedict, how came you to be so forward?"

"He said I might, as if I were a cousin or he a young uncle."

"I hope you would address an uncle as 'Uncle de Toledo' or at least 'Uncle Solomon.' "

"Portia, either of those would sound ridiculous. He is a friend. But using only his last name as we do at school sounds peculiar. Sometimes you have to do what makes sense instead of what's proper."

True, as she'd discovered after Papa's apoplexy. "I will rely on his giving me good counsel."

He stood and took two steps toward the door. "Portia, why did Sol come to see you?"

"He has misgivings about the marquess's character and thought it strange he would invite us to be his guests."

"Ah." Benedict nodded sagely and went off, leaving Portia no easier in her mind.

Chapter 21

Portia froze in the act of buckling her shoe, arrested by the soft double tap at her door. Her first thought was that her father had suffered another stroke, as Dr. de Toledo had called it, or her mother was ill. No, a maid sent to fetch her would have entered and spoken or shaken her awake if she had been asleep. Heart pounding, she hastened to open it, hobbling with only one shoe on.

"Portia," Benedict whispered, pushing his way into the room and closing the door carefully behind him. He was fully dressed, his greatcoat over one arm and hat clutched in the same hand.

"What is wrong?"

"I thought I might go with you this morning, as it does not suit my notions of proper conduct for my sister to be meeting a man unchaperoned," he said primly. Before she could raise her eyebrows at such a sentiment from her little brother, he added, "I wanted to see Sol."

"I suppose if you wish to come along—"

In the dim light of the candle, he shook his head impatiently. "I went down to the kitchen to get a slice of bread and butter or a bun because I usually wake early. The cook and the kitchen maid were talking about dinner the day after tomorrow. There are to be guests, and the cook is in a pother because the master wants a number of elaborate dishes. She's not used to cooking elegant meals on short notice." He paused to catch his breath.

"How inconsiderate of Furness."

"You don't understand, Portia. It's the wedding dinner."

"The wedding dinner." No one would plan a wedding dinner unless he were certain of his suit being accepted.

"I'm coming with you this morning to see Sol."

She nodded and put on her second shoe.

While the sleet had stopped during the night, when they slipped through the door into the garden, they found the ground still wet. The wind billowed her cloak around her as they hastened toward the three oaks.

The marquess ordering the wedding dinner—and therefore presumably the wedding—before her formal acceptance made it all but impossible to refuse him. Her father had virtually ordered her to accept and must assume she would obey for their family's sake. Still, it was presumptuous of Furness, even if he was a marquess and therefore a desirable catch. Her father had never made the slightest effort to provide her opportunities to meet men among whom she might have found a husband; indeed, he had often said he did not know what he would do without her assistance. To arrange a marriage for her without even asking her opinion of the man, was…was… Upwelling anger caused her to miss her brother's remark.

"Hmmm? I beg your pardon, Benedict. My mind was on my footing. What did you say?"

"Only that a greatcoat such as men wear would be more practical than your cloak, which is a nuisance in the wind. Warmer, too, I would think."

"Oh. In its favor, it does have a hood." A sudden gust blew it back, exposing her to the cold, damp air. Benedict clapped his hand to his tricorne before it could sail away. "And the hood, unlike your hat, cannot take leave of my cloak."

She clutched it around her more firmly and they trudged forward in silence until they drew near the oaks. Their branches stirred but the hedgerow marking the boundary of Blackwater Hay provided some shelter.

"What if he has not come today?" The question popped out. Portia had not intended to voice the fear; her mind must be more disordered than she had realized.

"If he said he'd come every day, he'll be there."

He left her huddling in the hedgerow's lee to approach the road. Just as Portia despaired of Solomon, Benedict called softly, "I hear a horse." He prudently drew back behind one of the trees. "In case it should be someone else," he muttered.

The clip-clopping stopped short of the hedgerow. Portia waited for the sound of creaking leather to signal a rider dismounting. She heard only the rustling of brush and branch until Solomon de Toledo stepped into the clearing, pausing abruptly as he noted Benedict's presence.

Portia's "Mr. de Toledo" and her brother's "Sol!" overlaid each other.

"What's amiss?" Solomon demanded.

Benedict spoke first. "Furness wants to marry Portia."

"My father is in favor of it." She did not want to admit her papa considered it her duty. Mayhap any parent would regard marriage to a marquess as the best way of providing for an undowered daughter. Considered logically, it made sense, yet she could not like the idea, either of the marriage or of her father and Furness arranging her future without reference to her wishes.

"I am not surprised."

Uttered differently, it might have been a compliment, implying she was an object of desire. Instead, Solomon's curt statement suggested something else. Before she could wonder what he meant, Benedict said, "It seems curst odd to me for a nobleman to want to marry my sister. I mean, Portia isn't bracket-faced, she's not a chattering ninny, and she is the best of sisters, but I can't see her as a bride for a marquess. Particularly not Furness."

"I agree. Except that I would rate her higher than you do, Benedict. Any man of sense might be proud to wed Mistress Portia."

He had a charming smile. Had Furness smiled at her in such a way, she might be tempted to accept him.

"I asked someone to make inquiries for me before I left London, and send his reply to the coaching inn at Maldon. It came yesterday. While I am sure Lord Furness welcomes your natural attractions, I fear his primary interest is your fortune."

"But I have no fortune. Father inherited some amount, which Benedict and I agree cannot be large, but 'tis surely not enough to dower me." Enough to send Benedict to Oxford or Cambridge, perhaps, but not enough to enable him to live the life of a gentleman, as Thomas Gillespie seemed to intend.

"As to that, I've learned more about Sturgis's will." She heard him take a deep breath. "When I heard your family had gone to visit Furness, I asked someone who might be able to learn more to investigate the question. His letter informed me that Mr. Gillespie was indeed left only a pittance, with the balance of Sturgis's money divided between Master Benedict Gillespie and Mistress Portia Gillespie, protected by trusts. Nathan Sturgis was a wealthy man."

Benedict exclaimed, "Blood and thunder!"

"I've heard nothing of this, Mr. de Toledo." If only it were true, life would be so much easier. They need not worry about school fees or using too many candles or too much coal.

"Nevertheless, 'tis true. It explains one or two remarks Mr. Gillespie made when he paid off my loan. He spoke as though he expected no future economic difficulties, and I wondered why."

Certainly it explained why the marquess might be willing to marry her. Did her father expect Furness would support the rest of the family, so Thomas Gillespie did not need to resume tutoring? Furness might be willing to do so, if only to avoid having a tutor father-in-law. Then she thought, *Benedict is a minor, and the family will live like gentry on his inheritance.*

Benedict asked, "Isn't Nathan Sturgis the one who improved the blast furnace?"

"That's the one."

This disclosure impressed her brother more than the inheritance. "Only think of Father being related to Sturgis. I wish I had known. Did we inherit the furnace works as well?"

"No, he left it to the man who had been his foreman and most valuable assistant. You and your sister will receive a small percentage of the profits during your lifetimes, however. I take it Sturgis felt some obligation to his cousin's children, if not to Gillespie himself."

"I should like to see it. Mayhap the new owner would let me visit sometime."

"Benedict, we have more immediate matters to discuss." She could imagine her father's reaction to his son touring such a place, and one associated with his detested cousin, at that.

The clouds were thinning, at least near the horizon, where the sun shone like a fuzzy lemon ball. The wind had not abated. As a stronger gust whipped Portia's cloak back, de Toledo shifted position, the better to shelter her from the wind.

"If we're rich, why would Father insist you marry the marquess when you have doubts about him? You did tell him how you felt, didn't you?"

"I did. He said it was my duty to marry Furness because being related to the marquess would benefit you in your career, and you could live like a country gentleman. A connection to a nobleman would benefit all of us."

"Huh!" Her brother snorted. "Some other titled fool would do as well. One you could like. And if I am not to have a career, where's the benefit?"

"I suppose our position in society would be improved. Is my inheritance truly big enough to outweigh the difference in our ranks and my unsuitability?"

"Furness does not possess as large an income as one might expect for a man of his rank. His father was a viscount, but not especially affluent. His uncle, the first marquess, was a mere country gentleman before he rendered some signal service to the Crown at Malplaquet."

She did not need Solomon to explain further. "My fortune really is the attraction, then."

"Oh, yes."

"But—" Her objection died on her lips. A woman's property became her husband's on their marriage. As her father had not even informed her she was an heiress, the money might pass into Furness's control without her knowledge. "Benedict's inheritance would allow him to go to university, and I suppose, pursue any profession he chose." Which meant there was no need for her to marry against her inclination to assist Benedict, losing control of her fortune and her life.

Her brother ignored the statement. He chewed his lower lip. "I don't see why he would insist on Furness when you don't like him. It's not the same as his wanting me to learn Greek and Hebrew. He would feel it was for my own good, whether it meant I could earn a living acceptable to him or even simply be well educated if I didn't have to work. It wouldn't matter to him that I'd rather do something else."

"I'm sure Papa believes marriage to the Marquess of Furness is for my own good." Why Furness, whom he had known less than a month? Was it simply a case of a bird in the hand is worth two in the bush?

"Certainly he would prefer you to marry a marquess unless you could marry a duke. But it doesn't seem like him to want you to marry against your wishes. He's not unkind."

"No, and he only wants what's best for us."

"I think this time he's wrong. If it won't advance my career because I won't need to earn a living, what's the point of making you marry against your will? We can live like landed gentry anyway, can't we?"

"Your father does not have access to your inheritance, Benedict. Mistress Portia's and your fortunes will be administered by three trustees. Mr. Gillespie is one of them. The other two are Sturgis's attorney and the new owner of the blast furnace works. Any two in agreement can disburse funds. I have little doubt they would have no objection to providing enough income for you to live comfortably if not luxuriously. But to be landed gentry, you would need to own property, and the other two trustees might consider that if Benedict wished to be a country gentleman, he could buy a manor when he comes of age. "

"I would be happy to contribute from my own money," Portia said.

There was a momentary silence, until Benedict, with his usual lack of tact, asked, "So why would our father want Portia to marry Furness, apart from puffing up his vanity?"

"Benedict!" It was too bad her protest was at his voicing the thought. In good conscience, she could not deny that her father was vain in some ways.

"Benedict, some things are best left unsaid." Solomon de Toledo smiled crookedly. "Besides, do you really think he would demand Portia wed a man against her will only for vanity's sake?"

"No, sir, that's exactly my point. Aren't there other noblemen who would like to marry a fortune? Unless Father doesn't think he could find one."

"There are, indeed. In fact, he even knows someone who arranges such matches, though never if one of the parties is unwilling."

Portia raised her brows. "Really? How does he happen to be acquainted with someone like that, Mr. de Toledo?"

He cleared his throat. " 'Tis a specialty of mine. As a favor, I made a match for someone who needed a wealthy spouse, and the next I knew, others wanted my help."

Had he had anything to do with this determination of Papa's to marry her to the marquess?

Mayhap he detected some question in her gaze, for he said, "This is none of my doing. When I act as a matchmaker, both parties are aware of it, and both are willing because there is advantage to both."

"I did not suppose you were involved, though if you mentioned your matchmaking, it might have given my father the notion. Why would you come here to warn me if you did arrange it? For that is why you came, is it not?" She did not believe the man who had loaned her father money for Benedict's education at no interest, with little chance of being repaid, would take part in such a scheme.

"It is. I was concerned to hear of your being Furness's guest."

With the persistence of a bulldog, Benedict returned to the point that worried him. "Father told Portia marrying Furness will help our family, but I don't see how merely being connected to him will help us. Father has mentioned we will live in the country like gentry, but that would cost a good deal, surely? Unless he's thinking of a cottage. But I don't think he is. He talks about how he lived when he was my age, with horses and a park and a home farm, which doesn't sound like a cottage. He can't be thinking of our living with Furness, can he? I wouldn't care for that!" After a moment's reflection, he added, "I don't think Furness would, either."

Portia was diverted from the matter at hand. "He spoke to you about his boyhood? I don't recall Papa ever saying a word about it." When others described their fond memories of childhood pranks or treats or their school days, she had supposed her father's youth had been unhappy.

"Well, he didn't, until recently. It was after he went to that manor with the marquess. 'A tidy little estate' he called it, that reminded him of the place where he grew up. Then he went on and on about riding around the countryside and fishing in the stream and how that was the life for a gentleman."

"What manor was it?" Solomon inquired. "Some neighbor of the marquess?"

From something in his tone, Portia thought it was not an idle question.

"Pipperidge Rise, it's called. 'Pipperidge' means barberry in Essex, they say. It belongs to Furness."

"The manor he inherited from his first wife."

Portia glanced at Solomon askance.

"It's not entailed," he said, as if that explained anything.

"Does it matter, Mr. de Toledo?"

"I'm not certain. Madam, do you intend to accept Furness?"

"I don't want to marry him. I thought perhaps I ought to agree to the match for my family's good, but if Benedict and I have substantial inheritances, is it necessary for me to sacrifice myself?"

De Toledo laughed. "I think you might describe it

as substantial."

At the figure he named, Benedict whistled.

"That much?" Portia asked faintly. "Are you sure?"

"Ay. My information comes from a source in the, ah, financial community. News like that gets around in those circles, if not in society."

Her muscles went limp as unstarched linen with relief from the anxiety she had not known she felt. "Then once my father knows of Benedict's and my inheritance, he will not ask me to wed the marquess."

Solomon shifted uneasily. "Mistress Portia, he did know. He must have been fully apprised of the terms of the will. Ordinarily, it would have been read in the presence of the beneficiaries. In this instance, there was some difficulty in locating Mr. Gillespie, and then his illness led to more delay, but you should have been informed."

"Why would he not have told us?"

"I don't know."

"I can guess," Benedict said. "You know how he felt about trade, and Sturgis, too, I suppose, for he never mentioned him, did he? I'd have been proud to know we had such a knacky relation. If he resented Cousin Sturgis and especially if he considered him common, he would go to the gallows rather than speak of him."

"That is no way to speak of our papa, Benedict."

"But 'tis true. How long was it before he told us his paper speculating on the historical basis of the Trojan War was rejected?"

"Well…" Not until she had asked about it, and then her father had been tight-lipped for days. "The humiliation of most of the money being left to us must have sealed his lips. The first time he was recovered sufficiently to go out, I recall he was annoyed when he came home." Sulky, she would have called it, had Benedict displayed the same behavior. "He brought tea, which he should not have been able to afford. And he had written to an attorney earlier." Why had she never wondered why he was writing a lawyer?

The pallid light made it possible to recognize Solomon de Toledo's expression. He must be suppressing a thought he did not like to share. She had felt the same way too often to mistake it. When he did speak, he said only, "I am surprised Nathan Sturgis's attorney did not inform you. Perhaps even law firms sometimes make mistakes."

Her brother put her own thought in words. "Father receives the letters and distributes them. They are not simply left on the hall table."

"Perhaps he felt we did not need to know, Benedict. You are a minor, and many men regard females, even those of us who are of age, as being no more than children." She had never thought her father one of them, when she had not only served as his amanuensis for years, but also managed the house when Mama did not feel able to deal with it. Papa would set no value on the latter activity, unless some domestic crisis inconvenienced him. As for her assistance with his work, he had sometimes complimented her on her ability to decipher his handwriting or her speed in copying. She had occasionally suggested better ways to explain an idea to his students or changes to his phrasing in an essay. He had never acknowledged those, even when he made use of them. Her father might indeed share the common male opinion of females' intelligence. Disappointment and annoyance battled for supremacy; she tamped them down.

"In that case, I will simply refuse Furness. Thank you for bringing this news, Mr. de Toledo. I fear it was at considerable inconvenience and took you away from your business."

"Damn the inconvenience!"

Her brother uttered a startled "Oho!" and grinned.

"I beg your pardon. I could not put trade above your happiness and safety."

"And I beg your pardon, sir. You have already taken more pains to help my family than anyone could expect."

"It has been my honor and my pleasure."

"Now that you and Sol have settled the matter, perhaps we can go find our breakfast."

She dragged her gaze away from de Toledo's face to reply. Before she could speak, Solomon's urgent voice stopped her.

"Mistress Portia, refusing his offer may not be enough. You are essentially his prisoner here. There is but one coach from Maldon each week. The next nearest is in Chelmsford, which is fourteen or sixteen miles away. Furness's coach brought you here."

"What would be the point in his trying to keep us at Blackwater Hay once I refused him?"

"I don't think it impossible he would attempt to persuade you to change your mind, one way or another."

The idea was ridiculous, something from a novel. *Pamela*, for instance. Yet her family did rely on Furness for transportation. They might be able to hire someone with a wagon in the closest village to convey them to Chelmsford. On the other hand, most of that village's inhabitants were probably dependent on the marquess's business or goodwill. Why was she even worrying about difficulties that could never arise? "Surely if he offers for me and I refuse, he will be only too glad to send us on our way."

"Furness's arrogance alone might lead him to refuse to believe you would turn down the chance to be a marchioness."

"I assure you, I would not be worn down by importunities, sir, even if he were discourteous enough to persist."

"Your father's approval and Furness's persistence are not the only danger. The marquess is not a good man, and he is a bad enemy."

"Your letter expressed concern about him, I recall, before you learned of our inheritance."

"I could not be easy about your presence at Blackwater Hay, whatever his reason for luring your family here. I did not like to go into detail on paper."

She searched his face and saw nothing but concern. His reluctance to write down his reason for it seemed to hint at something more than disinterested kindness. What a pity Benedict was present. Then again, perhaps it was wise to have a chaperon. "You had best tell me what you know about the Marquess of Furness."

"If Furness were merely a fortune hunter, I would counsel you not to marry him because you are worthy of a better man than he. But Furness attempted to hire a bravo to cripple his sister's preferred suitor as the marquess meant to arrange a marriage for her which would benefit himself. My informant—not the one who told me about Sturgis's will—also suspected he intended to compromise a well-dowered lady who was unwilling to marry him. I had the account from a friend who moves in the same circles as the marquess. Luckily, he and her friends prevented it."

"Are you sure of your facts, Mr. de Toledo?"

"I would trust the man who told me with my life. I have known him since he saved me from a pack of young miscreants when I was a child. Too, I have seen Furness in a rage. He was ready to destroy an innocent girl's reputation to strike a blow at a rival. He refrained only because it would have led to his own circumstances being revealed."

"You paint an ugly picture."

"No uglier than the reality. He has not provided his sister with the dowry to which she was entitled, and that matter is now before the Court of Chancery, which may be why he wants money very badly and is not particular how he acquires it. His late wife was unhappy in her marriage, I understand. At the best, he would not make a pleasant husband." He shifted uncomfortably. "Nor do I think he would necessarily limit his persuasion to refusing you the use of his coach. A lady who has been compromised has little recourse but to marry the man responsible."

"You think he might try to force me?"

He gazed at her very intently. "I think the marquess is capable of almost any villainy."

"Even then I could refuse and would."

"Mistress Portia, he has many chances to be alone with you here. If he raped you, to whom could you report the crime? As a nobleman, he can only be tried in the House of Lords, a body not known for disciplining its own."

"But Solomon, Mr. de Toledo I should say, what

am I to do? You would not suggest I marry him, but if I won't, I risk ruin."

"We need the wisdom of a more famous Solomon to work out that problem. You should leave Blackwater Hay at once, except that would also be ruinous to your reputation. When must you give him your answer?"

"This evening, I suppose. He proposed to me last night, and I asked time to consider, being overwhelmed by the honor and feeling myself unprepared for the dignity and responsibilities required of a marchioness." Her lips quirked in spite of her apprehension.

Benedict made an uncouth noise. "Oh, ay, he would believe such a tale."

"What will you tell him?"

The concern in Solomon's voice warmed her. "I think I must ask for more time, pleading that we are scarcely acquainted."

"Portia, you are forgetting the dinner."

Benedict's interruption took both of them by surprise. The meeting with Solomon had driven her brother's news from her mind.

"I overheard the cook and a maid talking. Furness is giving a dinner the day after tomorrow for some of the neighborhood gentry, including the parson. I don't think you have any more time, Portia."

"But I have not yet agreed to marry him,' she said foolishly. "The wedding could not be held so soon, even if I did."

"It could if he already has a special license."

"Papa mentioned the marquess wanted to marry soon and might acquire a special license." Solomon's warning began to seem less unlikely. "What can I do?"

Solomon frowned. "I could carry you away now,

but it would be better to make some arrangements first for your comfort and to preserve your reputation as much as possible."

"Elope?" The word popped out like a cork from a bottle of ginger beer too carelessly handled.

"Ah…I had in mind you should go to some good friend or relative your parents would be unlikely to think of. I would be no more than your courier."

"I see."

If he detected the faint tinge of disappointment in her words, he tactfully ignored it.

Benedict fidgeted. "I would think you should leave here this morning, Portia, except that you would be missed in an hour or two."

"That is an argument for leaving tomorrow," Solomon agreed. "I may be able to find some female to act as your maid on the journey. If you are willing to entrust yourself to me, that is, Mistress Portia."

She swallowed. "It's only that I don't know who I could shelter with. The people I know well enough to appeal to are equally known to my family."

"Can't see any of them standing up to a marquess, either," Benedict contributed.

"A good point, Benedict. In that case, I will take you to friends of mine Furness would never think of—and who need not fear him if he did learn where you had gone. Once you are back in London, you can visit Sturgis's attorney. A lady with money of her own can more easily resist an unwelcome marriage than one who is a dependent."

She swallowed hard. Both of her choices carried the risk of ruin. Only one offered a possibility of a happy outcome, or at least of avoiding misery.

"If you are willing?" Solomon asked.

"I must be. I will not marry Furness, and I begin to fear you are correct that he may not give me a choice."

"I will take you today if you wish, or tomorrow if you feel it safe to remain here until then."

"I agree with my brother that tomorrow would be better. I could bring a change of clothing and my remaining money for expenses along the way. Not that I have much more than a pound. Can that be enough?"

"I've got almost all of what Father gave me. I was saving it to buy a book I particularly want, but you may have it, Portia. You can pay me back."

"You will wish some pin money with you, Mistress Portia, but I have sufficient to get us to town."

"I will pay you back, too, Mr. de Toledo, as soon as I receive my inheritance."

"Time enough to think of that when we have you well away from here. Are you prepared to meet with Furness today?"

"You need not worry I will lose my nerve, sir."

His answering smile made the day seem less cold and bleak.

"I will meet you here tomorrow."

She nodded. "How will we travel? The marquess has given me riding lessons, but I have not ridden fast or very far. I can manage a trot."

"Our journey is the problem I have not quite worked out yet. I will take your limited riding experience into consideration. I've not spent much time on a horse's back myself," he admitted.

Chapter 22

Trotting along the lane leading to the road to Munden, he pondered the meeting with Portia. It had ended with agreement, yet still felt inconclusive. His suggestion that she run away was outrageous and might mean social ruination. She was relying on his account of Furness's past behavior and his suspicions of Furness's motives regarding her. At the same time, it would save her from a lifetime as Furness's wife. Portia now felt ruin preferable, and it might even be avoided.

In a perfect world, her father should have been the one to protect her from the marquess. In reality, once Furness had learned of Portia's inheritance, Thomas Gillespie had little chance of taking a principled stand. A nobleman could crush the Gillespies with a word or two, losing Gillespie his livelihood by spreading rumors among men whose sons needed preparation for university. Such extortion would be hard enough to ignore for a man already living at the limit of his means most years. Then again, for all his fine qualities, Gillespie doted on the nobility. The prospect of marrying his daughter to a titled man would have been beyond his imagining until it was presented to him. His family would be allied to a member of the upper nobility. How could he resist?

Portia was a dutiful daughter. Overnight, fear of the monstrous impropriety she was contemplating and guilt at refusing to sacrifice herself for her family (or for her father's ambition, not quite the same thing) might change her mind.

He was appalled, himself, when he thought how his meddling would seem to most. He was helping a young lady flee her family. Some would say he was luring her away from the protection of her relations. Worse, she was an heiress. Almost anyone would conclude he meant to marry her himself. He would think the same, given those facts about someone else.

He could imagine what his family would think of his current activities. His cousin David, who understood him better than anyone except Barlicorn, claimed he wanted to fix the lives of others. The accusation was probably true.

When I can't fix my own.

He was the changeling in his family. He was a moneylender who was not wealthy and a would-be rescuer who had no idea of what he was doing. His father would point out that Solomon supported himself comfortably and he meant well. His brother Vidal would smile and pat him on the shoulder; Daniel would tell him it was time he took a position with Levanter Trading Company, or one of their family's and friends' businesses. "Though not a bank, I think, Sol. You're too soft-hearted." Samuel would shrug.

He winced to think of his mother's reaction. On second thought, she might approve of his trying to save a lady from an unwanted marriage. No, there was no "try" about it. If he failed and Furness knew Portia had attempted to escape him, he would make her life a living hell. Being merely ruined for running away with Sol would be a comparatively benign fate, as Portia at least had the money to live in comfort. She would have chances to marry, too, given her fortune, whatever society thought of her. He could imagine his mother saying, "As she was willing to compromise her reputation by fleeing with your aid, you should offer to marry her."

It was true. He was ruining her or helping her to ruin herself. He should save her by wedding her. She was admirable: intelligent, devoted to her family, pretty. She was also a Christian, and he wanted a Jewish wife…when he was ready to marry, which would be when he could support a wife and children in some luxury. Still, mixed marriages were not uncommon. He knew several men with Christian wives and the children were still being raised as Jews, more or less. A strict rabbi (and maybe even a more lenient one) would disapprove, but it was not always possible to achieve the ideal in an imperfect world, as he knew from personal experience. He did not live in a community cut off from contact with Gentiles. If he did, his choices would be easier because they would be more limited.

He would not mind marrying Portia, if it were not for her fortune. What made her a desirable bride for anyone else made her impossible for him. He would not be called a fortune hunter. Well, never mind that now, especially as she likely had no interest at all in marrying him.

Concentrate on getting Portia well away from Furness.

His mind circled away from the final question regarding Portia's removal from Blackwater Hay. Meddling with Furness was not safe. He had offended the marquess once already, supporting the new Earl of Barlyon in their confrontation at Vauxhall Gardens. Furness had apparently ignored him then as insignificant. If Portia did leave and Furness learned of Solomon's part in spiriting her away, he could not hope to be overlooked again.

Grannie Irons's cottage came into sight. It was probably no more than a mile from Blackwater Hay as the crow flew. By the road, it might be two miles. Abe came out before Solomon had dismounted, face tense.

"I've news. In two days, the parson is invited to the Hay for dinner in celebration of Furness's marriage to Mistress Portia. It sounded as if the wedding was to take place then."

"The rumor came to her brother's ears, too. The marquess is putting the cart before the horse. She is to give her answer tonight—and in the morning, I will take her away. We have plans to make."

"There's a bucket of water for your horse in the shed. I was sure we'd have things to talk of," Abe said.

In the cottage, Grannie Irons poured them cups of small beer and seated herself at her spinning wheel near the table.

"How are we to get her away?"

"I had no set plan, not knowing what the situation was." Not knowing if Portia would want to marry Furness, or at least be willing to marry him.

Abe nodded thoughtfully. "We will need to have our plans completed to get her away before the lady's absence is discovered."

"There is no 'we' in this from now onward, Abe. You must not be involved further. Furness is dangerous."

"I don't intend to travel with you. I'll finish part of Isaac's route before I go home. Why should your evil marquess suspect me of anything? Still, I can help you plan, and Mistress Irons may have some advice."

"Advice will be welcome. My first thought was to take her to London by coach from Chelmsford, forgetting the question of how she was to get there. My second thought was that Furness would at once think of Chelmsford."

"The lady likely rides, being a gentlewoman. You'll want another horse," Abe said. "If you ride, you can avoid the roads."

Grannie Irons joined a twist of carded wool to the end of the wool already spun and commenced turning the wheel again. "A man might ride to London in a long summer day on a good horse, if he went by road and the weather did not turn foul. In the winter, you'd need to have a cat's eyes to follow the road in the dark."

"She is not skilled at riding. She learned only since coming to Blackwater Hay and is not sure of her ability to go faster than a trot. Whether we go by post road or cross-country, we cannot travel quickly, and she would be exhausted." Whoever would have thought rescuing a lady was this complicated? "I've never planned an elopement before."

"I shou' hope not!" Faded blue eyes skewered him. "I know something of gentlefolk and their ways, having been a maid up at the Hay afore I married. The lady needs to get away, but she don't need to be ruined. Not but what ruin wouldn't be better than his lordship."

"I have no intention of ruining her."

"Sol…mayhap what Mistress Irons is saying is, with a lady not used to riding, you'd have to allow two days or more. You would have to stay at an inn at least one night and maybe two."

The woman looked up, one hand still paying out the wool evenly while the other turned the wheel. "The young lady needs a maid with her for decency. My granddaughter would be willing."

"The one who works at Blackwater Hay? Would she give up her place there?"

"Ay. If you or the lady will get her a place in London, she would be glad to go. She wants to leave the Hay. The house is ill-run, and the wages are poor, taking into reckoning the amount of work. His lordship don't part with a farthing more than will keep the place from falling down. There's not many men around to choose from, neither. Mary would best be away from here."

"I can find her work in town," Solomon agreed. "But we'd need two more horses with their equipment.

"You'd only need another horse, if one of the females rides pillion." Abe turned to Grannie Irons. "I suppose your Mary can ride astride?"

"Ay, and she's a wentersome mawther."

"An adventurous girl," Abe translated.

"Tall and strong, too. Mary's not one to squeak and throw her apron over her head. Not much of a lady's maid, I guess, but she's a good worker and can protect the young lady. I know a man who'd sell a horse and hold his tongue, but he wouldn't have saddle nor bridle to sell, nor a pillion. You might get them in Maldon."

"I would call it a good idea except for certain difficulties. With Mistress Portia riding pillion, we could not travel even at the speed we would make without changing horses and with an inexperienced rider. Besides, a stranger purchasing a bridle, saddle, pillion, and horse only a day before a young lady vanished would cause talk. I know enough of country ways to be sure Furness would hear of it." Barlicorn would undoubtedly say he should leave no trace for Furness to follow.

"If you could hire a coach or carriage," Abe began.

"I don't know if it's possible in Maldon, but again, 'tis too close to Blackwater Hay. I've been staying at the coaching inn for days. It would cause talk. Hiring one in Chelmsford would be as bad as taking the public coach from there."

"If you cannot travel fast, you must travel slow. You cannot go by the stage or ride, and I misdoubt you will want to walk." Grannie Irons clucked in annoyance. "Let me think for a little on the way to do this."

"We must leave early in the morning, Mistress Irons."

"And you will. If you are set on taking your young lady away, I will have to visit the Hay to speak to my Mary. There's another I will see on the way." Coming to the end of her carded wool, she stopped turning the wheel, stood up and said, "I'll be away now. When I'm back, I will have thought how you can go."

"Can you visit Blackwater Hay without raising suspicions, mistress?"

She grinned at him saucily, and Sol could imagine her as a girl who had won a farmer's heart. "His lordship is so seldom here, those who work at the Hay do not live such narrow lives as the servants in most great houses."

"What of the ones hired for this visit?"

"They none of them love Furness, either. They'll all bow and scrape and speak respectful, but they won't tell him aught."

****

There seemed to be more hours in the day than usual, or else the hours were longer than sixty minutes each. Benedict was already at the breakfast table making labored conversation with Furness when she came down after changing into a suitable gown. They both stood when she appeared, Benedict a little tardily and still chewing a mouthful of bacon. The marquess came forward to take her hand and lead her to the chair beside his, ordering the footman to fill a plate for her. He did not ask her what she wanted to eat, though he did remember to ask whether she preferred tea or chocolate.

To her relief, it was not necessary to say much more.

"I must concern myself with estate matters later today, but I think this morning Mistress Portia and I will ride into Knight's Stow. Benedict, it may entertain you to see it, too. Blackwater Hay was first held by one of Duke William's knights. Our family has been elevated since, but our village's name has not changed. There is an ancient church, and some ruins that go back before the Normans. I've heard there are traces of the Romans, although I cannot swear to it myself.

"We will not make a long excursion of it, my dear, as you are not yet accustomed to spend hours in the saddle," he added to Portia. "I need not ask how Benedict means to amuse himself afterward, if he chooses to come. He will be off careering around the countryside, no doubt. I remember how I enjoyed riding around the estate by myself or with my brother. There cannot have been a fence, hedge, or wall we did not jump."

"I would like to see the ruins, my lord. I am fond of history." It would also prevent any tête-à-tête with Furness, especially if Benedict accompanied them. She directed a sisterly look at him.

"Excellent!" Benedict spoke after a slight pause occasioned by needing to swallow a mouthful. "I like ruins, too."

Her papa came in then and joined in the discussion of the antiquities to be found in Essex, relieving her of the need to do more than force down a few bites of breakfast. Her meeting with Solomon and Benedict's revelation had killed her appetite.

****

After they returned from their ride, Furness escorted her to the house, saying he hoped for a private word with her later in the afternoon but now needed to pay a call on a tenant.

His absence would give her a chance to speak with her father without the risk of being overheard. A question she had ignored until parting from Solomon stirred at the edge of her mind like the Thames lapping at the shore as the tide came in. She found Gillespie in the library, as expected. While she was not fond of confrontations, she owed him the chance to explain.

"Papa, you said my marrying the marquess would be an advantage to Benedict in his profession, but you have also spoken as if you expected him to live like a country gentleman, and I do not quite see how his being distantly connected to Furness could make both possible."

"'Tis possible to be a scholar and a gentleman. Indeed, most scholars are gentlemen, for the lower orders do not value education and do not go to university. You would not deny I am both."

"Certainly not. But several things you have said to Benedict suggest to me that you expect him to be a landowner. He cannot pursue a profession living in the country."

"Very true. However, when he is older and ready to take up my mantle"—as one of the preeminent scholars of Greek and Hebrew in England, he meant—"there is no reason he cannot reside in the country and write, without the annoyance of preparing dunces and the sons of cits for university."

Thomas Gillespie would enjoy the life of a pure scholar and country gentleman. She found it difficult to imagine Benedict being content in that role, though he did seem to enjoy riding and learning about agricultural matters. He had asked Furness's bailiff whether Tull's seed drill and horse-hoe were in use on Furness's land and received the embarrassed admission that they were not. "There is a small manor not far distant where they are employed to good effect, but his lordship prefers more traditional ways," the man admitted. This was likely a tactful way of saying he was unwilling to spend the money to acquire the new tools.

Portia drew a breath. "Is your inheritance sufficient to purchase a property that would permit my brother to retire to the country? I should think any property large enough to support a gentleman would be expensive, unless it were in poor condition through neglect."

"You need not concern yourself with such matters. They do not fall within a lady's proper sphere."

"Yet when you were ill and unable to tend to your affairs, sir, I necessarily became familiar with your finances. In similar circumstances, other ladies have found they must interest themselves in something besides needlework and chitchat." Not that she herself had been limited to those activities. "Now you are recovered, I cannot conveniently forget what I learned, as I would be unlikely to forget the Greek or Hebrew alphabets even if I never used them again."

"Then you understand why it is essential that you should marry Lord Furness."

Portia paused to be certain her growing annoyance did not show. "No, sir, I do not. You have yet to explain how such a marriage will benefit our family enough to make it possible for my brother to join the ranks of landed gentry."

"Rrumpf!" He began to frown.

She changed direction before he could take further offense. "I wish I understood why the Marquess of Furness would want to marry me when he must know so many more suitable ladies. Surely many of them would bring a dowry as well as noble antecedents. It cannot be for love, when he has not spoken a word hinting at any feelings for me, and how could he, when he hardly knows me?"

"I own I am surprised to find you expressing romantic nonsense at your age and with your education. Furness knows what will suit him."

"Yet he must know of others with the same qualifications. Why choose me?"

"He met you, formed the opinion you would be a well-behaved marchioness, unlikely to be extravagant or wish to figure in society or set up your will against his. He is ready to marry again as soon as may be. His reasons matter little. You should be rejoicing at this opportunity. As your father, I would be derelict in my duty if I failed to arrange such a very advantageous marriage for you."

"I see." Gillespie's evasiveness confirmed her formless suspicions. Some very significant benefit must attach to her marriage, not only to allow for the acquisition of even a small estate but to allow her father to dispense with her services as a copyist. He was not clever about money, but they had never exceeded their budget (except in the matter of Benedict's school fees) until his illness.

His face cleared. "Excellent! You are prepared to receive Furness's addresses, then. I knew your sense of duty would overcome any foolish female hesitation. The marquess means to seek you out before supper today, and we will toast your brilliant match in champagne tonight."

She dared not correct his assumption. "When we go back to town, I must purchase two or three things, like stockings and a night rail and one or two other items. If there is enough money, I would like a new gown as well." She disliked misleading him but saw no way to avoid it. If she had meant to marry Furness, it would be true that she would not wish him to see her threadbare night rails and smocks and darned stockings. Her father had seen no need to order new garments for the visit to Blackwater Hay, a decision she had endorsed, feeling that her papa's windfall should not be squandered, given how close they had come to disaster. But she had not known the real purpose of their stay with the marquess.

“There is no need. Furness means to wed before the end of the year and will see to clothing you as befits your new station.”

Benedict must be correct about the dinner party tomorrow celebrating the wedding. Her father did not notice her nervous swallow. “Then perhaps when you return to London, Mama can purchase one or two small wares for me and send them on.”

“Your mother and Benedict will be remaining in the country while I go back to take care of some matters. I will be too busy to shop for fripperies.”

“They do not go home with you?”

He was vexed, judging from a slight change around his eyes and lips, familiar to her when one of his scholars could not grasp some simple point.

“No. You will be pleased to know they—and I, once I return—will be living not far away, at a small manor Furness owns. ’Tis the one I visited with him. It needs a resident landlord, though the bailiff seems capable.”

“That is a surprise.” After a moment, she was able to say, “How pleasant for you.” She wanted to ask if Gillespie received the favor in return for pushing her into marriage with the marquess. Her father’s income from investments and writing was not adequate to support their family in London without the money he made from tutoring. It would be cheaper to live in the country, but there would be rent to pay, and if he meant to support the style of even the least affluent country gentleman, he would need more revenue.

Unless… He had used the phrase “resident landlord.” Thomas Gillespie was exceeding precise in his use of language. A landlord was by definition one who rented out property he owned, which would make her father a member of the landed gentry. Solomon had remarked that Pipperidge Rise was not entailed, meaning the marquess could dispose of it by sale or gift. If Furness was giving her father the manor in return for her own hand in marriage, it supported Solomon's contention that she was a great heiress. It would make sense for both parties: Furness would get her money, and Papa would be a country gentleman who could devote himself to scholarship without the need to tutor boys and young men or to write to earn money.

Her linen smock suddenly felt damp with perspiration. Forcing down her anger, she managed to murmur, "How convenient that will be. If you will excuse me, sir, I will see if my mother would enjoy a stroll in the garden."

"Pray do not mention this matter to her. The marriage is to be a surprise for her and for Benedict. I have no patience with the exclamations and endless discussion of unimportant details which would result if she knew of it."

He had kept one finger between the pages of the book he had been studying when she came in. Now he opened it and resumed reading.

She enticed her mother out to the garden for a short time, after convincing her that the walls around it would block the wind. Her poor mama clearly knew nothing of the matter except she had noticed the marquess paid Portia a flattering amount of attention, considering their respective ranks.

"But he should not slight you as he does, Mama."

"Nonsense, my love. I would be thrown into

confusion if he addressed more than the merest commonplaces to me. I find him quite terrifying. What a pity he will look high for a wife. How wonderful it would be if he chose to make you an offer."

Just as Portia began to feel guilty that Eliza would be disappointed, her mother's smooth brow wrinkled ever so slightly. "Although I am not at all sure I would care to marry him, if I were young and unmarried, I mean. I fear I would never get over being intimidated by his lofty manner. Which I think hardly justified by the state of this house and his table. Why, eight dishes in each course is no more than a decent family dinner," she remarked. "He must be stingy or else not plump in the pocket, as my father would have said. Not that you are to use such an expression," she added hurriedly. "Though it may only be that he does not keep servants enough in the kitchen to manage more dishes."

Chapter 23

She looked forward to her interview with the marquess with the dread of a felon awaiting the gallows and hoped it might not occur until evening. He did not grant her so long a stay, approaching her shortly before supper to beg a word with her in the gallery.

His choice of the gallery added another cause for alarm. It was distant from the parts of the house where her family was, and the servants would have no reason to enter it or use the passage in that wing except when cleaning it or laying a fire in the hearth. If he chose to assault her there, no rescue would come. Solomon de Toledo's warning about Furness was at fault for her apprehension, which must be unfounded. The marquess might have chosen the gallery because Eliza and Frances were working at their needlework in the drawing room and Gillespie had retreated to the library, the only two rooms which were comfortable and private. The others, apart from the bedchambers and dining room, seldom had fires lit in them, meaning the damp and chill would not easily be banished. Benedict might be anywhere, of course.

She hoped Furness had no reason to think she would be reluctant to marry him, and therefore no reason to compromise her, unless her father had spoken of her hesitation. Besides, to carry out a rape immediately before entertaining her family at the evening meal seemed…undignified, at odds with the marquess's correct manner. No, the time to worry about would be after she retired for the night, and she could prevent any intrusion by locking her door, which she would certainly do. She might put some piece of furniture in front of the door, too, the close stool perhaps, so that if he contrived to unlock it even with the key in the lock, the noise would alert her.

In any event, his proposal was not the ordeal she had anticipated. Fires burned at both ends of the gallery; the marquess must have given orders to make sure it was relatively warm. Several many-branched candle stands gave a cheering light.

Furness led her to the fireplace nearest the door, took her hand, and began, "You are aware of my regard for you, Portia…"

He did not go down on one knee. When her girlhood friends had spoken of their ideal imaginary proposals, Portia had wondered whether any suitor actually did so. It seemed like the action of a very callow young man. To expect it was a schoolroom miss's dream of melting glances, ardent sighs, and comparisons of her various attributes to the sky, the stars, pearls, gems, the sun, roses, ripe cherries, and the like.

The rest of his speech was as passionless as a lecture on Latin grammar, for which she was glad. He ended with, "I wish to make you my marchioness."

She raised her eyes from her shy contemplation of his hand, expecting his question. It did not come. He gazed down at her, all cool composure, eyebrows slightly elevated.

"I am overcome at the honor you do me, my lord."

Her voice catching in her throat, emerged timidly. She could not have acted the part as well if she had tried.

"My dear, you have made me the happiest of men. I believe you owe me a kiss."

He had not asked her to marry! He had taken her assent for granted, sparing her having to agree. Relief washed over her. Abruptly he tilted up her chin and pressed his lips to hers. It was not the kiss romantic tales had led her to expect. Its force pressed her own lips against her teeth almost painfully. When his tongue penetrated her mouth, she would have pulled away, but one of his hands was behind her head and the other was roaming over her bodice. When he finally released her, her reddened cheeks and palpitating bosom evidently pleased him, for he smiled.

"I believe we have time before supper to share the happy news with your father and mother."

She resisted the impulse to wipe her lips. The thought of eating turned her stomach. On the other hand, she would have had no appetite if she were still awaiting his proposal, either. Now it was past and had removed her last vestige of reluctance to flout decency by running away. Perhaps other men's kisses were as disgusting, though one or two old friends had gone into raptures over their first kiss or the kiss of their betrothed. One thing was certain: while she might not be able to prevent Furness kissing her once more today, she would not suffer a third.

She did endure Papa's self-congratulatory approval and her mother's exclamations. Benedict expressed his felicitations to Furness with a bland formality which might have been copied from a book on deportment. He possessed a greater talent for dissimulation than she had realized. He wished her every future happiness with becoming solemnity, though from the twitch of his lips she interpreted the sentiment as meaning "away from Furness." Frances Sedgewick smiled and twittered anxiously.

Champagne was served, and the marquess casually mentioned he had invited some of the local gentlefolk to dine in two days' time.

That night, Portia made a little collection of possessions she felt she must take with her: a simple wool gown, two chemises, a night rail, her prettiest cap, two pairs of stockings, her brush and comb, handkerchiefs (because it would be horrid to be without them if her nose should run in the cold), a pair of shoes for indoor wear once they arrived in town. She tied them all into her wool mantle, adding her Book of Common Prayer at the last minute. A few smaller items, like her spare hairpins and her remaining money she would carry in the pockets she could tie on under her skirt. She had only shoved her bundle under the bed when Mary came with hot water to prepare her for bed.

The maid saw her guilty start. "Are you truly meaning to leave with your gentleman in the morning?"

"What…?"

"My grannie come this morning to tell me he planned to take you away and wanted me to come for decency. He sent no written message as he and his peddler friend who's staying with Grannie had to make plans. She said you should dress warm and not bring too much with you. He sounds nice, your London gentleman. Will we go, mistress?"

"Do you want to come with me, Mary?"

"Ay, right glad to get the chance. Grannie says

working in a gentleman's house can be pleasant if there's a decent family. It wouldn't be bad even if they didn't live there, if there was enough servants for company and to share the work. I'd not have stayed at the Hay, but there's few folks that need maids around here and I won't live with my stepfather. Can't live with my grannie or he'd come and bluster and demand I come home to keep house for him and his brats. In London, I'll get work somehow. Grannie says your beau swears he can find me a place."

"Very well. You'll come here with what you mean to take at first light?" She ignored the girl's use of the word "beau" to describe Solomon de Toledo. What was the point of getting into that discussion?

"Before then, to help you dress. We'll be away as soon as we can."

Almost too nervous to sleep, Portia found it a comfort to know she would have someone with her.

****

Mary's presence was reassuring as they waited, screened from the road by the thicket. All the same, they had not spoken since leaving Portia's chamber, fearing to make a sound. They were too far from the house now to worry about being heard, yet even the maid's placidity must be somewhat daunted by the prospect of their flight. She herself was too nervous to make conversation.

The sound of a horse's hooves accompanied by rattling brought her out of her agitated musings about the wisdom and the impropriety of her actions. Her mama would be prostrated; her father would be disappointed and furious. Benedict would approve, though she wished she had had the opportunity to tell him all was settled. Perhaps it was for the best, as he would not have to exert himself to show surprise.

"That's no horseman," she whispered to Mary.

"No, mistress." She moved forward stealthily and peeked out. "I recognize the cart. That's how Grannie decided we're to go. Come." She picked up the burlap bag holding her spare clothing and pushed through the brush.

Portia had not considered how Solomon de Toledo would spirit her away, her mind having been too taken up with dread of Furness's proposal. Had she given it a moment's thought, she would have expected a coach hired from the nearest livery stable, as her rescuer knew she was no horsewoman. The sight that met her eyes in the gray dawn light gave her pause.

The cart rolled to a halt. By then, Portia had followed the maid, praying that it did indeed mean rescue. It looked like some of the farm carts she had seen: two wheels and high sides, drawn by a single horse, with the addition of supports at each corner to hold up an arched canvas cover. Panels of canvas were rolled and tied around the top, ready to be let down to enclose the cart bed.

A man and an old woman sat atop some sort of bench in the front of the cart. When the man saw them, relief lightened his somber expression, and he clambered down. Mary tossed her sack over the side, saying, "I'll take the reins from Grannie while you help Mistress Portia climb in." Somehow she scrambled up without assistance.

The man—could it be de Toledo?—wore a wide-brimmed hat, a long smock, and baggy breeches with coarse woolen stockings rolled up over the knee. His torso was strangely thick. Additional clothing underneath the smock? Or padding to make him look burly? He removed his gloves to take her bundle and his hands were the ones she remembered: well-manicured and uncallused. When he murmured, "You came. I feared you would not be able to leave the house or would have changed your mind. Come, let's be off," it was Solomon's voice.

At the cart's tail, he unfastened the latches that secured the back panel to let it down and slung her belongings inside. Bending, he offered his joined hands as if to help her mount a horse.

She placed her left foot on them, hoping she was not too heavy, and he lifted her with no obvious effort so she could step up to the cart bed. She preferred not to wonder if Solomon had caught a glimpse of her ankle…by the merest mischance, of course.

The cart held a long canvas bag stuffed full of something, her own parcel, two or three other bags and a valise. She hoped the floor was not splintery, if she must sit on it. Solomon raised the cart tail and fastened it.

"I'll assist Mistress Irons to alight." He strode toward the front. Mary was now sitting on what appeared to be a blanket chest, very old, very plain, and scarred by long use and water damage. She had the harness lines in hand. The other woman stood, and Solomon swung her down to the ground. She heard a few soft words, then he sprang into the cart more nimbly than she expected.

He tugged loose the ties binding the rolled canvas at the back and sides, enclosing three sides of the wagon.

"There's a mantle and a cap in the second largest canvas bag, and blankets. If you would put away your own cloak for now, the other garments will make you look like a country woman. It's best you stay out of sight, but if someone does catch a glimpse of you, he'll not see a young lady, only a farmer's wife or sister. You should be warm enough. You can sit on the biggest bag."

"Whatever is in it won't be damaged?"

"It's full of hay, oats, and a blanket for the horse."

Mary turned on the box. "We'd best be away."

"Ay. I promise you, Portia, it will be all ri—" The word was cut off as the cart jerked into motion. He caught his balance and took his place on the chest beside the maid.

"Once we're past Maldon, sir, I'll show you how to drive."

"My thanks, Mary." Over his shoulder, he added, "I've never driven a cart before. Thank God for Mary and her grandmother, who knew where to get one and how to drive it."

No one spoke again for some time. The dapple gray clopped along. Portia huddled in a blanket-like blue wool mantle that ended at the hip and smelled of lavender. Pulled up around her neck, it kept her warm. Bumpy as the ride was, she was glad they were moving along at a brisk pace; what if someone discovered their absence too soon? After a while, she pulled aside the curtain to peek out.

"Is this not the way to Maldon?"

"It is."

"Is it safe? Will he not expect us to take this road?"

Mary said, "His lordship lies abed later than this.

No one else will know you are gone as I made up the fire in the kitchen as if I had heated water for you." She ruminated. "When the servants breakfast, they'll wonder where I am. They'll not mention it, not to the marquess. His lordship does not like to be bothered with questions. Problems are always the fault of the servants."

Solomon turned on the bench. "The greater danger is your mother coming to your chamber early. Will she not be all a-flutter over your imminent marriage? I know my mother would want to help my sister decide what gown to wear and, er, talk to her about female matters."

Portia ignored the maid's snort.

"Yes, if she knew the wedding was to be tomorrow. Papa did not tell her because he dislikes female flutterings. He might also fear she would tell me. Neither my father nor the marquess mentioned I was to be rushed into marriage so soon."

Mary muttered something rude under her breath. Solomon's lips twitched.

" 'Tis at most five miles from Blackwater Hay to Maldon. We would be there within the hour, but instead, we will turn off short of the town to go south a little way. We have no other choice. Essex is a peninsula and singularly unsupplied with useful roads. The one that passes through Mundon ends at Fambridge on the River Crouch.

"In spite of the name, as best I can determine, there is no bridge. Like the Blackwater, it's an estuary rather than a river. There may be a ferry, but we cannot count on it, and if the weather turned bad, we might be trapped there. I dared not inquire much about roads at the inn at Maldon, but I have two maps I brought from London, though one is forty years old and the other fifteen. I don't know how accurate they are.

"The way we will take has several advantages: it's not a stage route until we reach Billericay, and then the coach runs but once a week. From there we go south, still not on a coaching road. When we are near the Thames, we are east of London. From the maps, it would not be above twenty miles or so from Maldon to the Thames if we could fly, but the road meanders somewhat until Billericay. Once we turn west, it's another twenty miles to London. More or less."

"More, if the weather does not hold," Mary interjected.

"We must get as far as possible before we stop. In any case, we will have to stay at an inn, given the shortness of the day at this season."

Once they left the road to Maldon, Mary commenced to teach Solomon how to handle the ribbons. Conversation lapsed except for Mary's occasional advice. "Tell Dumpling to gee-up and she'll turn right," and " 'Haw' for 'left,' now."

The rigidity of Solomon's shoulders either signified the stress of learning a new skill or apprehension they were being pursued. She certainly felt the latter, although the risk to her was only to be forced to marry Furness if he could make her say the vows. Surely no clergyman would perform a marriage if the bride refused.

But what would Furness do to Solomon de Toledo if he caught them? That question occupied her mind to the exclusion of all else. Would he murder him? Hale him before a magistrate and charge him with abduction? And the same with Mary, perhaps? Would her word that she had begged the maid and de Toledo to save her from an unwanted marriage do any good?

"Mistress, there's food in that covered basket. We should have some bread and cheese to break our fast."

Cutting cheese and bread and serving them out distracted her briefly. She discovered she was hungry and felt better after eating. Once Mary was done, she took the reins again to give Solomon a chance to eat.

"We are making good time, for which I am obliged to Dumpling. I bought her for riding, but fortunately she was also trained to pull a wagon. I meant to sell her in London."

"Have you changed your mind? I thought stabling was dear in town."

He swallowed. "It is. However, I've a family connection who has stabling, and I believe he will take her in for less than the usual rate. Her paces do not make her a comfortable ride, but…"

"You like her and would fear she would be mistreated."

He flushed. "Well…yes."

"I'm glad. You have rescued both of us." This comment must have rendered him speechless, for he applied himself to eating his portion.

Chapter 24

They went through Billericay at a sedate walk. The High Street was lined with substantial buildings both old and new, and the church testified to the town's age. It was midday, but no one suggested stopping for a hot meal, though there was a pleasant-looking inn. The farther they could get from Blackwater Hay, the better. By now, her absence would have been noticed.

"We should stop soon so we can eat a little more and water Dumpling, who might also like a bite. I hope we can make Orsett, or near it, before dark. Judging by the map, 'tis another twelve or fifteen miles."

By way of response, Mary encouraged Dumpling to trot.

Portia sensed Solomon was worried but only by the set of his shoulders, and that could be no more than tension at their situation and at learning to drive. When he remembered, he commented on the scenery, told amusing stories about his childhood and his siblings, and related some mildly scandalous stories about the court circle.

Twilight was on them when the cart creaked into Orsett and they beheld a timber-framed inn a little way beyond the church. Portia no longer worried about being caught by Furness; freezing seemed a greater danger. By now they were all wrapped in the blankets donated by Grannie Irons.

Dressed as they were, requesting hot baths was out of the question; Solomon had some difficulty convincing the innkeeper they needed two chambers, not a single one with a truckle bed. The man took them for a poor farm family.

"If you don't mind spending your coin, I'm agreeable to let you have two, as there's no gentry folk likely to come." He jerked his head toward the fireplace. "There's room to warm yourselves, and if you want supper, there's roasted cow's udder and roots."

"Ay, that'll do us well and the sooner, the better," Solomon said.

An hour later, full of roast meat, carrots, parsnips, and turnips, accompanied by bread and butter, Portia was glad to retire to the room she and Mary would share and latch the door, though she would not sleep until Solomon returned from the stable.

"Knock on the door when you come back," she said when he told her he wanted to make sure Dumpling was well settled.

He was not gone long, though Mary was already snoring gently when Portia answered the three soft taps and heard Solomon wish her a good night.

****

Solomon had slept undisturbed in the plain little inn bedchamber. Even so, he half suspected Furness or his henchmen would be waiting downstairs. Instead the room was empty but for two or three other travelers. His careful planning had won them a day. Unaccustomed to informal prayer, he found himself thinking, *Let me succeed in saving Portia. For once let me not make a fool of myself.*

He went up again to let Portia and the maid know it

was safe to come down whenever they should be ready. Portia opened the door, Mary close behind her. Both appeared none the worse for their hurried journey and consumed a hearty breakfast. Solomon avoided the bacon and ate cold mutton ham instead.

In response to his question, Portia admitted she was somewhat stiff, and Mary volunteered that her backside was sore, but both were cheerful, if anxious to reach town.

"We'll be in London before dark." *If nothing goes wrong.* After that, he was quiet. Now that the prospect of imminent pursuit was behind them—he hoped!—he needed to decide where they were to go once they reached the city. The question had not seemed worth worrying about when he had expected worse trouble on the road.

He had originally intended to take Portia to Hawkins's home on York Street. As they rolled down the Essex Road, certain objections arose. Hawkins was a friend and would take her in, but how would Lady Emily Hawkins react? Especially to their arriving in a farm cart, dressed like rustics? He had not met Lady Emily. All he knew of her was that she was the daughter of a duke and that Hawkins had married her for social advancement. Captain Easterday claimed she had been zealous in extricating Hawkins from the murder charge; she might be less straitlaced than one would expect. Still, it would be best not to cause a stir among their neighbors.

The same objections held true for any other reputable establishment he could think of. An inn? The tale would be all over town in a day. Portia felt it unwise to stop at her parents' house, even to change into her other gown and to collect whatever clothing she had left there. He inclined to think she was correct. Her father and Furness might have expected her to take refuge there. The Earl of Barlyon would have welcomed them at Barlyon House which had the advantage of being in a less exclusive part of town, but he and his countess were in Kent. He could take Portia to his mother. She would shrug off their absurd transport. She might welcome Portia with open arms, seeing her as a prospective daughter-in-law, and would bend every effort to making it so. His father would greet them absentmindedly and rush off to see one or more of his patients. By the time he returned, he would have forgotten they had a house guest until he saw her at supper. The rest of the family, unto the most distant cousins, would soon hear of it. The female cousins would assume he was courting Portia, and the men would conclude he had yet again done something ill-considered. They would all agree he must marry her.

The thought was not unappealing. His great-grandfather would have been appalled. Grandfather would have wished them well, if it were a love match. His own scruples in the matter of marriage were hardly rational, given that he did not live strictly according to Jewish law. He did not eat pork as a rule and tried not to eat meat and dairy products at the same meal. Some schools of thought would hold that their dinner of cow's udder the previous night was not lawful. But none of the meat he ate in inns and ordinaries was ritually slaughtered, and he had given up trying to determine which fish had fins and scales and thus was *kashrut.* He did not eat eels, less because they were *treifah* than because they looked like snakes. Ugh!

If he were inconsistent in his dietary observance, why boggle at marrying a Christian? Well, because he wanted his children to be Jews. Still, he had heard it alleged the tradition that only the children of a Jewish mother were Jewish went back no further than the Middle Ages. Would it really be worse than eating shrimp or oysters?

The Essex Road ran inexorably into White Chapel Road. They had traded off driving again, for while Mary handled the lines better than he, Solomon knew London and would not be distracted by its sights and sounds, or made nervous by the number of wagons, coaches, barrows, sedan chairs, and riders, not to mention the people and dogs cutting across the streets between vehicles.

The idea struck him with the force of a blow: the nearest and most private place he and Portia could go to make themselves presentable and leave the cart was his grandfather's house near the White Chapel Road, just outside the ancient City of London. They would attract no attention there. Taken on a long-term lease when his great-grandfather was still in the prime of life, Solomon's father had inherited it and his older brothers had lived in it at various times before acquiring better lodgings. He lived there now, with an elderly widow who kept house for him, and a boy to run errands, carry the coal and water and anything else too heavy for Mistress Wynn. Another woman came in once or twice a week to do the heavier work. It was perfect.

And it would be ruinous to bring a lady to his home when he had no mother, wife, or even a mature sister on the premises to chaperon her. If anyone found out, she would have no reputation left.

On the other hand, her flight from Blackwater Hay was equally damaging if it were known. Would her family cast her off if the events of the last two days were made public? Once he would have said no. In light of Mr. Gillespie's recent behavior, he doubted the man would defend her.

Gillespie stood to lose the confidence of the men who sent him their sons to tutor. God forbid their innocent boys should be exposed to a wanton female! He would face the choice of keeping his daughter or his livelihood.

If any of Portia's actions came out, she would have to marry any man who was willing to marry her. How could they keep the cat in the bag? Her family would not advertise her shameful behavior. Certainly neither he nor Portia would mention it. Mary was a sensible girl; a word to her would guarantee her silence. Besides, she counted on him to find her work. Furness was the real danger. Would the humiliation of having his suit scorned outweigh his determination to secure Portia's fortune?

All they could do was conceal the way she had arrived in London and hope it was enough. He signaled Dumpling to turn right, and they rattled down a street as familiar to him as the faces of his family.

"Mistress Portia, I think we must stop at my home long enough to change clothing so we look like respectable persons. I will send for a hackney, and we will call upon a friend to ask if he and his wife can take you in until we have made arrangements for you to see Sturgis's attorney." Once she had her inheritance, she would be able to hire a companion, lease or buy a house, start a new life. Probably not in London, but somewhere. "I realize it's not ideal…"

"It's certainly preferable to Blackwater Hay and the marquess." Beneath her briskly practical reply ran an undercurrent of anxiety.

"It will be all right." *I hope.* "You should write immediately to Sturgis's attorney to tell him you will call upon him tomorrow. His name is Bertram Keswick, in Chancery Lane."

"Will he see me without an appointment? I suppose he is very busy and will have to put me off for a day or two. Or more."

Solomon turned his head long enough to grin at her. "Oh, he will see you if you give him a day's notice. You are a great heiress, after all."

"It doesn't seem quite real."

"It will. You've only known of it since the day before yesterday."

He stopped the cart before the narrow house where he had spent five years as a child. It stood cheek by jowl with its neighbors, better kept than many in the street but still very simple. Passing the reins to Mary, he climbed down stiffly. "As soon as the cart's unloaded, I'll take it and Dumpling to an acquaintance in the neighborhood who's a carter and ask him to board Dumpling in exchange for the cart." Solomon could not think about asking his uncle to stable the mare until Portia's situation was resolved.

****

Two hours later he presented himself in his best suit, wearing the sapphire ring he had once taken as surety and the owner had never redeemed. It had not been his borrower's family heirloom; he had won it at cards. The ring was a handsome one, fit him, and gave him an air of fashion. The latter was desirable as he was calling on a very wealthy friend living in close proximity to St. James's Square. Still, they were oddly assorted: Portia's attire was plain though of reasonably good quality. Mary looked like an awkward country girl.

He introduced Portia to Hawkins, and Hawkins took them to Lady Emily Hawkins who was all that was gracious. Possibly she was misled by his velvet suit, the lace at his neck and cuffs, and the ring. Or perhaps she remembered his name, for she greeted him with unmistakably genuine warmth.

Hawkins added, "De Toledo is a friend of the Earl of Barlyon."

"It is enough that he is a friend of yours, Ambrose." Then she tactfully excused herself, saying, "Mistress Portia, while I have a chamber prepared for you, let us have tea in my sitting room. Do you want your maid to sleep on a truckle bed in your bedchamber or in the servants' quarters?"

"It might be best if she stays with me. Mary is not a London maid, merely a chambermaid from a country house, hired to accompany me on our journey. I realize this must seem very unusual conduct…"

"I have become accustomed to the irregular, these last few months. Your arrival does not compare with some of my actions since my marriage." With a nod to Solomon and a faint smile for her husband, she led Portia from the study.

"What a terrible experience you have had!"

Lady Emily's exclamation after Portia recounted the events leading to her arrival at the Hawkins house was reassuring. There had been no way of avoiding an explanation of why a respectable if slightly bedraggled spinster should suddenly appear on their doorstep in company with Solomon de Toledo. Any reasonable person would wonder, even if she had appeared with a nobleman. She had feared Lady Emily might be shocked. Instead she was sympathetic. Remembering a remark of Solomon's, Portia wondered if it was because Mistress Hawkins herself had been forced to marry against her inclination.

Yet if she had, the marriage had turned out well; Portia could not have mistaken the fondness in Lady Emily's expression when she looked at Hawkins.

"I know it must seem strange I would refuse an offer from a marquess," she began.

Her hostess ran her right thumb over the square emerald in her ring before responding. "While many might agree, I do not. Your situation, Mistress Portia, is almost the opposite of what mine was when I agreed to marry Hawkins. My cousin's financial difficulties, and hence mine, were extreme, and I need not hesitate to say as much because it was certainly no secret. It was absolutely necessary I wed a man of fortune, even if I would not have considered him otherwise. But having met Ambrose, I liked him and decided it would be no sacrifice.

"In your case, it was not clear why you were being pushed to marry the marquess, and you did not like him, understandably, given that he evidently planned a wedding dinner before receiving your agreement. Such arrogance would not be pardonable even in a duke. I do not wish to offend you, but I cannot think your father did right to promote the match without consulting you. My cousin discussed the matter of my marriage with me and would have accepted my decision had I refused."

"There is no need to apologize, Lady Emily. I am quite annoyed with my father." Bitter disappointment and anger were emotions too strong to confess, when she had told Emily Hawkins only that he wanted her to marry Furness for the family's good and had not mentioned how he had connived at it. "I believe his illness affected his brain." Or perhaps he had simply never before had an opportunity to sell her advantageously.

Lady Emily said tolerantly, "Men," and poured her another cup of tea. "How do you like Solomon de Toledo? I had never met him before you came, although he was the one who arranged my marriage. He gave my cousin excellent advice on several topics, too. And one would not know him from a gentleman, in spite of his business."

"He is a gentleman! In the best meaning of the word," Portia added. "His birth may not qualify him, but in honor, merit, and virtue, he deserves the title. To call a man of defective character a gentleman only because of his birth…"

"No, no, I agree with you. I was only voicing common opinion. Some would hold his origins against him, but in all respects I consider him a worthy friend. A lady might do far worse for a husband."

Struck dumb, Portia sipped her tea.

"I am not trying to be a matchmaker. However, I feel I must point out that de Toledo and Hawkins do not understand society as I do. No matter how careful de Toledo was in aiding you to leave Furness's estate, and however we try to conceal your return to London, there will be talk. Servants do talk—yours, mine, Furness's. It will all soon be an open secret. Be prepared for it. We may be able to avert the worst, but it may still come to your needing to marry. I would suggest asking de Toledo to find you a man who needs a wife with money, as he did such an excellent piece of work in matching Hawkins and me…"

"But his having been the one who helped me run off would make it awkward," Portia finished. "Unless no one knows that fact?"

Emily smiled wryly. "Someone knows he brought you here, and while our own servants might not mention it except to their particular friends and family members, someone in another house or who was passing by might well have seen."

"How would they know who he was? Or care?"

"While I may not know a great deal about the commercial world, since my marriage I have learned something of it. Solomon de Toledo is not some quaint foreign street peddler. He may not be a…a *personage*, but he is known to the segment of the beau monde which needs to borrow money, or marry it."

"Oh." She had not thought of Solomon being anyone in particular.

"I might have Hawkins sound him out on the subject of marriage. As you trusted yourself to him, you evidently do not hold him in aversion. While it might not be the perfect match, he is presentable and very sensible about finances, as I know from his advice to my cousin. The 'perfect match' does not exist outside the imaginations of schoolroom chits."

"I would rather Mr. Hawkins not broach the subject. I don't want Mr. de Toledo to feel he must offer for me when he has already saved me from Furness. He may have an understanding with some lady. I can live retired in some other town where no one has heard of me." The prospect was not a cheering one, but she made the effort to smile.

"Quite unsatisfactory. If you do not wish to marry at the moment, we must use social power to establish your good name. Which will be easier to do as you are now a lady of fortune."

Hawkins and Solomon entered the drawing room, fortunately too late to hear Lady Emily's suggestion he speak to Solomon and her reply.

"May we join you, Emily?"

She assented, smiling up at her husband. Hawkins seated himself beside Lady Emily on the settee. "We realized—de Toledo did—we needed to consult you about our plans."

Solomon, to Portia's regret, chose an armchair at some distance from her.

"Our plans meaning your plans, Lady Emily, Mistress Portia, as well as what Hawkins and I have talked about."

"That is most considerate, Mr. de Toledo." Lady Emily's voice hinted at laughter despite her composure. Portia smiled. She suspected the notion of speaking with them had come from Solomon.

"Mistress Portia, did you leave word where you would be staying?"

"At Blackwater Hay, Mr. Hawkins? No. I didn't know. I didn't leave a note of any sort. I wish I could say I hoped it would be assumed I was taking a longer walk than usual, but I simply didn't think of it," she admitted. "I cannot explain the turmoil of my thoughts when I believed I might be trapped in marriage with the marquess."

"All to the good, I'd say, if it's delayed pursuit. Otherwise, I'd expect Furness to be in town by now, hunting for you. De Toledo?"

Solomon addressed Portia. "Now we must decide how to discourage Furness and preserve your reputation."

She had given no thought to what was to come after her flight from Blackwater Hay. Herding her thoughts into some sort of order proved difficult. Solomon de Toledo appeared as comfortable in the elegant room in a velvet suit as he had in her father's shabby study, dressed in a professional man's plain clothing. He was not precisely handsome. He lacked the fashionable pallid complexion and languor thought appropriate for gentlemen. On the other hand, Hawkins, who had come of the gentry class, did not possess them either. While his suit and embroidered waistcoat belonged to the beau monde, the breadth of his shoulders, his calf muscles, and his ruddy complexion suggested a strenuous life spent outdoors.

How many men were truly handsome, after all? But somehow, Solomon was very attractive. Far more so than the Marquess of Furness or any other man she could think of.

As Portia dithered, Emily said, "I believe we might pay calls. My friends Anne Guysbridge and Aurelia Barlyon, and my cousin—" She added in an aside to Hawkins, "He's really grown quite ducal," then continued, "—are in the country at the moment, unfortunately. Olivia Easterday is expecting an addition to their family in the near future and not really well enough for visitors. None of them are the sort to spread on-dits, anyway. We will make do with a few choice gossips."

The prospect loomed as terrifying as her escape from Blackwater Hay. She was not known in Lady Emily's circles, but would it be safe? "What if Furness pays a call at the same time?"

"He is hardly likely to do so as I believe he has little patience with ladies' chatter. He could hardly abduct you from a lady's drawing room anyway."

"He would learn where you are staying, however." Hawkins did not quite scowl. "Not that he would be able to get to you here, but Emily should not be upset." Because she was *enceinte*, Portia gathered.

"Furness in a temper is not likely to overset me." Lady Emily and her husband traded secret-sharing smiles. "Besides, it's necessary to establish Portia creditably and scotch any talk about Portia's marriage to Furness, and how else are we to do it?"

Hawkins did not reply. Indeed, his blank expression suggested his thoughts were miles away from the pretty blue and white room. "Emily, why would there be talk of marriage? Wouldn't it be best to conceal the whole incident?"

"Why, the newspaper yesterday morning—or was it the day before?—announced the betrothal."

"Oh, no." Furness had not only arranged their marriage and the wedding dinner but notified the papers as well. All with her father's agreement, no doubt.

"Awkward! How can you explain it away, when everyone will have taken note of a marquess's marriage?"

"Very easily, Ambrose. It was no more than a

malicious prank meant to humiliate Furness."

Hawkins guffawed. "Very good, my dear. All the same, it might be best for Portia to keep to the house. If you must speak with your attorney, have him come here. Until Furness learns that he cannot control your money, he might resort to desperate measures."

"Mr. de Toledo explained how things are left, then?"

"He felt I should know in order to be on guard against any knavish tricks."

"I applaud his good sense," Lady Emily said. "It's a tiresome habit of men to hug secrets to themselves out of mistaken notions of honor or to protect ladies who could protect themselves if they were aware of the facts."

Her husband grinned at her.

"I shall write to my more loquacious acquaintances out of town to tell them the ridiculous joke someone has played upon Furness."

"You need have no fear, ma'am. My lady is a dab at rescuing reputations." Hawkins must have noticed her unease. "She has almost dragged me into the beau monde in spite of my business and some other matters."

Solomon had mentioned the rumor Hawkins had been a pirate and his stay in Newgate while awaiting trial for murder. His experience cast her own problem into the shade. With an only slightly effortful smile, she responded, "I have every confidence all will be well." *Eventually.*

"That should help." Solomon spoke for the first time in some minutes. "But I think Mistress Portia and I must go to Sturgis's attorney's office. If he is summoned here, his clerks will know where she is staying. Furness learned of the inheritance somehow, and the likeliest source of his knowledge would be someone in that office. Unless…is it possible Mr. Gillespie contacted the marquess?"

She could not rule it out, except, "I'm sure he was not acquainted with Furness before Furness inquired about my father's tutoring services. It's hard for me to believe he would have known the marquess was in need of a wealthy bride."

"My theory holds, then. It would take only one indiscreet word. Even I had heard Sturgis left a fortune and that his supposed heir was an academic, and I have no connections to the legal community." After a moment, he added, "We ought to take Attorney Brigginshaw with us when we see Sturgis's lawyer."

"A pair of my footmen will accompany you, Sol. I refuse to have a guest abducted or a friend assaulted if it can be avoided. Tomorrow?"

Hawkins's words served as a reminder she was not out of danger yet. She hoped Solomon had some device in mind for permanently dissuading Furness from pursuing her. Or Brigginshaw might; including him had been an excellent suggestion. She trusted him, and he was familiar with the law.

"Ay, tomorrow. The sooner Portia is safe, the better."

Chapter 25

" 'Tis a wonderful fine house, and the servants almost like gentlefolk, too," Mary said. "Even if I am in rags and jags beside Lady Emily's maid."

Understanding her attendant's phrase to mean shabby, worn-out clothing, Portia admitted, "I'm not much better. I wish I might have brought another gown with me, but I didn't expect to be staying anywhere so fine."

"Couldn't have got another into your bundle, anyhow. We're away and that's the thing. Maggie, that's Lady Emily's maid, says she will teach me to sew very fine if we stay here a few days."

"I don't like to impose, but I suppose we must until I can make other plans." *With Solomon's help.*

They had done what they could with the gown she had worn to meet Hawkins and Lady Emily. The wrinkles had been ironed out—by Maggie—but there was not much improvement. It remained simple, practical clothing. Lady Emily had offered something of her own, only to find that it would need far too much alteration to be ready overnight. Mary's spare gown was both faded and mended. Lady Emily's maid, unfortunately, was too slender to be able to lend Mary one of hers.

Then a footman tapped at their door to inform Portia that Mr. de Toledo had arrived and Mr.

Hawkins's coach would be brought around in a few minutes.

"Are you sure it's safe to go to the house?" she asked after greeting Solomon.

De Toledo smiled at her. "If your parents have already returned, you still have nothing to fear. You are of age, and Hawkins has provided two footmen who look as if they would be useful in a brawl. And Sturgis's attorney will want proof of your identity."

She had her Book of Common Prayer with her, a gift from her papa, inscribed with her name and the date of her confirmation. They had discussed the question of proving who she was, but the thought still made her nervous.

"I'm sure the attorney will be satisfied with your prayer book, the letters you will collect at your home, and Mr. Brigginshaw. Your birth should be recorded in the parish register, too. That is always acceptable proof."

"I suppose it must be. My parents were already living in our house at the time, so the parish register would be easy to consult."

To her relief, her family had not yet returned from Blackwater Hay. Abby and William were surprised to see her, even more surprised she had come only to collect some things from her chamber, and curious about Mary, the burly footman who had taken up a post in the hall, and the fine coach at the door.

"I do not have time to explain now. Here is a letter for my father when he returns."

Ten minutes later, she was out the door, followed by Mary, carrying two bandboxes filled with a number of letters and with another gown and a few other necessary items of apparel. She managed to deflect the servants' questions about where she was staying. That information she had not included even in her letter, merely saying she had gone to visit friends as she refused to be forced to marry Furness.

What did they think about her disappearance at Blackwater Hay? Mary's absence at the same time should indicate that she herself had not simply become lost and suffered an accident on her morning stroll. Her father and the marquess might be combing the countryside, as her papa would guess she did not have enough money for coach fare. And what was her poor mother feeling? And Benedict? No, Benedict would know Solomon had helped her get away. He was unlikely to reassure Mama, as to do so would lead to Papa finding out. She regretted the worry her mother at least must be suffering. She feared her father and Furness were simply furious. What a tangle!

****

"Upon my word," Bertram Keswick said, after scrutinizing the pile of letters, the inscription in the Book of Common Prayer, and a sample of Portia's handwriting and signature. Extra chairs had been brought into his office to accommodate Portia's retinue of Mr. Brigginshaw, Solomon de Toledo, and Mary. "My dear Mistress Portia, I am disconcerted to find I have been misled. I understood from Mr. Gillespie that you were a shy, retiring young lady. I did write to you for confirmation of his allegation that you were content to leave matters regarding your inheritance in his hands and received a reply to that effect signed with your name. I can have my clerk bring it for your review, but it's obvious to me now it was a forgery. Your own hand is very different from that in the letter, and while an impostor might have stolen the letters and prayer book, nothing will convince me my colleague Brigginshaw would lend himself to a fraud. Even Mr. de Toledo has a reputation for unquestionable honesty."

Here Solomon bowed ironically. Portia stole a glance at him, surprised that the attorney knew anything of him. Perhaps Keswick's clients sometimes needed to borrow money outside their usual bank.

"I fear Mr. Gillespie practiced a deception upon me." Skewered by both Brigginshaw's and de Toledo's eyes, he went on hastily, "Not that it was successful. As I explained to him, your inheritance being safely in a trust, there was nothing for him to do in regard to its management. I did advance a portion of the quarter's funds to him, but only a hundred pounds."

Only a hundred pounds? Poor families live a year on less. Keswick continued, "The rest is still available, of course, and the next quarter day is at hand." He wrote something on a slip of paper and folded it before passing it to her. "Have you a man of business, madam?"

She opened the billet and glanced at it, expecting Attorney Keswick had made a note of his name and direction. Struggling with amazement at the amount of the funds remaining for the current quarter, she managed to reply, "No, sir."

"I can recommend one or two. Mr. Brigginshaw may know several more."

Her eyes went to Solomon. "The man who handles my affairs represents at least one peer. I've found him more than satisfactory. Or Ambrose Hawkins would know of someone."

"You are in good hands, then. Would you like me to pay out the balance of this quarter's funds? You should open an account with whatever bank one of these gentlemen advises and deposit it. Once you have a bank account, if you let me know who your banker is, I will transfer each quarter's income to it. Unless you prefer I pay it out to you directly, a course I do not recommend."

Portia could not answer at once. She had still not caught her breath at the jotted figure. "I must think about what will be best. As to this"—she held up the slip, now folded again—"will this not deplete the fund too quickly?"

Keswick laughed heartily. "No, indeed. The majority of the quarter's income is only the interest on the principal for the period, with the addition of your percentage of the profits from the manufactory, which is a much smaller amount."

"Is my brother's portion equally secure?"

"His trust fund was set up in precisely the same manner as yours. It will pass to his control on his twenty-first birthday. Until then I will disburse to Mr. Gillespie only such monies as are reasonably necessary for Master Benedict's support: school fees, clothing, a portion of the household expenses." He steepled his fingers. "I think, hmmm, ay, I do think I shall require accountings from Mr. Gillespie regarding the said expenditures and also a private interview with the boy several times a year."

As Keswick walked with them to the door, Solomon asked suddenly, "Sir, do you know how the Marquess of Furness might have become aware of Mistress Portia's inheritance? Or someone else, for that matter?"

The attorney blew out a chagrined breath. "If his lordship learned of it, I am sorry to say I can guess. It's an accepted fact that men in the same trade or profession will, er, talk about their interests when they meet. While it's permissible for grocers or seamen or farmers to do so, professional men should observe stringent confidentiality regarding their clients' affairs." His mouth turned down. "Unfortunately, the lawyer who represents Furness occupies chambers not a quarter mile from here. Need I point out there is an alehouse nearby? I do not patronize it, but my clerks and others do. I will question them, if you wish." He glanced at their intent faces. "Is there a particular reason you ask, Mr. de Toledo?"

"The marquess attempted to entice Mistress Portia into marriage while she and her family were staying at his Essex estate. It's likely he meant to force the issue."

"Zounds! If I can determine which clerk spoke of it, I will turn him off."

"Thank you, Keswick," Brigginshaw nodded. "I'm much obliged."

"The obligation is all on my side. Your servant, madam, gentleman."

****

Brigginshaw suggested going first to a bank to deposit the greater part of the money and then to his own office. "I believe Mistress Portia has some decisions to make. It might be helpful to discuss them."

She agreed. She had not thought beyond the meeting with Keswick because she had not quite believed she really was an heiress, certainly not of such a fortune. She had thought she would simply hire rooms in a respectable lodging with Mary to attend her and continue her copying work.

Brigginshaw's bank was endorsed by Solomon de Toledo, who pronounced it well managed. The banker who arranged for her account bowed very deeply when Brigginshaw murmured to him that she was one of Sturgis's heirs. Even after depositing the greater part of the funds, she had more money at hand than she could imagine spending in several months, let alone the few days remaining before the quarter day. The banker changed three guineas for smaller coins, too, offered her sherry and biscuits and congratulations, and wished her a happy Christmas as he accompanied them to the door.

In Chancery Lane, they had tea and buns fresh from a nearby bakery. After consuming half a bun and all of her tea, Portia broke the silence. "Tomorrow I must begin looking for a place to live."

Solomon's head snapped up from his contemplation of his tea bowl. Brigginshaw had raised his own cup. He set it down without sipping from it.

"Portia, Christmas is almost upon us. I misdoubt much can be accomplished until after Boxing Day. Best to bide where you are staying."

Solomon spoke. "Nor is there any need for you to search. I suggest you put the task in the hands of your man of business."

"Whom I have not yet chosen."

"That decision should come first. Until he has found several suitable properties for you to view, you may as well enjoy the season with Hawkins and Lady Emily."

"I do not like to intrude upon them further, sir."

"Hawkins assured me they consider it no imposition. Many of their friends are at their country homes, including Lady Emily's only surviving relative. Hawkins is kept in town by his business, and Lady Emily will appreciate the company of another lady. There is another point in its favor, as well—"

Brigginshaw darted a warning glance at him, with a slight head shake.

"Mr. Brigginshaw, Mistress Portia is a lady of unusual courage and resilience. She needs to know the reason for our recommendation."

The attorney gave a little laugh. "She is all you say and more. However, it is difficult to overcome one's tendency to protect the fairer sex."

"Perhaps it would be easier to protect us if you told us what we are being protected from," she observed, echoing Lady Emily's tart comment.

"Mistress Portia, you will be safer from abduction in Hawkins's home than you would be in most others. First, it is in a fashionable area where crime is less likely to be ignored. Second, you may have noticed Hawkins keeps some rather rough footmen and grooms. What they lack in the approved manner, they make up for by their usefulness in a scuffle. They are all dead loyal to him. He has regained some polish since he sailed before the mast, but he still has the instincts of a man who lives by his wits and fists."

"I see, S—Mr. de Toledo." That explained why a household as elegant as Lady Emily's employed a number of servants who looked as if they would be more at home on shipboard or wharves, in spite of their livery. She clasped her hands tightly in her lap. Now that she knew the extent of her fortune, she understood

Furness's interest in marrying her. She had been naïve to assume that merely getting to London would end the problem. She might not be secure until she married. Unless—"Mr. Brigginshaw, did I understand Attorney Keswick to say that the greatest part of my inheritance would not be available to my husband?"

"You did. He would not be able to get his hands on it under any circumstances. Not even if you predeceased him," he added. "Though Keswick did not say as much, I glanced over the documents. He would receive one-half your quarterly payments for the remainder of his life. The rest would be held in trust either for your children, or if you had none or they also died, it would pass to your brother. Sturgis was, as they say in North Britain, a canny man. I salute his foresight and Keswick's skill at drafting a tight legal document."

"Then if Furness knew about the terms of the trust, he would lose interest in me, would he not?"

"Perhaps not."

"Possibly."

Solomon's and Brigginshaw's replies cut across each other. She raised her eyebrows and looked from one to the other.

The attorney said, "You might be able to access the monies held in trust over and above your quarterly payments if you requested it and the trustees agreed. He might believe he could cajole or intimidate you into applying to the trustees. They would not be obligated to release the money unless they were convinced it would benefit you or your children. Your father is one of the trustees; the other two are Keswick and Walter Wildblood, who inherited the blast furnace works, and they are shrewd men."

“If he were informed of those facts? Particularly if the trustees were warned against him?”

“Then if he has the wit of a louse, I should think he would lose interest.”

Solomon inquired, “Did his attorney not review the documents? Surely Mr. Gillespie must have received a copy? Or at least been informed of the terms?”

Brigginshaw uttered a dry “Ha!” and sipped tea. “Furness’s attorney is not a shining ornament to our profession. He does well enough at drafting a simple will or a lease or bill of sale, though he is lazy. He may have relied upon hearing that Portia had inherited half of the Sturgis fortune. He would have no access to Keswick’s documents, of course. We know Tom received a copy from Keswick. Had I been acting for Furness, I would have insisted on reviewing them. But Furness’s man might not take extraordinary pains for him, as he’s unlikely to be quick about paying. Furness should have read the will and trusts himself. Taken all together, neither may have read the documents carefully.”

“I do not like to suggest this…” She did not miss the reluctance in Solomon’s voice. “The marquess does not seem to be a perceptive man. Mayhap he relied upon Mr. Gillespie’s report of the details, unaware that Gillespie is unsophisticated in legal affairs?”

“I have never met the marquess, but it’s true his actions relating to the case currently in Chancery would lead one to believe he is not swift to take legal advice. And you are quite correct that my old friend Gillespie could have misunderstood what he was told about the trusts.”

Solomon and Brigginshaw were charitable in their

suppositions. Eyes upon her clenched hands, Portia said, "I am sorry to say it, but he may simply have lied to Furness."

"My dear girl."

"I realize 'tis unfilial of me to mention it. I am heartily sorry. Yet given my father's actions since his apoplexy, I cannot dismiss the suspicion."

Solomon sat biting his lip. He might understand how she could suspect her papa of dishonest conduct.

"Well," Brigginshaw remarked, "for our purposes, Gillespie's lack of legal sophistication works to everyone's advantage." Meaning Furness could not well accuse Thomas Gillespie of fraud only for being ignorant, when Furness or his attorney had not read the documents, or else not understood them. "Do you wish me to request that Keswick write Lord Furness to make it clear that marriage to you will not benefit him?"

She hesitated. "Could you wait until my family returns to town?"

"Do you think Furness would do them harm? I scarcely think it. Though I will write to Gillespie, suggesting he return home at the earliest opportunity. Once they are away from Furness, I will write Keswick. After that, it may be safe for you to set up your own household."

She turned to Solomon de Toledo to ask his opinion. His gaze was unfocused. "Mr. de Toledo?"

He shook off his brown study. "Write to Furness, ay, an excellent notion. I may be able to throw a red herring in his path to draw him off, too."

"Can you? What?"

He shook his head. "It depends on someone else. If I can, it should be sufficiently distracting to make him forget about the Gillespie family."

Would it be dangerous to Solomon? She wanted to ask. Brigginshaw's brisk "The more arrows to our quiver, the better" prevented her question long enough to decide she should not inquire. It was too personal a query, implying she was concerned about his welfare. Which she was, of course. The moment passed. The gentlemen were discussing the advisability of Portia's return to York Street before dark.

Chapter 26

Portia had expected time to hang heavy on her hands as the men had agreed she should avoid going out. Instead the next day found the Hawkins house a veritable beehive of activity. She had only just finished breakfast when Lady Emily's mantua-maker arrived with one of her assistants, a dozen or more lengths of fabric, and a box of ribbons, laces, cords, and every other sort of embellishment a lady could desire. They also brought a robe volante, nearly finished, which had not yet been delivered when the lady's husband found himself bankrupt.

Portia stood rigid while Lady Emily and Madame Poiret surveyed the effect. "It appears to need only the slightest adjustment," Lady Emily observed.

"Having the young lady's old jacket and petticoat made everything easy." Madame's voice hinted at the heather and moors of Scotland. She had acquired her name by marriage to a French tailor rather than by birth and scorned to adopt a French accent.

"I hope you like the colors of the dress lengths. Our hair and complexions are similar so I relied on Madame Poiret's judgment."

The mantua-maker's expression resembled nothing so much as that of a kitchen cat who had dined upon chicken and custard.

"If Mistress Portia prefers different colors or

shades of them, I will be happy to send samples for her convenience."

"That is not necessary, Madame Poiret. Everything you have brought is precisely what I would have selected." *Had I ever dreamed of having anything so lovely.* "I need only decide which one to have made up."

"Which *one*? You must have several different mantuas, robes à l'anglaise, a new jacket and petticoat, and all the other necessities. I suppose you need not order a riding habit yet."

The number of garments to be ordered struck Portia speechless, which Lady Emily took to be thriftiness. "You do need clothing. If you do not wish to incur so much debt all at once, which I completely understand, I will happily pay for them and you may pay me back as you are able."

Which seemed to indicate Lady Emily and her husband were unaware of how much her quarterly income was.

Madame Poiret clucked. "The ladies I gown seldom pay all at once. To pay in installments is quite *convenable* as my husband says."

"Please agree, Portia. I really cannot bear to see you so lacking in suitable dress."

The implication being that she would be embarrassed by such a meanly clad guest.

"Thank you for your kind offer, Lady Emily, and thank you both for your understanding. I can afford whatever I need. It is only to overcome old habits of economy."

A tap at the door interrupted a lively discussion of whether the sacque gown should be made up in the blue-green or the peach and cream striped silk. Maggie opened the door a crack, a footman murmured, and the maid closed the door and approached Portia.

"A letter for you, mistress." She held out a little tray on which lay a letter. The direction had been written in Solomon de Toledo's unmistakable—to her—hand.

"Do read your letter, Portia. Madame Poiret and I will glance over the trimmings."

Mistress Portia,

This morning I received a letter from Master Benedict reporting that your family is now back in town. He wrote to me, being certain I would know where you are. On discovering you gone, Furness sent out grooms and footmen allegedly to search for you, feigning belief you must have sprained an ankle or become lost. Furness and Mr. Gillespie were both exceeding upset, as indeed they would be if you actually had merely failed to return from your morning walk. Mistress Gillespie did not think of asking if Mary had been questioned; your brother is quite sure Furness guessed the truth as the marquess said nothing of Mary's absence.

The marquess sent your family off in his coach. Benedict did not know whether Furness also meant to return to London. He might even have ridden and arrived before them.

I trust you are remaining securely indoors. I have taken the liberty of writing to Mr. Brigginshaw to apprise him of this development and encouraged him to write to Keswick at his earliest convenience.

Your most obedient,

SdT

Portia was still enjoying the relief of knowing her family was gone from Blackwater Hay when she received another letter from Solomon de Toledo:

Mistress Portia,

Furness is in London. The knocker has been replaced on the door. I mean to pay a call upon Brigginshaw to find out if he has heard from Keswick.

SdT

****

Not caring to allow time even for the usually speedy penny post, Solomon betook himself to Chancery Lane on learning of Furness's return.

That news was quickly imparted. In Brigginshaw's cozy office, the attorney sat, hands folded on his paunch and said, "I wish we knew whether Keswick has sent his letter. Until Furness has received it, Portia is not safe."

Solomon rotated the glass of sherry in his fingers. "No. It's time for me to put into action an idea that came to me a few days ago when we met here. I—"

A discreet tap at the door, followed by the arrival of Brigginshaw's soft-footed senior clerk, interrupted him. "Sir, Mr. Thomas Gillespie is requesting a meeting. He says it is a matter of urgency."

Brigginshaw rotated one forefinger, which the clerk interpreted as an instruction to close the door. "Wait a moment. De Toledo, through the door behind my desk. Leave it ajar, and you'll be able to hear. Ay, ungentlemanly, but Portia's safety must take precedence over correct manners. Take your sherry with you. I'll see him now."

"You won't tell him where Portia is?"

"No. I do want to question him discreetly,

however."

Solomon found the little chamber equipped with more bookcases, a small desk and chair, a divan, and a close stool. With the sensation of taking part in a farce, he sat on the divan to the left of the door.

"Ah, Tom! Sit yourself down, and we'll drink a glass of sherry or claret, if you prefer. It's been too long since we last talked. I rejoice to see you recovered from your illness."

"Claret, Seth, if you please." Gillespie's unusually hesitant voice was clearly audible, as were Brigginshaw's movements as he poured wine.

"What's amiss?"

"I and my family were invited to spend Christmas at a country house. The gentleman had consulted me about his sons' education, and we became friendly."

A pause, perhaps while Gillespie fortified himself. "He formed an attachment to Portia, and why not? She's not young but he has heirs, and she's not a fool and would do well for a stepmother for his boys. It would be a very good marriage for her. He has a title, though only of rather recent creation…"

John Barlicorn always claimed too much explanation betokened nervousness or a guilty conscience; here was proof.

"Several days ago, Portia disappeared. Her betrothed and I, and her mama and Benedict, of course, are beside ourselves with worry."

"Good God! I should think you would be!"

"We searched everywhere and inquired at the nearest villages and towns. We returned home to see if she had somehow reached London, but there is no sign nor news of her."

A lie: Portia had left a letter for her father, explaining her flight and that she was staying with a respectable couple. The servants either had not noticed the livery of the footman who had accompanied her into the Gillespie house or had not reported it to Gillespie, or he had not learned it belonged to Ambrose Hawkins's household. It was subdued and not instantly recognizable, Lady Emily's influence, no doubt. Besides, while a nobleman's servants' livery might be familiar to many, a mere wealthy gentleman's (and he in trade, at that) might not be known.

" 'Pon my soul!"

"It is a damnable thing. I could think of no one else to ask how I can find her. If she was abducted and ruined while on her early morning walk, shame may have kept her from returning to the house."

No mention of the missing maidservant. Another lie.

"An early morning walk, eh? Could she not have become lost if she walked too far? Or broken an ankle and been unable to walk?"

"No, impossible. His lordship sent grooms and footmen out to hunt for Portia and not a trace did they find, as they must have done had she been lying helpless with a broken limb. Someone has carried her off, I know it."

This statement had the ring of truth. Gillespie must have guessed Portia had fled to avoid the marriage, and she could hardly have done so without an accomplice.

"Assuming your theory is correct, is it possible that she could have slipped back into the house and taken a few things, like a change of clothing and perhaps whatever money she had by her? If she could not bear the shame of telling you she had been assaulted and decided to flee to a friend?"

After a little hesitation, Gillespie said, "She took nothing with her, and I do not think she had enough money for coach fare. Where can she be? My poor wife is half mad with worry for her."

Regrettably, that too sounded true. How cruel not to tell Portia's mother the truth.

"I do not suppose your daughter would allow herself to be abducted without a fight. Did no one see or hear anything?"

Gillespie sighed heavily. "No, alas."

"Are you sure she has not returned to town, Tom? Have you spoken with her friends? Mayhap she is staying with one of them."

"To question our acquaintances would be to let the world know she is missing. She would be quite ruined. I do not care for that if only she can be found, of course, but how could she have reached London?"

"We do not always know members of our own family as well as we believe we do. I have often observed that fact in the course of my practice," Brigginshaw remarked. "Is it possible that rather than being abducted, she felt uncomfortable enough to decide she must leave?"

"With the prospect of a fine marriage and a title before her? What more could she want?"

"Mayhap she did not wish to marry your acquaintance or he frightened her by…er, his ardor?"

Finally Gillespie said, "She did not protest when I told her of his lordship's interest, or refuse him when he offered."

"She may have been reluctant to disappoint you."

"As well she should be! She must be found. The m—man to whom she is betrothed will still marry her once we find her."

"And if she does not agree?" Solomon heard the edge to Brigginshaw's voice.

Gillespie did not. "She has no choice. She is betrothed. If she refuses, she belongs in Bedlam."

"I see how it is, Tom. You meant to force her into an unwelcome marriage willy-nilly and thus made it necessary for her to run away. What were you offered for Portia and her fortune?"

The silence from Brigginshaw's office seemed thunderous.

"You'd best have a tumbler of brandy," Brigginshaw said. "I keep it for clients to whom I have given ill tidings."

"How the devil—" The rest of Gillespie's question would likely have been "—do you know that?" or some variation thereof.

"Oh, these things are gossiped about in my profession."

Gillespie responded with forced cheerfulness, "Well then, there's no more to be said about a marriage, if indeed you are correct. But she must be brought home, and we shall carry on as before."

A sigh. Solomon thought it was Brigginshaw's.

"Tom, Keswick has written to Furness to inform him that Portia's inheritance is as firmly secured as pudding in a pudding cloth for the boiling."

Gillespie's harsh intake of breath was clearly audible. "No."

"Yes. Your cousin Sturgis took precautions to prevent your daughter being the victim of a fortune hunter."

"Then when she marries, her husband would not have control of her inheritance?" Gillespie's voice trembled.

"He would not. Did you not read the will and the documents relating to the trust? Or take legal advice?"

"My son and daughter inherited fortunes. The Marquess of Furness said he had the news from his attorney, who would certainly know. Wouldn't he?"

"He heard it as gossip, I apprehend. He would not have been privy to the exact terms of the will, unless you provided Furness a copy."

"My God." A long, appalled silence ensued.

"Fortunately, Portia did not wed Furness, and while he may be disappointed or even furious to learn that he could not get his hands on her money, it would be far worse if the marriage had taken place. No harm done, Tom, except to your relationship with your daughter." To Solomon's ears, Brigginshaw sounded indecently cheerful, an emotion Solomon shared to the fullest extent.

"You have seen my daughter or had communication with her! Where is she?"

"I cannot divulge her location until she agrees. I doubt she will until it is accepted by Furness that there will be no wedding. I imagine he will be glad to end the betrothal once he knows he almost bought a pig in a poke. No disrespect to Portia intended! If he does not know yet, he soon will. He cannot even hold you solely responsible. He must share the blame, as neither he nor his attorney took pains to verify the details of the inheritance. I gather he approached you rather than the reverse?"

"You don't understand. I must speak with her. I have a right to know where my daughter is."

"She is of age, and she is not your dependent. Portia is now a lady of independent means. If anything, the situation is the reverse. While Mistress Portia and I have not discussed it, it's possible she may make you a little gift each quarter. You have not incurred a great deal of debt, I suppose."

"Not…not debt. You know I've always been careful with my money."

"You have, indeed. If you wish to write to make your peace with her, I will pass your letter on to her."

"I think I must speak to her rather than putting it in writing. Could we not meet here?"

"I will ask if she is willing to do so. But I will advise her against it. It is easier to be rational in a letter. One's feelings of anger and betrayal are less apt to be controlled when meeting face to face."

Not to mention that Gillespie might set someone to follow Portia after the meeting.

"I suppose I must settle for that crumb. I'll send it to you. Tell me, though, how did she get back to town? She did not go by the stage, for Furness inquired. That damned maid must have helped her, but what could she do without other assistance?"

"A friend aided her."

"Were you the one?"

Brigginshaw laughed. "No. Do I seem to you like a man who could help a lady escape from an unwanted suitor except by legal action?"

"You have seen her since she left Blackwater Hay, however. What did she tell you of how she came back to town?"

"She came to me for advice, as you have done. We did not discuss the details of her journey."

Which was true; they'd had quite enough to talk about without describing how she had returned. In fact, neither Portia nor he had said it was with his help, though Brigginshaw might have assumed it.

"Some man must have taken her away from Furness's estate. If he has ruined her, what will become of my poor daughter? Did she arrive at your door unaccompanied?"

"She had a maid with her, which is all the chaperon a lady needs in order to visit an attorney, Tom. This is hardly Vauxhall Gardens!"

"There must have been a man involved. Who could she—hmmpf!"

"Whoever enabled her to evade your and the marquess's scheme, she brought the maid with her from Essex. There's no point in discussing it further. I'll send your letter to her as soon as I receive it. Good day, Tom."

Gillespie grunted, "Servant, sir." A door slammed shut.

"He's gone. I think we'll have a glass of brandy now. That was most unpleasant." He poured out two tumblers of spirits. "Would you mind if I wrote a letter while we drink? The sooner Keswick informs Furness of the truth, the better. I am quite sure Gillespie won't tell him. My old friend was surprised to hear of the trust, wasn't he? I wondered whether he would fall into another apoplexy."

"Perhaps he fears Furness will blame him, though as you pointed out, Furness's lawyer should have looked into the matter."

"What was the notion you were mentioning when we were interrupted?" The attorney dipped his quill in the inkstand.

"I'll tell you if it bears fruit. Now I must set it in motion." He tossed off the last of his brandy and bowed himself out.

Chapter 27

Draft of a letter, never sent.

Lord Furness,

I beg your pardon for taking the liberty of writing to you unsolicited, but something has come to my attention which may be to your benefit, and as you may harbor some resentment toward me over certain events six months ago, I hope to make amends. That phrase was vague enough. *If you are desirous of marrying, I know of a widow of impeccable birth, large fortune, and presentable appearance who is out of mourning and hopes to replace her late husband with a man of title who is not sunk in age or vice.* Well, that description was accurate. As far as Solomon knew, Furness was not a rake or a profligate gambler. *Should you be interested in pursuing matrimony*—rather than Portia Gillespie—*I will be honored to present your qualifications for her review.*

Your most Obedient (ha!),

Solomon de Toledo

There should be no reason for Furness to suspect him of anything but a desire to earn a fee.

Opening his memorandum book, he dipped his quill in the standish.

He jotted a note to himself to write out the account of Furness's misdeeds in duplicate (or perhaps triplicate) and send it to Barlyon and Hawkins and perhaps David, as well, for safekeeping. By the time he had written replies to several men requesting appointments to discuss urgent personal business, he had begun to have serious doubts about the groveling tone of his letter. He would let it sit overnight.

He started out to the front office in time to hear a familiar voice remonstrating with Rafe.

"I must see him, it's important!"

"Boy, he won't lend money to no one that's in the schoolroom."

"Benedict?"

"Sol! Mr. de Toledo, I mean. I came to warn you."

The letter forgotten for the moment, Solomon gestured Rafe to go back to his chair. "I'll see Master Benedict. He's a friend."

Rafe studied Benedict Gillespie long enough to recognize him again and nodded. Then he resumed his earlier activity. Today he was carving a toy sheep, somewhat rough as to the head and limbs, but the curls of the fleece were executed in amazing detail.

"Come, we'll talk in my office. You said you wanted to warn me of something? Sit down. I'm afraid I have no suitable refreshments for you, but—"

"I don't care! I'm sorry, sir, but only listen, please."

The boy was red-faced, breathing hard and yet fidgety.

"What's wrong?"

"Father's in a fury. Usually he only sulks or makes one feel guilty for upsetting him, but this is beyond reason. I've never seen him so angry. He knows you helped Portia escape. Or thinks it, anyway." Benedict let out a breath. "By the way, thank you. I was never more glad of anything when Portia did not appear at breakfast that day. Father couldn't believe at first that she was really gone, and when he had to accept that she was nowhere to be found, he was too busy trying to soothe the marquess to fly into a passion himself. But now!" He ran down suddenly, like an unwound clock.

"How did he guess I was involved, do you know?"

"He came home yesterday afternoon from some errand with something on his mind. Then in the drawing room after supper, he asked Mama if Portia had any beaux. 'Beaux?' she says. 'I'm sure I can't think of any. Oh, to be sure, I've seen the apothecary look at Portia as if he admired her, but he's almost too shy to speak, never mind flirt.'

" 'Has she made a habit of going out and staying away longer than her errands require?' Father asks, and poor Mama was in a flutter and mentioned she took copying work to Brigginshaw's office every day or two but that she was never gone longer than it would take to walk there and back.

"That almost distracted him! He was not best pleased to find she had been working and might have held forth on that topic until he forgot his question. But as he was drawing breath to go on, my mother asked, 'How else were we to make ends meet? You cannot have considered the expenses of your illness, and while Mr. de Toledo would have lent us money in addition to Benedict's school fees, neither Portia nor I liked the idea of more debt. Fortunately she hit upon the idea of taking in copying and was well qualified to do the work.'

"Then there was a long pause before Father said, 'Hmmpf! That fellow!'

" 'Mr. de Toledo was as helpful as some relatives would be. More than my half brother has ever been, if I had chosen to ask him for help, which I never would. He brought his father who is a physician to see you, he made the arrangements to pay Benedict's fees, and took him to the coaching inn, and even provided the boys a basket of biscuits and cakes. I do not know how we should have managed without him.' I never heard her annoyed with Father before.

" 'Has he been encroaching?' Papa demanded. 'Not encroaching,' she said, and I could see her courage failing her. 'He consulted with Portia about the fees and the coach ticket.'

" 'And were you or the maid present at these consultations?' I wanted to ask how Mama or the maid could have been spared when someone was needed to sit with Father and the servants were run off their feet making invalid dishes or going out for special things like lemons and cordials from the apothecary, but if I'd spoken, he would likely have ordered me out. Mama only quavered, 'No. But some of the arrangements were made by letter.'

" 'They wrote to each other?' It didn't sound like a question. My mother answered it anyway. 'Yes, but if they had not written, Mr. de Toledo must have come here, which would surely be worse. It wasn't as though Portia is a young girl, and it was all for our son's sake.'

" 'Ha,' he said. 'He must be the seducer who lured Portia from Blackwater Hay.' She would have asked what he meant, but I caught her eye and shook my head, and for a wonder, Mother understood. Papa stamped out, and I had to explain certain things to my mother. All my father told her about Portia's disappearance was that she must have been abducted, which has kept her in a constant state of anxiety and tears. I did hint to her that perhaps Portia did not want to marry Furness, but I don't think she took my suggestion seriously. Then I mentioned, just casually, you know, about the wedding dinner being ordered before Portia gave her consent. She became very thoughtful, rather like the way Father looked before he left the room. Anyway, I thought you should know he's guessed you helped my sister."

"Thank you, Benedict." No doubt he would know soon enough what Thomas Gillespie meant to do with the information.

"Well, I thought you'd want to know." Benedict shuffled his feet. "It's not gentlemanly to pry into someone's affairs, but as it happens, he had our maid take several letters to the penny post this morning. I saw the one on top. It was directed to the marquess."

"Hmmm."

"He was still angry this morning, too. Not the way he was last night but tamped down and, er, simmering."

"I'm glad of the warning." The question now was, what would Furness do about it, assuming Gillespie had informed him?

"Is Portia all right, sir? I'm sure she's safe, but can I visit her?"

"I'm sure she would like to see you, but it might be best to wait a while. If your father asked you if you knew where she was, could you lie to him?"

"I never have. The most I've ever managed is to not mention anything that will, ummm, act as a priming charge. If you know what I mean."

For answer, Solomon grinned.

"Sometimes I can sort of lead the conversation away from awkward topics, too. I suppose we'd better not risk it."

"I don't think we'll need to conceal Portia much longer."

"Oh, good. I must say, apart from missing my sister, I'll be glad to go back to school."

"It's not been much of a holiday for you."

"Learning to ride was the best part of it, and seeing the countryside. The rest of it would sound exciting in a novel like *Moll Flanders*, but in real life it isn't actually enjoyable."

"You've read *Moll Flanders*?"

"There's a copy we pass around at Radford's School. Sir, do you think this business will spoil Portia's chances of marrying?"

"Any man of intelligence and character should be happy to marry Mistress Portia."

Benedict watched him expectantly.

"Benedict, are you asking my intentions?"

"Not exactly?" For once, the lad sounded hesitant.

"I would consider myself lucky to be a suitor for your sister's hand. But it would not be a good marriage for her: the difference of religion, my being a moneylender, which is not a genteel trade, and the fact I'm not wealthy or titled. Your father would likely oppose the match."

Benedict held up his right hand, fingers spread. "One, I don't think Portia has ever met a man who had a title or money except for Furness and isn't likely to meet another. Two, if Furness doesn't marry her, Father may not object, because who else would she marry? Three, the only other men she meets are old, like

Attorney Brigginshaw, or are haberdashers or butchers or servants, and they'd be less suitable than you. Four, in Sir Thomas Browne's *Religio Medici*, he says he would rather pity than despise a heretic or heathen. Something like that. If Papa did not object—oh! Your parents might not like the connection." Benedict bit his lip in chagrin.

"I think my mama would be happy with almost any lady I married, and we have relatives who have married Christians."

"Well, then. I don't think Portia would care. Five, you would be an excellent brother-in-law. And six, Portia is good at money matters. She's the one who figured out our budget problem when our father was ill, in case you didn't know. "

He gazed at Benedict. Everything seemed possible when one was a stripling. "I had formed that opinion from our conversations. But there is another difficulty. Everyone would think, and say, that I had married her for her money."

"Your pride is at stake."

He meant to say he was concerned for the embarrassment the talk would cause Portia. "Well…yes. But she would be humiliated, too."

"People marry for money all the time. Even chits in the schoolroom know it. And boys at Radford's, too."

Everyone knew and accepted it. "You are correct, I admit. But a man should be able to support a lady decently at the very least: keep a roof over her head, food on the table, provide servants, and clothing, and education for the children."

"You could do all of that, couldn't you? You must be plumper in the pocket than my family, or you wouldn't have been able to lend us the money for my school and the other things, or afford to go to Blackwater Hay and save Portia. She's used to our way of living, so yours would have to be an improvement."

However did a boy who had thought it would be interesting to go to sea as a powder monkey understand such things? He said carefully, "I have the greatest admiration and respect for your sister, and considering I removed her from the care and protection of her parents, I must offer for her. However, for the reasons I have given, I may not be accepted. In any case, we must be sure she is no longer in danger from Furness."

"That is a very good point." Benedict gave a brisk nod. "Do we know when she will be safe?"

"Your father learned only yesterday that your and Portia's money is protected by trustees. If Furness has not learned of it yet, he soon will. We believe that will cause him to break off plans to marry your sister. I won't say more lest you find yourself in a moral quandary."

"In case my papa asks? Then I'd rather not know."

Portia's brother departed. One thing was certain; Furness must be eliminated as soon as possible. Solomon would then ask for Portia's hand, which he really was obliged to do by common decency. The argument that Portia had a maid with her did not make their journey any less shocking. Several of Benedict's six arguments in favor of his marrying Portia were fairly convincing. The boy had not known of the seventh point, in some ways the most important. He loved Portia. He simply wasn't worthy of her.

That sparked a memory, something John Barlyon had told him during his stay with the Barlyons in the summer.

"I thought my past meant I could never marry her because a criminal was not worthy to wed a woman like Aurelia." Now she was the former John Barlicorn's countess.

What were the arguments against marrying Portia, assuming she would have him? Their differing positions in society: she was the daughter of a respected scholar who came from the gentry. *I am a moneylender, and not even to royalty or the nation, which would be acceptable, more or less. I come from a line of respected, successful physicians and rabbis.*

The difference of religion. Though it would not be the first time a Christian had married a Jew, nor the last. His grandfather's second wife had been a Christian; only his great-grandfather had really disapproved, and even he had been tolerant. Solomon's own mother had pointed out that he wasn't particularly observant. Mayhap the real question was, how would Portia feel about it?

The difference in their fortunes. Portia was a great heiress, whose inheritance would make her acceptable to the highest noblemen in the land, if they were willing to settle for their children inheriting the money. Most would want control of her money at once, though even her quarterly income would be irresistible to anyone not in immediate need of thousands of guineas. Any rational man could live very happily indeed on her annual income.

The bar to his offering marriage to Portia was not lack of money, but perhaps an excess of pride. He did not want to be seen as a fortune hunter.

But now that he thought of it, his income was not

much less than hers. He had a little from lending, more from rents, varying amounts from buying and selling odd lots of merchandise and matchmaking, a good deal from investments and the Funds. The latter were at least respectable. Somehow it all added up to a surprisingly significant sum. He reinvested most of his profit and lived simply.

Men of the highest rank improved their lot by marrying women with excellent dowries, even those whose fathers had made their money as tradesmen of the lowest sort. No one saw any harm in it; few would feel any shame. But his pride would suffer if he were suspected of fortune hunting.

His plaguey pride! He had inherited it from his great-grandfather. Alvaro de Toledo secretly cherished their family's history of rabbis and skilled physicians and their assistance to certain kings of Spain before the Expulsion.

At the same time, he taught Solomon to avoid making himself conspicuous: to dress decently but not richly, never to give offense to the English by presuming upon acquaintance with them, to be respectful of Englishwomen while never seeking their company. "Any failing will be used against you. Your safety lies in not being noticed." As a child, Sol had once said, "But I am English, sir," to which Great-Grandfather had replied with wintry humor, "In your own eyes, possibly, but never in theirs."

He might have been correct in the latter opinion. Solomon had changed his mind about some of Alvaro's other beliefs, mostly because of John Barlicorn. He had eaten food which was certainly not *kashrut.* He had been hesitant the first time, though he had been hungry and the pies smelled delicious. "You'd eat it if you were starving," John had told him. By then, he knew there had been times when Barlicorn likely had been very hungry indeed. "Ay," he admitted, and ended by sharing the meat pie. His conscience had bothered him for a while; no wonder Great-Grandfather disapproved of friendships with non-Jews.

On the other hand, he was not the first de Toledo to eat pork: their family had been *conversos* in Spain and Portugal before they left for more tolerant nations, like the Ottoman Empire and Italy. By the time he went into business, he had accepted that he would sometimes have to eat prohibited foods and occasionally do business on Shabbat.

Without Barlicorn's friendship, Sol would have been virtually a foreigner in his parents' home when he finally returned. His mother and father accepted the compromises necessary to take part in English life. As it was, they and his brothers assumed he was somewhat shy and considered him too well-behaved. "He'll grow up to be a rabbi," his brother Vidal had said. Solomon smiled at that: Vidal would not have made that mistake if he had ever seen Solomon in John Barlicorn's company. His family never knew where he went or what he did. They probably never noticed he was gone.

Chapter 28

Rafe interrupted his reverie. "D'ye want me to stay, Mr. Solomon?"

"Is it so late?" A glance at the window told him it was, and fog was thickening. "No, I'll leave now."

"I'll walk w' you."

"Thanks, but no need. I have the weighted cane." Rafe lodged in the other direction.

If not for John Barlicorn, Sol would have hesitated to make his way home through the foggy streets. A moneylender might seem a rich bird for the plucking, and attacks on Jews for no reason at all were not unknown. He locked the ledger in the concealed strongbox, put on his greatcoat, collected his stick, and made sure his notebook and the sheet with the day's transactions were in his pocket. At home, he would enter them in the duplicate ledger he kept. If his office or his house burned, he would still have records. Outside, fog made it hard to see the building opposite. As he turned toward Cheapside and Poultry Street, he thought he heard a murmur followed by the jingle of harness somewhere nearby and hooves in the road. Someone who had been visiting the Excise Office or the Mercers' Hall had been surprised by the fog, as he was. It would be a slow journey for a carriage or wagon, wherever he was going. A thick fog obscured landmarks and muffled sound so that one might come upon another walker or even a horseman or vehicle unexpectedly. The chances were anyone who was not compelled to be out, or not lost in thought, would have made his way home already. Still, if some footpad hoped to do business tonight, Sol had his cane. Plain, as befitted a tradesman, the engraved brass sphere at the top concealed its true nature. The lead ball inside could fracture a skull, he had been told. Thus far, he had only used it once, and a sharp rap on the attacker's wrist had sufficed to send him running.

He hardly needed the clues along his usual route: the scent of over-roasted coffee from a certain coffee house, the rough voices from a public house. On Cornhill he stepped out briskly. He need not turn off now until he reached the Commercial Road. He heard no more horses either driven or ridden.

The fog that muffled sound and sight sharpened his focus on his problems. Only two of them were important: he wanted to marry Portia, and he would not send a groveling letter to Furness in the hope of averting his displeasure. *Take the bull by the horns.*

By the time he reached his own door, he had drafted the message in his mind. While he ate supper, he refined it. He wrote it out at the little table in the parlor while his housekeeper sat knitting by the fire.

Lord Furness,

Last June I offended you one evening at Vauxhall Gardens. Let him begin by thinking I am apologizing for embarrassing him. *Recently, I helped a young lady who did not wish to be your marchioness to leave Blackwater Hay precipitately. I do not apologize for this, and by now you may be heartily glad of it, if you have looked into the terms of her late relative's will and the trust documents.*

I understand your need for money. In the course of my calling as a marriage broker, I am in a position to find you a bride of fortune and good appearance who would be pleased to wed you. I have a lady in mind who adds impeccable lineage to her other advantages. If you accept my offer, which I trust will resolve any awkwardness between us, please respond promptly with two or three dates and times you are available to meet the lady at the office of her man of business. Some urgency attaches to this—

Because one really could not be comfortable until there was no danger of his attempting revenge upon Portia for fleeing or her father for having misled him, or on Solomon himself. Furness might not commit a crime which would gain him nothing except satisfaction, but on the other hand, even if it were prosecuted, the House of Lords would never convict him.

—lest the lady be snapped up by some other.

Solomon de Toledo

Old Jury, Cheapside, at the Sign of the Scales

Was that tempting enough? He was not quite satisfied with the end. He wanted to hint that consequences might follow violence against the Gillespies or himself. One could scarcely write, "If you have me killed, my friends will see to it your reputation is left in shreds, even if you cannot be convicted in the House of Lords." On the other hand, Furness might take the suggestion of reprisal as a challenge. It would also imply he feared the marquess, which would invite an attack, as a mouse running from a cat would attract its attention and its own death. Better not to show any consciousness of danger.

Dropping molten sealing wax on the folded sheet, he imprinted it with his seal. His initials had been carved into the carnelian to match the monogram with which he signed letters to his borrowers, the ornate capitals S and T separated by a small d. The signet was instantly recognizable to those with whom he did business and meaningless to others who chanced to see it.

****

In spite of her unease, Portia found her days with Lady Emily full of diversions. First it had been the mantua-maker's visit, then Maggie, Lady Emily's maid, had gone shopping for her. She returned with shifts, stockings, caps, handkerchiefs, kerchiefs to wear when one did not wish to expose too much bosom, gloves, and two pairs of shoes. At Lady Emily's instruction, she also bought lengths of wool and linen, for as Lady Emily explained, Maggie was a skilled seamstress who would make several simple dresses for Mary. Portia was grateful for the suggestion, for as Mary had said, her two gowns were both "rags and jags."

Ambrose Hawkins showed her his collection of Chinese porcelain and jade one evening and on another told her about the voyages he had made.

Emily showed her the kitchen, in which she took justifiable pride as it was equipped with every modern convenience: a roasting jack which turned the spit by a clockwork mechanism, molds in various sizes, a biscuit pricker, a lemon squeezer. She also made a number of suggestions about what to look for in choosing a house, with hints as to suitable neighborhoods.

There were books to read, as well, a pastime for which Portia had seldom before had leisure, even if she had had access to novels, plays, poetry, and books of travel.

She was beginning to relax a little when Benedict's letter came, forwarded under separate cover from Solomon, who had added a note that he hoped to have good news regarding Furness in the near future.

Dear Portia,

I hope you are well and safe. Solomon says you are. I would visit you except that it's better I not know where you are staying, because while I would not tell Papa even under torture, it would be very uncomfortable to lie to him if he asked.

I am writing chiefly to let you know Papa has worked out that Solomon helped you get away. It would not have been difficult as Mr. de Toledo is the only man you know who might be able to do such a daring thing. No one would suspect Wilkes the apothecary or Smith the butcher or any of Papa's friends or scholars of it.

I hope Sol is being careful, as Papa wrote to Furness this morning. Mayhap the letter was only about your money being secured against whoever you married, which I gather he discovered only yesterday and which put him in a fury. He is nervous as well.

Mama is weepy and has taken to her bed, and I try to reassure her, but I dare not tell her I know you are safe. I am spending as much of the day away from home as I can, which is not as difficult as it would usually be because Papa has lost interest in my lessons, for which I am truly grateful, but it's worrisome, isn't it?

I went to Solomon to warn him, which is how I am able to write you. He said he could send it on. His office is nearly as nice as the headmaster's at Radford. Nicer, really, for although the walls are not paneled, the furnishings are newer and handsome. He has a hulking great fellow who sits in the outer office instead of a clerk, I suppose in case someone tried to rob Sol. Rafe sits and carves wooden toys and such things.

Solomon says Furness will lose interest in you as soon as he learns your money is safe from him.

Portia, I believe Mr. de Toledo is much struck by you. If he asked you to marry, would you? I understand our father might not care for the idea, but under the circumstances, I do not think I would let that weigh with me.

Your brother,

Benedict

Solomon might be in danger. She had not forgotten what he had told her about the marquess's attempt to harm his sister's suitor. That he had a man to guard the office was reassuring, but what about when he went out? Or was at home? Here she sat, enjoying her stay with Emily and Ambrose, when Solomon was in danger of being murdered or crippled or who knew what?

She read the last paragraph again. Why would he think Solomon was attracted to her? Benedict was more interested in whether steam could be used to fire cannon than in girls. Still, he did surprise her with some regularity.

Did Solomon find her desirable? He had been helpful to her father and brother as well as to her, but then, he had treated Mary no differently than he had Portia. Perhaps he showed everyone the same kindness and consideration. Had a certain warmth lurked in his eyes when he smiled at her?

She had never met a man she liked as well or respected as much. Once or twice (or several times) she had wondered what it would be like to be kissed by him. Her only experiences had been Furness's horrid kiss and a quick peck on the lips stolen by one of her father's university-bound scholars as he left the house for the last time. Insolent puppy!

If Solomon de Toledo did ask her to marry…it would bear thinking on. With the income she was to receive each quarter, she would not need to marry to escape poverty. What were the chances she would meet any man she liked as well in her family's constricted circle? As a single female living alone without a broad acquaintance, her choices would be limited to men met at church or the merchants or tradesmen where she shopped or at an occasional assembly. Mr. de Toledo's offer might be the only one she received, if indeed he did offer.

Could she live alone? To do so would be an insult to her family, and something of a scandal. Would it cause Papa to lose income? She was quite out of patience with him. If he lost work because of it, her mother and Benedict would suffer. At the moment, even if Furness were not a threat, she did not feel she could live in the same house with Thomas Gillespie.

She wished she could talk to Solomon. As Benedict had once pointed out, he gave very good advice, a commodity of which she felt she sorely in need. But since her problem involved marriage, he was almost the last one with whom she could discuss it.

Chapter 29

Rafe scratched at his office door.

“There’s a mortal fine footman come with a letter, but he caps he’ll put it into your own fambles.”

“What color is his livery?

“A kind of blue. Washed out. Silver buttons.”

The Marquess of Furness’s livery. “Tell him I’ll come out. Be on the watch.”

The footman, who really was a footman after all, proffered the letter, bowed minutely, and departed. Solomon tore it open where he stood. Furness had not wasted sealing wax on him, choosing to use a pale blue wafer seal. No one sealed a letter to a moneylender with wax and a signet.

Three dates and three times, and Furness’s name. Good. Now to reel in the other party.

****

Lady Isabelle Baldock sat at ease in the comfortably appointed room in which her man of business met with his clients. Solomon did not try to make conversation. One does not draw the attention of a lioness if one can avoid it.

The business agent himself, the grandson of an earl’s third son and proud of it, announced Furness and stood aside to let him pass. The marquess paused in the doorway. Solomon rose. He could not force himself to bow as deeply as he should. The nobleman’s gaze passed over Solomon as if he were invisible and stopped at Lady Isabelle. Lips pursed, he came forward and made her a leg elaborate enough to express respect but not so overdone as to constitute irony. She inclined her head without rising. The business agent's relief showed in the slight easing of his shoulders. The man began to follow Furness in.

Isabelle Baldock said, "I won't need you, Pierce."

"May I have a tea tray sent in? Wine?"

"That will not be necessary."

He bowed and withdrew, pulling the door closed behind him.

"Lady Isabelle, may I present the Marquess of Furness?"

Before she could speak, he replied, "We met years ago, when Lady Isabelle was hunting her first husband."

Her smile was faintly predatory. "And you were the younger son of a viscount without a pot to—"

Furness's unexpected crack of laughter took Solomon by surprise, as did the ungenteel expression the lady had been about to employ. "You were ever a saucy piece. If we are to talk of impecunious peers, your papa sold you to that fat Cockney." He sauntered over to the chair at right angles to Lady Isabelle's.

"Indeed, with my hearty agreement. I had no mind to freeze in winter and go without new gowns for the rest of my life. It served very well. Let us discuss business now. I did not know you were the prospect de Toledo found me." She tilted her head. "I believe I should like to be a marchioness, as no suitable duke is available."

Furness studied her with something akin to either

approval or amusement, or both. “You may achieve your ambition if we can come to terms. It is too bad you did not have de Toledo send your offer to me. Now we shall have to call your fellow back in.”

“There was no point in providing you the terms when I did not know the identity of my prospective husband. You might have been as much of a waste of time as the previous two. We will not need my man except to write out the settlements for the lawyers’ review, if we can come to an understanding. De Toledo can take notes.”

Without a word, Solomon took his place at the elegant desk. It seemed unlikely there would be anything to write, both parties being high-tempered.

“You have your requests with you, then?”

Her delicate arched eyebrows raised. “I do not need them in writing; they are simple enough. Nor are they requests.”

“You mean to make demands? Apart from pin money and the like?”

“Oh, ay. Pray, did you think me foolish when I was seventeen?”

He frowned. “No, you were a needle-witted chit. I think I never met a female as sharp as you.”

“Here is how it will go, if we are to marry. A great part of my inheritance is in trust. You will not have any access to those funds. A good deal more is in Bank of England shares. Which, in case you are unfamiliar with the Bank of England Act of 1696, means they are my personal property. I am able and willing to make you an allowance sufficient to live in the manner expected of a marquess, as I enjoy luxury myself.” Solomon’s quill stopped abruptly in mid-stroke at the figure she named.

He'd had no idea she was so wealthy. Baldock had not left her that much and mere accumulation of interest could not account for it.

"You mean to make me your pensioner?"

Solomon suppressed a sigh. The outrage in Furness's voice was indication enough that this meeting would be ending in a matter of minutes. What other peer could he think of who would fulfill Lady Isabelle's exacting requirements?

"I hope to make you my husband. However, great as your attractions are"—here she frankly ogled him—"the fact is, you are not good at managing money and I am. While marriage to Baldock was tedious, I did learn many useful things from him and his cit friends. I have substantially increased my money by wise investments.

"You ran through your first wife's money trying to live like a viscount though you were still a younger son. I shall not let you fritter away my money, except that which I allow you. I will not make an advance against your next quarter's…hmmm, let us call it a stipend. If you incur debts of honor you cannot pay, you will be shamed by having to ask time to make them good at the next quarter day. If the bailiffs dog your footsteps over your bills, you will have to suffer it until that time. Another thing I learned as a cit's wife was to be less concerned about appearances and more concerned about reality."

"You appalling woman." To Solomon's surprise, Furness did not sound angry. "You obviously have no interest in wedding me or any other man of spirit."

"The truth does not constitute an insult. Oddly enough, I would like to marry you, Robert, and not alone for your title. You know your own mind, you have almost the French nobility's manner, and I have no doubt at all that you are vigorous." Again, the calculating glance swept over him. This time Furness reddened.

"I think we might deal well together. I don't wonder at all if you found your well-behaved, docile wife boring. I suppose you bullied her, poor spiritless thing. I, on the other hand, will give as good as I get, and I will hold the purse strings." She rose. "You will wish time to contemplate whether an extremely comfortable life as my lord and master"—her voice quivered with suppressed amusement—"is preferable to your current state."

She leaned forward slightly to shake her petticoat free of creases. Solomon wondered if her stays would be able to contain her. Furness must be speculating also, as his gaze was fixed on that expanse of creamy skin.

"Ah…we might come to an agreement. Why drag out negotiations?"

Both smiled knowingly, their attention on each other. An embarrassing sight, altogether. Solomon cleared his throat. "Shall I give my notes to Pierce to be written up?"

"Will you do me the honor?" Furness inquired.

"With pleasure. Yes, de Toledo, go."

"Shut the door behind you," the marquess added, advancing on the grinning Lady Isabelle.

Solomon fled to the safety of Pierce's office; the agent looked up. "De Toledo? Do they want my presence?"

"No. I, ah, don't think I'd go in there at the moment. Best to wait for them to come out. These are the notes from which you are to draft the settlements."

A sigh. "I suppose this means I'll lose Lady Isabelle's business to Furness's man. At least I won't have to deal with milady any longer."

"Likely to be the other way around."

"What?"

"Read the notes." He took the client chair with the sensation of having escaped—barely—from a pair of the more savage beasts in the Tower menagerie.

"God save us all!" Pierce exclaimed a few minutes later.

"I don't think it's as bad as that."

The man of business looked up. "This is astounding. Did you extort these terms from the marquess? No, don't tell me. What I don't know I can't testify to."

"I'd nothing to do with it. Your client told him what she was willing to offer, that's all."

"He must be in a desperate case, then."

"What she was offering would be attractive to any man."

Pierce tutted. "I ventured to caution her not to be too liberal with him. If only she will refrain from pitching something at him before the vows. Will you take a glass of claret with me?"

****

Hearing the outer door burst open, Solomon jumped up from his desk chair, dropping his quill to spatter ink over the commonplace book's page, pausing only long enough to pull the pistol from the drawer. In the outer office, Rafe loomed before the passage to the inner offices.

"Can't see Mr. Solomon without a 'poin'ment. You

c'n write what you want on that paper." He jerked his head at his table with its slips of paper and pencil.

Solomon peered past his henchman's shoulder.

"Sol!"

"Rafe, you know Hawkins. He doesn't need to make an appointment. He can come in."

"If you're agreeable, Mr. Solomon." Rafe retreated to his chair and went back to carving a rectangular block of wood, apparently a tinder box.

Hawkins was flushed with exertion or excitement, a sight Solomon had never previously seen, except for his announcement of the expected addition to the Hawkins family. Without waiting to reach Solomon's office, he said, "The *North Sea Venturer* has been sighted in the Estuary."

"What?"

"She didn't sink." Hawkins threw himself into the armchair by the desk.

Solomon poured brandy while trying to adjust to the idea and passed one to Hawkins, who raised his tumbler and said, "Congratulations."

"Strike me dead."

"Not a good time for it. You're about to make an excellent profit by the sheerest good luck. Well, as soon as she makes the legal quays. You'll likely pay an extortionate duty on the pelts unless you re-export them directly. If you do, they abate almost the entire duty. If you need a loan to cover it, I'll lend it to you on good terms." Hawkins grinned piratically.

"Thanks. I can probably get even better terms from my cousin, if I need to borrow. Ah…how much duty is likely to be due?"

"I don't deal in furs or the Baltic trade, and I didn't

stop to look it up in the book of rates. I do recall hearing calabar skins are a shilling or two and ermine skins are eleven shillings the timber. I think sables are eight pounds the timber. Do you know what a timber is?"

"I looked the term up in Bailey's dictionary. There are forty pelts to a timber. The shipment is sixty timbers."

"Damme, you've had a stroke of luck. You might arrange to ship it to China; the East Indiamen should be sailing in late February or early March. There's always a demand for sable in China. Or Turkey. Olivia says they like fur there. She ships to the eastern Mediterranean. You'll make an excellent profit over and above the amount you lent that chousing bully-trap."

"I'll speak to Mistress Easterday's clerk. Turkey might answer well. What a stroke of luck for the ship's captain and crew that the ship did not founder, as well as for me. Did you hear how it came about?"

"We won't know the details until she anchors, but in short, though she was in grave difficulty and might have been expected to sink, her captain contrived to get her as far as some little Polish fishing village, where repairs were made. It took time, and there was no hope of sending a message." Hawkins swirled the spirits in his glass. "I don't know whether it's the unsettled conditions there or whether Poland simply doesn't have a decent system for sending the post. Whatever the reason, it's good news all around."

They both raised their glasses and drank.

****

The settlement documents were to be prepared by

the following afternoon. Surprising speed! Or perhaps not, considering the parties for whom they were intended. They meant to marry the day before Christmas by special license. Solomon returned to his office expecting to breathe a sigh of relief only when Furness and Lady Isabelle were actually married.

As it fell out, he scarcely had time enough to glance at his mail when Rafe informed him "that blue footman" had a message for him. Furness's servant presented the letter, saying he was instructed to await a reply.

Hades.

He opened the sheet with a premonition of doom.

Call upon me this evening at six of the clock.

Furness

He stared at it: not an invitation. Definitely an order.

"May I inform his lordship that you will wait upon him this evening, sir?"

"Ay."

The footman bowed a little lower than he had done on his last visit and departed. Solomon sat in his office writing out an account of his dealings with Furness which might lead to his being murdered, which he copied three times, addressing them to Barlyon, Hawkins, and David Mendys. He wrote a letter of instructions dealing with his business, copied it twice, and addressed those to his man of business and Mendys. A precaution only, of course. While answering the marquess's summons was the last thing in the world he wanted to do, he dared not refuse.

A minute or two before the hour, he was ushered into Furness's library, where Furness sat behind his desk, a glass of brandy at hand. "I hardly know whether to shake your hand or have you horsewhipped," he said.

At least Furness felt some doubt about his plans.

"Peter. A glass of brandy for my guest. Sit down, de Toledo."

Having seen Furness in a fury, he was somewhat reassured. He might still be murdered on his way home tonight, if Furness had been able to hire a bravo between leaving Pierce's office and summoning Solomon. However, he would have needed an intermediary like Barlicorn to supply one.

The footman poured out a measure of spirits, presented it, and left the room as silently as a wraith. Solomon sipped brandy. Why would Furness send for him?

"I was going to do it, you know."

"Do—?"

"Horsewhip you. Or have you beaten. My coachman lost sight of you in the fog."

"Fortunate for me."

"Ay. After I considered the matter, I concluded you'd done me a good turn," the marquess admitted after staring grimly at him for what seemed longer than it could actually have been, "much as it pains me to acknowledge it."

"I hope you are pleased with Lady Isabelle, my lord."

"Oh, in that, you have done better than you knew. We will be like flint and steel. No boredom there! I meant in your stealing away Portia Gillespie. Damme, I might not have learned of that curst trust before the wedding. I might as well have married a workhouse wench."

Considering Portia's generous quarterly income, Solomon was less angry than amused by Furness's slighting comparison. An amount many would envy apparently seemed a pittance to the marquess. He kept his face blank of either emotion.

"Gillespie came yammering to me that you had enticed away my intended bride." The marquess took a long swallow of brandy. "I suppose he wanted to distract me from his own crime."

"Was he dishonest in truth? Or did he simply not understand the terms of the will and trust?"

Furness stared moodily at the spirits in his glass. "I'm inclined to believe he knew. He's said to be a brilliant scholar, after all."

"He has a well-known reputation in the field of ancient languages. It might not enable him to fully comprehend a legal document, Lord Furness." It would not be wise to point out that neither Furness nor his attorney had verified the provisions of the will.

Furness snorted. "If he did not understand originally, he was yet guilty enough on other points. He led me to believe his daughter was willing to receive my addresses, in fact had already agreed to marry me. Plainly that was not the case."

"If Mistress Portia had expressed her unwillingness, you would have desisted?"

Furness stared at him. "Are you mad? With such a fortune at stake? Good God, what man would allow himself to be refused?" Amazement turned to vexation. "That's another point against Gillespie: he insisted the settlements be signed before the wedding."

"That's not the way it's usually done, is it? I confess I am not familiar with the procedures involved."

"I don't suppose settlements are necessary among the poor and the middling class. I agreed to execute the documents and have the deed enrolled before the ceremony as a favor to him. He claimed to be ignorant of such matters and feared the formalities would be delayed by Christmas. Or forgot after the wedding took place, I suppose. I forgave his implied questioning of my honesty…"

…because Furness had been desperate to get control of Portia and her fortune.

"When his daughter disappeared, I understood why he had wanted the settlements signed and the deed enrolled immediately. He must have believed he could use the fact to force her agreement to the match if she balked. Apparently he underestimated her. Of course he was then urgent to find her, knowing he had committed a fraud."

"I am surprised your attorney did not object to the proceedings. I would think some procedure exists to avoid settlements going into effect in case the wedding does not take place. And did he not explain the trust?"

Scowling, the marquess said, "Lawyers make snails look speedy. They must mull over every word, and their fees! Outrageous! Mine assured me the woman had inherited almost half of that tradesman's estate, which was well known to be enormous. It hardly seemed necessary to waste money and time on fiddling documents. I will be employing a new attorney."

"Ah." Something Furness had mentioned earlier came to mind. "What is the deed you mentioned, sir?"

"His price for selling me his wealthy daughter was a little manor I own. Owned, until he cheated me of it.

When Sturgis's attorney informed me Sturgis had tied up her inheritance, I taxed Gillespie with it. He was very nervous; evidently he was already aware of the existence of the trust."

Solomon cleared his throat. "Ah…I believe he learned of it at or very near the same time you did."

The marquess raised his eyebrows interrogatively.

"Mistress Portia consulted an attorney who went with her to see Sturgis's attorney. I understand he meant to write to you. Mistress Portia's lawyer spoke with her father as well, but it may not have been until after you were informed of the…er, problem. I think that would be enough to account for any anxiety."

"You cannot persuade me Gillespie did not know what he was about. I meant to bring suit against him for defrauding me of my property, but Lady Isabelle has convinced me that such proceedings are expensive and slow. The matter could as well be treated as criminal, which would be quicker. I have retained her attorney to deal with it."

"I suppose the man will give him the option of simply deeding the property back to you?"

"He advised doing so, and I agreed. My own former attorney seems to have been partly at fault. I am not a lawyer; I expected him to know how to prepare a conveyance of property in a marriage settlement. Why should you care what happens to Gillespie?"

"I know him slightly. While I think he was wrong to try to force Mistress Portia into marriage, I believe his actions were well intended." Misguided and wrong-headed but not criminal, at least. "It's too bad academic achievements do not necessarily mean common sense in practical matters. Many intelligent men are fools in legal matters."

"Including myself, I apprehend you mean; thank you!" After this ironic comment, the marquess drank off the rest of his brandy and poured himself another glass. He eyed Solomon's nearly full glass. "Drink up. You'll need it."

"Will I, my lord?"

"Oh, I think so. Why did you involve yourself in this farce?"

"I became acquainted with Mistress Portia when Gillespie suffered his apoplexy. When I learned she was in danger of being forced into an unwelcome marriage, I offered to help her return to London." Best to avoid explaining how he knew of it and that his disclosure of Furness's previous activities had influenced her.

"I have little doubt that Gillespie will return my manor rather than risk trial as a common criminal as there is no question he deceived me, whether intentionally or not. But that will be no punishment. It will merely restore him to his previous state."

"Isn't that punishment enough? He has lost his chance of being a country gentleman and likely his son's respect and his daughter's affection."

"No. Good God, the fellow's one step above a schoolmaster. He deserves a sharp lesson for thinking himself on a footing with me because he would be my father-in-law, if for nothing else. And he shall have it. Damme if I ever thought I'd be drinking with a curst moneylender."

He grinned disconcertingly. "Mayhap I'll reward you, pay off a score I owe you, and chastise Gillespie at the same time."

"Oh?"

The marquess reached across the desk to refill Solomon's glass which had mysteriously emptied. Furness in what passed for good humor was very nearly as terrifying as he was in a fury. "You have done me two favors: bringing me Lady Isabelle, who is monstrous pleased with you—and with me—and saving me from marrying a penniless female. You helped Portia Gillespie ruin herself. Had she actually possessed a fortune under her control…but she did not. Still, you meddled. I have not forgotten our meeting at Vauxhall Gardens, either." Furness lounged back in his chair. "Who do you think will marry a female so lost to decorum as to desert her betrothed bridegroom almost on the eve of their wedding, travel on her own or worse still, with some man, all the way from the Blackwater to London, and then conceal herself from her family who-knows-where? Anyone would conclude she was no better than a whore—"

Solomon lost the ability to control his expression. "My lord—"

"Don't issue me a challenge. You cannot fight me, and you would be ill advised to strike me. I should have to have my footmen thrash you. You would get the worst of it, for which I would be sorry, when you have rendered me good service."

"Thank you, my lord." He took no pains to conceal his ironic tone. The fact remained that all the advantage was with Furness.

"In any case, you ruined her. If not for the trust, some man who is not overparticular may be willing to marry her. She will have to accept him, for what father would permit his son to be tutored by a man whose daughter has such a reputation? He may have difficulty finding a publisher, too. Or perhaps she will not marry and will support her family on her quarterly allowance. Still, even in her family's plebeian circle, she will not be accepted."

Solomon did not point out that her income alone would make her an eligible wife for the majority of men, even of some of the lower aristocracy. He marveled briefly at how perceptions could differ. Nor did he mention they hoped Portia's leaving her family's protection would never become public.

"Yet while she may have injured your self-esteem by declining your suit in such a way, she is not guilty of deliberately injuring you. She would not have fled if she had believed a simple refusal would suffice. You had already invited the parson and guests to the wedding feast."

"To ensure my accepting it, she need only have told me about the trust. I would certainly not have pressed my suit knowing anything above her quarterly income would have to be approved by the trustees."

"But she didn't know about the trust or even how much she had inherited, until I informed her." Granted, she had learned of it the day before she had left Blackwater Hay. Solomon had considered informing the marquess of the will and trust's provisions and decided against it, as if Furness did not believe him, he would have lost the chance of getting Portia away. He had not mentioned the possibility to her, out of fear she would let it slip, with the same result.

"Sturgis's attorney failed to inform her?"

Was Gillespie's misleading Keswick and forging a letter purporting to come from Portia a prosecutable offense? As it permitted him to divert some of her income to himself, it might be.

He would have liked to avoid making it clear Gillespie had deliberately deceived both Furness and Keswick. There was no honest way to do it; and Gillespie, not Portia, deserved the blame. "I understand all correspondence to the Gillespie home is received by Gillespie." It was true. In many homes the head of the family distributed the post.

The Marquess of Furness stared at the empty glass clasped in both hands. After a time, he said, "In that case, I regret I acted hastily. It is a fault of mine, I am told."

"Lord Furness, what have you done?"

"I sent a notice to the papers announcing the end of the betrothal, the lady having fled before the wedding. Tomorrow all London will know she is ruined. Before I heard from Keswick, I hoped that making her an outcast would encourage her to reconsider our marriage. After I learned her departure had saved me from a terrible mistake, it seemed a way of punishing Gillespie."

It must be after seven in the evening by now. What time were the papers printed? While Solomon scrambled to think how to avert disaster, Furness continued, "If you were a gentleman, I would say you should feel it incumbent upon you to marry her, but as you are not…ah, well, at least she has the money to live quietly, out of the public eye. As she was never in society, it can make little difference to her."

"You are correct, sir. I should marry her, if she will have me. If you will excuse me—"

"I doubt her trustees will release her money to you any more readily than they would to me."

"It doesn't matter. I can support a wife in better circumstances than her father, at the very least, even without her income." As Benedict had pointed out.

Furness laughed. "If you are willing to live upon crumbs, all's well."

"My lord, why did you invite me here?"

"I hoped to see you squirm."

"I trust you are disappointed."

"I am…and I am not. If you were a gentleman, I would shake your hand. Good night." He picked up a finely bound book and opened it.

Solomon bowed—slightly—although Furness's attention was on his book. He did not add the courteous, " 'Servant, sir." The footman in the passage escorted him to the hall and held his greatcoat before bowing him out.

All's well indeed! He must offer for Portia, which he was happy to do; he only wished she and her father might be equally glad. Strictly speaking, he did not care if Thomas Gillespie was pleased, given the man's actions, but Portia might care. While she had been hurt by her father's scheming, they had been close. She might forgive him eventually.

Chapter 30

It was too late to pay a call upon Portia or upon Gillespie. It would also be a good idea to think about which he should approach first. Ordinarily one would request permission of the young lady's father. That rule assumed the lady was a minor and under her father's control. Portia was of legal age, and while it would still be correct to speak with her father, his recent actions, her absence from his home, and her current annoyance with him suggested that he should address Portia first. Ay, that would be best. Then—if she agreed to marry him—he would inform Thomas Gillespie. Probably. If Portia agreed.

In the morning he would write to her, asking if he might call upon her. No, he decided as he reached the hack stand. He would get to Hawkins's house as early as possible, to be there when the newspaper arrived. Hawkins would certainly be awake and at breakfast before leaving for his offices. He was not a man to insist on formality. Nor did Solomon care to risk either Hawkins or Portia seeing the notice before he came to offer for her.

He instructed the coachman to stop at Samuel's house and wait. His brother readily agreed to his request, not even asking Solomon's reason. That task done, he arrived at his own door in a far better frame of mind than he had left it.

Until on letting himself in, he found Billy dozing on the stairs. The lad was supposed to be off duty earlier: he had to be up at dawn to fetch and carry for Solomon's cook/housekeeper. As he closed and bolted the door, the boy jerked awake and shot up from the step.

"Mr. Solomon!"

"What's the matter, Billy?"

"A message come for you. By a footman, it was, and he told me to be sure you got it as soon as you stepped in the door, if I stayed up never so late." The letter he held out had been crumpled in his hot, grubby hand.

"Did the footman say who sent it?"

"No, sir."

He took it to the room he used for an office and lit a branch of candles. The wafer's simple cross-hatched pattern gave no indication of the sender.

...I heard today a rumor that Furness had been made the butt of a prank, that being the recent notice of his betrothal to a lady (not myself). I have endorsed the on-dit by mentioning that some malicious fellow who hoped to marry me must have published the announcement in the hope of improving his own chances. I do not want Furness embarrassed as, like all men, his self-esteem is fragile, and a wound to it makes him captious.

Here there was a sort of stutter in the elegant script suggesting the writer had been interrupted.

I am vexed to report that an ill-considered retraction has been sent to the newssheets. It is too late to have it withdrawn, and it may serve as a salutary lesson to the writer thereof not to be overhasty. You will see it in the morning, and I am sure you will deal with it in the most sensible way. I am doubling your fee, as you have thus far exceeded my expectations. It will be delivered to your man of business in the morning. Let me add a word of advice: be exceeding honest in all your dealings with any lady...

How delicately phrased in all its parts! What could he do but laugh?

****

Portia tripped down to breakfast in her pretty green petticoat and jacket. Lady Emily was unlikely to wish to go out this morning and probably not this afternoon, either. She was sitting up in bed only long enough to take a sip of tea or nibble distastefully at a bit of rusk. Informal attire was therefore acceptable.

At the door, she hesitated at the sight of Hawkins, silent and serious, his face half turned toward a man in a prodigious fine amber velvet suit with bands of gold lacing at the wide cuffs, and an embroidered waistcoat in amber and green. His hair was powdered, which was too bad, as it went ill with his rather swarthy complexion. A newspaper lay discarded on the table beside him.

Solomon de Toledo!

Seeing her, Hawkins lunged to his feet. With a moment's less notice, Solomon managed to rise more gracefully, and bowed.

"Portia," Ambrose Hawkins began. When it became clear he was at a loss for words, Solomon came around the table.

"Mistress Portia, I came here earlier than good manners ordinarily allow in the hope of speaking with you on a matter of some importance." He came to a stop. “Perhaps you would like to breakfast first?”

She swallowed. Something must have gone terribly wrong. “Thank you, no. I could not eat for wondering what has happened. Please tell me quickly.”

“Uh, perhaps in the drawing room?” That was Hawkins, strangely tentative.

Bad news, then. She essayed a slight smile, hoping it did not appear tremulous. “Certainly, sir.”

Neither of them spoke as she led the way and seated herself. De Toledo stood irresolutely, hand on the door lever.

Why—? Oh, propriety, of course. “If privacy is required for your errand, I think you might close the door. I cast propriety to the winds days ago. Tell me, what has gone wrong?”

This seemed not to reassure him. “Nothing. Indeed, almost everything has come right. The Marquess of Furness now knows he has no hope of your money and yesterday became betrothed to a rich widow who wants a titled husband. He—”

“The poor woman. Should she not be warned of his character?”

Solomon laughed, the tension ebbing out of his body. No wonder she had feared the worst; she had sensed he was ill at ease, recognizing it from their journey.

“Ma’am, I believe she already understands him well and will be a match for him. Last night he told me they would be like steel and flint, and it was no complaint. They knew each other years ago.”

“You spoke with Furness, Mr. de Toledo?”

“And escaped unscathed, oh ye of little faith,” he murmured.

“I don’t doubt you are a match for him,” she apologized because men were so easily offended. But Solomon was a commoner confronting a nobleman, and she placed no reliance in Furness’s honor.

“I could not meet him in a duel or in a fistfight. But I was able to arrange a very satisfactory match for him in addition to…mmmm…saving him from marrying you.” His lips twitched with suppressed merriment.

She could not restrain a laugh, partly at the notion of the marquess being saved from her and partly from sheer relief.

“Furness was willing to acknowledge he owed me some gratitude. I don’t think either of us need worry about him in the future.”

She drew in a shaky breath, limp with released tension. “Thank you. You cannot know how much that news eases my mind.”

“Oh, I think I can. I gave the marquess cause to notice me once before and have wondered ever since if it would occur to him to squash me like a beetle.”

“Are you sure you are safe now? How did you happen to meet with him?”

“He invited me to call upon him last evening.”

“And you *went*?” *Into the lion’s den?* He had not replied to her first question. While Solomon de Toledo had an advantage she did not possess, being male, as a commoner he was nearly as powerless against a nobleman as she was against any man. “Please, be seated.”

He ignored the invitation. “I thought I might as well get it over with. A friend of mine told me years ago it was a mistake to show fear. I took his advice.”

“But why did he want to see you if he did not plan

some revenge? Are you sure you are safe?"

Her heart lifted at his wry smile.

"He wanted to watch me squirm. Fortunately he was in a mellow mood as his financial worries are now resolved, or will be on Christmas Eve."

"Will it hold? I cannot help but be concerned for you."

He studied her face with a curiously intent expression which reminded her of Benedict's face as she had seen it years ago peering into a confectioner's shop window. Longing for something unattainable. She knew the feeling herself. Though she had just a wisp of hope…

"I am honored by your concern. But yes, I believe we are no longer of interest to the marquess. I think his marchioness will be an excellent influence on him."

"It is hard for me to believe."

"In the ordinary way, I would agree." His eyes crinkled with amusement. "However, she will hold the purse strings."

Which reminded her—"Mr. de Toledo, I fear you spent a good deal on rescuing me. The horse, the cart, travel, and I suppose you paid your peddler friend something. And oh, I never paid him for the lovely Alençon lace! I had only three shillings, and he returned them to me. Please tell me how much I owe you and him, and I will pay you immediately."

"It was my privilege to assist you. I did not expect or want payment."

"But I can easily afford it." She saw the tension returning. Was he remembering Furness's marchioness "holding the purse strings"? She had no wish to offend him, but he must have spent a great deal on her behalf, none of it benefitting him.

Emily's earlier remarks about Solomon de Toledo stuck in her mind like a burr in a stocking. Had he meant to make her an offer? Why was she thinking of such a thing? Surely not. Why, it would be like a Papist proposing marriage to a Protestant. Or vice versa. His family would disapprove. Her family would disapprove. Not that she cared if her father was upset, but her mother and Benedict were another matter.

Benedict would be pleased. Mayhap her mother would grow accustomed.

Had offering to reimburse Solomon for his expenses given him a distaste for her? If she lost his friendship, her world would turn gray and cold. She cherished more than his kindness to her and her family; she basked in his companionship.

She liked to look at him, in proof of which, she was staring at him like a goosecap or a silly young chit. When he had helped her into and out of the cart, she had felt the strength of his hands. She had wished he might court her, as one dreams of delightful but impossible things.

He was still standing, gazing down at her. How long had they been as motionless and silent as a pair of statues? There were sounds from the street now: pedlars' cries, wheels and hooves and jangling harness. Someone had to speak.

"I did not mean to give offense. If I did, I am sorry for it."

"I was not offended. It speaks well of your character. But P—Mistress Portia, the money was nothing to me, no more burdensome than buying you a sweetmeat or an orange. While I do not have such a fortune as you do, my income is more than adequate to support a family in some comfort." He ran out of words suddenly.

Come, this was encouraging. She rose and stepped forward. They were as close as they would be during some figures of the minuet. "Sir, was there a reason you requested a private interview beyond telling me Furness is no longer a danger to us?" Because why would he not have imparted that news in the dining room? Their situation was no secret from Hawkins or Lady Emily.

"Deuce take it! There was. Is."

He came to a stop once more. From his oath and the keenness of his expression, it was no paltry thing. Her heart misgave her. What if it were not what she hoped? He and Hawkins had appeared very solemn when she came upon them in the dining room. Too serious to have been discussing any pleasant matter, surely?

"Please tell me what you brought me here to say, whatever it is." It might break her heart but at least the suspense would be over.

He did not immediately speak. The moment felt brittle as the finest crystal. Like it, her heart would shatter.

"I was advised by a woman of sense to be strictly honest with any lady whose opinion mattered to me. With any lady for whom I cared. She added that the exception would be if the lady preferred not to be burdened by the truth. I think you would prefer plain speaking, particularly as you will discover it anyway, and I would not have you think me dishonest."

She looked down at her hands, clenched against her stomach, hoping he would not see gathering tears, and praying she could hold them back.

"I am not unaccustomed to harsh truths, sir."

"Here it is, then. A retraction of Furness's notice of your betrothal appears in the newspapers this morning. It is not kind. As I understand it, he submitted it while still furious you had rejected him. This is not to excuse him in any way. In fairness, however, when we spoke last night, he was sorry for it, or as sorry as he is capable of being. I believe his future marchioness brought him to an understanding of his error."

The idea surprised a short laugh from her. "Then I hope she may make him sorrier yet. And I am ruined in spite of all your care."

"Not necessarily. You know marriage will make everything right, or nearly. The beau monde may look askance, but do you want to enter that circle?"

Despite the gravity of her situation, that too made her laugh. "No, indeed. It was another reason I did not wish to marry Furness."

He cleared his throat. "Then perhaps I can offer a solution. I mean to lease a house. Lady Emily and Hawkins may have some suggestions. And there is a little manor for sale near Battlesbridge in Essex. I might be able to buy it with the profit I expect from a cargo of furs. Even without that, in a year or two I should be able to afford something in the country. It is presumptuous of me, I know—"

She smiled, because she had already committed so many offenses against propriety, one more could not matter. "Solomon, I am perfectly besotted with you."

Solomon appeared nonplussed or as if hit over the head. "You are? Are you sure?"

After a moment, he evidently gathered his wits. "I

love you, Portia, but I'm not foolish enough to think nothing else matters. What of the likely opposition of your family, the assumption I must be a fortune hunter, the religious differences, and my occupation?"

"Does my being an ape leader and having jilted a marquess and ruined myself, and the likely disapproval of your family trouble you?"

"You are not an ape leader. I helped ruin you by taking you from Blackwater Hay—"

"And I am so grateful that you did. As is Lord Furness, it would seem." She chuckled. What a pleasing thought, the marquess married to a woman ferocious enough to govern him.

"My family won't care. My mother will be happy. My cousin is betrothed to a baronet's daughter. No one opposed their match."

A baronet who must therefore be a Christian.

"Well, then. Benedict will be glad, and I think my mother will accept it. Perhaps I should care whether my father does or does not. However, I do not think myself obligated to sacrifice my happiness to conform to his wishes." Not when he had shown so little care for her happiness and wishes.

"*Haberes buenos!*"

The exclamation startled her. But whatever it meant, from his tone it indicated pleasure.

" 'Good news' in the Spanish dialect my great-grandfather taught me. I thought I'd forgotten most of it. Er…you'll want the children raised as Christians."

She was blushing at the thought of children. Or what led to children, which was seeming more appealing by the moment. "I don't care how they are reared as long as they grow up kind, honest, and knowing they are loved."

"If they're Christian, the boys could stand for Parliament. One might even gain a title."

"We can work out the details when there is a child, can't we?"

"We can, my sweet. May I conclude you accept my offer? I don't think I asked as I ought to have done. Will you marry me? Shall I kneel? I wanted to do this in the approved manner."

"Yes, I'll marry you. And no, please don't kneel. I always thought the 'approved manner' for a suitor to ask for one's hand, as discussed by my girlhood friends, sounded rather silly."

"Speaking of your hands," he began and groped in his coat's pocket. He brought out a snuffbox and opened it.

Her hands were unclenched now, but she kept them folded at her waist lest they wander to Solomon. A shocking thought! But she wanted to touch his hands, his shoulders, his hair…no, mayhap not his hair. The powder, after all. She would like to—

"I was not certain of getting the correct size, so I brought several. If there's one you like that does not fit, it can be altered. Or if none pleases you, we can—"

She gasped. Cushioned in black velvet in the plain snuffbox were half a dozen rings. "You went out carrying a fortune in your pocket?"

"They're not all of great value. I chose rings I thought you might like, in several sizes."

The clear, roughly cut stone in a heart-shaped setting must be a diamond. A circle of small diamonds surrounded a flat-cut red stone, pearls ringed a blue stone. One ring consisted of a cluster of opaque sky-blue stones—turquoise? A golden yellow square cabochon in a finely molded setting caught her eye. She ran a finger gently over its smoothly polished stone.

"Try it on, if you wish. Try them all."

It slipped onto her ring finger as if it were coming home. "This one."

"It's only a citrine set in rose gold."

"It's perfect."

He closed the box, returned it to his pocket, and then raised her hand to his lips. When he kissed each knuckle and then began working his way up to her wrist, her heart beat faster. He would have to stop there, where her sleeve ended. Then, *oh please*, he would kiss her lips. Put his arms around her. *Bliss.* She leaned toward him like a plant toward the sun. Then his arms were around her, and he was lowering his head to kiss her.

The third tap at the door, more of a rap, really, penetrated their mutual abstraction. They sprang apart as Lady Emily entered.

"Portia? Oh, you are here. My husband said you might be. Are you ready to come to breakfast? And you, too, Mr. de Toledo. I apprehend we have something to celebrate—"

Had Hawkins known Solomon meant to propose marriage and told his wife? Had she and Solomon been together in private so long that Lady Emily had felt she had to come in search of them to preserve decency? Ambrose Hawkins's grinning face appeared over Emily's shoulder. He held up a bottle of champagne.

"—now that Furness has given up his pretensions, according to the newssheet. And Mr. de Toledo can tell us what else he was urgent to impart to you. Pray, come to breakfast, and we will toast the good news in champagne."

A word about the author…

Kathleen Buckley has loved writing ever since she learned to read. After a career which included light bookkeeping, working as a paralegal, and a stint as a security officer (fascinating!), she began to write as a second career rather than as a hobby. Her first historical romance was penned (well, word-processed) after re-reading Georgette Heyer's Georgian/Regency romances and realizing that Ms. Heyer would never be able to write another (having died some forty years earlier). She is now the author of five published Georgian romances: *An Unsuitable Duchess*, *Most Secret*, and *Captain Easterday's Bargain*, *A Masked Earl*, and *A Duke's Daughter*. A seventh is in process. She is picky about accurate detail.

~

Warning: no bodices are ripped in her romances, which might be described as "powder & patch & peril" rather than Jane Austen drawing room. They contain no explicit sex, but do contain some bad language, as the situations in which her characters find themselves occasionally call for an oath a little stronger than "Zounds!"

A word about the author...

Thank you for purchasing
this publication of The Wild Rose Press, Inc.

For questions or more information
contact us at
info@thewildrosepress.com.

The Wild Rose Press, Inc.
www.thewildrosepress.com

www.ingramcontent.com/pod-product-compliance
Lightning Source LLC
LaVergne TN
LVHW020527100826
845148LV00010B/1371